THE TROUBLE WITH HONOR

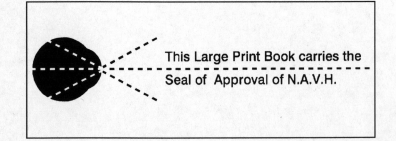

This Large Print Book carries the
Seal of Approval of N.A.V.H.

THE TROUBLE WITH HONOR

JULIA LONDON

THORNDIKE PRESS
A part of Gale, Cengage Learning

GALE
CENGAGE Learning·

Farmington Hills, Mich • San Francisco • New York • Waterville, Maine
Meriden, Conn • Mason, Ohio • Chicago

Copyright © 2014 by Dinah Dinwiddie.
Thorndike Press, a part of Gale, Cengage Learning.

Thorndike Press® Large Print Romance.
The text of this Large Print edition is unabridged.
Other aspects of the book may vary from the original edition.
Set in 16 pt. Plantin.

LIBRARY OF CONGRESS CATALOGING-IN-PUBLICATION DATA

London, Julia.
    The trouble with Honor / by Julia London. — Large Print edition.
        pages cm. — (Thorndike Press Large Print Romance)
    ISBN 978-1-4104-6826-0 (hardcover) — ISBN 1-4104-6826-7 (hardcover)
    1. Inheritance and succession—Fiction. 2. London (England)—Fiction. 3. Large type books. I. Title.
PS3562.O78745T76 2014
813'.54—dc23   2014000270

Published in 2014 by arrangement with Harlequin Books S.A.

Printed in Mexico
2 3 4 5 6 7 18 17 16 15 14

Dear Reader,

I am so excited to present *The Trouble with Honor* to you! This is my first book for the Harlequin HQN line, but I have written many historical romances, almost all of them set in the Regency period. I love the pageantry of the era and how society and the concern for appearances ruled the gentry. But I imagine that human nature being what it is, there were those who did not like to live by the rules, who chafed at being ruled at all and who dared to break the rules.

In this series about the Cabot sisters, I introduce four young, privileged women who are expected to aspire to a very good marriage and not much else. But when their fortunes begin to change, these four are determined to break the rules that bind them and define happiness on their own terms. However, when one is raised in the lap of luxury, and learns nothing more taxing than some intricate stitching, one may not be equipped to circumvent the rules. One's attempts to do so may go very, very badly. I hope you enjoy the Cabot sisters and their shenanigans as much as I enjoyed writing them.

Happy reading,
Julia London

For my mother,
who instilled a love of books and
reading in me from the beginning.

CHAPTER ONE

The trouble began in the spring of 1812, in a gaming hell south of the Thames, a seedy bit of Southwark known to be thick with thieves.

It was beyond comprehension how the old structure, originally built in the time of the Vikings, had become one of the most fashionable places for gentlemen of the Quality to be, but indeed it had. The interior was sumptuous, with thick red velvet draperies, rich wood and low ceilings. Night after night, they came from their stately Mayfair homes in heavily armed coaches to spend an evening losing outrageous sums of money to one another. And when a gentleman had lost his allotted amount for the evening, he might enjoy the company of a lightskirt, as there were ample private rooms and French women to choose from.

On a bitterly cold night, a month before the start of the social Season — when, inevitably, the gentlemen would eschew this gaming hell for the Mayfair assembly rooms and balls that had become a spring rite for the wealthy and privileged — a group of young Corinthians were persuaded by the smiles and pretty pleas of five debutantes to have a look at this gaming hell.

It was dangerous and foolish for the young men to risk forever marring the reputations of such precious flowers. But young, brash and full of piss, they'd been eager to please. They did not allow the hell's rule of no women to deter them, or that any number of mishaps or crimes could befall the young women in the course of their lark. It was a bit of adventure in the middle of a gloomy winter.

It was in that Southwark gaming hell where George Easton first made the acquaintance of one of those debutantes: Miss Honor Cabot.

He hadn't noticed the commotion at the door when the young bucks had arrived with their prizes, flush with the excitement of their daring and overly proud for having convinced the man at the door to give them entry. George had been too intent on divesting thirty pounds from Mr. Charles Rutherford, a notorious gambler, in the course of a game of Commerce. He didn't realize anything was amiss until Rutherford said, "What the devil?"

It was then that he noticed the young women standing like so many birds, fluttering and preening in the middle of the room, their hooded cloaks framing their lovely faces, their giggles infecting one another while their gazes darted between the many men who eyed them like a paddock full of fine horses.

"Bloody hell," George muttered. He threw down his cards as Rutherford stood, the poor lass in his lap stumbling as she tried to stop herself from being dumped onto the floor.

"What in blazes are they doing here?" Rutherford demanded. He squinted at the group of them. "Bloody unconscionable, it is. See here!" he rumbled loudly. "This is not to be borne! Those girls should be removed at once!"

The three young gentlemen who had undertaken this adventure looked at one another. The smallest one lifted his chin. "They've as much right to be present as you, sir."

George could see from Mr. Rutherford's complexion that he was in danger of apoplexy, and he said, quite casually, "Then, for God's sake, have them sit and play.

Otherwise, they're a distraction to the gentlemen here."

"Play?" Rutherford said, his eyes all but bulging from their sockets. "They are not fit to play!"

"I am," said one lone feminine voice.

Ho there, which of them dared to speak? George leaned around Rutherford to have a look, but the birds were fluttering and moving, and he couldn't see which of them had said it.

"Who said that?" Rutherford demanded loudly enough that the gentlemen seated at the tables around them paused in their games to see what was the commotion.

None of the young ladies moved; they stared wide-eyed at the banker. Just as it seemed Rutherford would begin a rant, one of them shyly stepped forward. A ripple went through the crowd as the lass looked at Rutherford and then at George. He was startled by the deep blue of her eyes and her dark lashes, the inky black of her hair framing a face as pale as milk. One did not expect to see such youthful beauty here.

"Miss Cabot?" Rutherford said incredulously. "What in blazes are *you* doing here?"

She curtsied as if she were standing in the middle of a ballroom and clasped her gloved hands before her. "My friends and I have come to see for ourselves where it is that all the gentlemen keep disappearing to."

Chuckles ran through the crowd. Rutherford looked alarmed, as if he were somehow responsible for this breach of etiquette. "Miss Cabot . . . this is *no* place for a virtuous young lady."

One of the birds behind her fluttered and whispered at her, but Miss Cabot seemed not to notice. "Pardon, sir, but I don't understand how a place can be quite all right for a virtuous man, yet not for a virtuous woman."

George couldn't help but laugh. "Perhaps because there is no such thing as a virtuous man."

Those startlingly blue eyes settled on George once more, and he felt a strange little flicker in his chest. Her gaze dipped to the cards. "Commerce?" she asked.

"Yes," George said, impressed that she recognized it. "If you desire to play, miss, then bloody well do it."

Now all the blood had drained from Rutherford's face, and George was somewhat amused that he looked close to fainting. *"No,"* Rutherford said, shaking his head and holding up a hand to her. "I beg your pardon, Miss Cabot, but I *cannot* abet you in this folly. You must go home at once."

Miss Cabot looked disappointed.

"Then I'll do it," George said and, with his boot, kicked out a chair at his table. Another murmur shot through the crowd, and the tight group of little birds began to flutter again, the bottoms of their cloaks swirling about the floor as they twisted and turned to whisper at each other. "Whom do I have the pleasure of abetting?" he asked.

"Miss Cabot," she said. "Of Beckington House."

The Earl of Beckington's daughter, was she? Did she say that to impress him? Because it didn't. George shrugged. "George Easton. From Easton House."

The girls behind her giggled, but Miss Cabot did not. She smiled prettily at him. "A pleasure, Mr. Easton."

George supposed she'd learned to smile like that very early on in life in order to have what she liked. She was, he thought, a remarkably attractive woman. "These are not parlor games, miss. Have you any coin?"

"I do," she said, and held out her reticule to show him.

Lord, she was naive. "You'd best put that away," he said. "Behind the silk neckcloths and polished leather boots, you'll find a den of thieves between these walls."

"At least we've a purse, Easton, and

14

haven't sunk it all in a boat," someone said.

Several gentlemen laughed at that, but George ignored them. He'd come to his fortune with cunning and hard work, and some men were jealous of it.

He gestured for the lovely Miss Cabot to sit. "You scarcely seem old enough to understand the nuances of a game such as Commerce."

"No?" she asked, one brow arching above the other as she gracefully took a seat in the chair that a man held out for her. "At what age is one considered old enough to engage in a game of chance?"

Behind her, the birds whispered fiercely, but Miss Cabot calmly regarded George, waiting for his answer. She was not, he realized, even remotely intimidated by him, by the establishment or by anything else.

"I would not presume to put an age on it," he said cavalierly. "A child, for all I care."

"Easton," Rutherford said, his voice full of warning, but George Easton did not play by the same rules as the titled men here, and Rutherford knew it. This would be diverting; George had no objection to passing an hour or so with a woman — anyone in London would attest to that — particularly one as comely as this one. "Are you prepared to lose all the coins you've

15

brought?"

She laughed, the sound of it sparkling. "I don't intend to lose them at all."

The gentlemen in the room laughed again, and one or two of them stood, moving closer to watch.

"One must always be prepared to lose, Miss Cabot," George warned her.

She carefully opened her reticule, produced a few coins and smiled proudly at him. George made a mental note not to be swept up by that smile . . . at least not while at the gaming table.

Rutherford, meanwhile, stared with shock at both Miss Cabot and George, then slowly, reluctantly, took his seat.

"Shall I deal?" George asked, holding up the deck of cards.

"Please," Miss Cabot said, and put her gloves aside, neatly stacked, just beside her few coins. She glanced around the room as George shuffled the deck of cards. "Do you know that I have never been south of the Thames? Can you imagine, my whole life spent in and around London, and I've never come south of the Thames?"

"Imagine," he drawled, and dealt the cards. "Your bet to begin, Miss Cabot."

She glanced at her cards that were lying faceup, and put a shilling in the middle of the table.

"A bob will not take you far in this game," George said.

"Is it allowed?"

He shrugged. "It is."

She merely smiled.

Rutherford followed suit, and the woman who had occupied his lap for most of the evening resumed her seat, sliding onto his knee, her gaze challenging Miss Cabot.

"Oh," Miss Cabot murmured, apparently as she realized what sort of woman would sit on Rutherford's lap, and glanced away.

"Are you shocked?" George whispered, amused.

"A bit," Miss Cabot responded, stealing a look at the young whore again. "I rather thought she'd be . . . homelier. But she's quite pretty, isn't she?"

George glanced at the woman on Rutherford's lap. He would call her alluring. But not pretty. Miss Cabot was pretty.

He glanced at his hand — he held a pair of kings. This would be an easy victory, he thought, and made his bet.

A servant walked by with a platter of food for a table that had resumed its play. Miss Cabot's gaze followed it.

"Miss Cabot," George said.

She looked at him.

"Your play."

"Oh!" She studied the cards and picked up another shilling and placed it in the middle.

"Gentlemen, we've had two bobs bet this evening. At this rate, we might hope to conclude the game at dawn."

Miss Cabot smiled at him, her blue eyes twinkling with amusement.

George reminded himself that he was not to be drawn in by pretty eyes, either.

They went round again, during which Rutherford apparently forgot his reluctance to play with the debutante. On the next round, Miss Cabot put in two shillings.

"Miss Cabot, have a care. You don't want to lose all you have in the first game," one of the young bucks said with a nervous laugh.

"I hardly think it will hurt any less to lose all that I have in one game or six, Mr. Eckersly," she said jovially.

George won the hand as he knew he would, but Miss Cabot didn't seem the least bit put off by it. "I think there should be more games of chance at the assembly halls, don't you?" she asked of the growing crowd around them. "It makes for a better diversion than whist."

"Only if one is winning," a man in the

back of the crowd said.

"And with her father's money," Miss Cabot quipped, delighting the small but growing crowd around them, as well as the birds who had accompanied her, as they now had the attention of several gentlemen around them.

They continued on that way, with Miss Cabot betting a shilling here or there, bantering with the crowd. It was not the sort of high-stakes game George enjoyed, but he did enjoy Miss Cabot, very much. She was not like what he would have supposed for a debutante. She was witty and playful, delighting in her small victories, debating the play of her cards with whomever happened to be standing behind her.

After an hour had passed, Miss Cabot's purse was reduced to twenty pounds. She began to deal the cards. "Shall we raise the stakes?" she asked cheerfully.

"If you think you can afford my stakes, you have my undivided attention," George said.

She gave him a pert look. "Twenty pounds to play," she said, and began to deal.

George couldn't help but laugh at her naïveté. "But that's all you have," he pointed out.

"Then perhaps you will take my marker?"

she asked, and lifted her gaze to his. Her eyes, he couldn't help noticing, were still sparkling. But in a slightly different way. She was challenging him. Heaven help him, the girl was up to something, and George could not have been more delighted. He grinned.

"Miss Cabot, I must advise you against it," one of the bucks said, the same one who had grown more nervous as the game had progressed. "It's time we returned to Mayfair."

"Your caution and timekeeping are duly noted and appreciated, sir," she said sweetly, her gaze still on George. "You'll humor me, won't you, Mr. Easton?" she asked. "You'll take my marker?"

George had never been one to refuse a lady, particularly one he found so intriguing. "Consider yourself humored," he said with a gracious bow of his head. "I shall take your marker."

Word that he had taken a marker from Miss Cabot spread quickly through the gaming hell, and in a matter of minutes, more had gathered around to watch the debutante lose presumably something of value to George Easton, the notorious and self-proclaimed bastard son of the late Duke of Gloucester.

The betting went higher among the three of them until Rutherford, who was undone by the prospect of having a debutante owe him money, withdrew from the game. That left George and Miss Cabot. She remained remarkably unruffled. It was just like the Mayfair set, George thought. She had no regard for the amount of her father's money she was losing — it was all magic for her, markers and coins appearing from thin air.

The bet had reached one hundred pounds, and George paused. While he appreciated her spirit, he was not in the habit of taking such a sum from debutantes. "The bet is now one hundred pounds, Miss Cabot. Will your papa put that amount in your reticule?" he asked, and the men around him laughed appreciatively.

"My goodness, Mr. Easton, that's a personal question, isn't it? Perhaps I should inquire if *you* will have one hundred pounds in your pocket if I should win?"

Cheeky thing. There was quite a lot of murmuring around them, and George could only imagine the delight her remark had brought the gentlemen in this room. He tossed in a handful of banknotes and winked at her. "Indeed I will."

She matched his bet with a piece of paper someone had handed her, signing her name to the one hundred pounds owed.

George laid out his cards. He had a sequence of three, the ten being the highest. The only hand that could beat his was a tricon, or three of a kind, and indeed, Miss Cabot gasped with surprise. "My, that's impressive!" she said.

"I've been playing these games quite a long time."

"Yes, of course you have." She lifted her gaze and smiled at him, and the moment she did, George knew he'd been beaten. Her smile was too saucy, too triumphant.

As she laid out her hand, gasps went up all around them, followed by applause. Miss Cabot had beaten him with a tricon, three tens. George stared at her cards, then slowly lifted his gaze to hers.

"May I?" she asked, and proceeded to use both hands to drag coins and notes from the center of the table. She took it all, every last coin, stuffing it into her dainty little reticule. She thanked George and Rutherford for allowing her to experience the gaming hell, politely excused herself, slipped back into her cloak and gloves and returned to her little flock of birds.

George watched her go, his fingers drumming on the table. He was an experienced gambler, and he'd just been taken by a debutante.

That was when the trouble with Honor Cabot began.

CHAPTER TWO

Lady Humphrey's annual spring musicale was widely regarded as The Event at which the ladies of the *ton* would reveal their fashionable aspirations for the new social Season, and every year, one lady inevitably stood out. In 1798, Lady Eastbourne wore a gown with cap sleeves, which many considered so *risqué* and yet so clever that tongues wagged across Mayfair for weeks. In 1804, Miss Catherine Wortham shocked everyone by declining to wear any sort of lining beneath her muslin, leaving the shadowy shape of her legs on view to all.

In the bright early spring of 1812, it was Miss Honor Cabot who left quite an impression in her tightly fitted gown with the daringly low décolletage. She was dressed in an exquisite silk from Paris, which one might reasonably suppose had come at an exorbitant cost, given the amount of embroidery and beading that danced across the hem, and the fact that Britain was at war with France. The silk was the color of a peacock's breast, which complemented her deep-set blue eyes quite well. Her hair, as black as winter's night, was dressed with tiny crystals that caught the hue of the gown.

No one would argue that Honor Cabot wasn't a vision of beauty. Her clothing was always superbly tailored, her creamy skin nicely complemented by dark lashes, full, ruby lips and a healthy blush in her cheeks. Her demeanor was generally sunny, and her eyes sparkled with gaiety when she laughed with her many, *many* friends and gentlemen admirers.

She had a reputation for pushing the boundaries of the polite and chaste behavior expected of debutantes. Everyone had heard about her recent foray into Southwark. Scandalous! The gentlemen of the *ton* had playfully labeled her a swashbuckler.

That evening, after the singing had been done and the guests had been invited to promenade across Hanover Square to the Humphrey townhome for supper, it was not the swashbuckler's exquisite and daring gown that caused tongues to wag. It was her bonnet.

What an artful construction that bonnet was! According to Lady Chatham, who was a self-proclaimed authority in all things millinery, the prestigious Lock and Company of St. James Street, a top-of-the-trees hat shop, had designed the bonnet. It was made of black crepe and rich blue satin, and the fabric was gathered in a tiny little fan on one side, held in place by a sparkling aquamarine. And from that fan were two very long peacock feathers, which, according to Lady Chatham, had come all the way from *India,* as if everyone knew that Indian peacock feathers were vastly superior to English peacock feathers.

When Miss Monica Hargrove saw the bonnet jauntily affixed atop Honor's dark head, she very nearly had a fit of apoplexy.

Word spread so quickly through Mayfair that a contretemps had occurred between Miss Cabot and Miss Hargrove in the ladies' retiring room, that it did, in fact, reach the Earl of Beckington's townhome on Grosvenor Square before Miss Cabot did.

Honor was not aware of it when she snuck into the house just as the roosters were crowing. She darted up the steps and into the safety of her bedroom, and once inside, she tossed the bonnet onto the chaise, removed the beautiful gown Mrs. Dracott had made especially for her and quickly fell into a deep and dreamless sleep. She was rudely startled from her slumber sometime later when she opened her eyes to see her thirteen-year-old sister, Mercy, bending over her, peering closely.

It gave Honor a fright, and she cried out as she sat up, clutching the bed linens to her. "Mercy, what in heaven?" she demanded.

"Augustine bids you come," Mercy said, examining Honor closely from behind her wire-rimmed spectacles. Mercy was dark haired and blue eyed like Honor, whereas her sisters Grace, who was only a year younger than Honor's twenty-two years, and sixteen-year-old Prudence, were fair haired and hazel eyed.

"Augustine?" Honor repeated through a yawn. She was not in a mood to see her stepbrother this morning. Was it even morning? She glanced at the mantel clock, which read half past eleven. "What does he want?"

"I don't know," Mercy said, and bounced to a seat at the foot of Honor's bed. "Why are there dark smudges beneath your eyes?"

Honor groaned. "Have we any callers today?"

"Only Mr. Jett," Mercy said. "He left his card for you."

Dear Mr. Jett — the man simply could

not be persuaded that Honor would never consent to be courted by him. It was her lot in London society to attract the gentlemen for whom she could never, in her wildest imagination, find an attraction for in return. Mr. Jett was at least twice as old as she, and worse, he had thick lips. It vexed her that women were supposed to accept any man whose fortune and standing were comparable to hers. What about the compatibility of souls? What about esteem?

The closest Honor had come to such depth of feeling was the year of her debut. She'd fallen completely in love with Lord Rowley, a handsome, charming young gentleman who had aroused her esteem to a crescendo. Honor had been so very smitten, and she had believed — had been *led* to believe — that an offer was forthcoming.

An offer *was* forthcoming . . . but for Delilah Snodgrass.

Honor had heard of the engagement at a tea and had been so stunned by the news that Grace had been forced to make excuses for her as Honor had hurried home. She'd been brokenhearted by the reality of it, had privately suffered her abject disappointment for weeks. She'd been crushed to see Rowley squiring Miss Snodgrass about, had felt herself growing smaller and smaller in her grief.

How could she have been so terribly wrong? Had Rowley not complimented her looks and accomplishments? Had he not whispered in her ear that he would very much like to kiss her more thoroughly than on the cheek? Had they not taken long walks together in the park, speaking of their hopes for the future?

One day after the stunning news, Honor had happened upon Lord Rowley. He'd smiled, and her heart had skipped madly. She'd not been able to keep herself from confronting him and demanding, as politely as she could, what had happened to the offer *she'd* been expecting.

She would never, as long as she might live, forget the look of surprise on his lordship's face. "I beg your pardon, Miss Cabot. I had no idea the strength of your feelings," he'd said apologetically.

She had been completely taken aback by that. "You didn't *know*?" she'd repeated. "But you called on me several times! We walked in the park, we talked of the future, we sat together during Sunday services!"

"Well, yes," he'd said, looking quite uncomfortable. "I have many friends among the fairer sex. I've taken countless walks and had many interesting conversations. But I was not aware that your feelings had gone beyond our friendship. You gave no outward sign."

Honor had been dumbfounded. Of course she hadn't given any outward, blatant sign! Because she was a good girl — she'd been proper and chaste as she'd been taught to be! She'd demurely waited for the gentleman to make the first overture, as she'd supposed such things were done!

"And I really must stress, Miss Cabot," he'd continued with that pained expression, "that had I known, it would not have changed . . . anything," he'd said, his face turning a bit red as he'd shrugged halfheartedly. "Ours would not have been a fortuitous match."

That had stunned her even more than his deceit. "Pardon?"

He'd cleared his throat, had looked at his hands. "That is to say, as the first son of an earl, it is expected that I should set my sights a bit higher than Beckington's stepdaughter . . . or the daughter of a bishop, as it were." He'd scarcely looked her in the eye. "You understand."

Honor had understood, all right. For Rowley, and for every other gentleman in Mayfair, marriage was all about position and status. He clearly did not care about love or affection. He clearly did not care about *her.*

The wound of that summer had scored Honor, and she had never really recovered from it. She had vowed to herself and to her sisters that she would never, *never* allow herself to be in that position again.

She yawned at Mercy. "Please tell Augustine I'll be down directly."

"All right, but you'd best not be late. He's very cross with you."

"Why? What have I done?"

"I don't know. He's cross with Mamma, too," Mercy added. "He apparently told Mamma that the Hargroves were to dine here last night, and she said he did not. She hadn't planned a supper, and they had quite a row."

"Oh, no," Honor said. "What happened?"

"We dined on boiled chicken," Mercy said. "I must go now," she added airily, and skipped out of the room.

Honor groaned again and pushed the linens aside. She was really rather fond of Augustine, all things considered. He'd been her stepbrother for ten years now. He was four and twenty, no taller than Honor and a wee bit on the corpulent side. He'd never been one for walking or hunting, preferring

31

to read in the afternoons or debate his friends about British naval maneuvers at his club, the details of which he shared in excruciating detail over supper.

But never mind his dreadfully dull life — Augustine Devereaux, Lord Sommerfield, was a good man, kind and considerate of others. And weak willed and terribly shy when it came to women. For years, Honor and Grace could easily bend him to their will. That had changed, of course, when he'd fallen in love with Monica Hargrove and made her his fiancée. They would have been married now were it not for the earl's declining health, as it hardly seemed the thing to celebrate a wedding of the heir to the Beckington throne when the old earl was only barely clinging to life. Honor's stepfather was suffering from consumption. The many physicians who had trooped through this house believed he had months, if not weeks, to live.

Honor dressed in a plain day gown, brushed her hair and left it loose, too tired to put it up. She made her way downstairs and found her sisters and Augustine in the morning room. She was not happy to see all of her siblings in attendance, particularly given the dark look on Grace's face — that did not bode well. The sight of food on the sideboard, however, suitably revived Honor's demeanor, as she vaguely tried to remember the last time she'd actually eaten anything. "Good morning, all," she said cheerfully as she padded across the Aubusson carpet to the sideboard and picked up a plate.

"Honor, dearest, what time did you return home, if I may ask?" Augustine asked crisply.

"Not so very late," Honor said, slyly avoiding his gaze. "I didn't intend to stay quite as long as I did, but Lady Humphrey had set up to play faro, and I was caught in an exciting game —"

"*Faro!* That is a rude game played by rowdy men in taverns! On my word, do you *never* consider that your behavior will give rise to talk?"

"I always do," Honor said honestly.

Augustine blinked. He frowned. "Well, what gentleman will want a debutante who gambles her stepfather's fortune until the wee hours of the morning?" he demanded, changing tack.

Honor gasped at that and firmly met her stepbrother's gaze. "I did *not* gamble the earl's fortune, Augustine! I gambled what I've fairly won!" She would not apologize for it — she was really rather good at winning. Not a month ago, she'd taken one hundred pounds from Mr. George Easton in front of everyone at a gaming hell in Southwark. She could still remember the shine of defeat in his eyes.

But Augustine was not appeased. "How does *winning* improve your reputation?" he demanded.

"Tell us about the musicale," Prudence said eagerly, ignoring Augustine's querulous mood. "Was the music divine? Who was there? What were they wearing?"

"Wearing?" Honor repeated thoughtfully as she took her seat beside Augustine, her plate full of cheeses and biscuits. "I didn't notice, really. The usual sort of thing, I suppose, muslin and lace." She shrugged lightly.

"Any *bonnets* about?" Augustine asked crossly, and swiped a biscuit from Honor's plate.

Honor knew then that he'd heard about her quarrel with Monica. She hesitated only a moment before she straightened her back, smiled at her stepbrother and said, "Only *my* bonnet that I recall."

"There you are, Augustine!" Grace said triumphantly. "Do you see? It's *impossible* that she would have taken Monica's bonnet."

"*Taken* it?" Honor repeated incredulously.

"I grant you that Honor can be vexing, but she hasn't a dishonest bone in her body," Grace continued as if Honor was not sitting just across from her. "Quite the contrary! If one can make a criticism of her, it is that she is *too* honest!"

"How can one be too honest?" Prudence asked. "Either one is honest or one is not."

"I mean that she often lacks discretion," Grace clarified.

"*Thank* you," Honor said wryly. "You are too kind."

Grace blinked innocently, as if it were beyond her capacity to deny.

"Neither is Miss Hargrove lacking in veracity," Augustine said sternly. "She would not bring such a complaint to my attention were it not true." He punctuated that statement by stuffing the rest of his biscuit into his mouth and chewing with enthusiasm as he glared at Honor.

Honor refrained from saying there were many things Monica Hargrove lacked, and Honor should know — she'd been acquainted with the woman since their sixth year on this earth, when their mothers had thought it expedient to employ one dance instructor for the both of them. That instructor — a simpering fool with a sharp nose and long, gangly arms, as Honor

35

recalled him — had taken quite a liking to Monica and had given her the best roles in all their recitals. Moreover, Monica's costumes always had wings and Honor's had not, a fact that Honor might have been able to bear had Monica not been so bloody smug about it. "Perhaps your dancing will improve, and next year, you might have this costume," she'd said as she'd twisted one way, then the other, so that Honor might see the thing in all its glory.

The competition between them had only intensified over the next sixteen years.

"Monica would bring even the slightest misunderstanding to your attention if it would mean you view her favorably and me less so," Honor said.

"Do you deny that Miss Hargrove commissioned a bonnet from Lock and Company," Augustine continued, having swallowed his biscuit, "and was dismayed to see it affixed to *your* head at the musicale? It must have been quite shocking for her, the poor dear."

Mercy, who was turning the pages of a book without glancing at the words, laughed at that, but was quickly silenced by a dark look from Grace, who said soothingly to Augustine, "It's surely a slight misunderstanding."

"No," Augustine said, shaking his head. "Miss Hargrove told me herself that she confronted Honor at dinner, and naturally, Honor denied it, and when Miss Hargrove mentioned she'd commissioned it for a dear sum, Honor said, 'It wasn't *that* dear.' There, you see? She all but confessed to Miss Hargrove that she took the bonnet!"

"I meant only that when *I* purchased the bonnet, I did not find the cost of it so dear," Honor said sweetly.

Augustine's cheeks began to mottle as they were wont to do when he was flustered and confused. "Honor, it . . ." He paused, his chest puffing a little as he attempted to display authority. "It will not do."

"What won't do?" Honor asked, holding out her plate to offer him another biscuit. "She admired my bonnet, then claimed it was hers. How could it be hers, I ask you, when the milliner sold it to *me* and it was on *my* head? You may inquire of Lock and Company if you please."

Augustine's look of confusion went deeper as he clearly tried to sort out the mystery of the bonnet in his mind. "I would not like to disparage your fiancée, Augustine," Honor continued. "I want us to be friends, I do! But I will privately confess to you that there

are times I very much fear her true intentions."

"Her intentions are pure!" Augustine said.
"There is not a kinder, sweeter woman in
all of London." He suddenly reached for
Honor's hand and, finding a plate there,
instead took her wrist beseechingly. "I really
must insist that you do not take her bonnets, Honor. Or . . . or buy those that she
fancies," he said uncertainly.

Behind Augustine, Grace rolled her eyes.

"You have my word," Honor said solemnly. "I will not take Monica's bonnets."
The snigger she heard was from Prudence,
doing her best to keep from laughing outright.

"I cannot have disharmony between you,"
Augustine continued. "You are my stepsister
and she will be my wife. I don't care for the
talk that goes around town about the two of
you, and it's not good for Papa."

"No, you're right, of course you are right,"
Honor said, feeling only slightly chastened.
"How is the earl this morning?"

"Exhausted," he said. "I looked in on him
after breakfast, and he bid me pull the
shades, as he wanted to sleep, having suffered another long night."

Augustine stood from the table, his belly
brushing against it. He tugged down his

waistcoat, which had a habit of riding up when he'd been seated, and removed his linen napkin from his collar. "If you will all excuse me?"

"Good morning, Augustine!" Grace said pleasantly.

"Good morning!" Honor called out.

She received a frown from Grace for it, who said, "All right then, Pru, Mercy, go and have your hair dressed, will you? We'll take Mamma riding in the park after luncheon."

Mercy hopped up from the table. "May I ride the sorrel?"

"Ask Mr. Buckley," Grace said to them, wiggling her fingers in the direction of the door, indicating they were to go. As Mercy and Prudence went out, Grace smiled sweetly at the footman attending them this morning. "Thank you, Fitzhugh. My sister and I can manage from here."

Fitzhugh followed the younger girls out, closing the door behind him.

When they were alone, Grace slowly turned her head and fixed a dark hazel look on Honor, who was eating hungrily from her plate and pretended not to notice.

"What did you do?" Grace asked low.

"Nothing." But Honor couldn't help it; a smile began to curve her lips. "All right. I bought a bonnet." She took a bite of cheese.

"Then why is Monica so vexed?"

"I suppose . . . because she'd commissioned it for herself." Honor's smile widened.

Grace gaped at her for a moment, and then burst out laughing. "Dear God, you're incorrigible! You will *ruin* us!"

"That is not true. I am very corrigible."

"Honor!" Grace said, still laughing. "We agreed that you'd not vex her *again.*"

"Oh, what is one bonnet?" Honor said, putting aside her plate. "There it was, in the window of Lock and Company, and I admired it. The shop attendant was perfectly happy to tell me that even though Miss Monica Hargrove had commissioned it one month ago, she'd not come round to pay her bill. It was languishing in the window, Grace, a beautiful bonnet, and if I may be frank, the wrong palette for Monica's pallid complexion. And the expense the poor shop had incurred in making it had gone unpaid! The attendant was quite happy to sell it to me, of course. And really, I don't care that Monica commissioned it in the least. She is so very disagreeable! Do you know what she said to me last night?" she said, leaning slightly forward. "She said, 'I know what you are about, Honor Cabot,' " Honor said, her voice mockingly low and menacing, " 'but it won't do you a bit of good. Augustine and I are going to wed, and there is nothing you can do to stop it. And when we are wed, mark my words, you may find yourself in a cottage in the Cotswolds without need for fine bonnets!' " Honor sat back to let that sink in.

Grace gasped. "The Cotswolds! Why not banish us to the African desert, for it couldn't possibly be worse! Oh, Honor, that is *precisely* what we fear, and now look what you've done!"

Honor snorted and picked up another piece of cheese. "Do you really think Monica holds so much sway with Augustine? Do you think he hasn't a care for his sisters?"

"Yes!" Grace said emphatically. "Yes, I think she holds quite a lot of sway with him! And Augustine may care for us all very much, but when the earl dies, do you really, truly believe Monica will share Beckington House, or Longmeadow in the country, or *anywhere,* for that matter, with all of us?"

Honor sighed. It was a true fact in their society that a new earl and his even newer wife would not welcome his dead father's third wife and his four stepdaughters into his household. Grace was right, but Monica was so . . . *imperious*! And so perfect, so modest, so demure, so pretty!

"Really, you can be so careless," Grace said. "What of Prudence and Mercy, then? What of Mamma?"

It would be difficult for their mother to find a new husband who would be excited about the prospect of providing for four unmarried daughters, particularly given their rather lofty expectations for a certain way of life, as well as the demands of dowries. The Cabots had come into this marriage with only a little money, certainly not enough to dower four girls. They were entirely dependent on the earl.

Worse, it was almost a certainty that the Cabots would find themselves on the fringe of society altogether if anyone suspected what Grace and Honor knew about their mother: that she was slowly, but demonstrably, losing her mind. It had begun two years ago, after a trip to Longmeadow. Their mother had been involved in an accident when a curricle had overturned, tossing her onto the road. Physically, the countess had recovered, but since then, Honor and Grace had noticed her mind was slipping. Mostly, it was unusual memory lapses. But there were other, less subtle signs. Once, she had blithely talked of seeing her sister at Vauxhall, as if her sister were still alive. Another time, she hadn't been able to recall the earl's title.

Recently, however, it seemed as if their mother was getting worse. Most days, she was clearheaded and a constant presence at her husband's side. Other days, she might ask the same question more than once or remark on the weather three or four times in the space of a few minutes. Once, when Honor had tried to speak to her mother about her increasing forgetfulness, her mother had been surprised by the suggestion and seemingly irked by it. She'd even suggested to Honor that perhaps *she* was the forgetful one.

"And I don't think I need to tell you that the earl has not been out of his bed in two days," Grace added.

"I know, I know," Honor said sadly. She curled her feet under her on the chair. "Grace . . . I've been thinking," she said carefully. "What if Monica did not marry Augustine —"

"Of course she will," Grace said, cutting Honor off. "Augustine is completely besotted with her. He runs after her like a puppy."

"But what if . . . what if Monica was lured away by a bigger fortune?"

"What?" Grace eyed Honor warily. "How? Why?"

"Just suppose she was lured away. It would give us a bit of time to settle things. Look here, Grace, if the earl dies, Augustine will take her to the altar as soon as he is able, and then what? But if they *don't* marry as soon —"

"Are you forgetting that Augustine loves her?" Grace asked, clearly struggling to remain calm.

"I've not forgotten. But he is a man, isn't he? He will soon forget her and find another."

"Our Augustine!" Grace cried with disbelief. "Monica Hargrove is the first woman he's ever so much as looked at, and even so, it took him several years to do it!"

"I know," Honor said, wincing a little. "I'm only trying to think of a way to put off their marriage for a time."

"Until what?"

"I haven't worked that out completely," Honor admitted.

Grace studied her sister for a moment, then shook her head. "It's ridiculous. Folly! Monica won't turn loose a bird in the hand — Augustine could turn mute and blind and she'd not care. And besides, I have a better plan."

"What?" Honor asked skeptically.

Grace sat up now. "We marry first. *Quickly.*

If we marry, our husbands will have no choice but to take in our sisters and our mother when the earl dies."

"Now who is being ridiculous?" Honor said. "What do you think, that we may summon up a husband with the snap of our fingers? Who would we marry?"

"Mr. Jett —"

"No!" Honor all but shouted. "That's a *wretched* plan, Grace. First, neither of us has an offer. Second, I don't *want* to marry now. I don't want to tend to a man and do his bidding, and be shunted off to the country where there is no society, all because *he* desires it."

"What are you talking about? Who do you know that has been shunted to the country?" Grace asked with some surprise. "Really, Honor, don't you want to marry? To have love and companionship and children?"

"Of course," Honor said uncertainly. She rather enjoyed her freedom. She didn't pine for marriage and children the way other women her age seemed to do. "But at present, I don't love anyone and I don't want to marry merely because it is expected. It vexes me terribly that we are expected to do as we are told and marry this man, or seek that offer," she said, gesturing irritably.

"Why? We're free women. We ought to choose and do as we please, just like every man is allowed."

"But we have others who must rely on us," Grace said, referring to Prudence and Mercy.

The reminder put a temporary damper on Honor's enthusiasm for women's equality.

"And besides, your perception is clouded by Rowley's rejection —"

"It was not precisely a *rejection,*" Honor began to argue, but Grace threw up a hand to stop her.

"I didn't say it to be unkind. But your judgment *has* been impaired, Honor. You won't allow anyone to come close."

Before Honor could argue against such a ridiculous notion, Grace said, "So we are agreed, we must do *something.*"

"Yes, of course, we are agreed. Which is why I want to seduce Monica away from Augustine. And I know just the man to do it."

"Who?" Grace asked skeptically.

Honor smiled at her own brilliance. "George Easton!"

Grace's eyes widened. Her mouth gaped. It took her a few swift moments to find her tongue. "Have you gone completely round the bend?"

"I have not," Honor said firmly. "He is the perfect man for it."

"Are we speaking of the same George Easton from whom you managed to divest one hundred pounds in that scandalous little game in Southwark?"

"Yes," Honor said, shifting a little self-consciously in her seat.

Grace made a sound of despair or shock, Honor wasn't certain, but her sister suddenly stood and walked in a complete circle behind her chair, one hand on her back, the train of her muslin gown trailing behind her. When she faced Honor again, she folded her arms across her chest and stared down at her. "To be *perfectly* clear, are you speaking of the self-proclaimed *by-blow* of the late Duke of Gloucester? The man who loses a fortune as easily as he makes one?"

"*Yes,*" Honor said, confident in her idea. "He is handsome, he is the nephew of the king and currently, he is quite flush in the pockets, as we know."

"But he is a man with no real name. Or connections! We may all very well believe he is the true son of the late duke, but the *duke* never acknowledged it. And I've not even mentioned that the current duke — Easton's half brother, if he is to be believed — utterly detests him and forbids anyone from even mentioning his name! For heaven's sake, Honor, he does not enjoy the privileges of his supposed paternity! Monica Hargrove will not give up the Beckington title for him, not if all of Hades freezes over."

"She might," Honor stubbornly insisted. "If she were properly seduced."

Grace blinked. She sank down onto her chair, her hands on her knees, gaping at her sister. "What a dangerous, *ridiculous* idea. You *must* promise me you won't do anything so entirely *wretched.*"

"Wretched!" Honor was miffed that Grace didn't see the brilliance in her plan. "I mean him only to lure her, not compromise her! He need only make her believe there are other interests in her, and then perhaps she will want to explore an option or two before marrying Augustine. It seems quite simple and brilliant to me. Your idea is superior to that?"

"Much," Grace said emphatically. "If *you* won't marry, then *I* will."

"Oh, and have *you* any offers you've not told me about?"

"No," Grace said with a sniff. "But I have some thoughts on how I might gain one."

"Such as?"

"Never you mind," Grace said. "Just

promise me you won't do anything so fool-ish."

"Very well, very well," Honor said with an impatient flick of her hand. "I *promise,*" she said dramatically, and picked up her plate again. "I'm famished."

In fairness, Honor had every intention of keeping her promise. In fairness, she *always* meant to keep her promises.

But then she unexpectedly encountered George Easton that very afternoon.

CHAPTER THREE

Finnegan, George Easton's butler-cum-footman-cum-valet, had pressed George's dark brown superfine coat, his gold-and-brown waistcoat and his dark brown neckcloth. He had hung them where George would see them: directly before the basin, blocking his sight of the mirror, of the razors and brushes and cuff links he kept there.

Until Finnegan, George had been perfectly happy to live his life with a pair of footmen, a cook and a housekeeper, but his lover, Lady Dearing, had implored George to take Finnegan after her husband had cast the valet out. Lady Dearing had said his dismissal was an issue of austerity. George was quite familiar with austerity, as he'd been forced to befriend it on more than one occasion in his thirty-one years on this earth.

It hadn't been until several weeks after he'd taken him on that George learned the real reason for Finnegan's abrupt departure:

he, too, had been invited to share Lady Dearing's bed. George had known the fair-haired vixen was a wanton, obviously, but the *valet*? That went beyond the pale. However, by then, George had grown accustomed to Finnegan's ways. So George had promptly discarded his lover and kept his butler.

He'd finished dressing when Finnegan appeared in the door of his master suite of rooms, a hat in his hand.

"What's that?"

"Your hat."

"I can see it is my hat. Why are you bringing it to me?"

"You've an appointment with Mr. Sweeney. From there, you will collect Miss Rivers and Miss Rivers at the Cochran stables. You have invited the young ladies to ride."

George's eyes narrowed. "I have? And when did I extend this invitation?"

"Last night, apparently. The Riverses' footman brought round a note with the ladies' delighted acceptance of the invitation." He smiled. Or smirked. George was never quite sure.

He didn't remember any invitation, but then again, he had been having a bit more fun than he should have had at the Coventry

House Club last night. That was a club for men like him, frequented by tradesmen and gentlemen of the *ton,* who, like George, had deep pockets for the gaming tables, a thirst for whiskey and an appreciation of cheroots made with American tobacco. It was the opposite of priggish, which is what he imagined White's on St. James to be.

Tom Rivers, the ladies' brother, had been at Coventry House last night, too, and George had only a vague recollection of too much drinking and laughter. "God have mercy," he muttered, and stood up, extending his hand for the hat.

He strode down the thickly carpeted stairs of the stately Mayfair home he'd purchased quietly from the Duke of Wellington. The duke had not wanted to sell to a man like George — that was, a bastard son of a duke and the half brother of a duke who despised the very idea of him — but the duke had wanted the cash George had offered.

The house was quite spectacular even for fashionable Audley Street in Mayfair. A crystal chandelier the size of a horse hung daintily from the high foyer ceiling, and the stairs curved down around it. The silk-covered walls of the foyer were adorned with paintings and portraits, all purchased by the duke.

George scarcely noticed them today, but many times, he'd searched them all, looking for any resemblance to him. In the end, he supposed any of them could have been his ancestors, and it hardly mattered if any one of them were. When one is the son of a duke and a lowly chambermaid — a chambermaid the duke had sent away upon discovering her pregnancy — one can be assured of many closed doors and painful silences when inquiring after one's heritage.

The footman, Barns, was standing at the door, and opened it before George reached it. That was Finnegan's doing. Finnegan was the only person in George's life, now or ever, who treated him like the great-grandson of a king, the nephew of another. George wasn't certain he liked it, however. He rather preferred opening his own doors. He preferred to saddle his own horses, too — he was fast, having learned the skill as a lad, working in the Royal Mews while his mother cleaned chamber pots.

"Thank you, Barns," George said. He stood a full head taller than his footman. George had the height of the royal family but the robustness of his mother's family, who had all worked with their hands and their backs for their livings. There was a portrait of his father that hung in Montagu

House, which George had studied on occasion. He believed he had his father's thin and aristocratic nose and his strong chin, the streaks of his mother's dark chestnut hair in his brown mop and her pale blue eyes. The other children who had worked in the Royal Mews used to say he was a mongrel. Not the nephew of a king.

George's horse was waiting on the cobblestones before the house. He tossed a farthing to the boy holding the reins, who caught it adroitly over the horse's neck and pocketed it as he handed the reins to George. "G'day, sir," he said, and was off, running back to the mews.

George fixed his hat on his head, swung up and spurred his horse into a trot down Audley Street.

He arrived at the offices of Sweeney and Sons a quarter of an hour later. Sam Sweeney, his solicitor and agent, was smiling broadly. "What's that look?" George asked as he handed his hat to an elderly woman in a lace cap in the foyer.

"One of joy, of happiness," Mr. Sweeney said, taking George's hand and shaking it with great enthusiasm. "Do come in, Mr. Easton. I have some wonderful news."

"Has the ship been found? Has it come to port?"

"Not exactly that," Mr. Sweeney said, showing George into his office. Once inside, he made a show of dusting off a leather chair with his handkerchief, and gestured with a flourish to the seat.

When George was seated, Mr. Sweeney said, "The *St. Lucia Rosa* is in port. I have personally spoken with the captain. He said that Godsey and his crew did indeed reach India and were to depart a week later for England. That means she should be in port within the week."

Relief. It flooded through George like a swollen river. He'd put a substantial portion of his fortune into this ship and couldn't bear the thought of having lost it all, of having to start again.

"And we must bear in mind that Captain Godsey is a captain of great experience," Sweeney reminded him.

Sweeney had found Godsey. George trusted his judgment — he and Sweeney had worked together for years now, first to invest the money the Duke of Gloucester had left George upon his death a few years ago. It was the only acknowledgment George had ever received from his father. The money wasn't much, really, merely enough to appease a man's guilty conscience when he was about to meet his maker.

Everything else had gone to the duke's eldest son, William, George's half brother, a man George had met only once and who had promptly decreed that he would never allow George Easton to step foot in any London establishment of which he was part.

George had become adept at brushing off the bruising disappointment of being judged by the circumstances of his birth, of being called a liar, a blackguard and a pretender after the Gloucester fortune. He'd focused instead on making a name for himself. He'd invested a lot of money in his latest venture: the import of cotton from India.

It was a great risk, but George had built his fortune by taking risks, then carefully tending them. As his fortune had grown, so had his confidence. Women liked him, but he never allowed himself to develop feelings for them. He played a man's game, taking satisfaction where he could and keeping them all at arm's length. Because if there was one truth in his life, it was that he would never be more than a by-blow to this set.

George was very clear about his place in the world. And he hoped that his place would soon extend to cotton.

The war with France had made it possible for men like George to discover untapped commerce potential. Two years ago, he'd struck a deal with an Indian man for the import of cotton to the British Isles. It had been a risky venture, one fraught with many opportunities for disaster. But that was how George chose to live his life — he took chances. Astoundingly big chances. He thrived on risk; it kept him on the edge, made him feel as if he were balancing on the knife's sharp edge.

In his initial cotton venture, he'd felt euphoric. The cotton had arrived as promised, and George had made an astounding profit. He had capitalized on that initial entry into the trade now by purchasing a ship and a crew to bring even more cotton to England.

It was by far the riskiest thing he'd ever done. The crew could make off with the cargo and sell it themselves. The ship could sink along the way. It could be overrun by pirates. Any number of things could happen, more than George could possibly imagine, because he'd never sailed anywhere in his life. But if he was right, the reward would make him an unfathomably wealthy man. If not, well . . . George would find something.

He would start again.

He and Sweeney talked about how quickly

they would sell the cotton once it arrived, and George left his offices with a considerably lighter step than when he'd gone in.

The twins, Miss Eliza Rivers and Miss Ellen Rivers, were waiting for George at the Cochran stables. They were accompanied by a sour-faced woman whom George could only assume was their nurse, given that these young ladies were of a tender age, which he found almost laughable for a man who'd just marked his thirty-first year. But the young ladies were giddy and bright eyed on that cool spring afternoon, their cheeks like pairs of apples. "By my oath," George said, "I cannot determine which of you is the lovelier."

The girls giggled, and George liked the sound of it; it sounded like spring. He was glad to set out with the little birds onto Rotten Row, their smaller horses trotting alongside his Arabian, who ambled along at a leisurely pace.

George quickly discovered that the young debutantes liked to finish each other's sentences, which made it difficult for him to follow their conversation. He was calculating how many steps it would take to return the young ladies to the stable — he liked to distract himself with mathematical practices from time to time — when he was startled by a cloud of blue headed directly at him at a reckless speed.

He leaned forward in his saddle, peering at the blue cloud, and realized it was actually a woman riding so fast and hard that he thought perhaps the horse had gone wild with her on his back. He was fully prepared to chase the animal down and save the woman when she pulled up directly before them and smiled broadly. "Good afternoon, Miss Rivers. Miss Rivers," she said with jaunty breathlessness, and touched her gloved hand to her hat.

George's companions were so astonished by her approach that they could only gape at her, but George recognized her instantly: Honor Cabot.

She smiled brightly. "Mr. Easton!" she said, as if she'd just noticed him. "A pleasure to see you again, sir!"

"Miss Cabot," he said, dipping his head. "You gave us a fright."

"Did I?" She laughed gaily. "I beg your pardon, that was not my intent. I meant only to stretch the old girl's legs," she said, and leaned over her horse's neck, patting her with enthusiasm. "Miss Rivers, how are your parents?" she asked.

"Very well, thank you," said one of them.

"I'm very glad to hear it. I did not mean

to interrupt your ride, and I shall leave you to carry on," she said. "I do beg your pardon for the fright."

"Quite all right," said another of the twins.

"Good day!" Miss Cabot's smile turned the tiniest bit sultry when she glanced at George. "Mr. Easton," she said, and let her gaze slide over him as she turned her horse about and moved away. Curiously, George felt that gaze run down his body.

Miss Cabot suddenly reined up and glanced over her shoulder. "Pardon me, but it just occurred to me! Mr. Easton, I understand you will be among those dining at Gunter's Tea Shop at five o'clock this afternoon with my brother, Lord Sommerfield."

Sommerfield? Hardly. George did not have much use for soft men who preferred books to sport. He looked at her curiously, wondering how she might have confused it.

"I was wondering if you would be so kind as to pass a message to him? I shan't see him today due to prior commitments."

"I had not —"

"If it's not a bother," she quickly interjected, "would you please relay to him that I shall come round in the earl's coach at half past five to fetch him? I would not want to intrude on your meeting."

He opened his mouth once more to explain that she had confused him with someone who actually took tea in tea shops, but she quickly interjected before he could speak. "Thank you. You won't forget, will you? Half past five outside Gunter's Tea Shop. I'll be in the earl's coach."

George had the strange, preposterous idea that Miss Cabot was trying to arrange a meeting with *him*.

No. Impossible. That was not something that a proper young miss would do. But she'd just done it. What could she possibly want? It was baffling. And damn well intriguing. "I should be delighted to deliver the message," he said. "Half past five. I'll not forget."

She smiled. "Thank you." She turned about and spurred her horse, riding hard, catching up with other riders down the way.

George happened to glance at Miss Eliza Rivers.

She was staring at him. "Are you acquainted with Miss Cabot?"

"I've been introduced," he said, and left it at that. "Shall we carry on?" He spurred his horse and made a remark about the fine weather.

He hadn't been introduced, precisely, but he had indeed met her in Southwark, when he'd been charmed to the tips of his toes and played like a harp.

If there was one thing George Easton hated, it was losing.

If there was one thing he hated worse than losing, it was losing to a handsome woman.

If there was one thing he hated even worse than losing to a handsome woman, it was losing to a handsome woman before a bloody audience, and all because he'd preferred to admire her delectable décolletage than his own damn hand.

He couldn't begin to imagine what Miss Cabot was about today, but he had every intention of being at the tea shop this afternoon. It was a daring move for her to conspire to meet him, alone. Away from prying eyes.

That was not an invitation a man of *any* stripe would turn down, and George Easton least of all.

CHAPTER FOUR

Honor dressed carefully for her meeting with Mr. Easton. It would not do to give him the wrong impression, as she was walking on treacherous ground as it was. She remembered how he'd looked at her in Southwark, his gaze penetrating and boldly moving over her.

She needed something demure. Reserved. She chose white muslin with a high neckline, trimmed in green, and topped it with a dark green spencer. She donned a bonnet with matching trim, and dark green gloves.

Honor studied herself critically in the mirror above her vanity. It would do — no one would suspect she had gone to Gunter's for anything more than a cup of tea or an ice. Certainly not to meet a gentleman alone, unchaperoned. "Certainly not," she muttered and smiled at her reflection.

But her smile looked forced. As if her lips knew how dreadful she was behaving.

She dropped a few coins in the beaded reticule Prudence had made her, then made her way downstairs, taking care to avoid any place that Grace might be. She asked the Beckington butler, Mr. Hardy, to bring round the coach. As she stood waiting in the foyer, Augustine walked through the door.

"Honor!" he said, surprised to see her there. "Are you going out?"

"To tea," she said breezily, hoping she didn't appear as nervous as she felt. "Shall I see you at supper?"

"Supper? No, no, afraid not." He handed his hat to Hardy and added proudly, "I'm to dine with Miss Hargrove and her parents this evening." He glanced back at Hardy and whispered loudly, "Shall I tell you a secret?"

"Why, yes! I adore secrets."

Augustine yanked at his waistcoat where it had inched up over his belly. His brown eyes were shining, his smile irrepressible. "I've not told anyone, but Papa agrees with me that Miss Hargrove and I should marry this spring."

Honor's heart hitched. She'd believed there would be no possibility for Augustine's marriage to occur before the earl's death. "This spring?"

"Yes, isn't it marvelous? When I explained to Papa that Miss Hargrove is anxious to be wed — and so am *I,* naturally — Papa reasoned that he could very well linger for *months,* and that there was no point in putting it off indefinitely. I rather think he'd like to see me wed before . . . the, ah . . . inevitable."

Honor tried to hide her shock behind a bright, happy smile.

"I should very much like to announce a date at our annual affair at Longmeadow," he added happily.

The Beckingtons hosted a country-house gathering at the earl's seat of Longmeadow before the opening of Parliament each year. The stately Georgian home had thirty guest rooms, and at least one hundred guests attended every spring.

"What better time and place?" Augustine happily continued.

"What better?" Honor echoed, her mind suddenly whirling. The Longmeadow soiree was a mere three weeks away.

"Monica is a bit anxious. I have counseled her she should not fret so, that my sisters have always been *quite* welcoming." He looked pointedly at Honor.

"*Particularly* to dear friends, I should like to think," Honor said. And she would like to think that precluded Monica, but there was no need to confuse the issue at the moment.

Augustine glanced slyly at Hardy, then leaned closer to Honor and whispered, "I think she feels as if the four of you might all see her as an intrusion into our happy family. I assured her *nothing* could be further from the truth. She was eased when I said so and reminded me that in any event, you will all have husbands of your own soon enough." Augustine smiled indulgently at Honor. "I should not like to speak out of turn, but I believe she would take great pleasure in helping those happy events along in some way."

"I have no doubt of it," Honor said sincerely.

"You should think of it, Honor. One cannot live under one's father's wing forever, as I am discovering myself."

"No, of course not." Monica was already beginning to sow her seeds, was she? Honor was now determined more than ever to intervene before it was too late. "What a happy occasion," she said to Augustine. "You must impress on our friend that she will not be intruding *in the least,*" she said, tapping Augustine's chest with each word for emphasis.

The door opened; a footman stepped in. "Ah, there is your coach," Augustine said happily. "I shall give Miss Hargrove your felicitations, shall I?"

"You *must*," Honor insisted, and pictured herself with her hands around Monica's neck.

"Good day, sister," he said jovially.

"Good day, Augustine." Honor watched him toddle off, whistling as he went. She turned to the door. Hardy was waiting, holding it open for her. "Lord help us all, Hardy," she said as she swept past him.

"Indeed, miss."

Honor saw Mr. Easton the moment the coach turned onto Berkeley Square. How could she miss him? His was an imposing figure. He was leaning up against a railing, one leg crossed over the other, his arms folded loosely across him, watching people stroll across the square. That night in Southwark she'd been properly titillated by his comely face and virile presence. She now understood why he was rumored to be London's greatest rake, his affairs numerous. His looks stirred something deep inside her.

Honor pulled open the vent to the driver. "Jonas, please stop at Gunter's and open the door to the gentleman in the black coat and gold waistcoat," she called up.

The coach turned the corner and began to slow. Honor nervously adjusted her bonnet. She had only to think of Monica and an imminent wedding to find her resolve.

A moment later, she heard Jonas's deep voice. The coach door swung open, and Mr. Easton, still perched against the railing, leaned to his right and looked inside. Honor smiled. "Good afternoon!"

He pushed away from the railing and came to his full height. He was *quite* tall, wasn't he? With his muscular legs and broad shoulders he looked too big to fit into the coach. He strolled toward it now, his expression inscrutable. Just like that evening in Southwark, he had an uncanny way of looking at her that made Honor feel as if he was seeing right through her, seeing her cards, even the thoughts in her head. She'd felt fluttery that night, as if a thousand butterflies had nested within her chest.

She was feeling fluttery again.

He paused just outside the open coach door, arched a brow and said, "Your stepbrother must be dining elsewhere."

Honor swallowed down her nerves. "Won't you come inside, Mr. Easton?"

He cocked his head to one side, assessing

her, his gaze nonchalantly taking her in, from her bonnet to the hem of her gown. The slightest shadow of a smile turned up one corner of his mouth. He reached for the coach handle and easily came inside, swaying the coach as he settled heavily across from her and the door swung shut behind him.

Honor had guessed right — he was too big for the coach. His knees framed both of hers, and his body very nearly filled the bench. He sat casually, one arm stretched across the back of the squabs. He reminded her of a wolf, calmly watching a hare hop across the path.

He inclined his head. "Miss Cabot."

"Mr. Easton, how do you do?" She rapped on the ceiling and called up, "A drive around the park, please, Mr. Jonas." She closed the vent and smiled at her guest. "Thank you for coming."

"How could I possibly resist such an unusual invitation?" His voice was smooth and low, and it sent another little shiver winging through her, fluttering in her chest, in her groin.

The coach took an unexpected turn; Mr. Easton's knee bumped her leg. He said nothing, but he smiled as if that amused him, too. "Well, Miss Cabot?" he asked.

69

"What has brought on this unprecedented ride about the park in a Beckington coach? Do you desire to seduce me? If so, I am favorably inclined. His gaze slid down to her well-covered bosom. "I find seduction one of the greatest pleasures in life."

Honor had the strongest urge to look down and assure herself that her spencer was properly buttoned.

Easton lifted his gaze. "Well? I am filled with curiosity."

Her palms were suddenly damp, her heart fluttering still, making it feel impossible to speak. But speak she must, for here it was, the moment of her greatest folly. "I am in need of a favor, Mr. Easton."

One brow arched above the other.

"Of you. . . . That is, if you would be so kind." She smiled.

Mr. Easton's gaze flicked over her again, lingering a little longer on her chest. "Do you believe we are so well acquainted that you might ask a favor?" He touched her foot with his boot.

"I . . ." She hesitated.

Now he smiled, as if he had the upper hand, as if there was no possible answer to that but *no.*

He was certainly right about that — there was no possible answer to that beyond *no.*

But it was his faintly smug expression that gave Honor the swell of pluck that she needed. "One might agree that one hundred of your pounds suggests I do, sir."

Mr. Easton very nearly choked on his smile. His eyes, Honor noticed, were an amazing shade of blue, the color of pale china silk. She had a fleeting thought of what it must be like to lie beneath this man and gaze up into those eyes.

"Touché, Miss Cabot," he said. "I have never been asked a favor in quite this manner, but you are so comely, I can't possibly refuse. Lift your skirts, then, allow me to gaze upon the valley I shall be pleasuring —"

"What?" she gasped as a hot bolt of awareness shot through her. "No, *no,* Mr. Easton, you misunderstand!"

"Do I?" he asked with an easy smile.

"*Yes.* I am in need of a different sort of favor. Not . . . not *that,*" she said breathlessly.

He laughed. "I do not frequent the same assembly rooms as debutantes."

He didn't what? Honor blinked with surprise. The tingling in her was momentarily forgotten in favor of her indignation. "For heaven's sake, I am not asking you to *dance* with me. My dance card fills the moment I step into an assembly room."

"Fills right up, does it?" he asked wryly.

"I mean that I do not arrange to meet gentlemen so that I might ask them to stand up with me. Or anything else," she hastily added.

"I didn't think that you invited me to ask me to stand up with you, Miss Cabot. I thought you had invited me for more obvious and —" He paused, ran his tongue over his lip as he took her in again, and added, "*Diverting* reasons. But now I am fairly certain that you have invited me here to engage in some duplicitous debutante scheme. That," he said, "is not appealing."

Her heart was beating wildly now, her mind sorting through all the diverting reasons. "How odd," she said, trying desperately to ignore her thoughts. "You make it sound as if debutantes are frequently scheming." Which, Honor was all too aware, she was doing in that very moment.

"That, or sleeping. Come now, don't be shy," he said, gesturing for her to carry on. "I suppose I am not generally opposed to granting favors . . . particularly if there is some hope I might personally *enjoy* the favor after all." His gaze fell to her bodice again. "Open your spencer."

"No!" Honor said, appalled and titillated

at once.

"Then I suppose we are finished," he said, and moved as if he meant to knock on the ceiling.

Honor quickly unbuttoned her spencer. He arched a brow; she frowned slightly and pushed it back from her bosom.

He eased back, studying her casually. Honor was accustomed to the way men looked at her. But she had never felt it quite like this, so intently. Honor's blood began to race. She wasn't certain if she was appalled by him or entirely aroused.

"Hmm," he said thoughtfully as he gazed at her collared gown. "That is not an improvement."

Honor yanked her spencer closed. "As I said, Mr. Easton, I did not come here for a dalliance."

"Apparently not," he said. "Or you are woefully unimaginative in your seductions." His slow, deliberate smile made the fluttering in Honor's breast skirt merrily down her spine and land squarely in her belly. "Nevertheless, I should think it would be pleasurable for us both."

Honor couldn't think. Her imagination was galloping away from her.

"Go on, then, Miss Cabot. You have me on tenterhooks. If I will not be allowed to show you the pleasure your young heart has imagined, then please, do say what it is you want."

Steady on. Honor ignored her breathlessness, the heat in her veins, the desire to remove her spencer entirely, and said, "I will not lie, Mr. Easton. This favor involves a bit of . . . persuasion."

"Even more interesting." His gaze drifted to her lips. "I knew that you were a bold one, Miss Cabot. A young lady of your stature does not appear in a Southwark gaming hell without a river of audacity running through her veins." He smiled as if that pleased him. "What sort of persuasion did you have in mind?" he asked, and reached out, taking the end of her bonnet's ribbon between two fingers, rubbing the velvet.

She pulled the ribbon from his grasp. "I need you to seduce someone."

He reached for her ribbon again and smiled so charmingly that Honor felt a bit of herself melt. "I am trying, Miss Cabot."

She pulled the ribbon free once more. "Not *me.*"

He chuckled, the sound of it reverberating in her chest. "A pity. But I suppose you are too tender after all. Is it anyone I know, or anyone I choose?"

"Someone I know." She prepared to explain herself, but George Easton abruptly reached for her wrist and wrapped his fingers tightly around it, the thumb pressing against her vein. Could he feel how her heart raced? Her heart skipped — she knew a slender moment of terror as she looked at his hand on her wrist; it looked enormous compared to her arm. She was so *foolish* — she had no idea if he would harm her, if he would force her —

"What the devil are you talking about?" he asked silkily, rubbing his thumb across her inner wrist.

God help her, she couldn't falter now — she'd already walked out on the plank away from propriety and decency. "As I said, I very much need you to seduce someone."

He lifted her arm, touched his lips to her inner wrist through the keyhole of her glove then lifted his head with a knowing smile. "It would seem I am more successful at seduction in this coach than I thought." He pulled her forward. His eyes were blazing. "If not you, little bird, then *who*?"

"Miss . . . Miss Monica Hargrove."

Mr. Easton blinked. He suddenly let go of her wrist and fell back against the squabs. "Miss Hargrove," he repeated disbelievingly.

Honor nodded, thankful for the opportunity to catch her breath. She pressed her palm to her chest, took a breath.

"Isn't Sommerfield affianced to Miss Hargrove?"

Honor nodded again.

"Your stepbrother," he announced, as if she had not realized that Viscount Sommerfield was one and the same as Augustine.

When Honor said nothing, Easton surprised her with a laugh to the ceiling. "Of all the *reprehensible* —"

"Reprehensible!" Honor protested. "Goodness, Mr. Easton, I am not asking that you *ruin* her. I merely ask that you direct her attention elsewhere," she said, and fluttered her fingers in a vaguely "elsewhere" direction.

"For what purpose should I direct her attention elsewhere?" he asked, mimicking her finger fluttering.

"Surely it is clear as to *purpose.*"

"The only purpose *I* can see is to make your stepbrother cry off his engagement, and I cannot imagine what reason you would have that is in any way founded —"

"I have my reasons," she said crisply.

"Do you," he drawled, folding his arms across his chest. "What are they?"

"You need not know —"

"Bloody hell I need not know. You ask me to turn the head of your brother's fiancée and tell me I need not know *why*?"

"I certainly hadn't counted on you *arguing* with me," she said petulantly, and toyed with the fringe of the window's sash, thinking quickly. "I cannot divulge what I know about Miss Hargrove," she said hesitantly, "but I can assure you I have very good reason to wish that she not marry Augustine." She glanced at Easton again, who was now looking at her with complete disdain. His eyes were still blazing, but in a strangely different way. Honor swallowed. "No good can come of their union. You must trust me," she insisted. "And I thought . . . I thought that perhaps you might agree to help me."

"Of course," he said with mock sincerity. "Because of who I am."

"Yes! Because you are a man who takes risks and you are rather . . ." She couldn't help but take him in, his broad shoulders, his muscular legs, his fine mouth.

"Rather *what*?" he prodded her, nudging her leg with his knee again. "Rather a *bastard*? A man whose mere association with a debutante casts a shadow on her?"

"No!" Honor said, feeling herself color. "I meant you are *handsome,* Mr. Easton. And . . . and wealthy. At least there is some speculation that you are. Naturally, I would

77

not know firsthand."

"Naturally," he said a bit derisively.

Lord, when she said these things out loud, she sounded absurd. She glanced to the window again, trying to find her way back to her plan, which she was having trouble remembering around the man's sensual gaze and masculine presence. This plan had seemed almost flawless when she'd first conceived it, but Grace was right. This was a ridiculous thing to have done.

She was startled by a nudge of her knee again. She glanced at Easton.

"And if Sommerfield cries off? With that tiny bit of conscience you might have salvaged after requesting a favor such as this, you believe you will have saved him from some great embarrassment and spared his suffering?"

He had not completely dismissed her? "Well," Honor said, shifting uncomfortably in her seat. "I wouldn't put it *precisely* that way, but —"

"But," he interrupted, and leaned forward again, so that his face was only inches from hers. His hand found her knee and squeezed, causing Honor to lose track of what she was saying altogether.

"With Beckington on his deathbed, you fear that a new countess will not look kindly to keeping four stepsisters as they should like to be kept."

Honor gasped — how had he divined *that*?

"And therefore, you wish to keep Sommerfield from marrying Miss Hargrove so that you might continue to live as you please. And that, Miss Cabot, weighs more than a bit on the side of reprehensible." He squeezed her knee once more as if to punctuate it, then leaned back, both arms now spread along the back of the squabs, looking as if he thought himself vastly superior to her. He cocked a brow, silently daring her to disagree with him.

Honor could hardly disagree with him, but she would not be chastised by him, either. Who the devil did this man think he was? She suddenly leaned forward and put her hand on *his* knee — but her fingers scarcely reached the breadth of it. She tried to squeeze, but his knee was as hard as stone. "And what if that is my intent? What possible difference should that make to *you*?"

He laughed with delight. "By God, you *are* bold! You admit it is true!"

"I understand how these things work, Mr. Easton. I am not some debutante freshly picked from the garden."

"No, you certainly are not that," he said jovially.

"Before *you* think to scold *me,* I shall remind you that you are also guilty of pursuing *your* singular happiness without regard for the consequences to others." She squeezed as hard as she might, but it seemed to have no effect on him.

"Pardon?" he said, laughing outright now. "What do you mean?"

She sat back, folded her arms tightly across her. "Please," she said with roll of her eyes. "*Everyone* in town knows about your affair with Lady Dearing. And that is on top of the rumors surrounding you and Lady Uxbridge and Mrs. Glover as well, who you apparently seduced at the same time you were courting her daughter —"

"All right, all right," he said cheerfully, holding up his hand to stop her. "You have made your point."

"I should think I have," she said primly, and brushed the lap of her gown. Another thought flitted through her head — was this how he had seduced Miss Glover? "As to Miss Hargrove, the truth is that I am in a bit of a bind."

"Are you?" he said skeptically, and waved his hand grandly at her, indicating she should continue.

"It is a simple fact in our society that women who don't enjoy the protection of a brother, a father or even an uncle are rather helpless. It's not as if we can make our own living, is it? The only way we might get by is to marry well."

"As Miss Hargrove clearly intends to do," he pointed out. "As *you* should do, if you want my opinion."

"Thank you, but I do not want your opinion."

He grinned, and that fluttering started in her all over again.

"Miss Hargrove would have any number of offers if she liked," Honor said, and it was true. As much as it pained her to admit it, Monica was a beautiful woman, her looks admired by men and women alike. "It needn't be Augustine. But as it *is* Augustine, the stakes are quite high for me."

"I would think you'd have any number of offers, as well," he said. "Is that not a better solution?"

"Yes, of course, a woman's only hope — marry well. Thank you for your confidence, but we aren't discussing me."

"Perhaps you should have asked for an offer as your favor, Miss Cabot. I find the request for conjugal bliss *far* more enticing."

"I beg your pardon," Honor said, taking great exception. "I would *never* ask a gentleman to offer for my hand!"

"I see. You will not ask a man to marry you, but you will ask him to seduce the woman who would be your sister-in-law." His brows rose dubiously.

"Two entirely different points, Mr. Easton!" she argued. "My sister Grace and I, we shall make our way in society with or without Augustine's support, but my younger sisters are not yet out, and they cannot hope to fare as well without proper introduction. And my mother —" She caught herself, took a deep breath.

"Your mother?" he prodded.

Now she'd gone and done it. She anxiously smoothed the lap of her gown again. "My mother is unwell," she said, and looked up. "No one knows."

He eyed her shrewdly a moment. "I am sorry to hear it," he said softly.

His tenderness surprised her. And strangely enough, it made the fluttering in her spread across her skin. "I rather doubt my mother will find another situation that will provide the same sort of opportunities for my younger sisters that Grace and I have enjoyed. I fear they will be pushed from society altogether."

"Why not take your fears to Sommer-field?" he asked. "He seems a rather fair fellow to me. Surely he would provide a stipend —"

"He is too easily persuaded by Miss Hargrove's opinion. And Miss Hargrove is . . . That is to say, she will . . ." Honor sighed again with frustration, finding her reasoning so bloody difficult to explain. "Well, I shan't lie about it," she said wearily. What was the point in that? "Miss Hargrove doesn't care for me in the least."

"Aha. And you are certain of this?"

"Oh, quite," Honor said with a flick of her hand. "She finds me unlikable."

"Oh?" He smiled again. "Passing strange, as I find you quite likable."

That remark sent a little thrill down her spine. Honor didn't want to smile, but she could feel one playing at the corners of her lips. "Even so?"

"Even so." He smiled warmly at her.

There was nothing wolfish about it, and yet . . . and yet Honor was breathless once more.

"So then, tell me, Miss Cabot, if I were to agree to your outlandishly reprehensible and ill-advised request to save your poor sisters and ailing mother —"

She gasped with surprised delight. "You

will?"

"I said *if,*" he cautioned her. "But if I were to agree, what will I have in return?"

"What do you mean?"

"Come now, lass, I've seen you with cards in your hand. You are far too astute to believe I'd not want something in return for this favor."

Apparently she was not as astute as he thought, for that had not crossed her mind.

He abruptly shifted forward again and deliberately allowed his gaze to wander the full length of her body, then up again. He touched her jaw with his knuckle, tracing a slow, deliberate line, sending Honor's heart into another wave of wild beating. "What are you willing to trade?" he asked, his voice low and silky.

She leaned away from him. "How dare you —"

Easton took her by the arm and pulled her back. "How dare *I*?" he asked, admiring her mouth. He reminded her of a cat with a mouse, determining just how much to play before making the kill. "How dare I ask for recompense for a wretched deed?" He abruptly cupped her breast as if it were the most natural thing to do. Honor caught her breath; he smiled a little and began to massage it. "How dare I ask for a favor in return?" he asked silkily as tiny fires of desire erupted and sluiced down Honor's spine.

"You ask too *much*," she said, and pressed away from him. "How can you call yourself a gentleman?"

"I've not called myself anything, love." He brushed his knuckles across her breast, sending another shaft of fire down her spine, then cupped her face, his thumb stroking her cheek.

Honor's heart was beating so quickly she wondered how it did not leap from her chest. She understood how he would seduce and claim a woman. She understood why so many women had taken him as a lover. She was drawn to him, to his intense gaze, admiring and ravenous at once. To his touch, unyielding and yet soft. "Allow me to suggest a suitable trade," she said quickly, before this cat devoured its prey. "I will pay you," she said, alarmed that her voice shook ever so slightly. "There is the one hundred pounds I won from your purse. I could return that in exchange for your help."

"You would return one hundred pounds, fairly won, for this?" he asked silkily, and flicked his finger across the tip of her breast.

"Actually," she said, her gaze on his mouth, "I would return ninety-two pounds."

She did not think it necessary to tell him that she'd bought a bonnet, some shoes and some underthings with the money.

"Enticing. But money is not what I have in mind." He slipped his hand to her nape and pulled her closer. "I have in mind something just for you." He put his mouth to her ear and said low, "Something that will make your timid heart shatter and bring a glow to your fair cheeks." His hand was in her lap, his palm pressing against her abdomen. "Do you know what will bring a glow to a woman's cheek, Miss Cabot?"

She tried to turn her head, but she couldn't seem to force herself to do it. "I am not a girl, Mr. Easton."

"Aren't you?" he whispered, and drew her earlobe in between a pair of soft, moist lips, nibbling it.

Dear Lord, she would expire. She closed her eyes, taking in his scent — spicy and warm — the feel of his hands on her. She could imagine his hands on all of her, and feared that her heart would give in, and she would die here on this bench. And yet, somehow, she managed to keep calm. "I can offer you ninety-two pounds, nothing else. There is nothing else I will trade, sir."

He shifted closer, his lips against her cheek now, and Honor thought he intended to kiss her. Her mind screamed for her to bang on the ceiling to cry out to Jonas to save her. But another, wanton part of her was whispering *kiss me. Kiss me, kiss me. . . .*

He slid his hand up her rib cage, to the side of her breast. "I will think on your ninety-two pounds," he murmured, his breath warm and moist on her skin, tantalizing her almost to the point of madness.

"You mean to do it," she said softly, surprised, and opened her eyes. "You will grant me this favor."

"Now you are reprehensible *and* presumptuous. I haven't said I would."

"But I can see that you will," she said, and twisted about to face him, beaming. "Thank you, Mr. Easton!"

He wrapped his fingers around hers.

"Call on me tomorrow, at Beckington House, please. I can explain more openly there."

"I cannot, for the life of me, imagine how much more open you could *possibly* be, Miss Cabot."

"I *knew* you would agree," she said, suddenly full of delight.

"I have not agreed to anything."

"I shall be waiting for you at half past two. The girls will be at their studies and Augustine at his club. Thank you, sir," she said again, her voice full of the gratitude she felt. "I am in your debt." She moved to knock on the ceiling to signal Jonas that this ride was over.

Only then did she realize that Mr. Easton was still holding her hand.

CHAPTER FIVE

Honor returned to Beckington House breathless from her dangerous rendezvous, her heart still beating wildly, and floated into the foyer where she found Prudence and Mercy quarreling loudly.

"Honor!" Prudence cried the moment she saw her older sister. "Please do tell Mercy she is to return my slippers at once!"

"Mercy, please return Pru's slippers at once," Honor said without looking at Mercy's feet.

"But why must she have them always?" Mercy countered. "I can't see what harm there is in borrowing them on occasion."

"You don't see the *harm*?" Prudence demanded. "Honor, you really must *do* something. She's completely without scruples! If you don't insist she hand them over, I shall remove them from her feet myself!"

"Mercy, really," Honor said absently as

she untied her bonnet, her fingers running over the same velvet fabric Easton's fingers had stroked. The fingers that had stroked the skin of her arm, her face; she shivered lightly at the recollection. "They belong to Pru, and you have a wardrobe full of slippers."

"What's this about slippers?" The girls' mother, Joan Devereaux, Lady Beckington, appeared from the corridor. "There will be no forceful removing of slippers, my dears." Her blue eyes were bright; there was no sign of the distant fog Honor noticed in her mother's eyes when she wasn't entirely present. Joan Devereaux was a regal woman, the epitome of elegance and grace, and had once been considered one of the more handsome women of the *ton.* She smiled warmly at her daughters, looking between them. "What are you girls about?"

"Only the usual sort of thing, Mamma," Prudence said imperiously, and began striding for the grand staircase. "Mercy has a wretched habit of borrowing things without permission, and with no consequence!"

"That's a bit dramatic, my darling Pru," Lady Beckington said as she watched her daughter flounce up the stairs.

"Of course you would say that — you're not the injured party!" Prudence tossed over her shoulder, and disappeared into the corridor at the top of the stairs.

Lady Beckington sighed and looked askance at her youngest daughter. "Mercy, darling, you really *must* learn to ask to borrow things instead of taking them. I suggest you go and apologize to your sister and return the slippers. Now go and dress for supper."

"But we've only just had tea," Mercy complained.

"Go on, darling," her mother said, giving her a gentle push in the direction of the stairs. To Honor, she offered her arm, which Honor was happy to take. She let the ribbons of her bonnet flutter behind them as they walked. She noticed that the embroidery on her mother's sleeve was damaged — the threading was coming loose. "What's happened here?" she asked, bending over it to have a look.

"What?" Her mother scarcely glanced down at her sleeve. "Never mind it. Where have *you* been this afternoon?" she asked as they began to make their ascent.

"Nowhere, really." She gave her mother a sheepish smile.

"I know you better than that, Honor. I would guess that your absence from tea involved a gentleman."

Honor could feel herself flush. "Mamma —"

"You don't have to tell me," she said, squeezing her hand fondly. "But your poor mother hopes that you are at least considering the idea that the time has come for you to settle on a single suitor and think of marrying as you ought."

"Why ought I marry now?" Honor asked. The thought of marrying now was unnerving. She felt too . . . unfinished.

"Because you should," her mother said. "There is a whole new world awaiting your entry. You needn't be timid about it."

"Timid! They call me a swashbuckler, Mamma."

"Yes, well, perhaps you are a swashbuckler in the ballroom. But I know my girl, and I think your heart is yet bruised."

In moments like this, it was difficult to believe that her mother was slipping. In moments like this, Honor believed she wasn't, that she and Grace had imagined it all. Her mother seemed at ease, very present in the moment and *quite* motherly. "What shall I wear to supper?" Honor asked, blatantly changing the subject before her mother could question her further.

Her mother laughed. "Very well, have it your way. The blue silk," she said. "It complements your coloring so very well."

"The blue, then," Honor said.

She accompanied her mother to her suite of rooms and rang for Hannah to attend her. She moved on to her suite of rooms. She was not surprised to find Grace within, standing on the new Aubusson rug, her arms folded tightly across her body. Light streamed in from windows opened to late afternoon sun, casting shadows across the silk-covered walls of Honor's rooms and Grace's face.

But the shadows did not hide Grace's ire. "Where have you been?" she demanded.

"Out."

"Yes, yes, quite obviously you have been *out.* Hardy said you took the coach to Gunter's."

"What of it?" Honor asked with a shrug.

"I can't imagine why you would venture out alone to Gunter's, *alone.* One does not enjoy an ice *alone.* I can't help but wonder if there was someone there waiting for you. Was there? Perhaps a certain unclaimed son of a duke who might have been taking his tea?"

Honor blinked. "How could you possibly *know* that?" she exclaimed.

"Mercy saw you speaking to a gentleman in the park, silly bird. She described him perfectly."

"It would seem those spectacles are improving her sight better than we'd hoped," Honor drawled, and carelessly tossed her bonnet onto her bed.

"Then you don't deny it?"

"No," Honor said.

"Lord in heaven!" Grace exclaimed to the papier-mâché ropes and cherubs that adorned the ceiling. "You *promised* me!"

"I know."

"Think of the scandal you invite!"

"Grace! There is no scandal. I am sorry if —"

"Spare me your apologies, please," Grace said, and dropped dramatically onto the chaise longue before the hearth. "You never mean to do it, you are always sorry. When you suggested this ridiculous plan, I laughed. I was naive to think that even *you* wouldn't go through with it, that even *you* wouldn't risk so much for a lark."

Honor frowned, miffed that Grace knew her so well. "It's not a lark, at least not to me. And really, Grace, you bear some responsibility, do you not?"

"Me!"

"Wasn't it you who insisted that I accompany you and Mamma and the girls riding in Hyde Park? If I hadn't seen Easton there, I should have carried on without giving the matter another thought."

Grace gaped at her. And then she burst out with wild laughter and fell back against the cushions of the chaise. "That is the most absurd reasoning I have ever heard!"

Honor couldn't disagree with that, either. "All right," Honor acquiesced, sinking onto the end of the chaise next to Grace. "I will allow that I was a bit impetuous. But, Grace, the idea was so fresh on my mind, and there he was, escorting the *Rivers* twins, of *all* people. It occurred to me that if he would squire those two magpies, he would most certainly think Monica an improvement."

"Of *course* he would think Monica an improvement over those two, but that is hardly the point, is it? The *point* is that you went to meet the man quite alone, a man you scarcely know, and you proposed something absurd and reckless and full of ruin."

"That's one view," she said wearily. "If a woman is to make her way in this man's world without a husband, she must risk quite a lot to succeed. It's not as if I have a solicitor to call upon his solicitor. It's not as if I can offer Monica money to find another suitor. I am a female, and as such, I have nothing available to me to change anything about my life but my hand in marriage. I find it altogether infuriating if I allow myself to dwell —"

"Honor —"

"Yes, well, to put your mind somewhat at ease, I met him in front of Gunter's Tea Shop. No one saw me but Jonas. Easton stepped into the coach, and we talked."

Grace seemed genuinely distressed by that revelation, judging by how she buried her face in her hands. Honor tried to soothe her by stroking her hair. "I don't see another option for us, dearest."

"You *must* have a care for your reputation, which, I might point out, has already been suspect on several occasions." Grace lifted her head to arch a golden brow high above the other, daring Honor to challenge that.

"I've not been *that* bad," Honor muttered.

"Can you imagine the talk that would gust like winter winds around this square if anyone were to see you?"

"I am acutely aware." Honor knew she was too impetuous for her own good. She had no desire to see her reputation ruined, and she understood Grace's concern.

"Never mind all that, then, you've gone and done it." Grace suddenly twisted around to face her "*Well?* What did he say?"

Honor smiled slyly at her sister. "He said that I was reprehensible."

Grace gasped.

"But that he would consider it."

Her sister didn't breathe for a moment. "*What?* He will?"

"I will know on the morrow." Honor stood up and began to unbutton her spencer. "If he agrees, he shall call here."

"*Here!* That's all well and good for outsiders, but what will Augustine think?"

"Grace, calm yourself. Augustine can think of nothing but his nuptials. I asked Mr. Easton to call at half past two, when the girls are in their studies and Augustine is out at his club for the day."

Grace looked set to argue, but the sound of a painful racking cough drifted down the hallway to them; they both paused. A moment later, they heard their mother's steps hurrying in that direction.

Grace sank back onto the chaise. "It's getting worse, isn't it?" she asked morosely, referring to the deteriorating health of the earl.

"I think so," Honor agreed.

"Your plan is utter madness, you know."

"That is the kindest thing you might say for it," Honor said, and squeezed in next to her sister, nudging her with her shoulder.

"But at least it's diverting madness."

Grace smiled ruefully. "I fear you are far beyond hope."

"Not at all, dearest — I am absolutely *bursting* with hope," Honor said. A movement caught Honor's eye; she sat up and turned toward the door. Her mother was standing in the opening, staring into the room.

"Mamma?" Honor said, coming to her feet. "Is something wrong?"

Lady Beckington frowned slightly.

"Mamma," Honor said again, moving to her mother's side. "Did you mean to see to the earl?"

"Oh, Honor," her mother said, her relief clearly evident. "You're home! Yes, the earl is unwell. I should see to him," she said, and squeezed Honor's hand affectionately as she turned and hurried down the hall to the earl's rooms.

Honor looked back at Grace. "I don't understand it. Not a quarter of an hour ago she was perfectly all right."

"We should have Dr. Cardigan come," Grace suggested.

"And risk the *ton* knowing before the earl is even gone? Dr. Cardigan sees every old biddy in Mayfair! We can't, Grace. Not until we absolutely must."

It was heartbreaking to watch a beloved mother slide ever so softly into senility. Joan Devereaux, so charmingly clever — Honor could not think of a single person who had a poor opinion of her. She'd been amazingly resourceful, too — she'd known how to navigate a ballroom better than anyone, and had managed to keep her daughters well after her husband had died. Honor had been only eleven years old, but she could recall her mother taking two old gowns to a friend, and together, they'd created a stunning ball gown. Her mother had donned it and gone off to a grand ball and the next morning had gathered her four daughters in her bed and told them about the Earl of Beckington.

It was necessity that had driven her mother to seek the earl's attentions, but Honor truly believed that her mother had come to care very much for the older earl. Certainly no one in Mayfair would blame Lady Beckington if she left the earl's care to a nurse, but she'd refused to do so. She saw to him every day.

The sound of the earl's racking coughs reached them again. "I'll go and help her," Grace said, and stood from the chaise to go. At the door, however, she glanced back at her sister. "Do have a care, Honor. You are playing a very dangerous game."

"I will," Honor promised.

Later, Honor would recall that moment with Grace and her easy promise. She hadn't believed George Easton would really come to Beckington House.

But he did.

CHAPTER SIX

It took quite a lot to astonish George, but Honor Cabot had done just that. From her bold invitation to meet, to her ridiculous, *preposterous,* cake-headed suggestion, George could not have been more astonished than if the king were to recognize him as his legitimate nephew.

Yesterday, he'd left Berkeley Square stewing in his own juices, aroused as he always was by prettiness, and as disgusted with Miss Cabot as he was with himself for somehow softening to her charm again. He couldn't fathom what it was about this debutante that could so keenly capture him with a smile, but he'd been determined to never see her again. She was trouble. In fact, he'd even been of half a mind to ride directly to Beckington House and explain to the dimwitted Sommerfield exactly what his stepsister was about. She deserved no less.

But George hadn't gone to Beckington House. He'd gone home, riding hard from a pair of dark-lashed blue eyes shimmering in his mind's eye.

Bloody, bloody hell.

Still, he thought that after a good night's sleep, that would be the end of it, that he'd not give as much as a passing thought to the young woman again. He'd gone out last night as was his custom, had dined with several gentlemen at the Coventry House Club. But he'd had no interest in cards or prattling, and had returned home before midnight.

Finnegan had not said a word when George had stalked into his house far earlier than was his custom. He'd merely arched one dark brow high above the other as he'd taken George's hat. "Don't look so smug," George had snapped as he'd strode past.

George had gone to bed quite early, but then had tossed and turned. He'd finally settled on his back, one arm draped above his head, the other on his bare abdomen, and had glared at the canopy above him, his jaw clenched, mulling over that absurd meeting.

Honor Cabot's suggestion was the most fatuous thing he'd ever heard in his life. Furthermore, it was the very thing that made him cringe when he saw squads of young debutantes milling about Mayfair — silly girls in pretty colors playing silly courtship games.

But worse, the game Honor Cabot played was harmful.

The problem, George had mused, was that he was the sort of man who was intrigued by dangerous women. He had no illusions — Honor Cabot was a dangerous woman by nature, and she was made all the more dangerous because of her beauty and her incandescent smile. Regrettably, cunning and beauty were his primary weaknesses when it came to women.

Why was it, he'd wondered in the dark, that he could not be the sort of man who was pleased with a woman of virtue? The sort of chaste woman who would make him a fine wife and bear him beautiful children, someone who would make him attend church services on Sunday and give alms to the poor and dutifully open her legs to him? He supposed that one day, he would settle on a woman for that reason, for her goodness and purity, and he would have his slippers and his spectacles, and he would while away his evenings with a book while his wife attended her needlework.

Someday.

But he had no patience for it now, not with a ship late to port and buyers awaiting his cotton.

So how was it, then, that George found himself the next afternoon at half past two at Grosvenor Square, staring up at the impressive Beckington House with its row of windows that looked black in the afternoon sun? *Utter, indefensible folly.*

No one answered straightaway when George rapped three times, and he had all but turned about, prepared to make his escape when the door suddenly swung open and a man with thinning hair stood imperiously before him.

George fished a calling card from his interior coat pocket. "Mr. Easton for Miss Honor Cabot, if you please."

The man nodded and disappeared for a moment, reappearing again with a silver tray, which he held out to George. When George had deposited the card onto the tray, the door opened wider. The man stepped aside and inclined his head, indicating George should step inside, which he did. Just over the threshold. He tentatively removed his hat.

"If you will kindly wait here, Mr. Easton, I shall inform Miss Cabot that you have called," the butler said, and marched briskly away, the silver tray held high.

George looked up at the soaring entry and the elaborate chandelier hanging high above him. There were paintings on the walls, portraits of people, of landscapes. The marble floor was polished to a sheen, and gold candelabras with new beeswax candles stood in neat rows on a table nearby.

He heard the butler again before he saw him, his brisk walk echoing down the corridor he'd disappeared into. The man bowed. "If you will allow me to show you to a receiving room, sir," he said, and carefully put aside the silver tray — empty now — and moved in the opposite direction from where he'd come, walking into the west corridor.

George followed. They moved down a carpeted hallway past polished wood doors and wall sconces and more beeswax candles. George was reminded of how pleased his mother had been when she could afford to buy one or two beeswax candles and rid their rooms of the smell of tallow for a time.

The butler entered the last room on the right. He opened the pair of doors wide, pushed them back and nudged a doorstop into place with his foot. He strode across the small room to the windows, opened the drapes, tied them back then faced George.

"Is the comfort in the room to your liking, sir, or shall I send a footman to light a fire?"

"That won't be necessary," George said stiffly. "I do not intend to be long."

"Very well, sir. If you require any assistance at all, the bellpull is just there," the butler said, nodding toward a thick velvet braid of rope near the door. "Miss Cabot will join you shortly." He quit the room.

George put his hat aside and examined a painting on the wall as he waited, staring up at the puffy face of a Beckington forefather. He always looked at the portraits in homes like these, looking for any similarity to himself, any hint that he might somehow be related. This man looked nothing like the late Gloucester, except perhaps for the slightly aquiline shape of his nose. George was so intent on that feature that he did not hear the advance of Miss Cabot until she swept into the room on a cloud of pale yellow, her train swirling out behind her as she twirled around to peek out the corridor and then draw the doors quietly closed.

She twirled back around, her smile luminescent, her hands clasped just below her breast, reminiscent of a choirboy preparing to sing. But all similarity to anything remotely angelic ended abruptly when he noticed that the gown she was wearing did not conceal her up to her chin like the one she'd worn yesterday. This gown was cut fashionably low, and creamy mounds of her breast appeared to almost burst from her bodice . . . a mishap George would delight in seeing.

She was oblivious to his fascination with her décolletage. "You *came,*" she said breathlessly.

Bloody fool that he was, yes. George inclined his head in acknowledgment of that.

"I scarcely believe it! I was so certain you'd not come, and I had no good idea of what I might do if you didn't. But here you are!" she exclaimed, casting her arms wide. "You will help me!"

"Before you take flight with joy, Miss Cabot, understand that I came here not to help you in your lunacy, but to dissuade you from it."

She blinked her lovely blue eyes. "*Dissuade* me," she repeated, as if that were a foreign concept to her, which George suspected was highly probable. "But that's not possible, Mr. Easton. My mind is quite made up. When I am fixed on something, I am very dedicated to it. Now then — will you help me?"

George couldn't help but chuckle at her

dogged determination. "No."

"*No?*"

"It is madness, complete and *utter* madness," he said. "It is a loathsome thing to do to a brother and a friend, and I feel it is my duty as a gentleman to direct you away from it — not abet it."

Now her bright smile faded. She folded her arms. "Very well, Mr. Easton. You have done your gentlemanly duty," she said, sounding irreverent. "*Now* will you help me?"

George stared at her. And then he couldn't seem to help himself — he laughed. "You may very well be the most obstinate woman I have ever met."

"Then perhaps you have not met as many women as I've heard tell," she said pertly. "Do you think I make this request to you lightly? That this is a girlish whim? Not at all, sir. Monica Hargrove intends to turn my family out when she marries my brother. She has said as much to me. Further, I don't believe for a moment that you came all the way here to tell me you *won't* help me. You might have sent a note or ignored me altogether, is that not so?"

That was so, and it made George a bit uncomfortable for her to point it out so bluntly. He shrugged.

"That you did not suggests to me that you must have at least *considered* my request. Have you?"

He felt as if he were a naughty boy, caught in the act of mischief. She had him, this shrewd and wily young miss, just as she had that night in Southwark. And she knew it, too, for a smile appeared on her lush lips, ending in little dimples in either cheek. That smile was a small gust of air to smoldering ashes, and George felt a tiny flame ignite.

"It would seem we are agreed," she said silkily.

"Not so fast." He let his gaze slide slowly down her curves and up again. He would like to sink his fingers and his tongue into that flesh, to smell her hair. "If I cannot dissuade you —"

"You cannot —"

"Then it is now my duty as a gentleman to ensure you do no harm to Miss Hargrove."

Miss Cabot beamed, knowing she had won. "How *kind* of you."

"I am not the least bit *kind,* Miss Cabot. But I do have some principles. I'm not sure the same can be said for you."

"I am touched by your concern for Monica," she said sweetly. "My desire is only that she is made aware that there are other, perhaps more attractive possibilities for her so that she will not rush to the altar as she seems to want to do. No harm."

"Debatable," he said, his body caught in the snare of feminine mystique as he moved closer to her. "There is still the matter of what I will have in return for this . . . abominable favor."

"Of course," she said demurely, and folded her arms across her body tightly.

"Let's begin with the agreement that you will return to me the one hundred pounds won in Southwark."

"Ninety-two pounds," she corrected him.

"Ninety-two pounds, then," he said, his gaze falling to her mouth, "will earn you one round of rakish behavior designed to turn Miss Hargrove's head. That ought to suffice."

"Ah . . ." One of Miss Cabot's finely tweezed brows rose high above the other.

"What?" he demanded.

"Nothing, really," she said lightly, and shrugged. "Only that you seem rather confident of that."

George stared at her. He wished to high heaven that such bloody impertinence from a pampered, privileged woman didn't fascinate him quite as much as it did. "Of course I am *confident,* Miss Cabot."

"Oh, dear, I didn't mean to insult you," she said, and her tender smile shot through him. "I have no doubt that you would turn the head of most debutantes —"

"You are not improving the situation."

She bit her lip.

He very much wanted to bite that lip, too. George frowned — he didn't like that, not at all. When he began to want things like that, he did very foolish things. One could inquire of several women in this town and find it was so. "Well, then? I will agree to speak to Miss Hargrove and pay her a . . . foppish compliment or two," he said, with a flick of his wrist, "in exchange for ninety-two pounds." He extended his hand, offering to shake on it.

But Miss Cabot gazed reluctantly at his hand.

George sighed. "For heaven's sake, what now?"

"I will agree on one condition," she said, holding up a finger.

"You are in no position to impose *conditions* —"

"Agreed," she said quickly. "Nevertheless . . . you must allow me to instruct you."

It took a moment for those words to sink into George's brain. "I beg your pardon, but I am most certainly not in need of your *instruction,*" he said irritably. "You have come to *me* for my experience, is that not so? I think I am a fair judge of what effort is involved in chatting up a young debutante," he added with an indignant snort.

"Yes . . . but I know her better than anyone," she said, tilting her head back to look him directly in the eye.

"Good God, you speak as if I come to this in short pants —"

"That is *not* what I —"

George suddenly grabbed her by the waist, yanking her into his body.

"Mr. Easton!" she exclaimed. "What are you doing?"

He didn't know what he was doing, honestly. Reacting to some primal drumbeat in his veins. "I don't need your instruction," he said in a low voice, and brushed his knuckles against her temple.

"You are too *familiar,*" she objected crossly, but her hands curled around his upper arms, and she made no move to escape him.

"I am aware." His gaze moved over her face. "And yet you enjoy it. That is my point."

"Are you always so assured, sir?"

"Are you?" he retorted.

"You mistake my offense for misunderstanding," she said to his mouth, and the drum beat louder in George. "But make no mistake — I am *offended.*"

"If you were *offended,*" he said, mimicking her, "you would kick and claw like any prim little lass to be set free." He cocked a brow, daring her to disagree.

She frowned darkly at him.

"Aha," he said, brushing his fingers against her collarbone. It felt small and fragile to him. "It would appear that I know women far better than you."

Honor Cabot responded to that with a firm kick to his shin.

George instantly let go and reached for his leg. "Ouch," he said with a wince.

Miss Cabot put her hands on her waist and glared at him as he rubbed his shin. "I grant that you are acquainted with women, Mr. Easton. Everyone in Mayfair is aware of just how *well* you are acquainted. But *I* am acquainted with Monica Hargrove. I know what will entice her and what will turn her away, and I must insist that you allow me to at least prepare you!"

He was acquainted with women, all right, but he'd yet to meet one like Honor Cabot. And it didn't help matters when she sensed a crack in his facade, for a smile slowly began to light her face. Bloody hell, but those smiles were his undoing! They fairly sang through him, made his blood rush, his body tense. How was it possible this wisp of a young woman could affect him so? He straightened up with a sigh of resignation.

"I happen to know she will be attending the Garfield Assembly this Friday," Miss Cabot said.

Lustful thoughts gave way to terror. George knew of the Garfield Assembly; everyone in London knew of it. The *haut ton* in its entirety would attend. All his life, the world of the *ton* had been held out to him as the ideal, as the world in which he would never be welcomed. He was well aware that were it not for his wealth, he would not be tolerated at all. He feared that if he lost his wealth — which, arguably, he was on the verge of losing — he'd be shunned as a pariah. Nothing was more loathsome than someone who had tried to become one of them and had failed.

George had been treated all his life as if he were deficient, that he was less than mere mortals because his father had not claimed him. His father's refusal had become George's burden of shame to shoulder. He had trained himself to keep his heart at arm's length from anyone, to maintain an emotional distance. He fancied himself like the magnificent show horses of the royal cavalry he'd brushed when he was a child. Like them, he was proud and high-stepping, his movements precise, his looks enviable. But he never looked right or left, never wanted anything that wasn't in his prescribed path. He kept trotting forward, his steps high, his head held higher.

George had known his share of bruising disappointments, and yet he did not think himself a bitter man — quite the contrary, he thought himself generally a happy one. But then again, he took great pains to avoid venues like the Garfield Assembly.

"No," he said instantly.

"Mr. Easton! What better opportunity?" Miss Cabot asked, her eyes shining with the victory of his giving in to her. *Again.*

"I think I was quite clear at our first meeting. I will not frequent assembly rooms."

"But I can facilitate your entry —"

"Pardon, you can *what*? I do not need you to *facilitate* anything on my behalf, Miss Cabot. It may astonish you to know that there are some such as myself who simply don't care to spend an evening surrounded by vapid, simpering debutantes!"

Miss Cabot's smile only deepened with happy skepticism, and the drum began to beat again. "You surely do not think me so naive as *that,* sir," she said pertly. "You do not want to attend the assembly because you can't gain entry without proper invitation. But I can get you that invitation. And you must agree it is the perfect opportunity. Augustine will not be in attendance, and you need only speak with Miss Hargrove to put the suggestion in her head that you find her appealing."

"I don't need to attend an assembly for that," he said crisply.

"What, then, do you think to do it on the street?" Miss Cabot asked gaily. She suddenly took him by the hand. "Come," she said, and pulled him to the center of the room. "Stand just there, if you please." She pulled a chair from the hearth and positioned it before him, sat down, and arranged her skirts before gracefully folding her hands in her lap. "All right, then, we are in an assembly room."

George stared down at her.

"Go on," she said with a charming smile. "Pretend I am Miss Hargrove and you wish to talk to me." She settled herself once more, then looked away.

George could not believe he was standing in the Beckington House receiving room, engaged in some foolish courtship game. "This is daft," he groused.

"Please," she said angelically.

God in heaven. He muttered a curse to himself, pushed a hand through his hair, then bowed. "Good evening, Miss Hargrove."

Miss Cabot glanced at him sidelong. "Oh. Mr. Easton," she said, and nodded politely before looking away again.

George stood there. This was not the way he would go about turning Monica Hargrove's head, not at all. In fact, he had never approached a woman in this manner and wondered at those who did. It felt a bit desperate. Is this how the young bucks behaved in the storied drawing rooms of Mayfair?

Honor looked at him sidelong again. "Sit next to me," she whispered.

"Why?" George demanded.

"You should be at eye level. You look so . . ." Her gaze swept over him, and if George wasn't mistaken, she blushed slightly. *"Big,"* she said. "You look very big, towering over me as you are."

George did not see the significance. "I *am* big."

"But that is rather intimidating to an impressionable woman," she said. "Please, do sit."

"Intimidating!" He laughed. "I think there

is nothing that will intimidate you, Miss Cabot."

"Certainly not! But we are not speaking of *me.* We are speaking of Miss Hargrove."

George couldn't help his chuckle. "Bloody hell," he said, and reached for a chair at his elbow and set it next to Miss Cabot. He sat. She looked away. She did not speak. What was he supposed to do, then? He racked his brain for what to say. "The weather is fine," he said.

"It is indeed." Her gaze was not on him. "I beg your pardon, Mr. Easton, but I am wanted across the room." She abruptly stood and glided away. When he did not follow — was he to chase after her like a puppy, too? — she twirled around and frowned at him.

"What in the devil is the point of that?" George demanded.

"The *point,* Mr. Easton, is that you did not engage me. All I saw was a big man with nothing to say."

Her remark struck a nerve in George — it was precisely the thing he feared, that he somehow would never reach the measure the *ton* put on him. "That's quite enough," he said crossly. "I refuse to be part of some elaborate, choreographed courting dance." He suddenly stood up and strode directly toward her.

"What are you doing?" she exclaimed.

George didn't answer. He stepped around a chair, continued moving toward her. Miss Cabot quickly scrambled out of his path, but found herself caught between a table and the door. She whirled around, pressed herself flat against the door, her eyes widening as he walked up to her and brazenly braced himself with one hand beside her head.

Miss Cabot blinked big blue eyes up at him. Silly young woman. She had no idea that she roused the beast in a man. "I'll show you how to attract an impressionable young woman's attention, Miss Cabot."

"Is this how you will do it? Because you are too forward *again.* This sort of thing requires a bit of finesse."

He suddenly smiled and took in her delectable figure once more. "I've not even begun to *finesse* it," he muttered, and leaned in, his head close to hers, his breath in her hair. "I know precisely what needs to be done," he added softly, and turned his head so that his lips brushed her temple. "You need not fret."

"Then, for God's sake, do not mention the weather," she said low.

He was of a mind to take her in hand now,

to show her how a man enticed a woman. But he kept his desire in check; he was a man who enjoyed the pleasures of a woman's flesh, of giving her pleasure, yes — but he was not a man to dally with a young woman with no more experience than a goat. "To hell with the weather. I shall mention the ivory of her skin," he said, brushing his lips against her cheek. "The scent of her hair," he added, touching his nose to her hair. "And then I will quietly mention the desire that wells in a man when he is graced with her smile."

Miss Cabot did not move. The color bloomed in her cheeks, and she drew another, deeper breath before slowly releasing it and saying, "That would do for a start, I should think."

He heard the slight tremor in her voice and smiled to himself as he shifted closer, his hand finding her waist. "You want me to turn Miss Hargrove's head, love? Not only will I turn it," he said smoothly as he caressed her side, his hand sliding down her hip, squeezing the flesh of it as he pressed against her body, "I will make her want to open her legs like a flower."

Miss Cabot sucked in a sharp breath, her chest rising with it. *"No,"* she whispered.

"No? I won't put my cock in her, if that's

what you fear. In spite of what you think you know, I am a discerning man." He pressed his erection against her hip. "I only put my cock where it is most appreciated." He kissed her temple, feeling the frantic flutter of her pulse beneath his lips. "I plow only fields of pure spun gold," he muttered, and put his mouth against her neck, sucking lightly, his tongue on her skin as he ran his hand up her side to her breast, filling his palm with it, kneading it.

"No self-respecting gentleman would put his hand on a woman," Miss Cabot said breathlessly, her eyes fluttering shut as she bent her neck to give him better access.

He almost laughed as he moved to her ear, nibbling at her lobe. "No. But you did not come to me because I am a self-respecting gentleman, Miss Cabot. Now hush," he said, and slid his hand around to her hands, which she held clasped tightly at her back, and pulled one free of its grip of the other. He lifted that hand to his mouth. Miss Cabot's lips parted slightly; her eyes fixed on his face. George turned her hand over and licked the inside of her wrist before kissing it. Her skin was warm and fragrant, and smooth as butter against his tongue. It was dangerously provocative, and he could feel his own heart beginning to race with want. He slipped one hand beneath her chin, tilting her head back. Her eyes were as wide as saucers, her lips slightly parted. He was out of his mind to go any further, but George couldn't help himself; he lowered his head, touched his mouth softly to hers, lingering there, his tongue teasing her lips, one hand boldly caressing her breast, squeezing it, then sliding down to her hip, squeezing it, too. When he felt her begin to soften, felt the familiar curve of a woman's body into his, felt himself grow harder, he lifted his head and said, "Perhaps you will do me the honor of saving me a dance, Miss Hargrove?"

Miss Cabot nodded. *"Yes."* Her voice was a bit shaky, and she quickly cleared her throat. She said again, more firmly, "Yes. Thank you."

Satisfied with the knowledge that he'd succeeded in showing her a small step in the dance of seduction, he stepped back, putting a respectable distance between them.

Miss Cabot did not move. She stared at him, her gaze sliding down to the protrusion of his desire in his trousers.

Unabashed, George cocked a brow. His response was as natural as breathing, and if she had not seen a man's desire, more was the pity. "Well, then?" he asked her.

"I think," she said, nervously touching the strand of pearls at her throat, "I think that will do." She continued to stare at him, her eyes locked on his mouth, and it stirred dangerously deep and devilish in him. He needed to leave. Now. Before he did something that he regretted. "Then we are agreed, Miss Cabot. Now then. When is this assembly?"

"Friday," she said. "Half past eight."

He nodded, picked up his hat and fit it on his head. "Then I shall make a point of attending."

"Thank you again, Mr. Easton. You can't know how much I appreciate your help." Her smile was tremulous, but there was no mistaking the glow in her cheeks.

That was it, then. George had made his deal with the devil, all for the sake of a bloody smile. He'd come very near to undoing her gown, too, and lest there be any more thoughts along those lines, he would remove himself from Beckington House. God help him, but this irresponsible and devious woman captivated him in a way he did not care to be captivated. "Good day, Miss Cabot."

"Good day, Mr. Easton," she said, still absently fingering the strand of pearls as she eyed him curiously as he strode through the door.

CHAPTER SEVEN

Honor and Grace Cabot entered the Garfield Assembly like a pair of princesses, but tonight, Honor outshone her younger sister in a gown of pale blue silk with pearl trim. She was so stunning, Monica turned away, holding out her cup to the footman to refill with punch.

The many gowns and shoes and accoutrements Honor and Grace possessed amazed Monica. She had once teasingly inquired of Augustine if the family coffers had been robbed to support his stepsisters' wardrobes, but Augustine had earnestly assured her that the funds had come from their late father.

Of course Augustine had believed it, the poor man — he hadn't the slightest notion how much a wardrobe such as the one Honor possessed might cost. Monica was not even slightly convinced that the late Richard Cabot, who had risen as high as bishop in the Church of England, had left enough of his family's money to outfit his daughters in such an extravagant manner. Monica imagined that Honor had somehow managed to take terrible advantage of her ailing stepfather. She had no evidence to support that, naturally, but it seemed quite impossible that one woman, as yet unmarried, could be so *fashionable*.

Honor annoyed Monica. Honor had once been Monica's closest friend, but Monica disliked that Honor had everything. *Everything!* She had fine looks with her dark hair and astoundingly blue eyes and smooth skin. Monica had auburn hair and brown eyes, and when she stood next to Honor, she could almost feel herself seeping into the wallpaper.

Honor also had the unflappable, unfailingly cheerful disposition, whereas Monica was, at times, prone to dark moods that she could not, no matter how hard she might try, seem to keep from her expression.

Honor also had the privilege of making her life at the palatial Beckington House in London, or at the earl's majestic country seat of Longmeadow. It was as if when her father died, Honor had fallen into the lap of luxury. And now that she was grown and out in society, men *adored* Honor — one

126

need only look about this room and see how many of them glanced at her admiringly to see it was so. Honor squandered that attention. So many young women would appreciate the options of suitors, but Honor never seemed to move beyond only a cursory courtship.

And what did Monica have? Two older brothers, that was what, with not a single thought of society or fashion between them. Her family lived in a respectable house just outside Mayfair, and her father was an esteemed scholar of law. Not an earl. Not even a baron. A scholar.

Monica considered herself fortunate to have been accepted into such august society as the one that surrounded her this evening. She herself had never wanted for admirers, but she wasn't the type to flirt and invite the attentions of several gentlemen at once. In truth, Monica felt intimidated by many men and considered herself fortunate to have caught the eye of Augustine, Viscount Sommerfield.

Augustine didn't intimidate her; he was genuinely adoring of her. Her parents were over the moon at her engagement, and the sooner Monica married Augustine, the happier they would be. Who would have thought that their daughter would marry a titled man and become a countess?

Monica knew that Honor believed her understanding with Augustine was all by design, but in truth, it had happened quite honestly. At first, Monica had been amused by Augustine's attentions. He was a bit too round for her tastes, and he could be a bit of a bumbler at times. But as days turned into weeks, she'd grown rather fond of him. He was very attentive and sincere in his devotion to her. It certainly didn't hurt that he would one day be an earl, or that Monica would preside over the Beckington estates as Lady Beckington. Monica had grown accustomed to the idea, and she truly believed that she and Augustine would have a family, and she would live quite contentedly.

She hadn't really given any thought to his stepsisters until her mother suggested that six in a marriage of two might be a bit crowded. "I hope you won't need to vie for Sommerfield's attentions with all those girls," she'd said laughingly. Or, "Ah, isn't Honor's gown lovely? I hope there will be enough money for *you* to be clothed in that manner when you are countess."

Now Monica did not see a gaggle of stepsisters in her rosy view of the future.

Speaking of which . . . Monica glanced

over her shoulder now. A pair of gentlemen had intercepted Honor, and they were laughing as if she'd said something terribly witty. Even from here, Monica could see the twinkle in Honor's eye.

Monica turned away from that scene and was startled by Lady Chatham, who had appeared from seemingly nowhere to stand directly beside her.

"Lady Chatham," Monica said, dipping a curtsy.

"Good evening, Miss Hargrove," she said cheerfully. "Have you come alone? Where is your handsome fiancé?"

"He won't be attending this evening. He had a prior commitment."

"I see," Lady Chatham said.

Monica could almost hear the little mice wheels turning in the woman's head, stuffing away gossip to be doled out in enticing little bits to her friends on the morrow. "I have come in the company of my cousin, Mr. Hatcher," Monica added.

"Mr. Hatcher is a *dear*," Lady Chatham said, as if she knew him. "I see the Cabots have arrived. At least Miss Cabot is wearing pearls in her hair and no one's bonnet this evening."

Really, that entire incident had spiraled out of control. Monica *had* commissioned the hat, but when she'd gone round, the price was much greater than the proprietress had led her to believe it would be. She hadn't intended to purchase it — but why did Honor have to be the one to take it?

"That was just a trifle, really. I didn't care for the bonnet at all." She smiled, hoping that bit of untruth was not noticed.

"Well, neither did I," Lady Chatham agreed. "It seemed to me designed to draw attention, and that, Miss Hargrove, is *not* the way young ladies should behave."

Monica didn't think that the bonnet was as showy as that, and neither did she think for a moment that Honor was concerned about appearances to old women like Lady Chatham. Quite the contrary — Honor was perfectly happy to take risks, to flaunt society rules. That was the difference between them — Honor always pushed, and Monica followed the rules.

"Miss Hargrove."

Monica turned slightly to see Thomas Rivers standing beside her.

"Lady Chatham," he said, inclining his head to the older woman, before smiling at Monica again. "Miss Hargrove, will you do the honor of standing up with me?"

Lady Chatham waved her fingers and trilled, "Of course, of course! You must dance and be merry, Miss Hargrove, for soon you will be a married woman."

"Pardon?" Monica said, confused as to what, exactly, Lady Chatham had meant, but she'd already swanned away.

Mr. Rivers led her onto the ballroom floor. The dance began with a pair of turns, one way, then the other. On the second turn, Monica happened to catch sight of George Easton, who, surprisingly, was watching her. Monica twirled the other way.

George Easton, *here*? She knew Easton instantly, of course — everyone knew him. One did not claim to be the nephew of the king and escape attention. Recently, she'd heard he had jeopardized his fortune.

How had he gained entrance? Lady Feathers, the lead patroness of the assembly, was quite strict in her rules of entry, and Monica could not imagine that she would ever allow the bastard son of the Duke of Gloucester to enter, particularly as the current duke was disdainful of the man he called a pretender.

The dance came to an end, and Mr. Rivers escorted Monica from the dance floor. She declined his offer for a drink and watched him move away, searching for his next dance partner.

Monica scanned the crowd — there was

Honor again, dancing now, her step light and free as she skipped around Charles Braxton in her figures, while Braxton admired her like an adoring child. Grace was on the dance floor as well, her smile brilliant beneath the candelabras, her dancing more elegant than her sister's.

Monica turned away, unwilling to watch. She was seeking a familiar face to talk to when she felt a tingling in her spine — she could *feel* someone looking at her, and when she turned about, she was surprised once again to see George Easton staring directly at her.

Not only was his gaze locked on her, he was walking purposefully in her direction. Monica thought perhaps she was mistaken, but Easton headed right to her. He smiled charmingly and bowed low. "Miss Hargrove, may I be so bold as to present myself to you? I hope you will forgive me, but I saw you with Rivers and I've not been able to turn away. I am George Easton, at your service."

Was he not aware that a gentleman did not approach a lady without invitation? Monica glanced slyly around the room to see if anyone had noticed this breach of etiquette. "How do you do, Mr. Easton," she said, smiling a little. She found his approach completely suspect, and yet she couldn't help but be a bit flattered by it.

He gave her a dazzling smile. "I confess I am quite captivated."

Gentlemen had, at times, been captivated with her, but they hadn't admitted it quite like that. "Are you, indeed?" she asked, smiling coyly. "How unusual it is to have a gentleman approach without invitation, and make such a proclamation."

"I am an unusual man," he said cheerfully. "But I see I've been too forthright. I've been accused of being so in the past, but when it comes to beautiful women, it is a habit I cannot seem to break. May I offer you a glass of punch, Miss Hargrove?"

What was happening here? Why was he talking to her like this? She didn't believe for a moment that a man of his charm and fine looks and reputation would be the least bit captivated by her. She was suddenly wildly curious as to what he was about. "You may."

He led her across the room to the sideboard, nodded at the footman attending and accepted a glass of punch to hand to Monica.

"Thank you."

Easton smiled again, his eyes softening around the corners. He really was *quite* handsome, what with his square jaw, blue eyes and brown hair streaked with gold. Monica wished Augustine had more hair, really; his was beginning to thin on top.

Easton touched her elbow lightly and led her away from the sideboard. "You will undoubtedly think me bold again if I were to proclaim there is not a lovelier woman in attendance tonight, but I must say it is so."

He was perhaps a bit blind. "But there are so many women here tonight," Monica said.

"None that can compare to you." With his finger, he casually caressed her wrist. His eyes seemed almost to dance, and Monica was beginning to appreciate how the man might have earned his notorious reputation of bedding women with ease.

"I was watching you dance with Rivers," he said, his gaze sliding to her décolletage. "Admiring your figure."

"I saw you," Monica said.

He leaned closer, his head next to hers, and whispered, "I found myself rather envious of Sommerfield."

"Perhaps you should tell that to Lord Sommerfield."

"And have him call me out?"

Monica couldn't help but smile at that preposterous notion. A man like Easton had nothing to fear from Augustine when it came to duels or fights, or however men settled challenges between them. Monica was intrigued by Easton's sudden interest in her . . . but not fooled by it. She wondered what gain he sought from it. An introduction to someone, perhaps? To Augustine? She looked him squarely in the eye and said, "I cannot help but wonder at your interest in me."

He looked surprised by her forthrightness. "I should think a woman as comely as you must have gentlemen admiring you at every turn, Miss Hargrove."

He didn't *truly* think she would believe him? It was so wildly preposterous given the differences in their stations and circumstances.

"I had rather hoped you would do me the honor of standing up with me so that I might admire you a bit longer than decorum will allow," he said, and put out his hand for hers.

Monica laughed. She had no intention of standing up with him, of starting any sort of rumor. She pressed her cup into his hand. "Thank you, but I should not like to be the subject of any undue speculation. Good evening, Mr. Easton," she said airily, and walked away.

She glanced back over her shoulder as she

moved away.

He was watching her, his head down, his smile a bit smug.

Really, what the devil was he after?

CHAPTER EIGHT

George Easton left the assembly in the company of a gentleman Honor didn't recognize. He had not so much as looked in her direction in the short time he was there, but she nevertheless assumed he'd lived up to his end of the agreement.

She also assumed that if he'd been even a fraction as potent as he had been with her at Beckington House, Monica was properly reduced to a bag of weightless feathers by now. God knew that Honor had been so reduced by him, her heart racing well after he'd gone, that ethereal kiss lingering on her lips for hours afterward. That Monica would be suffering so was something Honor really had to see for herself.

Honor searched the crowd for Monica, finally spotting her at table in the company of Agatha Williamson and Reginald Beeker.

She did not look like a weightless bag of feathers.

She actually looked a little sullen.

Oh, no. No, it couldn't possibly be. Honor was marching across the room before she even realized it.

Monica was so intent on what Mr. Beeker was saying that she did not, at first, notice Honor. "Oh," she said, clearly surprised to see Honor standing before her. "Good evening."

"Good evening," Honor said brightly. "Miss Williamson, a pleasure to see you again. Mr. Beeker, how do you do?" she asked politely as that gentleman scrambled to his feet.

"Likewise, I'm sure," Miss Williamson said.

No one invited her to sit, but that did not deter Honor. "May I join you?" she asked pleasantly.

Mr. Beeker eagerly pulled a chair out for her. Honor sat and smiled at Monica.

"Shall I fetch us some drinks?" Mr. Beeker asked.

"Would you be so kind?" Honor asked before Monica could speak.

"You'll need some help," Miss Williamson said.

"Thank you," Mr. Beeker said, and smiled at Honor before departing with his trusty aide on his quest to bring back four drinks.

"Well, then? To what do I owe the pleasure of your company, Honor?" Monica asked drily.

Honor laughed. "Only a desire to greet my old friend."

"Mmm," Monica said, taking Honor in. "Your gown is lovely."

If there was one thing that could be said of Monica, she appreciated a fine gown when she saw one. "Thank you," Honor said. "As is yours," she added, thinking the dark green suited Monica's complexion very well. "Did Mrs. Dracott fashion it?" she asked, referring to the much-sought-after modiste.

"No," Monica said tightly. "Mrs. Wilbert. Mrs. Dracott has many commissions at the moment, what with the Season. But she's done very well by you, hasn't she? I suppose there is even a bonnet that matches the gown?" she asked, her gaze narrowing slightly on Honor.

"Good Lord, you're not still angry about the bonnet, are you?" Honor asked with a dismissive flick of her wrist.

"No angrier than I was the summer you wooed Mr. Gregory away," Monica sniffed.

Honor laughed with surprise. "We were sixteen years old, Monica. Really, why must you always bring up old hurts?"

"I'm not bringing up an old hurt, but an old scheme," Monica said. "That's always the way with you, isn't it? One scheme or another?"

"Scheme!" Honor protested. "Shall we speak of schemes? Do you recall the Bingham dance, and how you and Agnes Mulberry took the last two seats in the Bingham coach, when *I* was the one who'd been invited and, in turn, invited the two of you? I had no other means of attending and you knew it very well."

"Just as well as you knew that you had not invited me to the soiree at Longmeadow." Monica clucked her tongue. "A lost invitation, indeed!"

Honor lifted her chin, wisely choosing not to recall that summer after all. "Never mind that, Monica. I came to offer my felicitations, not rehash the summer of your sixteenth year."

"Felicitations? For what?" Monica asked.

"Am I mistaken?" Honor asked. "Augustine said that you were very keen to marry and that it may occur sooner rather than later."

Monica suddenly laughed; her light brown eyes sparkled. "My dearest Sommerfield!" she said gaily. "You misunderstood him, Honor. He is so keen to marry *me* that he speaks of Gretna Green with alarming frequency."

"Then you'd best marry him straightaway," Honor said. "One can hardly say when another man might come along so keen to marry you, can one?"

"Pardon?" Monica said laughingly. "Really, Honor, I know you too well, and I know you did not traverse the ballroom to ask after my wedding. That's not the least bit like you. Or me, for that matter."

Honor couldn't help but laugh. "True," she agreed. "But as we are to be sisters, I hoped we might turn over a new leaf," she said. "No more bickering over bonnets and whatnot."

Monica's arched a dark brow. "Indeed? If you *truly* wish to turn over a new leaf, then neither of us should be surprised to discover unpleasant facts about the other . . . such as scheduling a tea the very day the other has scheduled one. Is that what you mean, in turning over a new leaf?"

Monica had her there — last Season, Honor had indeed scheduled a garden tea on the very day and at the very hour of Monica's tea — to which, Honor graciously declined to point out, she and Grace had not been invited. But in Honor's defense, she really didn't believe they would be inviting the same people. She'd supposed Monica would invite all the tedious, lifeless acquaintances, while she would have the lively, diverting guests at hers.

"And neither shall we publicly speculate as to each other's whereabouts," Honor said, reminding Monica that during last Season's Jubilee Ball, Monica had openly suggested that Honor had snuck away with Lord Cargill, when in fact Honor had been in the retiring room with Grace. It had caused quite a *lot* of speculation.

"We'll mind that we don't," Monica said, graciously inclining her head.

Honor smiled. "So then, have you had a nice evening?"

"Passable."

"Did you make any new acquaintances?"

Monica cocked her head to one side. "What do you mean?" she asked suspiciously. "Why have you this sudden interest in my evening?"

"Dear God, but you are suspicious!" Honor said. "It's just that I find this crowd so terribly tiresome in its sameness, don't you? I should like someone new to divert us all. There you have it, the root of our disagreements — you always misunderstand me!"

"Or perhaps it is because I understand

you completely," Monica parried. "If you are seeking diversion, darling, perhaps you ought to consider a trip abroad. I said as much to Augustine just this week," Monica said, and began to straighten her glove as if she were speaking about the weather. "I said that perhaps you might find new and different things more to your liking in America."

An alarm sounded in Honor's brain. She tried to laugh. "What a lark."

Monica lifted her gaze from her glove. "Augustine was rather intrigued. He said he would very much like to see you and Grace enjoy a more worldly education. It seems to me if you find our society so tiresome, maybe you will find another society more diverting."

"I didn't say I found our society tiresome, Monica. I said I found the company this evening tiresome. I will kindly ask you not to put thoughts into Augustine's head."

"As part of our new leaf," Monica suggested slyly.

"Precisely," Honor responded firmly.

"Here we are!" Mr. Beeker's voice rang out. He and Miss Williamson suddenly sailed into view, each of them holding two glasses of wine.

"Oh, dear, look at the time. I'm afraid it's gotten away from me," Honor said, rising to her feet. "I really must be home to wish the earl a good-night." She looked pointedly at Monica. She might be out on her arse when the earl died, but today, she still held the upper hand. "Good evening, then," she said pleasantly.

"Good evening, Honor," Monica said, just as pleasantly.

Honor walked away, her back straight, her chin high, as if she hadn't a care in the world.

When in fact, she suddenly had many.

America! The devil take Monica Hargrove.

CHAPTER NINE

How was it possible that her plan had not worked?

The question caused Honor to toss and turn all night. She herself had been on the verge of being swept away by Easton's pretend seduction in her own receiving room, so how had Monica possibly resisted it?

There was only one explanation: George Easton had not kept his word. Or worse, he'd kept his word and had failed.

The next morning, Honor woke tired and cross. She pulled on her dressing gown, sat down at her writing table, and dashed off a note to Easton: *You gave me your word.*

She was still wearing her dressing gown when she went down to the foyer. The old footman, Foster, was at the door; she pressed the note into his hand. "Please deliver this to Audley Street."

Foster looked at her letter. "Easton," he

said out loud.

"*Shh!*" Honor hissed, and glanced quickly behind her, lest anyone had wandered into the foyer and overheard Foster. "*Discretion,* Mr. Foster."

"Aye, Miss Cabot," he said, a twinkle in his eye. "Ain't I always discreet, then?"

"You are," she said with a fond pat of his arm. "I have long depended —"

"*Honor?* What in heaven?"

Honor whirled around. "Augustine! Good morning!"

Augustine was standing with a linen napkin, presumably from breakfast, tucked into his collar. "I was coming to find you." He looked past her, to Foster. "What are you doing at the door in your dressing gown?"

"Aye, miss, looks like a lot of rain today," Foster said quickly. "Quite a downpour, really."

Honor adored the stately old footman. "Thank you, I shall dress accordingly." She turned back to Augustine with a bright smile.

"Then hurry along and dress, will you?" Augustine asked. "Mercy insists on regaling us with some gruesome tale of walking cadavers," he said, wrinkling his nose. "It has put me off my breakfast. The lass could

146

use a firm hand if you ask me."

"Oh, no, we can't have that," Honor said, wondering where Augustine's firm hand had gotten off to this morning. She gave Foster another sly smile, then darted up the stairs to her rooms to dress.

Rain continued to pour through breakfast and into the noon hour with no sign of abating. Honor spent the late morning reading to her stepfather. The damp weather did not help the poor man's situation, and he lay against the pillows, his eyes fixed on some point well beyond this room. He looked sad and exhausted. His once robust cheeks were sunken, his hands bony, his eyes rheumy.

At some point during her reading of Wordsworth's *Lyrical Ballads,* the earl closed his eyes. Honor quietly closed the book of poetry and carefully rose from her seat. She tiptoed across the carpet and had all but slipped through the door when the earl said roughly, "Honor, darling."

She turned back. His arm was outstretched, as if he'd tried to touch her as she'd slipped by him. "Are you all right?" she asked, moving back to his side. "Is anything the matter? Shall I fetch Mamma?"

He gestured for her hand, and she wrapped her fingers around his. "You must look after your mother when I'm gone," he said, his voice hoarse from coughing.

"Of course."

"Heed me, Honor — she'll have no one but her daughters to ensure she comes to no harm. Do you understand?" he asked, his eyes searching hers.

He knew. The earl knew what she and Grace suspected — that her mother was slowly losing her mind. "I understand you very well, my lord."

"I have loved your mother these many years," he said. "I believe Augustine is quite fond of her, but my son is weak. He is easily influenced. He is a good man, but I think too eager to please others."

"Perhaps," Honor reluctantly agreed. "My mother has loved you, my lord, as have we all. I give you my word I shall look after her."

The earl patted her hand. "How will you do it, my dearest Honor? I've been too lenient with you, haven't I, allowing you to flit about. Is there no one who might have caught your eye?"

Honor's heart fluttered; she thought of Rowley, how she had pined for him. "There was one, but he didn't desire me."

The earl made a clucking sound. "Then he is a fool. I suppose the thought of keeping a beautiful woman in style can seem quite daunting to some gentlemen."

"But I don't care about things so much," Honor said.

The earl smiled. "No? You've certainly made use of my coffers."

She smiled guiltily, but shook her head. "I like things well enough, my lord, but they are only things. If I loved someone, *truly* loved, nothing else would matter."

"If you find love again, my darling, latch on to it and hold tight. It's a rare bird, far too fine to let go. And don't be afraid of hurt. It serves its purpose and makes you appreciate love even more."

"Yes, well," she said, and glanced down. She did not care for the pain of losing love. She preferred to avoid it at all costs.

"You're a good girl, Honor. I don't care a whit what anyone else may say." He sighed, let go of her hand and let his head loll to one side. "Send Jericho in, will you?" he asked, referring to the man who had been his valet, and had, in the past two years, become one of his closest caretakers. He closed his eyes with a heavy sigh.

Honor found Jericho and sent him to check on the earl, then followed the sound of sprightly music downstairs. As she walked through the foyer, Foster happened to step in through the main door, pausing at the threshold to shake the water off his cloak and his hat.

"Foster! Have you delivered it, then?"

"Aye, miss," he said as he put his hat aside.

"And? Was there a reply?"

"No, miss. The butler said the gentleman had not yet returned home from the evening, and he'd hand it over when he arrived."

Not yet returned home? A curious little tickle went through Honor — there was only one place a man might stay all night and well into the morning, wasn't there? A warm bed, she reckoned, with a curving body to warm it. *Fields of gold.* Another, stronger, tickle went through her.

"Thank you," she said to Foster distractedly.

She carried on to the music room, imagining Easton with a woman, linens sliding away from his nude and rigid body as he demanded more from his conquest. *Who was the woman?* Lady Dearing?

In the music room, she found her sisters. Prudence was playing the pianoforte — she was the most musically inclined of the four of them, with an ear that Honor envied. Grace was seated at a table, her quill dancing across the page as she penned a letter.

Mercy was on her belly before the hearth, her knees bent and her ankles crossed. She was slowly turning the pages of fashion plates in *Lady's Magazine*. A soft fire glowed in the fireplace, and candles were lit around the room to chase away the gloom of the rainy day.

"Who are you writing, Grace?" Honor asked as she took a seat on the settee and curled her feet beneath her.

"Cousin Beatrice."

"She's not our cousin," Honor corrected her.

"No?" asked Prudence, pausing in the midst of her music.

Honor shook her head. "She and Mamma were childhood friends, so close that they took to calling each other cousin. Why on earth are you writing her, Grace?"

"Because she resides in Bath, and I should like to know if perchance she has seen Lord Amherst there. I understand he is not yet in London."

Honor blinked. "Amherst? Why?"

"Honor, really!" Grace said with a pert smile. "It's a private concern that I would think you'd have *guessed*." Honor could not guess, but Grace glanced meaningfully at Mercy, who had stopped flipping the pages of the magazine to stare intently at Grace.

"What is it?" Mercy demanded. "Why do you never tell me anything?"

"Because you are a child. What do you think of this piece?" Prudence asked, and began to play another sprightly tune.

Mercy pushed back onto her knees and adjusted her spectacles as she listened. "I adore it!" she said a moment later, and leaped to her feet. She began to do the figures from a reel around the salon, her arms outstretched, light on her toes.

Honor smiled at her younger sister. Dancing was the thing she needed to banish the gloom from her thoughts, and hopped up to bow and extend her hand like a gentleman. Mercy eagerly caught it, and the two of them began to dance to Prudence's airy song. Grace put down her pen, clapping in time to the music. "Higher, Mercy," she said when the steps called for a hop. "Don't drag your foot, dearest — *jump.*"

Mercy jumped. Prudence began to play faster, forcing Mercy and Honor to quicken their steps, spinning around and around. All of them laughed at the absurd pace of the music, and didn't notice Hardy until he stood at the pianoforte, his silver tray in hand.

"Hardy!" Honor said breathlessly as she and Mercy collided to a stop. "We didn't see you there."

"No, miss. I could not be heard over the music and the giggling," he drawled.

Prudence stood, stretching her arms high above her head. "What's that?" she asked, nodding at the silver tray.

"A caller," he said, bowing lightly. "For Miss Cabot."

Mercy was too quick for Honor — she darted in front of her sister and tried to grab the card before Honor could reach it. In spite of looking rather ancient, Hardy was a nimble man — he quickly lifted the tray above Mercy's head, and her leap fell short.

"Hardy!" Mercy complained.

"Behave," Honor said, and reached high above her sister to take the card from the tray. Her heart instantly did a bit of a flutter when she read the name: George Easton.

That little flutter of hesitation cost her, for Mercy was able to read it. "Who is George Easton?"

Grace gasped and stood from the writing desk, hurrying forward to have a look. "You didn't *invite* him, did you?"

"No! That is, I sent a note, but I didn't think he'd come —"

"Who is he?" Prudence demanded, crowding in beside her sisters, trying to view the card.

"Not someone you should know," Grace said quickly, and to Hardy she asked, "Where is Augustine?"

"At his gentlemen's club."

"Hardy, will you please ask Mr. Easton to wait a moment while we . . ." She fluttered her fingers; Hardy apparently thought the gesture meant that he should quit the salon, and bowed before going out and shutting the door behind him.

Honor whirled about and stared at the windows, her heart racing as quickly as her mind. "Good Lord, he has come *here*!"

"Who *is* he?" Prudence demanded. "I've never heard of him."

"Thankfully, because you are not yet out and not aware of the sort of men that lurk," Grace said darkly.

"Grace! That is hardly fair," Honor protested. "It's not as if he is *courting* me."

"Then why has he come at all?" Mercy asked, confused.

Honor ignored Mercy — she had just realized that her hair was down, and she was dressed in the plainest gown she owned. She quickly pinched her cheeks for a bit of color.

"And why are you doing *that*?" Grace demanded.

"Because she fancies him!" Mercy said delightedly.

"You're not going to *receive* him," Grace said, aghast. "Prudence and Mercy are here!"

Prudence took great umbrage to that. "*I'm* not a child, Grace. I'll be seventeen in three months' time."

"I don't fancy him, Mercy," Honor said as she hurried to the sideboard and the mirror hanging over it. She needed a comb! Her hair looked wild.

"Then why are you making those faces?" Mercy demanded as Honor squinted at her hair, quickly twisting it into one long rope.

"I am hardly dressed for callers!" Honor said with great exasperation.

"Then perhaps you shouldn't take the call," Prudence said imperiously.

"Perhaps I shouldn't," Honor agreed, and whirled around, and held her arms out to her sisters. "How do I look?"

Grace sighed. "Lovely. On my word, there is hardly a thing that could make you less lovely. It's really very irksome."

"Thank you, darling. All right, then, now the three of you stay put. Do you understand?"

"Why?" Mercy said. "I want to see him."

"No, Mercy. It's none of your affair —"

Mercy suddenly darted for the door, wrenching it open and running down the corridor.

"For heaven's sake!" Honor cried.

"If she will see him, then so will I," Prudence said, and swept out of the room very regally, hurrying after Mercy.

Honor looked at Grace.

"Now you've gone and done it," Grace said. "If you think for a moment that those two will keep your secret —"

"Oh, for heaven's sake! For once I wish you'd tell me something that would surprise me," Honor said, and grabbed Grace's hand, pulling her along as she hurried to catch up to her younger sisters.

CHAPTER TEN

George was taken aback by the sudden closing in of so many females, but he quickly regained his composure when the smallest, and presumably the youngest, peered up at him through spectacles that made her blue eyes look quite large and asked, "Are you a suitor?"

"God *help* me, Mercy, where the devil are your manners?" Miss Cabot said sternly, sailing in behind the girl and firmly planting her hands on her shoulders. "I do beg your pardon, Mr. Easton," she said as she wheeled the girl about and very nearly gave her the boot. "My sister Mercy's social graces are shockingly absent. May I introduce you? This is Miss Mercy Cabot, Miss Prudence Cabot and of course, you know my sister, Miss Grace Cabot."

"Those are quite a lot of virtues gathered in one small room," George quipped, inclining his head. "My pleasure, ladies."

"Mmm," Grace Cabot said, eyeing him suspiciously, as if it wasn't his pleasure at all, as if he had come all this way in this deluge to fabricate his pleasure at meeting the Cabot girls.

"Have you come for Honor?" the youngest one inquired. "Or Grace? Sometimes callers really don't care which of them will receive them."

"Mercy!" Honor Cabot gasped, her face going a bit white. "Please, all of you, return to the salon, and, for heaven's sake, if Augustine returns, *divert* him!"

"Why?" Prudence asked. "What are you going to do?"

"She's not going to *do* anything," Grace said with a dark look for one sister as she took the other by the arm. "Come on then, you two —"

"But can't we invite him in for tea?" Prudence asked as Mercy twisted about in Grace's grip to peer at George over her shoulder. "We always invite them in for tea."

"He's not *that* sort of caller," Grace insisted, ushering them along. "Honor, you'll be along shortly, won't you?"

Miss Cabot responded with a dismissive little wave of her fingers that made her sister's expression go even darker. When the girls had disappeared into the corridor, Miss

158

Cabot grabbed George's elbow and began to propel him along in the opposite direction. "Hardy, this is a private matter —"

"Aye, miss, of course, miss," the butler said reflexively, making George think that Honor Cabot was frequently engaged in "private matters."

"One moment, if you please, Miss Cabot," he said, trying to stop her. "I am not *calling* —"

"Yes, but I need a moment of your time," she said, urging him along. Or rather, tugging him.

She herded him into the same small receiving room he'd seen before and shut the door.

"Miss Cabot —"

"Didn't you speak to her?" she exclaimed, whirling about from the door.

"What the devil do you mean? Of course I spoke to her!" George said, miffed that she would doubt it. "She is undoubtedly whiling away this torrential rain reliving every moment of it," he added confidently. He knew how young women were — their imaginations were almost as ridiculously grand and expansive as their bonnets.

But Miss Cabot gaped at him. "*You* are rather cheerfully assured of yourself!"

"Why shouldn't I be?" he asked cavalierly,

and took a seat on the settee, crossing one leg over the other. "It's not as if I am new to games of courtship, Miss Cabot." He chuckled at the idea. "Miss Monica Hargrove was not only stunned by my approach, but dare I say, *delighted.*"

"Delighted, was she? Then how would you explain her response when I asked after her evening? She said she'd met no one new, and suggested there was no one new but the usual crowd in attendance."

George shrugged. "And so?"

"And so, clearly you did not make *any* sort of impression at all!"

George bristled at the insinuation and coolly narrowed his gaze on Miss Cabot. "I made an impression," he said clearly. "Your friend was suitably flummoxed. Naturally she would not admit it, for it's none of your concern." He articulated every word for the foolish chit and tried not to ogle her figure.

"Yes, well, you don't know Monica Hargrove as I do," she retorted. "She would not miss an opportunity to tell me that a gentleman of *your* reputation had shown her the slightest regard."

George was about to argue, but he was pulled up short by the words *a gentleman of your reputation.*

"Meaning," she said hastily when she saw

his expression, "that you are . . . Well, you are, ah . . ."

"Pray tell, Miss Cabot, I am *what?*" he drawled. *Bastard. Pretender.* He knew what he was, and if she thought differently, she was even more foolish than he believed.

"Ahem." Her cheeks began to color. "Appealing. As it were," she said, gesturing vaguely.

Appealing? That took George back. *That* was his reputation? Her awkward admission could not have pleased him more. He grinned. "Why, Miss Cabot, I had no idea the true depth of your esteem."

"Don't tease me."

"I wouldn't dream of it," he said, spreading his arm casually across the back of the settee. It was his gift, he thought with a deepening smile, the ability to bring a bloom to the cheeks of young women . . . as well as to the cheeks of women who didn't bloom quite as brightly as they once had. He was a man with a calling, and that calling was to pamper and pleasure women across London.

Miss Cabot's bloom, however, was fading quickly underneath her scowl. "You promised, Easton."

"I did as I said I would, Cabot."

"Then you must have done it wrong," she

said pertly.

"Wrong!" he sputtered. He had the sudden urge to turn her over his knee, lift her skirts and strike her bare bottom like a child. "By the saints, you are incurably impudent!"

"And you are positively bursting with conceit!" she exclaimed, and began to pace, her brow furrowed, her lips pursed. She suddenly stopped her pacing and faced him. "You must do it again."

"I beg your pardon, I will do no such thing. I *did* it. And to my way of thinking, you owe me one hundred pounds."

"Ninety-two pounds," she said. "We agreed."

"Ninety-two, then," he snapped, and came to his feet. "You may send it to my agent, Mr. Sweeney —"

"The Prescott Ball will be held this Friday evening," she interjected, as if he hadn't spoken, and began to pace again. "I can secure you an invitation."

Indignation soared in him. She spoke as if he were some underling, a charitable endeavor, and no amount of imagining her naked body writhing beneath his would ease it. *"No."*

"You must dance with her," she said, and suddenly stopped her pacing, eyeing him up and down critically.

"What are you looking at?" he demanded, glancing down his body. "Listen to me, Honor Cabot, you may send to me the ninety-two pounds as per our agreement —"

"No," she said, lifting her chin. "Not until you have done as you promised."

George gaped at her lovely face, her glistening blue eyes. Was she mad? Afflicted? He could not recall having ever been quite so affronted. "I find it ironic that a woman with the name of Honor would fail to do just that with *her* word. Or that she would toy with the happiness of two people who have done her no harm, just so that she won't have to give this up," he said, gesturing to the well-appointed room in which they stood.

"Is that what you think?" she asked, looking almost surprised by it.

He snorted. "I know it, Miss Cabot. Your motives are quite obvious."

For a moment, she looked as if she were about to shout, which would not have surprised him in the least, given the bats floating about her pretty head. But she pressed her lips together, folded her arms, and said, "You need not concern yourself with my motives, sir. And do not doubt that I will honor my word," she said confidently.

"Just as soon as you honor yours. I understand that *you* believe you have charmed
the stockings right off of Miss Hargrove,
but clearly you have failed to do it. I will
not hand over the money promised merely
because your esteem for yourself has
clouded your vision of the truth."

One fist curled at his side, squeezing
against the strange mix of angry lust rising
up in him. "Good *God,* if you were a man I
would call you out for such an insult."

"And if I were a man, I'd be quite happy
to oblige you," she shot back. She began to
pace again. "You must dance with her, and
show her that you are *quite* earnest in your
esteem. That will impress her."

Why was she so bloody insistent? George
forgot his anger a moment — he *had* turned
Miss Hargrove's head . . . hadn't he? He
tried to recall the events precisely now. He
remembered the woman's smile — quite
lovely, it was. Not as lovely as this imperti-
nent excuse for a proper English debutante,
but still. Miss Hargrove had giggled and
smiled and had eyed him coyly. Hadn't she?
No, Miss Cabot was wrong. George was
confident he'd done as she'd asked. "No,"
he said. "I don't know what brings you to
believe that you are the arbiter of seduction,
madam, but I did as I promised."

164

She sighed as if *he* were the mad one in this room. "All right, then. What did you say to her?"

George lowered his head. "Now you are making me quite cross."

"I beg your pardon."

"You want to know what I said?" he asked, and shifted closer, startling her as he cupped her chin and stroked her cheek with his thumb. "I said that I found her lovely." He lifted her face to his. "And that I admired her," he added, allowing his gaze to skim Miss Cabot's figure. He shifted even closer, lowered his head so that his mouth was just a fraction of an inch from hers. "And that I was *quite* envious of Sommerfield."

Miss Cabot's eyes fluttered. "And?"

"*And?* I asked her to stand up, but she very demurely declined," he said, his gaze on plump, wet lips that looked as if they were begging to be kissed again.

"There, you see?" she said softly, her eyes falling to his mouth, her suddenly shallow breath stirring him.

"Are you surprised? I am a man of a certain reputation, and she is a blushing fiancée. She declined for the sake of propriety."

"She is not a blushing fiancée, she is seasoned and shrewd."

Naive, he thought, and moved his hand to the side of Miss Cabot's slender neck, feeling the warmth of her skin radiate through his palm. The feminine form never ceased to astound him — so soft, so fragile, with the power to incite wars among men. "She didn't seem terribly seasoned to me. She seemed flummoxed. . . ." He paused to breathe in her arousing scent. "Not unlike how you seemed earlier this week in this very room."

Miss Cabot turned her head slightly, away from his mouth. "I beg your pardon, I was *not* flummoxed."

"Tsk, tsk, Miss Cabot. It won't do to dissemble now."

She frowned, but she did not deny it. "You must speak to her again," she insisted. "Invite her again to stand up with you."

George sighed. He slipped his hand behind her back and pulled her into his chest. For once, she didn't say anything, just gazed up at him with clear blue eyes. He frowned down at her, brushed his knuckles against her temple. "I think I should kiss you again. Only quite thoroughly this time. And against all my better judgments."

"I forbid it," she murmured. And yet she did not move.

"You are too trusting, Miss Cabot. You

should never forbid a man and yet allow him to hold you like this if you have a care for your virtue." Least of all, *him.* "You don't yet understand the mind of a man. When a woman is this close, he . . ."

He couldn't finish; he gazed into her eyes as myriad ideas raced through his mind of what he would do to a woman like her.

"He what?" she asked.

He couldn't say what was suddenly raging through him: that a man could not be satisfied until he'd been inside her. But for the first time since meeting Honor Cabot, George saw her innocence. It was there, buried under the mantle of privilege and sophistication, and it made him feel strangely protective of her.

Lord, no, not that. He was a high-stepping horse, trained to never look away from his path. Bloody innocence! Whether it was an instinctive need to distance himself from such protective thoughts or his growing, maddening desire, George didn't know — but he said, "He does this," and put his mouth on hers, kissing her.

He did not expect Honor Cabot to kiss him back. She sank into him, her back curving as she melted against him. She ran her hands up his arms, put them around his neck and angled her head slightly as she opened her mouth beneath his. George felt almost weak in the knees as he took full advantage of it, his tongue tangling with hers. He drew her tighter into his body to feel her soft curves pressed against the hard length of him. He slid his hand down her back, to her derriere, his fingers sinking into the soft flesh of her hip. He kissed her until he began to feel that primal thrumming, the call of his body to move against her, to be inside her.

He lifted his head, and with two hands to her shoulders, he set her back. Miss Cabot very gracefully ran her thumb across her bottom lip and smiled sheepishly at him.

"There, do you see?" he said sternly. "You should *not* have trusted me."

"But I *do* trust you."

He braced one hand against his waist, determined to talk some sense into her. "If you were mine —"

"But I'm not."

"But if you *were,* I would teach you that you cannot be so careless with your virtue. Or anyone else's virtue, for that matter! What you are doing is beyond comprehension."

She folded her arms. "I didn't ask you to defend my virtue," she said silkily.

"Don't push me, Cabot," he warned her,

his gaze taking in her face, her hair.

"Do you think that men are the only ones allowed to desire?"

That certainly sparked his interest. George arched a dark brow. "Do you desire me, love?" he asked silkily, and reached for her hip once more, abruptly pulling her forward so she might feel just how much he desired her.

In all his years, he had never met a woman who could not be intimidated, if only a little. But Miss Cabot looked him in the eye and said, with a coy little smile, "You profess to know women, Easton. What do you think?"

He chuckled low. "I think you've not the least idea what you want, lass," he said, and lowered his head to hers again to trace a line across the seam of her lips with his tongue.

Honor gasped at the sensation, but George had only just begun. He lifted his hand to her jaw and angled her head, nipped at her bottom lip. "Is *this* what you want?" he asked, crushing her pelvis to his as he slipped his tongue into her mouth.

She made a little sound in the back of her throat. Her hands found his shoulders, and for a moment, he thought that she might push him away, but she merely opened her mouth beneath his as she slid her hands down his arms, then up again, so that she might tangle her fingers in his hair. He brushed his hand against her breast, cupping it, squeezing it, his fingers finding the turgid tip through the fabric of her gown. He was hurtling headlong down that slope of physical desire, of emotional entanglement, and with a growl deep in his throat, he picked her up with one arm about her waist and twisted about, putting her down on her back on the settee.

Honor gasped again; her breath lifting her chest. George traced a wet path to her bosom, his tongue finding the valley between her breasts, his hand pressing against her flesh, kneading her, tantalizing her. He lifted one breast free of the confines of her gown, and Honor made a sound — of protest? Of delight? Whatever it might have been, George caught it with his mouth as he kissed her again, before moving to her breast and taking it into his mouth.

She suddenly fell back on a very long sigh and sank her fingers into his hair. George suckled her, his eyes closed to the storm brewing inside him, to the sparks that were igniting and filling him with rivulets of fire. He tasted her fragrant flesh, felt the hardened nipple in the crease of his tongue. He was hard, the pulse of desire thrumming in him, the image of his body sinking deep into hers as he lifted the other breast from her bodice.

But there was something else in him, too. The faint clatter of hooves, the high-stepping horse marching steadily forward, looking neither right nor left. As much he wanted to undress her, to spread her legs and deflower her, to feel the wet warmth of her desire, he could not. He could not ruin one debutante or entice another. This was not the sort of man he was, no matter what people said, and it took all the strength he had to push himself up and away from her, to move his lips from her breast. He braced himself with both hands on either side of her, gazing down at this young woman with the shining blue eyes.

"Never," he said angrily, "*never* trust a man in that circumstance." He pushed himself up off the settee, then caught her hand, pulling her up.

Honor Cabot looked slightly chastised. She took a moment to arrange herself into her gown and looked contritely at him, on the verge of saying something when the door suddenly opened.

She whirled about, shaking out her skirts and pulling her long hair around to cover the flush of her bosom.

A woman stepped into the room. George recognized her instantly — she was an older, graying version of Honor.

"Mamma!" Miss Cabot exclaimed, and quickly put some distance between herself and George. "Ah . . . may I introduce you to meet Mr. George Easton?"

God help him but he was still hard, still wanting Lady Beckington's daughter. Fortunately, the countess seemed unaware and looked blankly at George. "My lady," he said, bowing low.

She looked at him curiously, as if she were trying to place him. "Ah, yes," she said, nodding. "Of course. You've come about the horses, haven't you?"

Horses? George looked at Miss Cabot for help. "I beg your pardon, I think there is some confusion —"

"The earl has all but sold them, hasn't he, Honor? I think the sorrel is left."

"Mamma," Miss Cabot said gently, "the horses . . . We sold them ages ago."

"What?" Lady Beckington gave her a nervous laugh. "We haven't! We have the sorrel. Please, do wait here, sir. My husband will be along shortly to settle the terms with you."

George didn't understand what was happening, but he could see a slight tremor in Miss Cabot. "I shall wait with Mr. Easton until the earl arrives, then," she said. "Shall I ring for Hannah?" she asked, moving to her mother's side.

"Who? Oh, no, that's not necessary," Lady Beckington said, and turned around to the door. "Good day, sir." She walked out of the room without looking back.

Miss Cabot did not speak; she lowered her head a long moment, closed her eyes then slowly opened them and lifted her gaze to George.

"I don't understand," he said simply. How could a mother see her daughter in such an obviously compromising position and merely walk out the door?

"Perhaps if I tell you that two summers ago, my stepfather sold some horses at Longmeadow. But not the sorrel," Miss Cabot said. "And even if he were so inclined to sell more today, he could not walk down here to settle terms with you without as-sistance."

Understanding dawned. When Miss Cabot had said her mother was not well that afternoon outside of Gunter's Tea Shop, George had vaguely thought of pleurisy. "How long has she been like this?"

"This?" Honor said, looking at the door.

"Moments? Weeks? Months? Sometimes she is perfectly fine. And sometimes not at all. . . ." Her voice trailed away and she looked at the carpet.

"Why didn't you tell me?" George asked. "When you first came to me, why didn't you tell me?"

"And have half of London know it?"

She was speaking to a man who had protected his mother all his life. "Miss Cabot, on my honor, I'd not tell a soul. You have my word."

She flushed, her fists curled at her sides. "You can see, then, my dilemma, Mr. Easton. I do not think Miss Hargrove will be keen to have four sisters and a madwoman under her roof. *No one* will want a madwoman under their roof, will they? I need . . . I need *time* until Grace and I can marry or . . . something," she said, her eyes blindly searching the ceiling. "If I could take up a sword and fight for it, I would. If I had a vast fortune at my disposal, I would use it. But I am a woman, and the only options I have are to connive as I promise myself to the highest bidder before all is discovered." She lowered her gaze to him again. "That may seem as if I am lacking in honor to you, but on my word, it is all I have. I don't want to hurt Augustine or Monica. I truly want only to divert her until I can think of *something*. What else can I do?"

George's heart went out to her. He'd loved his mother dearly, a lowly chambermaid with the duke's bastard son to raise by herself. She'd never been accepted anywhere. The other servants judged her to be without morals. The duke had used her and left her to her own devices.

But Lucy Easton had been determined, and when she'd learned the duke was ill, she'd somehow managed to convince him to give George a stipend. He didn't know how she'd done it — he didn't *want* to know. He knew only that his mother had sacrificed everything for him, and that the stipend had enabled George to attend school, to meet young men who would become his peers, even if they did view his claims of having been fathered by a royal prince with great skepticism. Had it not been for George's mother, he would be mucking stalls in the Royal Mews yet.

"Please, help me," Miss Cabot said, her voice meek. "Please, come to the ball."

God in heaven, how could he look upon the worry and sadness in those eyes and refuse her? "Even if I come, even if I might divert her as you wish, there are any number of things that might happen afterward. What will keep her from telling everyone what you've done when she discovers it? What will keep her from taking her suspicions to Sommerfield? Don't you see? It could be even worse for you then."

"I know. But I have to try. So I will take that risk."

George gazed at her beguiling face. He supposed he'd done some things that would be considered mad by most when he'd seen no other option.

"Will you?" she asked softly.

"I will do it once more, Honor," he conceded. "*Only* once."

She smiled in a way that began to burn in the soft part of his gut. "Thank you, George."

Another deeper trickle of warmth rushed down his spine at the use of his Christian name. He was standing on dangerous ground here, soft pliable ground into which he could sink quickly and become mired. That it had happened so quickly shook him enough that George abruptly moved to the door. "*Once* more, Miss Cabot. No more than that. But don't mistake me for someone who cares for you or the consequences of what you're doing."

"Oh, I won't," she quickly assured him. *"Never."* And she smiled.

CHAPTER ELEVEN

"Why are you smiling in that way?" Grace demanded when Honor finally emerged from the receiving room. Prudence and Mercy flanked her, and all three of them eyed Honor suspiciously. Such distrusting young things! Clearly, Honor had taught them well.

"Am I smiling?" she asked quite honestly. She thought she'd waited long enough to remove any stain of delight from her cheeks at that unexpected, remarkable experience on the settee. "I'm happy that the rain has eased, aren't you? It's dreadful being cooped inside."

"But it's raining even harder than before," Prudence pointed out.

"For heaven's sake, are you going to stand there gawking at me, your mouths open wide enough to attract nesting birds?" Honor demanded, and pushed through the wall of sisters on her way to the stairs.

The wall was instantly on her heels.

She was not going to tell them anything. It was none of their concern. None of them could be *completely* trusted to keep a confidence. And there was simply no way to describe such a tantalizing, exceptional moment with George Easton. It was the sort of erotic experience that curled one's toes, and upon which one might reliably dream for years or decades to come. She was certain of it, for she would never forget it.

"Why are you scurrying away like a guilty cat?" Grace called out from behind her.

"Because I wish to be left alone!" Honor tossed back. Not that her declaration had even the slightest effect on her sisters; they remained on her heels.

"Must you all follow me like a flock of sheep?" she demanded crossly. She wanted only to float into her rooms and recline on her chaise longue and recall the way Easton's eyes sparkled so enticingly when he was cross with her. To privately study exactly *how* those moments on the settee had occurred and to devise a way to make sure it never happened again, no matter how much she might yearn for it! As much as she had enjoyed it — breathed it, felt it in every bit of muscle — that sort of thing could ruin everything, her whole wobbly little plan! She could *not* entertain his advances again, not more than once, and most assuredly no more than *twice* more.

She walked into her room, her sisters right behind her. Mercy immediately fell onto Honor's bed as she had dozens of times before, sprawled across the silk coverlet with her fists propped under her chin, waiting for the chattering to begin. Prudence, likewise at home in Honor's room, went to the vanity and began to sort through her jewel box without the least bit of consciousness.

But Grace remained standing, waiting impatiently for Honor to speak. "Will you say nothing of your private meeting?"

"Grace, darling, you know how these things are," Honor said airily. "A gentleman calls. He inquires after your health, and that of your family —"

"You're to have a chaperone when a gentleman calls," Mercy said. "Miss Dilly said."

"I am aware of the rules," Honor said. "Did your governess also tell you that sometimes rules are meant to be broken?"

Mercy gasped. *"No,"* she said, her eyes widening with delight. "Are they?"

"No," Prudence said firmly. "You mustn't listen to Honor or Grace, Mercy. They don't

do as they should." She frowned at Honor. "I beg you, don't give Mercy the slightest encouragement."

"We are moral women," Grace said, gesturing to her and Honor. "It was perfectly all right for Honor to receive Mr. Easton. She does not require someone in the room to protect her virtue, because she guards it quite closely."

Honor pretended to be busying herself at the wardrobe so that Grace would not see her blush.

"Pardon, Miss Cabot."

Kathleen, the housemaid who often helped them with their hair and with dressing, stood at the threshold, her cap a bit askew. "His lordship Sommerfield asks that you come to tea, as we have guests."

"Guests?" Honor repeated. Her heart skipped a beat or two — Mr. Easton had only just left Beckington House. "Who?"

"Miss Hargrove and Mr. Hargrove. He asks that you join them and Lady Beckington in the green salon."

Honor's heart plummeted; she could imagine the Hargroves arriving just as Easton had left the house. She exchanged a fearful look with Grace, who, judging by her expression, was undoubtedly thinking the same thing. "We'll be down straightaway," Honor said. "Thank you, Kathleen." She turned to her younger sisters. "Go, go, and keep Mamma company while I don something more presentable. Pru, offer to play your new song for Miss Hargrove until Grace and I arrive."

Fortunately, Prudence and Mercy were so delighted to be included, they didn't argue and went off to do what Honor had asked.

"Help me change," Honor said to Grace, grabbing a sunny yellow gown. "I can scarcely abide when she appears unannounced. And already sitting with Mamma! How long has it been since Mamma has received guests?"

"A month or more," Grace said, quickly undoing the buttons of Honor's gown.

Their mother had begun to withdraw from society when the earl's health had worsened, but Honor wasn't certain that was the only reason. Her mother had, at times, seemed particularly baffled when in the presence of guests. Monica, on the other hand, could be terribly shrewd in her study of everything and everyone around her. "Hurry," Honor urged her sister.

"Will you tell me what happened with Easton?"

"Nothing really." Honor hoped she sounded more convincing to Grace than she did to her own ears. "He promised to try again at the Prescott Ball."

"The Prescott Ball!" Grace echoed incredulously. "Has he received an invitation?"

"I'll arrange it," Honor said. She donned the yellow dress and presented her back to Grace to be buttoned.

"How?" Grace exclaimed as she quickly buttoned the gown. "Lady Prescott would *never* invite him. She counts Gloucester among her closest friends."

"Yes, I know," Honor said. "But I think Lord Prescott might be persuaded."

"And who will persuade him, pray tell?"

Honor arched a brow at her sister.

Grace groaned as understanding dawned. "For heaven's sake, Honor, you scarcely know the man."

"I know him well enough."

"You wouldn't!" Grace said, with not a little bit of awe in her voice. She dropped her hands from Honor's gown, having finished the buttoning of it.

Honor picked up a comb. "I don't know," she admitted, and undid the knot in her hair. "I should like to think I wouldn't, for it seems dangerous even to me."

"Thank goodness for that, at least," Grace said, and took the comb from Honor's hand to help her. "At times I believe you've lost all your good sense."

Honor didn't admit it, but she thought she'd lost all of her good sense the moment she had approached Easton on Rotten Row.

The green salon was the smallest common room in the house, but the coziest of them, with thick rugs and wall tapestries to keep its inhabitants comfortably warm. The furnishings were more worn here than anywhere else in the house, having suffered through several winters of lounging girls and one rather clumsy boy.

Honor swept into the salon just behind Grace. Her mother was seated at the small table where tea was often served, next to the earl, who sat hunched over the table, a woolen blanket draped around his shoulders. Monica, Augustine and Mercy were on the settee, and Prudence at the harp. Monica's brother had taken his place at the hearth.

"Good afternoon," Grace said to those assembled. "Mr. Hargrove. Miss Hargrove," she added, nodding politely as she walked across the room to stand by the earl.

Honor smiled at Monica's eldest brother, whom she'd always known as Teddy. He was a thin man with a large angular nose, and had already followed his father into academia. She extended her hand to him and said, "Teddy, dearest, how do you do?"

"Quite well, thank you," he said, and limply took her hand as he bowed over it.

"And your parents? They are well?"

"Very well, thank you. But the weather is too foul for my mother to be away from her hearth this afternoon."

That was a pity. At least when Mrs. Hargrove was present, Monica was less inclined to speak. As to that, Honor whirled around to the settee. "Monica, *dearest,*" she said, holding out her hands to her nemesis. "How lovely you look!"

Monica stood, took Honor's hands and squeezed them a little too hard. "A pleasure to see *you,* Honor."

There were many things Honor could fault in Monica, but her looks were not one of them. She eyed Monica's pale green gown. "You should wear it to the Prescott Ball," Honor suggested. "You'll be in attendance, won't you?"

"I wouldn't *dream* of missing it," Monica said, letting go of her hands.

The Prescott Ball was the Season's opening salvo, the event that would launch a dozen or two freshly minted debutantes, having been just presented in court, into high society. *Everyone* would attend.

Honor moved to the earl. "How do you fare this evening, my lord?"

"Passable," he said, and took her hand. "A spot of tea will warm me."

"I'll get it for you, darling," Honor's mother said, and stood from the table, moving toward the bellpull.

"But we've just rung Hardy," Augustine said. "He's not had time."

"Have we?" Honor's mother said lightly, and resumed her seat.

"Speaking of the Prescott Ball, Honor, I assume you and Grace will attend?" Monica asked amicably. "These events are so important when one is searching for a match." She smiled sweetly.

So did Honor smile, although it hurt her to do so.

"Oh, my dear, Honor doesn't concern herself with such things," Augustine said jovially.

"Well, I'm all aquiver with anticipation," Grace said as Hardy entered that moment with the tea service.

"Shall we see you at the ball, Honor?" Teddy said as Hardy filled china cups and plates.

Teddy had arranged himself artfully at the mantel, an elbow on the polished mahogany, one leg crossed so casually over the other it must have taken him several minutes to perfect.

"Me? I'd not miss one of the most important balls of the Season," Honor said laughingly.

Augustine chortled. "Yes, for what is a London ball without the Cabot girls to grace it?"

"How glad I am to hear it!" Monica said. "I sincerely hope that a bachelor gentleman might catch Honor's eye. On my word, Lady Beckington, sometimes it seems as if your eldest daughter does not want an offer for her hand!"

"That's quite true," Honor said pleasantly. "I don't attend balls to seek an offer. I attend for the pure diversion of it."

Monica laughed as if Honor had intended that as a joke.

"You've no interest in marriage?" Teddy asked.

"Not at present," Honor said. "Contrary to what you might believe, Teddy, not every unmarried female is in singular pursuit of marriage."

"Well, of course not," Monica agreed. "However, some *should* be. After all, your sisters' collective happiness rather depends on you, doesn't it?"

Augustine looked confused. "How do you mean, dearest?"

"Just that I should think the younger girls would not be free to accept an offer if the eldest is not yet married." She smiled and shrugged lightly and turned her attention to her plate. "But I suppose that can't be helped if you are against it."

"Honor has been against it since the business with Rowley," Augustine said casually. "I think she still carries a bit of a flame for him, do you not, darling?"

"Pardon?" Honor could feel her face warming. "No! Of course not. Not at all." She looked frantically to Grace.

But it was her mother who saved her. "My daughters have always been in high demand in our society, and I think it must be rather flattering and pleasurable. Why ever not should she enjoy it?"

"They take after their mother," the earl said, and Honor's mother beamed at her husband.

Hardy served tea, and when he was satisfied that everyone had been suitably attended, he quit the room.

Prudence asked, "What will you wear, Grace?"

"Wear?" Lady Beckington repeated.

"To the ball, Mamma," Grace said.

Her mother's face suddenly lit with excitement. "A ball!" she said. "Who is kind enough to host one?"

It seemed to Honor as if the entire room ceased to breathe. Every head turned toward her mother, and she looked around at them, expecting an answer.

"The Prescott Ball, Mamma!" Mercy said, as if the lapse in her mother's memory was not the least bit curious. "Don't you recall? We were only just speaking of it."

The countess looked blankly at Mercy.

"Goodness, Mercy, she could scarcely hear a thing, what with all the prattling between us," Grace said quickly.

Monica, Honor noticed, was staring intently at her mother. Panic began to pound in her veins, and she quickly interjected, "Mercy, darling, we've not had the pleasure of hearing you play the harp."

Mercy looked startled.

"Go on, then, Mercy. Don't be shy," Honor said, and waved at her youngest sister to play.

Mercy took a seat behind the harp. She looked uncertainly at the room. She adjusted her spectacles, put her hands on the strings, and with a great frown of concentration, she plucked a loud, disharmonious chord.

"E-sharp," Prudence whispered loudly.

Mercy nodded and tried again. At least the chord seemed to be in tune, but Mercy's handling of the harp was far from delicate. She played a truly torturous rendition of the song. Honor noticed how often Monica stole a glimpse of her mother, who sat staring at the table, nervously picking at the cuff of her sleeve.

As Mercy laid heavy hands on such delicate strings, Honor moved to take a seat between Monica and her mother and smiled broadly at Monica. "Does she not show promise?" she whispered.

It had the desired effect — Monica shifted her gaze to Mercy.

When Mercy had finished the song — at least, Honor thought she had finished, although it was impossible to know — the earl asked her mother to return him to his rooms. He walked stiffly and slowly across the room, pausing to speak to Monica and her brother, his breath shallow and wet as he moved.

On the morrow, Honor would devise a way to ask Lord Prescott to invite George Easton to his ball. With a glance to Monica, who was watching Lord and Lady Beckington's laborious departure, she realized Monica knew something was amiss, and she was

far too clever not to guess at it, and sooner
rather than later.

CHAPTER TWELVE

Good God, she'd done it, George thought as he read a personal invitation to the Prescott Ball two days hence. He'd strongly doubted that a woman who had scarcely entered her third decade could persuade influential persons such as Lord Prescott to issue a coveted invitation to a man like him. "Who delivered it?" he demanded of Finnegan, who had swept into George's cavernous study and presented the thick vellum with a flourish.

"Prescott's man."

George grumbled a few curse words under his breath. Part of him had sincerely hoped that Miss Cabot would experience a divine slap of good sense. And yet another part of him, existing right alongside the wiser, moral part of him, thought of little else other than the afternoon in the small salon.

Quite frankly, it irked George. Not the physical tangling, Lord, no — *that* was the only thing that didn't irk him. But what bothered him, in a manner he could not recall having ever been bothered, was that he was a man who had sampled women across England, women who were far more experienced than that virginal little debutante. And yet it was *her* kiss that was living in his memory. It was *her* image on the settee that had bedeviled him. It had all kicked up quite a lot of dust in him that still hadn't settled.

"Shall I press your dress coat?" Finnegan asked as he folded the vellum and tucked the ends together neatly.

George waved him away. "I know you'll not rest until you've pressed the last thread within a breath of its life."

"Very good, sir," Finnegan managed to say without smiling. "And shall I send your affirmative reply?" he asked, placing the invitation on the desk.

George eyed the man. "You're trying my patience, Finnegan."

"I will send it promptly," he said crisply, and walked out of the room, unabashed.

George frowned at Finnegan's trim back as he disappeared from the room. He'd been in a foul mood for a pair of days now, owing to those blue eyes, and worse, owing to the little trip he and Sweeney had made down to the West India Docks yesterday. Two ships had come into port this week, both having sailed from the west coast of India. George and Sweeney had hoped to learn some news of Captain Godsey and the *Maypearl.*

They had been fortunate to find the captain of the *Spirit of Whitby* still aboard and had inquired after their ship. "Three-masted privateer ship, British flag," Sweeney had explained. "Sits low in the water and built for speed."

The captain had shaken his head, his beefy, sunburned cheeks bouncing. "I've not seen her, but that's not to say she's not sailing up the channel now, aye?" He'd laughed roundly, displaying a row of yellow teeth with one missing. "Might be nothing more than prevailing winds, sir. Then again, perhaps she was caught up in the blockade. 'Course, she might not have made it around the Cape. And there's always pirates."

It had been all George could do from putting a fist in the captain's mouth and dislodging another tooth or two. George could very well imagine any one of those scenarios befalling his ship. In his mind's eye, he watched three dozen men and cargo sinking into the inky blackness of the ocean.

George was worried, but like Sweeney, he

had confidence in Godsey. He was a capable captain, and he'd not seemed the least bit concerned about war or pirates when he'd set sail, his hold full of provisions for the long voyage. "Quite a lot of sea out there," he'd said when George had voiced his concern even then of what might happen in the course of his journey.

But then again, that was precisely what had George in a foul mood today — there *was* a lot of sea out there. Plenty of places and people for a ship to get lost or find harm. And that he was thinking of a pretty debutante with a foolish drawing room scheme instead of his ship made him quite cross. He was completely at odds with himself.

No matter how captivating Honor Cabot was, she had no place in his life. She was too young, in spite of seeming much wiser than her age would suggest. And she was too . . . *proper.* She was a well-heeled woman of impeccable connections, a debutante, a woman who would, undoubtedly, receive a handsome offer of marriage. This was nothing more than a diversion, a game. He had only to keep the stakes from getting too high, because he could not win this game.

George was quite realistic — he knew he

could never inhabit her world. He could never be good enough for her in society's eyes. Wanting a woman of the *ton* put him at great peril for heartache, for rejection, for all the things that he'd learned at a very early age to push down and ignore, pretend were not part of him.

He was reminded that as a world-wise thirteen-year-old lad, he'd developed quite a heart song for Lady Anna Duncan, the daughter of a prominent London magistrate. She had given George every reason to believe that she, too, felt esteem for him. But on a day she'd come to the Royal Mews with her father, George had tried to kiss her, and she'd laughed at him. "I shan't give my first kiss to a stable boy," she'd said, as if he were so far beneath her that he might have been her boots.

It was a stinging rebuke, and though George had become a man and had put that incident in perspective, he still believed Lady Anna Duncan had taught him an invaluable lesson: he would never escape the shadows that surrounded his beginnings. No lady of the Quality would ever have him.

Honor Cabot was Quality. And she was trouble; he could feel it in his bones. And yet he could not stop thinking of her, of the feel of her in his arms, of her lips and her mouth beneath his. He could almost feel her sheath around him —

George suddenly realized he was holding something and glanced down. He'd picked up the invitation she had secured for him without thinking, and now it was crumpled. He threw it across the room.

CHAPTER THIRTEEN

George had to admit, Finnegan turned him out quite nicely the night of the Prescott Ball. He admired the green waistcoat with black embroidery — its appearance in his wardrobe a surprise, and its origin, at least to George, unknown. His neckcloth was black silk, and his dress coat made of the finest superfine wool. Finnegan had sent up a barber, and George was clean-shaven. His hair was trimmed and combed back so that it brushed his collar, and his boots polished to a high sheen. To his own eyes, George looked like the nephew of the king. He supposed others might think so, too . . . and then, inevitably, the sniggers behind their hands would begin.

George no longer took offense to the skepticism as he had when he was a lad. Now he knew who he was. He was an honest man with strong convictions, and if that didn't suit the titled lords and ladies of this town, so be it. He reminded himself that he'd had the wherewithal to pull himself up to these social heights. He didn't want to acknowledge the bit of queasiness at the thought of entering the highest reaches of society tonight.

He struck out on foot for the evening, having the luxury now of living within walking distance of the fashionable Grosvenor Square. Carriages were queued up around the square, waiting to disgorge their passengers into this prestigious event.

He strode briskly past them all, his crumpled invitation in his pocket, and jogged up the steps of the home of Lord and Lady Prescott.

It was quite impressive, indeed, taking up one-third of the north side of the square. Grecian columns marked the entrance; lights blazed in every window. George stepped into the entry and was instantly surrounded by a dizzying swirl of pastel gowns, headpieces and feathers. Jewels glistened at the throats and wrists of lovely ladies, who were accompanied by lean men in long tails and embroidered waistcoats. They reminded George of cranes as they bent their heads to hear the ladies speak, then lifted them again.

He stepped to one side to avoid the beaded train of a woman's gold gown, and very nearly collided with a footman who was moving with alarming speed through the crowd, his tray of champagne flutes carried high above his head to avoid any disastrous encounter with the feathers that grew out of the ladies' elaborate hairstyles.

George swallowed down his boyish angst and stood in line to be presented to the viscount and his wife. He handed his invitation to the butler, who in turn announced George in grand fashion as he neared the receiving line. When he stepped before the viscount, his lordship looked curiously at George, as if he couldn't quite make him out.

Lady Prescott, however, curtsied graciously and slipped her hand into his, her gaze fluttering up to his. "Mr. Easton," she said with a soft smile. "Welcome to our home."

"My lady," he responded, bowing over her hand. "Thank you."

She did not remove her hand from his but held his gaze, smiling up at him. He knew that sort of smile, and one of George's brows rose slightly above the other in silent question, and her smile seemed to deepen. *Women,* he thought as he let go of her hand, bowed and walked on. Either they were fearful of associating with his bastard self or were wanting more than he cared to deliver.

He moved on, scanning the crowd. He saw several acquaintances — some who looked the other way — and paused to speak to those who did not while surreptitiously looking for Honor Cabot. He didn't see her. Nor did he see Miss Hargrove. If Honor had forced him into attending a ball where Miss Hargrove would *not* be, he was afraid of what he might do to that impudent young woman.

He continued on, snatching a flute of champagne from a footman as he admired more of the women in attendance. He felt a light touch on his arm and turned, expecting — *hoping* — that it was Honor. But it was an old friend, Lady Seifert.

"Mary," he said fondly, taking her hand and bringing it to his lips. He and the auburn-haired, green-eyed beauty had been . . . associated, a few years ago.

"George, my dear," she said, smiling fondly. "I've not seen you in an age! I hear you've been rather well occupied. Women and ships, is it?" she asked with a slight wink. "All of them sailing beyond your reach?"

He was surprised she'd heard. "Not all," he said with a wink.

She laughed. "I can't believe you're here,

darling."

"Why is that? Because I don't dance?"

"Because *Gloucester* is here." She glanced around, rising up on her toes to see over the heads of those who crowded around them. "You really shouldn't have come."

He privately bristled at the idea Gloucester's invitation meant more than his. "I have an invitation," he said.

"Best not let him see you."

"Lady Seifert!"

Lady Seifert and George both turned round; what was that, his heart skipping a beat or two at the sight of Miss Cabot?

"Miss Cabot," Mary said graciously. "How do you do?"

"Very well, madam. And you?"

"Quite well. May I introduce Mr. George Easton?" Mary asked, gesturing to George.

"A pleasure, Miss Cabot," George said, clasping his hands behind his back and bowing.

Honor's eyes sparkled with amusement as she curtsied. "Thank you, Mr. Easton. A fine night for a ball, is it not?"

He could not begin to guess what a night must include to be considered *fine* for a ball. He smiled. So did Honor.

Mary, he noticed, looked intently at Honor, then at him, her eyes narrowing slightly above a wry smile.

"I think fortune has smiled on Lord and Lady Prescott and sent the rain away for the day," Honor said, and glanced about the room, as if she were looking for someone.

"Has it?" George asked amicably. "Personally, I don't give much thought to weather."

Honor looked as if she had just swallowed something.

"One can't help but wonder what you *do* give thought to, Mr. Easton," Mary purred next to him.

"My guess is that the gentleman gives thought to all the newly presented debutantes," Honor suggested. "There are quite a lot of them this evening."

"Would that include you, Miss Cabot?" George asked.

She laughed. "I was presented three years ago, Mr. Easton! I fear I've lost that glow."

"Oh, I think not, my dear," Mary said.

Another gentleman appeared in George's peripheral vision. "Lady Seifert," he said, greeting them. "Miss Cabot."

"Good evening, Sir Randall!" Mary said.

"Miss Cabot," the young man said, "if you will allow, I request the honor of standing up with you on the next set."

"I would be delighted," Honor said, and

looked as if she meant it. "Please, excuse me, Lady Seifert." She glanced slyly at George, a smile playing on her lips. "Mr. Easton."

Sir Randall quickly offered his arm to her; she put her hand lightly upon it, cast George a quick but sparkling little smile and glided away at the fop's side. George tried not to gape at her back.

That was it?

She would toddle off and dance while he did her dirty work? He watched until they'd disappeared into the crowd. He didn't realize he was staring until Mary touched the tip of her fan to his shoulder. "Drink your champagne, George, darling. She's not for you."

He chuckled. "No? Tell me, love, who is for me?"

"Certainly no debutantes here," Mary said with a lilting little laugh. "Their mothers would never allow it." She winked at him. "Enjoy yourself all the same." She moved away, her hips swinging suggestively.

George turned from that delectable sight, and his gaze landed on none other than Miss Monica Hargrove, standing beside Sommerfield. At least he might get his mission over and done, he thought, and casually walked to where she stood.

She glanced up as he approached and blinked with surprise. "Oh!" she said. "Mr. Easton!"

"Miss Hargrove," he said politely.

She looked at her fiancé, who was eyeing George curiously. "Lord Sommerfield, may I introduce Mr. Easton?" she asked.

"Easton, yes, of course!" Sommerfield said jovially. "Yes, yes, it *is* you. We've met," he said.

"Oh?" Miss Hargrove said.

"Quite right. At the club, I do believe. Was it not the club, sir?"

George was not welcome in Sommerfield's club but said, nonetheless, "Good to see you again, Sommerfield. Your family is well?"

"Exceedingly. That is, with the exception of my father. He ails terribly, what with the consumption."

"I'm saddened to hear it."

"Thank you," Sommerfield said perfunctorily.

"I had hoped," George said, turning his attention to Miss Hargrove, "that I might entice Miss Hargrove to take a turn about the dance floor."

Miss Hargrove blanched at the invitation and looked at Sommerfield, who looked just as flustered. He smiled nervously and patted her hand. "Of course you must, my dear."

"But I . . . I thought that perhaps . . ."

"I vow not to step on your toes," George said, and offered his arm. Miss Hargrove looked uncertainly at his arm, then at Sommerfield. Her fiancé nodded encouragingly.

She reluctantly put her hand on George's. "Thank you."

George moved quickly, forcing her to come along before she leaped into Sommerfield's arms. He led her out onto the dance floor, and they lined up across from each other.

Miss Hargrove frowned at him. "*That* was rather brazen."

"That is the least brazen I can be, Miss Hargrove. You may as well accept that I am a determined man." He smiled.

The music began, and he bowed. She curtsied. They moved forward, and she skipped around his back.

"What could you possibly want from me?" she asked, taking her place in line again.

He stepped forward and around her back. "To convince you that there are more potent choices than Sommerfield for a beautiful woman such as yourself."

She gasped as he stepped back into line. They came together in the middle, their hands meeting above their heads. "I am *affi-anced* to Lord Sommerfield."

He twirled her around in a tight circle and smiled down at her. "I know."

As they started through the paces again, she said, "What do you possibly hope to gain, Mr. Easton?"

"I think you know the answer to that." He allowed his gaze to drop to her lips as he stepped back.

"And how do you propose to lure me?" she asked skeptically as they clasped hands overhead and turned. "You've no connections, and rumor has it that your fortune has been lost."

George smiled. "Rumor has been unkind to my fortune, but I've not lost it. And I happen to think I am very well connected. I am the nephew of the king." He let go of her hands and stepped back.

So did Miss Hargrove. "You can scarcely expect me to believe it," she said laughingly.

"Then perhaps you will believe this," he said, stepping forward again. "I am capti-vated by you."

She didn't respond to that but with a smile, and continued to study him. George danced as well as he was able, meeting her gaze at every turn.

When the music drew to a close, he bowed

low and reached for her hand. He gave it a tender squeeze before placing it on his arm, covering it with his hand. "I beg your pardon if I've offended, Miss Hargrove," he said as he led her back to Sommerfield, who shifted from one leg to the other, anxious to have his prize back at his side. And beside him, standing innocently with her hands at her back, was Honor. She didn't look at George, and in fact, she made a point of looking away so as not to suggest any sort of familiarity between them.

"I am not offended, Mr. Easton," Miss Hargrove said, smiling up at him. "But I *am* taken."

"I will concede that you are . . . for the time being."

Her smile seemed to go a little deeper, the color in her cheeks high.

That was it, the unmistakable sign of being smitten. No doubt he could invite her into the garden now to take full advantage of her. But as they had reached Sommerfield and Honor, George took her hand from his arm, stepped back and bowed low over it. "Thank you for the dance, Miss Hargrove," he said. "A finer partner I've not experienced."

Miss Hargrove laughed as if she found that quite impossible, but Sommerfield was quick to agree. "She is indeed a *fine* dancer. I confess, I could learn a thing or two from you, Mr. Easton." He laughed as he nervously rubbed the side of his nose. "I should employ you to teach me the steps to our wedding dances."

"I am not a very good dancer, my lord. I'm more of a horseman."

"Nothing like a good horse race to get the blood flowing, eh?" Sommerfield agreed. "We are very proud of our horses at Longmeadow," Sommerfield continued. "Some of the finest horseflesh in the country —"

Honor suddenly gasped. "Augustine, you must invite him to Longmeadow!"

Sommerfield and Miss Hargrove looked as stunned as George felt — he could not find his tongue immediately. "Pardon?"

"Oh, dear," Honor said with a pretty smile and a curtsy. "I do beg your pardon, sir. Please, forgive my outburst, but it occurs to me that there will be quite a lot of horse racing at Longmeadow this spring."

"Well, yes," Sommerfield said uncertainly. "But I didn't . . . That is to say . . ." Terribly flustered, the poor man smiled nervously at those around him, looking for help.

Honor's face fell. "Well, now you've made me seem perfectly foolish, my lord."

"No, I — I don't mean *that,*" Sommerfield blustered. "I mean to say of *course* you are *very* welcome at Longmeadow, Mr. Easton. But the racing is all in fun."

"Dearest —" Miss Hargrove said, and laid a finger on her fiancé's arm.

"And it's rather a lot of fun," Honor quickly interjected before Miss Hargrove could persuade her fiancé differently. "A lot of friendly wagering. You *must* come, Mr. Easton. There's always need for a gentleman to serve as dance partner, and I am certain we will all appreciate an experienced card player."

Sommerfield's eyes widened, but Honor was on a mission and would not allow anyone to speak.

"Are you familiar with Longmeadow?" she eagerly continued.

George stared at Honor. He knew precisely what she was doing, arranging another "invitation." It grated on him, but at the same time, Miss Hargrove was watching him expectantly.

"It's my stepfather's seat, just one hour to the northwest from here," Honor continued.

"Yes, you must come, Easton," Sommerfield said now, nodding his head firmly. "That's that, my good man. We *must* have you at Longmeadow!"

He turned his happy smile to Miss Hargrove, who said, with much less enthusiasm, "Yes, we must have you, Mr. Easton."

"That's very kind," he said. "Thank you." George was glad that the music had begun again, giving him an escape from what was to him his own personal nightmare. "Miss Cabot, will you do me the honor?"

"Have a turn, Honor. He's a grand dancer," Sommerfield said, as if he had stood up with George himself.

"Well, then, I'd be delighted," she said and held out her hand.

George took it and gripped it hard. Her expression did not change. "Will you excuse us?" he asked Sommerfield.

Neither he nor Honor noticed Monica's thin smile fade behind them.

"*You* are a splendid dancer, my love," Augustine said to her. "I *do* wish I was a better companion for you."

"You are the perfect companion for me, Augustine."

"Are you certain?" he asked, taking her hand and squeezing it much too hard. "For I would be lost without you, my darling."

"I am certain." She meant that with all her heart. Augustine was a kind soul, a gentle soul. She was happy with him. So why, then, would Honor wish to draw them asunder? That was precisely what she was doing — Monica was certain of it. "Let go of my hand before you break a bone, dearest."

"Oh!" Alarmed, Augustine quickly relinquished it.

Monica glanced once more in Easton and Honor's direction. They were standing on the dance floor, waiting for the musicians. Honor had turned away from him, was speaking to Miss Amelia Burnes while Easton watched the orchestra.

She saw nothing that should make her the least bit suspicious, but Monica knew that somehow, Honor had put Easton up to this. She was very astute when it came to these things, and she had not been the least bit swayed by Easton's pretty words to her. It made no sense; there was no reason that a man like George Easton should suddenly discover an interest in *her,* particularly as everyone in town knew she was to marry Augustine.

She'd understood that Honor was involved the moment she'd invited Easton to Longmeadow. Honor, who never gave men another thought, so determined to have Easton, of all gentlemen, at Longmeadow. Oh, yes, Monica had known Honor Cabot far too long, and she *knew* when that one was up to mischief.

"I'm positively parched," Augustine said, as if he'd danced the last three sets. "Shall we fetch some champagne and perhaps sit a bit, my love?"

"Yes," she said, and moved along with her fiancé, her mind whirling.

CHAPTER FOURTEEN

Easton looked perturbed when the orchestra began to play. Honor stepped forward, curtsied as she ought. "You have me at a disadvantage," he said. "I am not familiar with this music."

"It's a waltz. You've not seen it danced?"

He frowned at her as she took his hand and placed hers in it, then held it out. "You know very well that I do not inhabit ball-rooms or assembly rooms."

"Then perhaps you should engage a dance instructor. I understand Monsieur Fornier is excellent. He counts the French nobility among his students."

"I don't *need* a dance instructor," he huffed. "I don't intend to dance. I am only here because of *you,* for which I am questioning my sanity."

"And I am forever thankful," she said graciously. "Your other hand should rest in the middle of my back," she said, and put her other hand on his shoulder.

He put his hand on the small of her back, just above her hip, and arched a brow. "This seems rather scandalous for a group of blathering debutantes."

Honor arched a brow, as well. "And it is quite diverting for them, too. Your hand should be higher on my back."

He smiled wolfishly. "I like it here."

So did she, very much so. She liked standing next to him — he was so much larger, so much stronger — but she could well imagine Lady Chatham and Lady Prescott's fit of apoplexy if they were to see it. Unfortunately, the song's introduction was over, the dancing had begun and Honor had no time to argue the placement of Easton's hand. "All right, follow me — *one,* two, three, *one,* two, three," she muttered, moving him first one way, then the other.

After a few stumbling tries, he found the rhythm of the dance.

"There!" she said as they moved forward, "I think you have it! You're a natural."

"Then perhaps you will allow me to lead," he said, and suddenly twirled her, very nearly colliding with another couple.

Honor laughed. "You can't do that — you must turn in the direction of the other dancers."

"I beg your pardon? I may do as I please, just as you seem to do. *Longmeadow,* Honor? You've made too much of this scheme now."

He was cross with her. The truth was that Honor had blurted it without thinking, which, upon reflection, she'd been doing quite a lot of lately.

Easton's foot collided with hers, and they faltered for a step or two before he quickly righted them. "Pardon," he said apologetically, and twirled her in the wrong direction again, heedless of the other dancers.

"The wrong way, Mr. Easton!"

"Say you," he said irritably. "And by the by, did it occur to you that perhaps I am not at liberty to leave London just now? That perhaps I might have more pressing issues than you?"

She wanted to know what those pressing issues were, if they involved women. "Impossible," she teased him.

"Oh? Well, here's a novel thought for you, madam — I don't want to go to Longmeadow. And if I did, I wouldn't need you to so bloody blatantly wrangle an invitation for me!"

So there it was — he was embarrassed. Honor was slightly chagrined by that — she never meant that. "I didn't *wrangle* an invitation for you, Easton. The thought occurred to me, and I said it. And why ever would you not want to go to Longmeadow? It's beautiful! The house is truly magnificent. And frankly, sir, I had to do it, for I never once considered that you'd not do as you've promised. I am merely providing you the opportunity."

That remark caused him to stop midstep.

"Move on!" she frantically urged him.

He grudgingly did so, but his expression was full of vexation. "Honor Cabot, I have done as I said," he snapped, and moved off step, so that she had to hop on one leg to catch up to him. "I have come to this wretched ball, I have *danced* with her," he insisted, bumping into the couple behind them and tossing a curt "pardon" over his shoulder. "I have engaged her, seduced her — I've done all but ask for her fragile little hand in marriage!"

Honor was not the least bit chastised; she rolled her eyes at his declaration.

He looked surprised, but then his eyes narrowed. "By *God,* someone should have turned you over a knee long ago. I would take great delight in doing it myself."

It surprised Honor that those words should send a delightful little shiver down her spine. "Don't be so cross with me,

George. I will concede that you've managed to make some headway, but you haven't *done* it."

"How do you know?" he demanded. "Your path has scarcely crossed Miss Hargrove's this evening!"

"I know," Honor said with confidence. "She's not watching you now, is she?" She did not expect him to suddenly twirl her about as he did. He squinted in the general direction of where they'd left Augustine and Monica.

"Well, then?" Honor asked. "Are the eyes of a doe fixed upon you now?"

"For the love of God, she is with her *fiancé.*"

Honor shrugged. "That hardly keeps others from it, does it? Lady Seifert has openly admired you, and she is married."

That news seemed to interest him in a way that Honor did not care for. "*Has* she?" he asked, and smiled as if that pleased him. "Where is she?"

"I don't know!" What a rooster! Now Honor was cross. "Seems rather vulgar to me, to be ogling a man who is not your husband."

"Spoken like a true innocent," Easton said with a patient smile as he searched the crowd, presumably for Lady Seifert. But then his blue eyes flicked to her; he studied her a moment and suddenly smiled so charmingly that Honor felt a little unsteady. "Oh, my," he said as they woodenly maneuvered the corner of the dance floor. "I sense you would like to convince me you are *not* an innocent, but couldn't possibly say so for the sake of propriety."

That was precisely the thing that had flitted through her mind, and Honor could feel her cheeks heating. She was very practiced in the art of courting, but she was an innocent in the purest sense of the word. In spite of all outward appearances, Honor guarded her virtue very carefully. In fact, Easton was the first man who had ever kissed her so thoroughly, and the memory of that kiss, of his mouth and hands on her skin, made her feel too warm all of a sudden. She should have guarded herself with him — he was a potent and very virile man. "That is not at all what I was thinking. You needn't tease me — I merely wondered after your association with Lady Seifert."

"That," he said, clearly still amused, "is not for an innocent such as yourself to wonder. I fear it would bruise your maidenly sensibilities."

"How foolish I've been. I thought you merely a rooster, but it would seem you're an *imperious* rooster. Just as I should not wonder about you, neither should *you* wonder about *me,* Mr. Easton."

His charming smile broadened with delight. "What is it that raises your hackles, love? One moment I am George, and the next Mr. Easton, depending upon just how cross you are with me, eh? Allow me to enlighten you, *Miss* Cabot. The difference between us is that it is not necessary for me to wonder about you. I know an innocent when I see one."

Honor gasped indignantly, but before she could argue, he whirled her about and her back brushed against another dancer. "Will you have a care!" she whispered hotly.

"*I* should have a care? That's rich — surely even *you* see the irony in that statement."

"At least I'm discreet when *I'm* careless and don't bump into this person or that."

Easton laughed. "Do you hear yourself, madam? You are quite possibly the most indiscreet woman I have ever met!"

"Me?"

"Absolutely you, love," he said, smiling. "You are a careless, indiscreet, absurdly brazen young woman, who wishes she were not as innocent as she is, and honestly, I have never been more goddamned intrigued."

Honor had already opened her mouth to argue, but warmth ballooned through her, puffing her up. She wanted to cover her entire body with it. With *him*. She really wished George wouldn't smile at her so charmingly, so warmly, so deeply. It shone inside him, glittered in his eyes. She tried to keep from smiling in return, to show him that she was quite offended, but try as she might, she could not keep the smile from her lips. "Well, you needn't *shout* it."

He laughed, pulled Honor into his body and twirled again and again to the edge of the dance floor, where he caught her hand and pulled her off.

"Wait, what are you doing?" she exclaimed, glancing nervously about them. Two gentlemen smiled knowingly. At least she worried that was so.

"I am giving my poor feet a much needed rest," he said, and glanced back. "Come, then," he said, and put his hand to her back, ushering her forward more quickly, to the buffet and footman. "A glass of champagne will quench your thirst, Miss Cabot," he said, rather loudly.

"I don't want —"

He squeezed her hand so tightly that Honor squealed a bit. But Easton ignored her and deftly steered her past the buffet, slipping into the corridor, then practically pushing her up the servants' stairs.

"Wait! I should go back."

He reached around her and pushed the door open onto a darkened balcony.

Honor stepped cautiously onto the balcony that overlooked the entrance below. She glanced around; it was dark, but there were couples walking about. Across the space she could see a pair of lovers, their arms entwined around each other. "Oh, no," she said, but Easton had already grabbed her hand and tugged her to stand behind a big display of chain mail. He slipped in behind her.

She twisted about in that crowded space and frantically swiped at a cobweb that touched her hair. Easton was standing so close that she could feel the heat of his body. "What in blazes are you doing?" she demanded.

"Removing some of the innocence from you," he said, and grabbed her waist with both hands as he kissed her.

Honor was so taken aback, she slammed her fists against him. He lifted his head. "Bloody hell, I've wanted to do that all night."

Oh, God, so had she. "Are you mad?" she

whispered hotly. "What if we are discovered?"

"What if?" he said, his mouth on her neck, her shoulders, his hands on her waist, her hips.

Honor heard the sound of someone approaching and caught her breath, digging her fingers into his arms. Easton stilled. They waited, her breath about to explode from her chest, until the person had walked by. When they did, George looked at her. She felt something very odd, like a whisper of silk across her chest. His eyes were darker, swimming with . . . with *affection.* Affection! She knew it was so because she felt it, too, a shock through her heart. She hadn't felt anything like it in so long, and certainly never as ardently — Rowley suddenly seemed like a puppy compared to this wolf.

Honor surged forward and up on her toes, her mouth landing on his.

George lifted her off her feet and twirled around, put her up against the stone wall behind the chain mail, trapping her there with his body. He put his arm around her, anchored her tightly to him and kissed her, his tongue in her mouth, teasing hers, his lips on her cheek, her neck, against her lips. With his free hand, he stroked the skin of her décolletage, his fingers sliding into her gown, brushing against the rigid nipple and sending violent waves of desire through her.

Honor's breath began to evaporate — she couldn't breathe, didn't *want* to breathe. She sought him with her hands, sliding down his arms and around his waist, up his chest again to his face, her fingers carelessly sliding in between their mouths, down his hard chest and boldly over the ridge of his erection. She caught her breath at the feel of it — so hard. Her body was responding, getting damper, softer somehow.

George reached for the hem of her gown, gathering it in folds until he could find her leg. His hand slid up past her stocking to the bare skin of her thigh, leaving a burning trail wherever he touched. Honor feared herself in danger of being swept under by the tide of hunger building in her, of rolling and tumbling along helplessly as it rushed through her, and still, she did not care.

How had he fanned so much desire in her? How had she come to esteem him so completely? He had seduced her thoroughly. "You are a *scoundrel,*" she said lowly, and splayed her hands against the wall at her back. "I could scream," she said breathlessly into his ear.

"Then do it," he challenged her. "Scream.

And still you will not scream as you will when I make love to you."

"Libertine," she breathed, and propped her foot against the stone spindles of the railing so that his hand could reach the damp warmth between her legs. She gasped at the sensation when his fingers closed around the core of her pleasure, then slid deep inside her.

"Lover," he whispered into her ear.

Honor closed her eyes and leaned her head against the wall. "I'm mad," she whispered. *"Mad, mad. . . ."*

"Enjoy it, lass," he said, and kissed her mouth, the hollow of her throat and, moving down, put his lips on the skin of her bosom as he began to stroke her, his fingers swirling around the slick folds, sliding in and out of her, stroking the hard core.

With some primal rhythm pulsing through her, Honor began to ride his hand, pressing harder against his fingers, seeking release. She gripped him as he increased the intensity of his strokes, swirling, dipping, rubbing against her slick sex. She could hear voices, the laughter of people below, the whispers of other people on the balcony. It only served to heighten her experience, to realize in that moment how overpowering desire could be. She didn't care if she was discovered. As her body tensed, coiling, preparing for release, she suddenly pitched forward, put her mouth against his shoulder and cried out against the wool of his coat with delirious pleasure as she shuddered around his hand.

They were both gasping when he withdrew his hand and dropped her skirts. She managed to lift her head and opened her eyes. She couldn't look away from George Easton, couldn't push back and put some distance between them as she did when gentlemen drew too close. She tried to think of something to say, but no words came to her. She felt breathless, weightless, and strangely erotic emotions swirled in her.

His hand slid down her arm, his fingers tangled with hers. He kissed her temple and said softly, "There you are, Cabot, a taste of your own medicine. And now the evening has come to its regrettable end."

"What?" Honor tried to hide her fluster, but it was useless. She had stepped beyond an invisible curtain and could not hear very well.

He dipped his head to look her in the eye. "In spite of our disagreement about the effectiveness of your absurd ideas, the pleasure has truly been all mine."

Honor couldn't look away from him. She

was stunned by what had happened, stunned by what he'd just done to her. "Will you come to Longmeadow?" she asked, far too anxiously.

"No."

She nodded as if she accepted that, but then grabbed his fingers more tightly and said incongruently, *"Please."*

"I've done all that I might do for you." His smile was prurient.

He couldn't mean it, *surely* he didn't mean it. "We shall expect you in a fortnight," she said stubbornly, panicking. "The guests begin to arrive on Thursday."

He shook his head, then gave her an indulgent look as he touched her temple, brushing a strand of hair away from her eyes. His gaze was so soft that Honor felt a little fluttery. *Light.* As if she could float away into the chandeliers like a tail of smoke.

"You must go and dance straightaway," he murmured. "Let everyone see you smile at someone else. You'd not want their last impression of you to be leaving the dance floor with me."

"I don't care," she said earnestly, but Easton put his hand on her arm and gently held her back.

"Yes, you do. Go now, before people talk."

Was he right? Honor truly didn't know anymore. Everything was beginning to feel turned on its head. She didn't care if people talked. She didn't care that he was a bastard son. She didn't want anything but him.

"Go," he said, more sternly, giving her a bit of a push.

Honor moved without thinking. She walked around the balcony to the main staircase, aware that he was watching her. She told herself not to look back, *begged* herself not to look back —

Honor looked back.

George Easton was standing where she'd left him, his gaze fixed on her. And she could feel it in her, burning a path all the way down to her toes.

CHAPTER FIFTEEN

When Monica had accepted Augustine's offer of marriage, her mother had promptly brought in a maid. "A future countess must know how to use the services of a lady's maid," she'd explained.

"But she's not a lady's maid," Monica had pointed out, watching the industrious girl polish the panes of her window.

"She will do," her mother had said confidently.

But Violet didn't do. The girl was as ignorant of what was required of her as Monica was about what a lady required. Privately, Monica didn't believe she needed a lady's maid. She was perfectly capable of donning her own clothes and rising on her own volition every morning.

Her mother, however, was determined that her daughter would know what was expected of her as a lady of privilege and leisure. Monica's future as a countess was a topic that greatly interested her mother and her eldest brother, Teddy. They talked about it at every opportunity.

This morning, Monica could smell the hot chocolate from across the room when Violet entered and placed a cup next to her bedside.

Monica yawned, stretched her arms overhead and pushed herself up, propping the pillows behind her back. She picked up the cup of chocolate as Violet opened the draperies. Rivulets of rain coursed down the windowpanes.

Violet began to pick up the articles of clothing Monica had tossed aside as she'd come in this morning. "Did you enjoy the ball, miss?" she asked.

"Very much," Monica said through another yawn. "But I thought it overly crowded."

"Aye, I'm not one for crowds," Violet said, moving about the room. She had no reservations about chatting freely with Monica. "I accompanied Mrs. Abbot to the market this morning, and such a crowd you never did see!" she said, and began to talk excitedly about her trip to the market.

Monica scarcely heard anything she said — something to do with figs, she thought — and was contemplating what she might wear for the day when she heard the name Beckington. Monica paused. She turned to look at Violet. "Pardon?"

Violet looked up from her work. "Miss?"

"What was that you said about Beckington?"

Violet frowned thoughtfully. "Oh!" she said, as recollection dawned. "Naught but that we saw a footman from Beckington House searching about. Mr. Abbot, he was there, and he said he knew the lad, as he's driven you to Beckington House and said the fellow was always there to greet him."

"You went to the market in Mayfair?" Monica asked, confused. It seemed quite out of the way.

"Oh, aye, to Mayfair. Mrs. Abbot, she prefers the butcher there. But the ham was *dear*! I said to her, Mrs. Abbot, you might have a ham for a few shillings in Marylebone, but she said the ham was not the quality Mrs. Hargrove preferred —"

"Violet, what about Beckington?" Monica interrupted before Violet explained different cuts of pork. "You said the footman was searching."

"Oh, him! Aye, he was searching for Lady Beckington." Violet smiled and picked up the wrap Monica had worn to the ball the night before, running her hand over the silk.

"For heaven's sake! He was searching for Lady Beckington in what way?" Monica prodded.

"Aye, she was lost. He said she'd gone for a walkabout and hadn't come back when they'd expected her. I said to Mrs. Abbot, a walkabout, in this foul weather? And Mrs. Abbot, she says, she no doubt has a boy to hold an umbrella over her head." Violet giggled.

Monica blinked. "Do you mean Lady Beckington was lost?"

"Oh, that I don't know, ma'am. The footman found her quick as you please, buying hothouse flowers of all things. Mrs. Hargrove, she'd send someone down for flowers, I think. She'd not walk to Mayfair on a day like this."

Violet folded the wrap as Monica pondered the news. Things were beginning to make sense, pieces of a puzzle falling into place.

After her chocolate, Monica dressed and made her way to the drawing room, where she found her mother and father. The room was small and dark, what with the wood paneling and worn draperies. Her mother wanted new drapes, but her father would not allow it.

This morning, her father was reading, jotting down notes on a sheet of paper at his elbow. Monica's mother was on the settee, busy with her needlework. Her hair was still strawberry-blond, still caught the candlelight, even on a dreary day such as this. "There you are, darling!" she said, and put down her needlework. Her father paused in his study of the book and glanced at Monica over the top of his spectacles.

"How did you find the ball?" her mother asked.

"Lovely," Monica said.

"And our Lord Sommerfield? Did he enjoy it, as well?"

Monica shrugged and sat next to her mother. She'd never known Augustine to be unhappy. "I think so."

Her mother patted her knee. "You should make sure of it, my dear. It's very important to keep a man happy. Is that not so, Benjamin?" she said to her husband.

Monica's father had gone back to his study and said absently, "Is it, Lizzy?"

"Mamma," Monica said, "how does one know if someone is going mad?"

That brought her father's head up. "Feeling a bit mad, are you, darling?"

"Not me, Papa," she said with a smile. "But . . . how does it descend on a person?"

Her father put down his pen and pivoted

around in his seat. "It depends on the sort of madness, I should think. If one suffers from senility, it might come on gradually. A lapse here or there, unusual forgetfulness. I knew of a chap once who lost his young son to fire. Madness came on him overnight. Why do you ask?"

Monica was almost afraid to say aloud what she was thinking. It seemed at best disrespectful, at worst scandalous. But it was the only thing that made sense, and her parents were looking at her expectantly. "I think that perhaps Lady Beckington is going mad."

Both of her parents stared at her, neither of them moving for a moment. Her father asked, "What do you mean, darling?"

"It's difficult to explain. But she seems rather too forgetful." Monica told them about the last time she'd been at Beckington House, and how Lady Beckington couldn't seem to follow the conversation. She told them what Violet had said. She told them how, at times, Lady Beckington's eyes looked strangely vacant, as if she weren't there at all.

Her father listened intently, and when she'd finished, he nodded and sat back in his chair, templing his fingers. "I don't see any reason for alarm, love. As people age, they become forgetful."

"Benjamin, she is only a year older than myself," Monica's mother pointed out.

"As I said," he said, and turned back to his book.

"When we were young, before you were born, Joan and I would go to the Mayfair flower stalls together," her mother said. "The flowers always seemed so much prettier than the hothouses where we lived." She looked wistfully away for a moment, seeing something in the distant past. "I've always enjoyed Joan's company."

"You will enjoy it again, Lizzy," Monica's father said. "She has forgotten a thing or two, nothing more."

Monica noticed the slight change in her mother's expression. She smiled at Monica. "Come, darling, let us go and dress your hair, shall we?" She stood up.

"Lizzy, do not put ideas into our daughter's head," her father said without lifting his gaze from his book. "You and Teddy have already suggested she turn the Cabot girls out to pasture."

"I've done no such thing, Mr. Hargrove," her mother protested, and took Monica's hand, pulling her along.

But that wasn't precisely true — her mother and Teddy had suggested more than once that perhaps the Cabot girls and their mother would be better suited to the dowager house at Longmeadow . . . or something even farther afield.

As they entered the narrow hall, Monica's mother put her arm around her shoulders. "I daresay your father is right, you've seen nothing more than a bit of forgetfulness in Lady Beckington. It happens to all of us. However . . ."

"However?"

Her mother glanced at her from the corners of her eyes. "However, if you were to notice a change, you might think again about the importance of finding a comfortable place where she and her daughters might reside. Out of the public eye, naturally."

Monica looked at her mother curiously.

"Are you aware that, in some cases, madness may turn to violence?"

Monica gasped. "You don't think Lady Beckington —"

"No, no, no," her mother quickly assured her. "But if she *were* mad, I don't think one could predict if or when she might be prone to violent outbursts. But I think such unpredictability would not be safe for the new earl's heirs."

Monica's heart began to pound in her

neck. She had visions of a madwoman stealing her babies from their cribs. Hadn't that happened a year or so ago? A madwoman had taken the child of her mistress, and they'd found the child dead some days later?

"Oh, dear, you are fretting!" her mother said. "Darling, I am *not* suggesting it would *ever* come to that, but . . . Well, you are my daughter. I am thinking of you, Monica."

"But . . . but shouldn't Augustine and I care for her if she's mad?"

"Yes," her mother said firmly. "However, that doesn't mean you must *reside* with her. I should think there would be some place quite safe for her and her daughters that would not require the expense of ball gowns and such."

Monica could not imagine Honor without fashionable gowns. But her mother smiled and gave her an affectionate squeeze. "You mustn't fret. I am certain it's nothing over which you should concern yourself."

CHAPTER SIXTEEN

The journey to Longmeadow took its toll on the earl; he was confined to his bed for two full days before he would feel strong enough to enjoy the warm weather that had followed the family from London.

That meant that the annual soiree at Longmeadow began without him for the first time. Barring some miracle, it likely would be the last time the earl attended the Longmeadow spring soiree, and the realization cast a pall over the entire family.

Prudence and Mercy took to disappearing to the stables to escape the somber mood, which, Grace opined, was not because of a sudden interest in all things equine, but a sudden interest in the strapping young men employed to keep the horses and the stables.

When the guests began to arrive, Grace kept a diligent eye on their mother, taking her for long walks in the gardens. It was clear that their mother was slipping further and further from them, and familiar pieces were disappearing every day.

Honor would do anything to have her loving, confident, sophisticated mother back. She thought of the carriage accident that had injured her mother. That had been the start of her mother's troubles, and Honor believed that she would give up all that they had to go back to that day, forgo the material things, the *haut ton,* the soirees — anything to keep her mother from that carriage. If her mother had never married Beckington, if they'd remained in the modest house with only Hannah to tend them, would they not have been happy and whole?

Honor was determined to keep her mother from the Hargroves if at all possible this week, but it was difficult to do, as Monica had made it her task to advise Augustine on the preparations for the next three days.

Honor stumbled upon the pair of lovebirds and another gentleman in the green salon, which happened to be her favorite room in the sprawling Georgian mansion. The house itself was one of the largest manors in England. It was so big, four stories high, that there had been plenty of places four young girls had found to escape in years past. It was built on a square with a central courtyard and had been lovingly tended; ivy covered the front entrance, roses the back.

The green salon overlooked the private rose garden from a pair of floor-to-ceiling French doors through which the heavenly scent wafted into the room during the spring and summer, when the doors were left open. The walls of the salon were painted a soft green, the draperies sheer white silks. It was cozy and comforting, bright and airy. Of the twenty-some odd guest rooms, as well as salons and drawing rooms and morning rooms, none appealed to Honor more.

"Honor!" Augustine said delightedly when he saw her. "Thank goodness you have come," he said, looking relieved. "You really *must* have a word with Mercy. She's got Mrs. Hargrove in quite a dither with her gruesome tales of ghosts."

"Longmeadow lends itself to gruesome ghost tales, Augustine."

"Perhaps. But dear Mrs. Hargrove assured me she scarcely slept a wink last night."

Having been subjected to Mercy's tales for many years now and being very familiar with Mrs. Hargrove, Honor couldn't imagine that she was the least offended by Mercy's tales of headless ghosts with bloodied necks.

"You'll speak to our Mercy, won't you? I

mentioned the problem to your mother, but she merely laughed and didn't seem inclined to help."

Honor's breath hitched at the thought of Augustine speaking to her mother for any length of time. "My mother is occupied with the earl. I will be happy to speak to Mercy."

"Augustine?" Monica said softly.

He looked at his fiancée, then said, "Oh, yes! Forgive me. Honor, I should like to introduce you to Mr. Richard Cleburne. He is the new vicar at Longmeadow."

The young man straightened, clasped his hands behind him and bowed reverently.

"How do you do, Mr. Cleburne," Honor said. "Welcome to Longmeadow."

"Thank you." He smiled.

Honor shifted her gaze to Monica. "I hope the fine weather at Longmeadow suits you?"

"I daresay *everything* at Longmeadow suits me."

Honor hadn't the slightest doubt of that.

"And Monica suits Longmeadow!" Augustine said proudly. "She's had some *wonderful* notions for how to improve this room."

Honor had already begun to back out of the room, but that remark gave her pause. "Improvements?" She looked around at the room with its floral chintz furnishings and paintings of serene landscapes. "But it doesn't need the slightest improvement. It's perfect as it is."

"I thought perhaps it might be better suited as a breakfast room," Monica said.

"She's right," Augustine agreed enthusiastically. "I can't believe we've not thought of it ourselves."

Honor suddenly had visions of guests trampling in and out of her favorite room in search of sausages. "*This* room, a breakfast room!"

"Yes, *this* room," Monica said airily. "The garden is the perfect vista for breaking one's fast, and it's not too terribly far from the kitchen."

"But neither is the current breakfast room, which has a lovely view of the park," Honor pointed out.

"Yet not enough room to accommodate all," Monica countered.

"And it's drafty," Augustine said, wrinkling his nose.

"Nothing that can't be repaired," Honor insisted. "Perhaps you and Monica might turn your attention to supper arrangements rather than worrying about this particular room."

"We've already done so," Augustine said proudly. "Monica and Mrs. Hargrove determined the seating this morning." He smiled as if that were perfectly brilliant.

But Honor was appalled. "Where was *my* mother?"

"Indisposed?" Augustine said uncertainly. "My father, you know."

"Don't fret, Honor," Monica said soothingly. "I personally saw to it that you will be seated next to Mr. Cleburne." She smiled, and it was a devilish one. Mr. Cleburne's smile, on the other hand, was uncertain.

"What a pleasure," Honor said sweetly, nodding at the vicar. "And where will you sit, Monica? In my mother's chair?"

"Honor!" Augustine said, glancing at his fiancée to see if she was offended.

But Monica merely laughed.

A footman stepped into the room. "My lord, Mr. Hardy asks that you come to the foyer."

"Oh, dear, probably something to do with the horses again, do you suppose?" Augustine said to Monica, wincing. "I beg your pardon, ladies. Cleburne, what do you know of horses?" he asked.

"I am woefully uneducated, my lord."

"Oh, you surely know more than me. Come, will you?" he asked, and walked briskly out of the room, forcing Mr. Cleburne to hurry along behind him, leaving Honor and Monica alone.

Honor frowned when they'd gone. "My mother is not yet a widow, Monica. Aren't you a bit too eager to take over as mistress?"

"What are you implying?" Monica asked indifferently. "Lady Beckington was quite agreeable this morning when we suggested it. She scarcely seemed to care what the seating should be. She seemed more interested in planning an excursion to Scotland." She paused. "At least I think that's what she meant."

How Honor managed to keep from gasping with alarm was a feat of her iron will. "Augustine should have consulted with her."

"He did, Honor. We have all consulted with Lady Beckington, and as I said, she is quite agreeable. Perhaps *she* understands that I shall be mistress here one day, and that there is no point in resisting it. Perhaps you should do the same."

Small truths like that made Honor feel defeated . . . almost. "I should like to think I'd not brag of it until I had stood at the altar."

"Don't be cross, dearest," Monica said sweetly. "I am confident you will scarcely give this room, or the supper, or even Longmeadow another thought once you have an offer for your hand and are planning your own wedded bliss."

Honor could feel herself bristling, which was precisely what Monica wanted. She forced herself to smile. "I beg your pardon — am I in imminent danger of receiving an offer?"

"One never knows," Monica cheerfully avowed. "Sometimes, things have a way of happening that defy all reason, do they not? People appear in our lives so suddenly and change things about completely."

"What are you talking about?" Honor asked, a sense of foreboding growing in her.

"Nothing! I am merely supposing that someone will appear to you, and then happily you might put the business with Rowley behind you."

Honor could smell something quite foul in this room and in those words, and folded her arms defensively. "There is no *business* with his lordship. I've not seen him in more than a year. I understand he is ensconced in the country with his lovely wife and their new son."

"I know you were stung by it, Honor," Monica said with great condescension. "But you can't allow it to color your opinion of all gentlemen."

"For heaven's sake!" Honor complained. "You've not the slightest idea what you are talking about!"

"I am only trying to impart that times are changing. The earl is quite seriously ill. Augustine will marry — even if it were not me, he'd marry someone, wouldn't he? You can't avoid the natural progression of things. You really should think of marrying a good man."

"A good man such as Mr. Cleburne, I suppose?" Honor said wryly.

Monica smiled broadly. "He *does* seem very kind, does he not?"

How Honor wished Monica was standing next to a window so she might push her out of it. "I am so thankful to have you looking out for my happiness," she said. "And while you impatiently wait for that happy moment that I am wed, I shall leave you to your renovation of Longmeadow and seek out Mercy. Good day, Monica."

"Good day, Honor," Monica responded, her voice singing with delight.

Honor walked from the room, leaving not the slightest trace of unhappiness behind her, lest Monica sense it. She would find Mercy and suggest that her tales of ghosts and goblins were not gruesome enough.

She stalked past the portrait gallery, the "drafty" breakfast room, the library, the formal dining room and the ballroom. She walked past the smaller salons and the yellow drawing room that took the western sun. She imagined what Monica might do with it all, and felt a knot of anger curling in her belly.

But she had no right.

As much as it galled her to admit it, Monica was right — Longmeadow was not her house; it was never intended to be her house. Honor *would* marry one day, and no doubt she'd live in a respectable house with a respectable man. But that house would not be Longmeadow with its hidden staircases and cold river and miles of green fields for girls to run and play. It would not be Beckington House in London with its marble foyer and grand salon where tea could be served to dozens at once. It wouldn't be this life at all, and the only way that Honor might hold on to it, at least until her sisters were out, was to keep Monica from destroying it, from unraveling it a thread at a time, just like her mother's sleeve.

Honor had steadfastly put off the inevitable these past two years, unwilling to feel the sting of disappointment again. Lord Rowley had broken her young, foolish heart, and Honor had found refuge in the Beckington wealth. The trappings of it had given her the freedom to keep a distance from her heart as she flitted to this event and that. She no longer knew if she was desperate to save the cocoon the earl's wealth gave her, or her sisters.

Honor didn't know her own mind any longer. Everything was so muddied now, and growing murkier every day. She couldn't keep Easton from her thoughts. Not for a moment.

Her heart was filling with that man. He was haunting her dreams, lurking in the shadows of her every waking thought since the Prescott Ball. He had resided like a brilliant comet in her memory — he had streaked across her night sky and had disappeared. But he was a bastard son, so wrong in so many ways, and yet so *right* . . .

Dear God, was he coming?

She clenched her fists at her sides and marched on. She despised the way women pined for men, hoping they would appear at this event or that. Easton had said he wouldn't come, and yet here she was, *hoping*. She looked expectantly toward every coach that pulled up before the massive stone columns that marked Longmeadow's grand entrance, hoping for him. But coach after coach had come and gone, and George Easton had not come.

He is not coming.

Surely she might admit that to herself now. Surely she might make an effort to stop reliving the moments she'd spent in his arms, awash in the mysterious connections between man and woman, her heart singing, her body yearning for his touch. Surely she might allow that George Easton was a dangerously sensual man, and while he had opened a carnal world to her, it had not been as meaningful to him as it had been to her. He had indulged her far more than she might have hoped, had made her heart flutter madly, had filled her mind with lustful images and tender thoughts . . . but it had been all play to him.

She had known from the beginning that he would not indulge her scheme forever; of course he wouldn't. What man would? Even she had never believed her plot would accomplish anything but to perhaps postpone the inevitable. Honestly, she couldn't even think of Monica now. Everything seemed so different.

If she admitted all of this to herself, she could reason that her disappointment in his not coming was absurd! She should *not* be disappointed in being relieved of his wretched dancing. Or that he didn't fawn over her as the young bucks of Mayfair were wont to do. She rather liked fawning and dancing! She should not admire his blue eyes that seemed to always shine with amusement, and neither should she be enamored of a man for the sole reason he would share her general annoyance at the grand form Monica had displayed at supper last night.

Because the moment she allowed those disappointments to gain ground, the ache in her head would move to her heart, whittling away at it until there was nothing left but dust.

The next afternoon, after luncheon, while the gentlemen rode about the thousand acres that made up Longmeadow, young Lord Washburn, who had graciously offered to stay behind and entertain the ladies, treated them to a poetry reading in the chapel. The ladies gamely trooped down the tree-lined lane to the small medieval church that had, at some point, been renovated to suit the needs of an earl.

Honor was well acquainted with Lord Washburn. He'd come into his title of viscount when his father's heart had suddenly stopped beating one day. He'd always been brash, loud and vexing, and then suddenly, with a title, he'd been one of the most sought-after gentlemen in all of Mayfair.

Washburn had taken to his new role with great enthusiasm, and on more than one occasion had insinuated to Honor, and then to Grace, that either of them might be the lucky young woman to win his heart.

Neither of them had the slightest desire to even try.

Today, Washburn randomly chose a young woman to affix his brown eyes upon as he read, and Honor was not pleased to see him affix them so often on Prudence. She was not yet seventeen, and frankly, her head was too easily turned.

Honor gazed at the rafters and idly wondered how long she might be trapped here. She sighed and glanced to her right — and gasped so loudly that Miss Fitzwilliam, sitting directly in front of her, glanced back over her shoulder with a look of alarm.

Honor quickly put a finger to her mouth and smiled apologetically, then glanced to the window once more.

He had come.

It was him, Easton! He and another gentleman trotted on horseback down the lane to the house. His back was to her, but Honor recognized the way he sat his horse, the broad shoulders and the glimpse of his brown hair brushing over his collar beneath the brim of his hat.

Her heart felt as if it was swelling in her chest with happiness. She could scarcely catch her breath, her heart was pounding so. Had he come for her? Had he missed her, had he thought of her as she had thought of him?

Honor was suddenly and violently desperate to quit the chapel.

Washburn had reached the crescendo of his current sonnet, had stepped away from the pulpit so that he might wave his arm around a bit. When he finished his sonnet, he crossed his arm across his heart and bowed deeply, graciously accepting the polite applause from the group of assembled young ladies. As two young women in the front row urged him to continue, Honor made her escape.

She fairly dashed out the back, bursting into the bright sunlight and pausing a moment so that her eyesight might adjust. She hurried along until she rounded the corner of the stables, taking care to walk and not run, smoothing her hair when she dipped behind the well house. She ran up the steps from the stable to the main drive, and walked quickly around the corner of the house, arriving on the drive just as Easton removed a bag from his horse's rump and handed it to a footman.

Honor paused to take a deep breath, then walked serenely and slowly into the men's midst. She stepped around the head of his horse. "Oh! Mr. Easton! You have come," she said far too breathlessly to convince anyone she was surprised to stumble upon him there in the drive.

His smile was so warm that it quietly filled her up like a tub of honey. He tipped his hat. "How do you do, Miss Cabot? Begun any new schemes? Created any bedlam in anyone's life?"

She laughed quickly, loudly, then took another steadying breath to reduce her ardor before smiling brilliantly at him. She could scarcely contain her joy at seeing him, or the urge to throw her arms around his neck and kiss him.

Easton frowned. "I will ask you kindly not to smile at me quite like that, Miss Cabot. I have come against my better judgment, and frankly, I've lost all respect for myself." He bowed.

"Then why did you come?" she asked cheerfully.

"Because I feared the chaos that would rain down on this august occasion if you were left to your own devices. It is my duty as a gentleman to spare these good people your unhinged thinking."

His declaration made her deliriously happy. She could feel her smile widening.

"Don't," he said brusquely. "I will not be swayed by your charming smile again."

"You find my smile charming?" she asked, taking a step closer.

"I find it dangerous." He bent over and picked up a valise. "I find everything about you dangerous."

A strong shiver of longing skirted up her spine; Honor took another step closer. "You'll be glad you have come, sir. You will have a very fine time at Longmeadow. I am certain of it."

"I won't," he said adamantly. But his eyes were twinkling with mirth.

The man who had ridden in with him stepped up, took the valise from his hand and inclined his head at Honor.

"Oh, yes. Miss Cabot, may I present Mr. Finnegan. He claims to be a valet."

"Madam," the gentleman said, and walked on.

"You've arrived just in time, too," Honor said to George. "There is to be a croquet tournament on the west lawn this afternoon."

"That settles it, then — I may now expire from joy."

Honor laughed. "I won't have you expiring at Longmeadow. Think of the scandal! Come, I'll show you to the house. Hardy has a room for you."

She began to walk and Easton fell in beside her. She could feel him, his body so close to hers, the strength of him beside her. She was so enthralled with it that she was startled when Augustine suddenly bounded out the entrance with Hardy on his heels, looking very nervous as he surveyed the ladies coming up the path. "We really must hurry things along," he said to no one in particular.

Honor guessed Monica would be close behind, and as much as she would have liked to engage Easton a bit longer, she thought she might succumb to her desire to touch him if she did not take her leave. Her thoughts began to tumble over each other as she plotted how to speak to him alone, away from prying eyes. But it was impossible to say the things that were bubbling up in her on the drive, so she called out to her stepbrother, "Augustine, look who has come!"

Augustine whirled about, squinting. And then he smiled. "Easton, yes, yes, of course! Welcome!" he said, and gestured to Hardy to follow him as he closed in on Easton.

"You're in excellent hands, sir," Honor

said. "Hardy will see you properly situated."
She turned about before he could respond
and said, "Augustine, you must tell him
about croquet! Mr. Easton said he is keen
to play."

"Croquet!" she heard Augustine say.
"Then you must play, Mr. Easton! We will
have a spectacular course, naturally," he
added, and began to explain in enthusiastic
detail the plan for croquet on the west lawn.

Honor could feel Easton's gaze on her
back as she practically skipped into the
house, her step suddenly lighter, her heart
still racing.

CHAPTER SEVENTEEN

Longmeadow was as impressive as George had heard, perhaps even more so. The Beckington butler led him and Finnegan down wide, carpeted corridors that turned into more wide, carpeted corridors, each one lined with paintings and portraits that George did not have time to study, artful little consoles that held Ming vases and hothouse flowers, and all of it illuminated by sunlit windows whose velvet drapes had been tied back with thick, gold silk cords.

The guest room George would inhabit was large, with a four-poster canopied bed and a view of the forest. As he stood in the middle of the room, looking up at a ceiling that had been painted with ropes and Grecian urns, he could certainly understand that Honor would not want to lose these surroundings. He really didn't know how exactly marriages were arranged among the very privileged, but from what he did know, he believed it was doubtful that she would marry into such opulence as this, only because there were so few families that enjoyed such wealth.

He was beginning to feel a bit foolish; he'd come here after a long internal debate. He'd told himself that he was helping Honor Cabot. His body had said otherwise. His body, his heart had said that he had to see her again. But toward what end? That was the murky mystery brewing in him.

Finnegan seemed perfectly at ease, putting George's things away as George stood by, uncomfortable in his uselessness. He'd not wanted Finnegan to come, but Finnegan had explained to Easton that if he arrived without a manservant or valet, he'd appear out of place.

"I *am* out of place," George had pointed out.

"Only if you believe yourself to be," Finnegan had said curtly, and had begun to fill a valise, his jaw set with determination. George knew better than to argue with the man when he was like that, and now here he was, brushing down George's formal dinner coat. "I suggest you have a walkabout," Finnegan said without looking up from his work. "You might prepare yourself for croquet. Perhaps it will improve your disposition and put you into a proper frame of mind for society here." He glanced up at George. "If I may, sir, it is vastly different than the society in which you typically associate."

George couldn't help but grin. "Do you know, Finnegan, that there are days I have the strongest urge to put my fist squarely in your comely face?"

"That would not become a gentleman," Finnegan said, and went about his business.

George couldn't watch Finnegan any longer; he ran his fingers through his hair, straightened his neckcloth and went out. He walked out into the gardens and paused to admire the fine specimens of roses rivaled only by those he'd seen around St. James.

He heard the sound of feminine laughter and was unthinkingly drawn to it, making his way through the maze of roses to the gate that led to a large expanse of manicured lawn. Beyond the vast lawn, he could see a lake shimmering in the sunlight, bounded by forest on two sides.

He walked through the gate and carried on down the slope, his gaze on footmen who were busily setting the croquet hoops. He approached a trio of ladies seated near a large fountain where three enormous cherubs streamed great arcs of water from their pursed lips.

One of the ladies glanced up from her wide-brimmed hat and blinked. "Mr. Easton!" she said, gaining her feet.

George had been so taken by the giant cherubs that he'd failed to recognize Miss Hargrove at first. He quickly recovered and bowed low. "Miss Hargrove," he said. "My day has just been immeasurably improved."

The two ladies in her company tittered at that.

"I wasn't aware you'd come," Miss Hargrove said.

"I only just arrived."

She nodded; her gaze flicked over him. "Miss Ellis, may I introduce Mr. George Easton," she said, her hand gracefully indicating the fairer of the two young women seated on the bench. "And Miss Eliza Rivers."

"We are acquainted," George said. "Ladies, how do you do?"

"Are you lost, Mr. Easton?" Miss Hargrove asked, eyeing him closely. He noticed that she was holding a croquet mallet, which she swung casually at her side.

"I am hopelessly lost," he said cheerfully, earning a titter from Miss Ellis. "I was in search of your very affable fiancé. He had mentioned a croquet tournament."

259

"Yes, it will begin shortly. You will need a mallet."

"And a partner." He looked pointedly at her. "Will you do me the honor, Miss Hargrove?"

Miss Hargrove studied him a moment, clearly debating his invitation.

"I might partner, if you like," Miss Rivers said shyly. "I am certain Miss Hargrove will want to partner with Lord Sommerfield —"

"Thank you, but I had agreed to partner with Mr. Cleburne," Monica interjected. "I'm certain he won't mind another partner now that a new guest has arrived so unexpectedly. Shall we fetch you a mallet, Mr. Easton?" She gestured to the path.

George smiled. He would delight in explaining to Honor Cabot that he was right, he had indeed turned Miss Hargrove's head, and one need only see how quickly she leaped at the chance to be his partner to know it. He graciously offered his arm to her, wished her companions a good day and began to walk with her. "Such lovely roses at Longmeadow," he observed. "Beauty is surrounded by beauty." He smiled.

Miss Hargrove sighed. "Quite flattering, Mr. Easton. Miss Rivers would have swooned. But I've never been swayed by poetic overture."

George was only slightly taken aback. "Should I take that to mean you are immune to honest admiration?"

"I am not immune to *honest* admiration," she said. "But how can you claim to have any admiration for me when there are so many lovely debutantes around you? I daresay my fiancé's *four* unmarried sisters are ripe for admiration."

She watched him closely for his response, but George was practiced in getting his way when it came to matters female. "Surely you must know that when one's heart has divined toward someone in particular, one cannot simply will it in another direction?"

Miss Hargrove suddenly laughed at that. "You're a rake, Mr. Easton! It would seem that all I've heard tell about you is true."

He didn't know precisely what she meant, but he was beginning to wonder if he'd ever worked so hard to entice a woman. "I am certain I am guilty as charged, but I am a man, first and foremost, and when I admire a woman, I cannot deny it."

They reached the stand where a footman was handing out croquet mallets and balls. She took a mallet and handed it to him. "You'd best admire someone else."

What had happened here? The woman had practically been melting at the Prescott

Ball. Had she heard the rumors of his missing ship, that his fortune was gone, as he'd heard round his club? Was that the reason for her aloofness?

He decided to resort to more salacious tactics. "You may be engaged, Miss Hargrove, but to a man who cannot possibly please you as I would." He paused, let his gaze drift down her body, then looked into her eyes. "In every manner your body might imagine."

He fully expected her to succumb to that suggestion, but she didn't. She took the croquet balls from the footman and handed them to George and pointed to the ground. "We will begin there when play is called." She glided away toward the start of the course.

George followed her and carelessly dropped the balls at the starting point, his gaze on her.

Miss Hargrove glanced at him sidelong. "Perhaps you should have a look about this weekend and set your sights on someone who is more accepting of your attentions." She glanced around and nodded to something over his shoulder. "Miss Peeples has no understanding with anyone."

George didn't even bother to glance at the Peeples girl. "I think her mother would not approve." He was certain of that — he'd enjoyed a brief but passionate affair with Mrs. Peeples a year or so ago. The woman had been frightened of pregnancy and had preferred to please him. Which, George thought, had been pleasant enough once or twice. But he'd discovered he'd rather be the one to do the pleasing.

A sudden and unwanted image of Honor Cabot danced in his mind's eye, and he was reminded of how lustfully she had received his advances at the Prescott Ball. So much so that he had struggled quite desperately to keep from taking it further.

"Well, there are plenty of others," Miss Hargrove said with a shrug. "Ah, there he is, my future husband." She gave George a pert little smile as Sommerfield began to wave his arms, seeking the attention of the players.

Bloody hell, Monica Hargrove *was* a tough little nut, George thought as Sommerfield bellowed out the rules of the tournament. He'd said things to her he'd said to far more experienced women, and which had produced *far* more satisfying results than this one would give him.

Dear God, was Honor right?

The more he thought on it, the more vexed George grew. He was a grown man, for heaven's sake, an *experienced* man. And when a man like him said that he desired to please a woman, she should slap him or eat out of his bloody palm. But she should *not* give him a coy smile and chassé away.

So what was it, George wondered irritably, that would turn Miss Hargrove's stubborn little head? He was feeling rather determined to find it.

CHAPTER EIGHTEEN

The beautiful sunshine of the afternoon had given way to rain, and the guests were in the foyer, filling the hallways and grand ballroom. It had been set for a night of gaming with card and casino tables, as well as roulette. The formal dining room was likewise set with tables, but for dining. At half past ten, a buffet would be provided.

Honor walked through the throng, pausing to accept the greetings of several guests and the compliments of more than one gentleman. She had dressed for the evening in anticipation of seeing Easton again. She wore a crimson satin trimmed with black lace and beaded embroidery that swirled about the hem of the gown and her train, and the front panel of the underskirt. The décolletage was scandalously deep, edged with more black lace. Around her throat she wore a choker of black obsidian stones, a gift from the earl on the occasion of her twentieth birthday. It was amazing to think that had been two entire years ago. Most of her friends that age were married now. Lucinda Stone was expecting her first child.

Honor felt a curious little draw of something when she thought of Lucinda that felt almost like regret.

But that was impossible. Honor didn't regret anything. She'd lived her life as she'd wanted, taking advantage of every opportunity to be as free as she pleased. So why, then, had that freedom begun to feel a little like a noose? No, no, that was *not* what she believed.

She believed in her freedom when she wasn't thinking of George Easton.

Speaking of Easton, where was he? She tried not to imagine him befriending any other woman here — the thought was a bit nauseating.

She could not see him in the throng.

A current seemed to run through the house; laughter crackled, the crowd's jovial mood helped along by unimaginable quantities of champagne and wine, served by a team of eight footmen.

Even the earl had come down, Honor was pleased to see. He was dressed in formal tails, his neckcloth snowy white against the sickly pallor of his skin. He looked rather small in the large, upholstered armchair where he sat, a footstool under his feet, a blanket over his lap, Jericho standing behind him.

Honor's mother was sitting beside him, beautifully regal in the silver gown. She was laughing at something Mr. Cleburne was saying. Mr. Cleburne was suddenly ever present, wasn't he? She supposed Monica had seen to that.

Honor made her way to the earl's side and crouched beside his chair, covering his hand with hers. "How do you fare this evening, my lord?"

He smiled at her, touched the back of his hand to her cheek. "I am fatigued, darling, but otherwise, I feel well enough, I suppose. You look beautiful." He cocked his head to see the obsidian choker and smiled. "Look at your daughter, Joan," he said, putting his hand on his wife's hand. "Isn't she beautiful?"

Honor's mother turned a bright smile from the conversation with Mr. Cleburne, Augustine and Monica to Honor.

Honor smiled and touched the black choker. "Do you remember the necklace his lordship gave me on my birthday, Mamma?"

Her mother's gaze dropped to the necklace a moment, then slowly lifted to Honor's

267

eyes again. "Of course I recall it. You've taken it from my jewelry box."

Augustine chuckled and said to Mr. Cleburne, "There is never a moment's peace with so many women, sir. But you will grow accustomed to it."

Honor was so anxious to dispel any idea that she might have taken the necklace from her mother that she only vaguely wondered why Mr. Cleburne would need to grow accustomed to sisters. "No, Mamma! The earl made a gift of it to me, remember?"

"You *stole* it," her mother insisted, her gaze suddenly dark and distant. Standing just on the other side of her, Monica's gaze widened with surprise.

"She's not stolen it, Joan," said the earl. "I gave it to her."

Her mother yanked her hand free of the earl's. "Why would you lie to protect *her*?"

Stunned, Mr. Cleburne looked from Honor to Lady Beckington. "May I be of some help?"

Augustine was gaping in shock at his stepmother, and Monica . . . Monica's gaze was fixed on Honor, neither surprised nor smug. She seemed only curious as to what Honor would say next.

God in heaven, she *knew.* She knew Honor's mother was going mad.

Honor's heart began to race. She quickly took off the necklace. "Here, Mamma. You are quite right, I have taken it without permission." She held the necklace out to her mother.

Lady Beckington turned away from it, as if looking at it hurt her. "I don't want it *now,*" she said, as if the necklace had been ruined. "Oh, there she is! There is my daughter Grace!" she said, and rose, almost pushing Mr. Cleburne aside as she reached for Grace.

Grace looked curiously at them all, but when her gaze met Honor's, the color seemed to bleed from her face. "Good evening, Mamma," she said, and kissed her mother's cheek.

Her mother grabbed Grace in a tight embrace. "How *thankful* I am that you have come," she said. "She stole my necklace!" She glared at Honor.

The earl very shakily reached his hand up to his wife's arm. "Sit, Joan, sit, sit. I should like you near."

Honor's mother looked as if she meant to refuse her husband, but Mr. Cleburne put a hand on her elbow, guiding her into the chair. With one last glare for Honor, she smiled up at Mr. Cleburne as if everything were quite normal, as if she hadn't just accused Honor of stealing from her.

But Augustine, Monica and Grace were all looking at Honor uncertainly, not knowing what to say. And what was Honor to do?

It was the earl who saved her. He subtly touched her hand. "Bloody women," he said, his voice rough. "Always arguing over this jewel or that shoe, are they not, Cleburne?" he said with a dismissive flick of his wrist.

Mr. Cleburne laughed with anxious relief. "Quite so, my lord."

"If you will excuse me, my lord, I should make sure the kitchen is in order," Honor said, to which Grace's eyebrows rose nearly to her hairline, seeing as how Honor rarely set foot in the kitchen. Nonetheless, Honor walked on, the necklace still clutched in her hand.

But as she moved away, she couldn't seem to settle her heart, racing with fear.

She wished she knew what to do, she wished, oh, God, how she *wished* that she had taken her responsibility to marry more seriously. If she had married, she would be in a position to care for her mother without fearing what would become of her.

Honor needed air, a moment of quiet to think. She stepped out of the ballroom and into the crowded hallway.

A touch to her arm startled her; she looked up to see George Easton.

He gave her a subtle wink as he bowed before her. "There you are, Miss Cabot. I thought perhaps you had returned to London, as I've seen hide nor hair of you since I left all my cares behind to come to your aid." He cocked a brow, a playful smile on his lips.

Her foolish heart skipped several beats at the sight of him. She suddenly didn't feel quite so alone. "Perhaps you've not seen me about because you were well occupied?" She arched a brow right back at him.

"Indeed I was," he said agreeably. "I spent the afternoon playing croquet with your future sister-in-law and charming her into submission. You do recall, do you not, the reason for our acquaintance?" he asked, gesturing back and forth between them.

She did not like to think he was here because of Monica. She wanted him to be here for her.

"It went exceedingly well, if you're wondering," he said. "Much like humoring a child —"

"Humoring a — *oh!*" Honor exclaimed. "It is comforting to know that your esteem for yourself never wavers!" She stepped around him, intending to stalk away before she said something she'd regret, but Easton was not content to let her go. He stopped her with a hand to her abdomen as she tried to pass.

"Don't you dare flounce away from me in a snit, madam."

"I am neither flouncing nor in a *snit,*" she said, pushing his hand away.

"Yes, you are. You're angry that your little scheme is not working and are directing your frustration at me."

That wasn't it at all. Her frustration was too ill defined, directed at everything and everyone. "You are quite right, Mr. Easton," she said imperiously. "I am directing my frustration at you. I truly believed you were the man for this, could turn *any* woman's head —"

"I beg your pardon once more, but *you* claimed that. I never did."

"I don't want you to do it!" she blurted.

Easton blinked. "Pardon?"

What was she doing? Honor put her hand to her forehead and closed her eyes, trying to make sense of her feelings. "You were right. It was a ridiculous notion, and one that has failed miserably."

"Have a care, love," Easton muttered, and smiled reassuringly. "I've not given up, and

272

frankly, I never thought *you* would. I've never met a more tenacious and stubborn —"

Honor lifted her head, her eyes narrowing.

"Pardon," he said with an easy smile. "*Determined* person in my life."

"I was. I *am,*" she quickly amended. "But this . . . this is folly. Childish folly. I don't want you to do it. Please."

"Well, yes, but . . . Good God, you *are* defeated," he said, pretending shock. "Where is the swashbuckler?"

The swashbuckler had deserted her. She felt nothing but fear and uncertainty and a strong desire for the man standing before her. She shrugged halfheartedly. She felt torn and pulled in so many conflicting directions, everything twisted all around, and in the midst of it were her growing feelings for Easton.

"Dear God," Easton muttered, his gaze sweeping over her face. "Stand right where you are, Miss Cabot." He walked a few feet away to hail a passing footman with a tray laden with champagne flutes. He returned and handed a flute to her. "Cheer up. That's a command," he said. "I won't allow the one shining star in this bloody *ton* to lose her flame. I'll even dance if I must."

That brought her head up with a swell of tenderness. "Really?" she asked hopefully.

He smiled at her earnestness. *"Really."*

That admission gave Honor a new breath of exhilaration for reasons that didn't seem prudent or even reasonable. She suddenly felt much lighter as she sipped her champagne. She looked into his pale blue eyes, filled with the warmth of his concern for her. "I need some air," she said simply.

His eyes sparked in the low light of the hallway. "I thought you'd never admit it."

CHAPTER NINETEEN

She glided down the hall before him, the train of her gown sweeping elegantly behind. George had no idea where she was going, but when they passed the French doors that led out onto a viewing balcony, he caught her hand in his. "Here," he said.

"It's raining," she said, but she did not pull her hand free of his.

"If I am not mistaken, there is an eave over the balcony." George opened the door and with a quick glance behind them, he stood aside so she could slip out.

Honor stepped out into the cool, damp air and took a breath. She closed her eyes and lifted her face to the fine mist that hung over Longmeadow. Given the weather, there was no one wandering the grounds, no one outside at all. George pulled the door shut and the cacophony of so many people gathered in one place fell away. It was quiet out here, the only sound the slow patter of rain on the eaves.

"I feel as if I can breathe for the first time tonight," Honor said, and bent her dark head and looked down, over the railing. She placed the flute of champagne on the railing and brought her hands to her bare arms.

George put his flute aside and shrugged out of his coat. He draped it over her shoulders; Honor smiled gratefully. "Thank you." She dipped her head, touched her nose to the shoulder of his coat, as if she were breathing it in.

"Now then," he said, picking up his flute and sipping once more. "What has happened to bring about this sudden melancholy?"

Honor sighed as if she carried a great weight. "My mother," she said simply. "She's getting worse. Soon, I think everyone shall know about her." She looked down at something she held in her hand. "I realize now I should have been more inclined to accept the attentions of gentlemen after I came out. If I had, I'd be married by now and I'd have the means to care for her."

George didn't like the reminder that Honor was a privileged debutante, or that she would marry one day, probably to someone here in this house this very weekend. It made him feel strangely adrift, as if he was being cast out into the stream while she remained anchored behind.

"I wonder," he said, taking in a face that seemed almost perfectly sculpted, "on whom you might have set your cap had you accepted their attentions? Perhaps he is stumbling about in his cups now, just beyond that door."

She smiled. "No. There is no one."

He didn't believe that for a moment. "No one," he repeated dubiously, and very casually brushed her earlobe with his thumb. The little black jewel that dangled there bounced a bit. "The most desirable bachelors among the Quality are gathered here this weekend and Miss Honor Cabot sees no one who might serve as a suitable husband? A father to her children? A companion in her dotage?"

She lifted her face a little. "Not in there."

"Washburn," George suggested.

Honor instantly burst out laughing. "Washburn! Do you think I would subject myself to simpering poetry readings every night of my life?"

"Ah, he is a poet," George said. "How appalling for you. Then you must at least find young Lord Desbrook appealing. I have it on good authority that he is one of the most sought-after young men in all of London."

"Well, of course he is — he will one day be a duke. But in the strictest confidence I may tell you that as a man, Desbrook is exceedingly dull. I once spent an entire supper party seated next to him, and all he could speak about was the stag he had shot."

"He's a hunter? The bounder," he teased her. "There is always Lord Merryton, who has, as far as I know, resisted the many attempts to lay a dainty finger or two on his fortune."

"Lord Merryton is not here. And if he was, I assure you, he'd be *quite* imperious. He's too proud, if you ask me."

"All right then, we have a poet, a hunter and a proud man who are all wholly unsuitable for the fair Honor Cabot."

"Precisely."

"Then who?" George traced a path down her neck, his finger sliding into the indention of her throat at the base of her neck. *Yes, who, Honor Cabot? Who would you take to your bed? Who would you allow to father your children, to love you every day of your life?* "You are a beautiful young woman with the best of connections. Surely there is *some* one you might imagine joining you in conjugal bliss? Or are the rumors perhaps true that Lord Rowley has ruined you for any other man?"

Honor looked up at him with surprise. "Is it truly said?"

"Not by everyone, but a few, yes."

She sighed. "I grant you that my unpleasant experience with Lord Rowley did not persuade me to other courtships . . . but it is not *entirely* true, Easton."

He couldn't imagine a greater fool than Rowley, and moved his hand to her décolletage, his fingers sliding across her soft skin. "Poor Honor. It must have been painful for you."

"At first," she admitted, and looked away. "It was really more surprising. Until then, I didn't know that life could be so terribly cruel."

How he hated that she'd discovered that sad truth. He wished that he could keep her from discovering other cruel truths about life, but that was beyond his capacity. The most he could offer was some advice. "Not every man is unkind, love."

She looked up at him, her eyes swimming in an emotion he could not name but could feel reverberating in his chest. "I know," she said softly. "You're not unkind. I can trust you."

George's heart hitched painfully. The words were erotic to the bastard child in him. They meant acceptance, respect.

"Don't trust me, love," he warned her. As much as it meant to him to hear those words from her lips, he knew that he could never be what she expected him to be. He was too much of an outsider, a man with no home.

Honor seemed to understand; she averted her gaze, swallowing hard.

George admired her slender neck and gentle jaw. A moment passed as the two of them gazed out into the night. Honor said, "I've not wanted to marry these past two years." She peeked at him again and smiled sheepishly. "I have valued my freedom and have believed that until Augustine shoved me out into the cold world so that his new wife might turn my favorite green salon into another breakfast room, I would enjoy the privileges I have somehow been fortunate enough to enjoy."

"But won't you still be a free woman if you are married?"

She clucked her tongue at him. "Of course not," she said. "Really, Easton, surely you understand that a woman is not *truly* free if she is married. Some husbands are benevolent, but others are not, and if your husband is not, there is very little a woman can do for it."

George had had liaisons with married

women, and none of them had ever complained particularly about their lives. But he did recall when Lady Dearing desired to see a sister in Wales who was near death, Lord Dearing refused her, claiming he could not be parted from his wife for so long, and she was not allowed to go.

He shook off the memory. "You want freedom to do what, precisely?" he asked as he cupped the back of her neck with his hand — it felt so small to him. "To attend teas and parties and ride about in Hyde Park?"

"No, I want to be free as *you* are," she said. "To not care about society, to do what I please, to go where I desire."

George snorted. "Do you truly believe what I have is freedom?"

She blinked up at him. "Well, yes . . . The best kind."

He laughed low, stroked her cheek. "It is a puzzle to me how one woman can be so clever and fearless, and yet so naive all at once."

"Naive!"

"Quite. How can you even think I am free, when you yourself have had to seek invitations for me? Admit it, Honor — we are all prisoners of our society in one way or another. Don't mistake loneliness for free-dom."

She looked startled. "Are you lonely, George?"

"At times, yes," he admitted. "I've no fam-ily, have I? There are times I'd rather have a family than all the ships in the sea." He laughed, the sound of it a little bitter to his own ears. "And now it looks as if I shall have neither."

"Oh, George . . ." She slipped her hand into his. "I . . . I think . . ."

He smiled at what he assumed was an awkward attempt to soothe him, caught her hand and brought it to his mouth to kiss it. "Don't fret for me, Cabot. I make do."

But Honor didn't smile. Emotion was swimming in her eyes again, and it seeped into George like good whiskey on a cold winter's day. He could feel a beast awaken-ing in him, rising up, wanting to take hold —

Honor abruptly looked down as if she couldn't bear it. She opened her palm, and he saw the necklace there. "Is it broken?"

"No. It's the casualty of a misunderstand-ing."

He had no idea what she meant, but he took it from her hand, turned her around and draped it around her throat. She bent her head slightly forward so that he might fasten it. When he'd secured it, he slid his hand over her shoulder, pressed his palm to her collarbone and pulled her back into his chest.

He could feel her shift closer, her weight leaning against his. "What are you doing?" she whispered.

God, but he wished he knew. He was falling. Off a mountain, down into a strange ravine whose bottom he could not see. It was dark in that ravine — he could not see where he was heading. "I wish you the freedom you seek, Honor."

She didn't move at first, but then she turned slightly, glancing over her shoulder at him, her blue eyes glimmering with desire.

He slid his hand down into her bodice, dipped his head and kissed her neck. "Freedom to experience all that life is."

"You are a curious man, Easton. Dangerous and unpredictable and unexpected. I don't know quite what to make of you."

He smiled against her cheek. "You might have considered that before you galloped up Rotten Row to intercept me."

"I mostly certainly *did* consider it," she said, and twisted around to face him.

He gazed down at her, taking in every freckle, every crease. He slipped his arm inside the coat, around her waist, and pulled her into his body.

But Honor put her hand between them and pushed back. "Don't you dare kiss me here," she warned him. "I can't bear it."

Neither could he. He gathered her closer. "Darling, you should never dare a ravenous man," he said, and dipped his head to kiss her.

She instantly softened into him, her hand sliding up his chest.

George's response was a guttural sound, deep in his throat. He slipped an arm around her waist, moved his mouth to her neck, her earlobe and across her jaw to her mouth again. It wasn't enough; it was never enough with Honor. He abruptly pushed her up against the wall, pressing his body against hers as his tongue dipped hungrily into her mouth. He needed to be inside of her, needed to fill her with the emotion that was damming up inside of him.

He thought she might protest and appeal to his sense of decency, but Honor didn't attempt to stop him — if anything, she curved more deeply into him, and her kisses became more urgent.

He paused for a moment, braced his arms on either side of her head.

Honor smiled at him like a woman who

knew she was in control and on the verge of carnal pleasure, and the effect on him was maddeningly strong. It sent a quake of desire rumbling through him. He allowed himself a moment to take in her fine figure, the swell of her bosom, the inky dark hair that smelled of roses.

He touched her collarbone with the back of his hand. "If you were mine, I would remove every stitch of clothing and kiss every inch of your skin, Cabot," he said, his voice rough with need. He dipped his hand into her cleavage, traced a line up to her neck again. "I would make myself mad thinking of all the ways I might have you."

She sucked in her breath and held it; her lashes fluttered.

"I would use my hands," he said, cupping her between her legs. "My mouth," he muttered, brushing his lips across her temple, "and my cock." He pressed his erection against her abdomen and could feel the shiver of anticipation course through her body.

"But you're not mine," he muttered, and began to trace a line from her chin, down her neck, between her bosoms, and to her groin. "I must then improvise." He began to gather her skirts.

Honor glanced anxiously at the balcony door.

"Does the threat of discovery excite you?" he asked, slipping his hand beneath her gown and between her legs.

Her answer was swallowed by a soft gasp at the sensation of his fingers sliding deeper into the slit of her body, twirling suggestively around the hardened nub.

Honor splayed her hands against the wall at her back as if she were trying to hold herself up. Her head dropped against his shoulder as he moved inside her, and her breathing began to grow ragged.

But for George, it was not enough. It could never be enough. He suddenly withdrew his hand. Honor's lips parted with surprise, and she opened her eyes. "We'll not go as quickly this evening," he said, and took her leg in his hand, lifting it to prop her foot against the railing.

"Easton!" she whispered hotly as she glanced frantically at the door.

He peeled one of her hands from the wall and stuffed the voluminous skirts into it. "Hold it," he commanded her, kissed her with all the desire that was building to a fevered pitch in him, then slid down her body, his hands following, raking across her breasts and waist, until he was on one knee

286

and his hands had settled on her hips.

He could smell her potent desire, could feel the dampness between her legs. Above him, Honor was gasping for air. George couldn't contain himself; he dipped in between the curls and the folds of skin, his tongue sliding into the valley. Honor gasped again and clutched at his head and hair.

George flicked his tongue against her again, gripped her hips, and began to lick her, dipping deep into her slit, exploring her, teasing her at the core of her desire then sliding down the slick pathway again, to where he could feel her throbbing for him against his tongue. Her moans of pleasure were incredibly arousing — he would not have thought himself capable of restraint, but he felt an intrinsic need to pleasure her, to give her this. The stroke of his tongue turned harder until he covered her completely with his mouth, sucking her as she moved against him, pressing against his tongue, seeking her fulfillment. He slipped his hand between her legs, used his fingers and his mouth to carry her over the edge.

When she came, she fell over his head, her arms around his neck.

George was breathing as hard as Honor. Harder. His breath was full of pent-up desire, of the physical toil of his restraint.

He kissed her belly, then lowered her skirts and stood up, dragging her up with him.

Honor was spent, her body limp as she sought her breath. She slowly straightened, brushed her hand against her hair — one thick strand had come undone from the neat little arrangement at the back of her head. She tucked it in and lifted her gaze to George. "You have destroyed me."

He shook his head and casually removed a handkerchief and wiped his hand and returned it to his pocket. "I have opened the door to a different sort of freedom," he said, and brushed her face with the back of his hand. He thought he should speak, but the taste of her was still on his lips, and he couldn't find the appropriate thing to say. *I adore you. I need you. I can't possibly have you.*

Honor rose up on her toes and kissed the corner of his mouth. She slid down again, removed his coat from her shoulders and said, "I don't know what to do with you, George Easton."

"The feeling is entirely mutual."

"I should go," she said, but her gaze was searching his face, as if she weren't certain what she should do.

George's body answered for them both. He could not stand on this viewing balcony with the taste of her on his mouth, her pleasure still thrumming in his trousers. "You should," he said, and ran his thumb across her lip. "Go now, little lamb, before I devour you." He leaned down, kissed her lightly on the mouth. *"Go,"* he said, more urgently. His high steps were faltering. He was off course. He needed a moment, several moments, to find his pace again.

"George —"

"No. Go now," he said, more forcefully.

With a hint of a smile on her face, Honor stepped around him and walked to the French doors. With one last swipe of her palm against her hair, she opened both doors and disappeared inside.

George donned his coat, walked to the railing and stared into black, willing his body back to its natural state.

Willing his heart back to its natural state was not as successful.

CHAPTER TWENTY

Three hours past midnight, Honor finally collapsed into bed, her head aching from exhaustion. She was emotionally drained after the evening.

But mostly, Honor was oddly euphoric, her senses still filled with the extraordinary moments with George on the viewing balcony.

George.

What was happening to her? When had she become so wanton? Her thoughts raced with the memory of his arms around her, his lips on her flesh, the scent of his coat enveloping her. She had been truly transported by him, carnal pleasure introduced to her and settling deep. Honor had believed herself ready for potent sexual advances from any gentleman . . . but nothing could have prepared her for what had happened on the viewing balcony. She'd tasted that secret world between men and women, the thing that brought them together, and now she wanted it all. She wanted to feel his body inside hers, to feel his hands on every inch of her body. She wanted to look into those pale blue eyes for as long as she could, to see the shine in them when he looked at her.

But such want was heart-wrenching. Honor was not naive — George Easton was the sort of man no woman could *ever* possess, she knew that. He was a man without connection, a man that no father, no brother, would ever allow a daughter or sister to wed. He was a man who brazenly and openly risked all for the greatest pleasures in his life. That sort of man had no room in his life for a wife. A lover, certainly. But not a wife.

He was precisely the sort of man who made her heart race with excitement.

But did she want to be his *wife*? Was that the fullness she was feeling in her chest? Was that the desire that lurked in her, the need to be with him always, to hold him, to see his smile? Realization of what she truly wanted dawned slowly, spreading softly like morning's first light. How interesting that Honor had believed herself to be the same at heart as George — no desire for entanglements, but only excitement and enchantment. How ironic that it would be someone just like her who would show her that what she *really* wanted was love. *She wanted love.* She wanted to feel love again, to feel the comforting security of sitting across from someone every day, of sharing a life, a family, the heartaches and triumphs of life.

She wanted George. God, how she wanted him. He was exciting, so different from the gentlemen of the *ton.* He was not afraid to risk all, he was not afraid of anything. He was the perfect man for her.

Except for the fact that he was a bastard, involved in trade and reviled by half the *ton.*

Honor tried to sleep, clutching the coverlet as if it were a rope tethering her to earth. She gripped it to keep herself on firm ground, to remember who she was, what her destiny was to be — safely married to someone of standing in the *ton.* An obedient wife, a perfect hostess, protector of her family. Safe in the bosom of the society she had been reared to accept.

But what did that all mean without someone she loved to share it with her? An empty life.

Honor must have slept — she was startled awake when someone grabbed her foot. Honor came up with a gasp and blinked sleepily at Prudence standing at the end of her bed.

"What in heaven?" she asked grumpily, and fell back onto the pillow.

"Why aren't you awake?" Prudence demanded. "You've missed breakfast."

"Because I had my supper at two in the morning." She yawned and stretched her arms high above her head. "Why? Is something wrong?"

"No. But the cricket tournament is today. Augustine is in a dither about it." She sat on the end of Honor's bed. "Lord Washburn intends to play."

"How perfectly lovely for Lord Washburn," Honor said. She pushed herself up, propped herself against the pillows. Oh, to be sixteen years all over again, Honor thought wistfully.

"He's rather athletic," Prudence added, and restlessly stood up. "Grace is looking for you. She said if I found you, I was to send you to her."

"But I want to *sleep*," she complained. Really, to think of George. "Tell Grace I will come to her just as soon as I'm able, will you?" Honor asked.

An hour later, Honor found her sister outside beneath a parasol. Like Honor, Grace had dressed in white muslin, the traditional color of the cricket tournament.

She looked as fatigued as Honor felt.

"Were you late to bed?" Honor asked. "You look as if you've not slept."

"I haven't," Grace admitted. "I shall be very merry when everyone leaves Longmeadow."

That wasn't like her sister — Grace, of all of them, seemed to love these annual gatherings at Longmeadow. "Is it Mr. Pritchard, again?" she asked, referring to one of Grace's more ardent admirers.

"What? No, no, not him," Grace said with a distracted shake of her head. "It's Mamma. This morning, over tea, she very carefully explained to me that we must be vigilant, for some men have come to take the earl away against his wishes, and we aren't to allow it. When I asked her what men, she said they were Scots."

"Scots?"

"She's getting worse, Honor, so much worse. It's a wonder people haven't noticed it. Or perhaps they have and they are too polite to mention it."

Honor snorted at that. "I can assure you, if they've noticed, they are mentioning it to each other with great enthusiasm."

Grace looked out across the field where footmen were setting up stumps and wickets for the match this afternoon. "I've done something quite horrible."

That surprised Honor; she looked curiously at her sister.

Grace's eyes were filled with tears. "Something that will surely condemn me to hell."

A million thoughts went through Honor's head, all of which she quickly discarded. She put her arm around Grace's waist. "That's impossible."

"I gave Mamma some laudanum," Grace said flatly.

Honor gasped. "Oh, dear God, you *didn't*!"

"You see? It's horrible!" Grace whimpered as a tear slid from her eye. "On my word, Honor, I had to do it. There she was, talking about the men from Scotland who would take the earl away, and I thought, how disastrous it would be if she were to say that to *anyone*, most particularly the Hargroves —"

"Where is she?" Honor demanded.

"Sleeping," Grace said. "Hannah is with her. Poor Hannah! She didn't approve of what I'd done, I could plainly see it, but I didn't know what else to do." She gave Honor a beseeching look. "What else could I do?"

Honor thought it was the worst thing she might have done, but Grace looked so hopeless, she couldn't say it. She hugged Grace to her. "We should not do that again, I think."

"No," Grace said weakly.

"Don't despair, Grace. When everyone is away, we will think with clearer heads."

"Perhaps," Grace said, and dabbed at her nose with a handkerchief. "How was your evening?"

Glorious and wretched. Honor averted her gaze — Grace could read her too well. "Quite all right, I suppose, in spite of being accused of thievery. Dearest Monica has determined Mr. Cleburne is a perfect match for me, I think."

"Who?" Grace asked, then gasped. "The new vicar?" She laughed. "She has smelled the countess's coronet and it has made her ravenous. Look, the gentlemen are beginning to come down for the match. Shall we go and watch?"

"I have it on great authority that Lord Washburn is to play and likely to win."

Grace laughed at that.

They walked down to the awnings that had been set up for the ladies observing the game, and took seats at a linen-covered table as the gentlemen divided into teams.

"There are the lovely Cabot girls!" a voice familiar to them both trilled.

"Good morning, Mrs. Hargrove," Honor said, and came to her feet, offering her chair. A footman quickly placed another chair at the table.

"Thank you, dear," Mrs. Hargrove said as she settled into the seat. "Where is your mother?"

"Resting," Honor said.

"Oh, good. She looked quite exhausted last night. No doubt the soiree and the earl's health have taken their toll."

"No doubt," Honor said, and looked pointedly at Grace, silently warning her not to burst into tears as she seemed on the verge of doing.

Augustine and Monica arrived, dressed in cricket whites. Augustine's white waistcoat, which Honor believed he wore once a year at this very tournament, was a bit more snug than last year. "I've *much* to do," he said anxiously, depositing Monica at their table and hurrying off to review the rules with the players.

Monica said, "Lovely day for cricket."

"Isn't it!" Mrs. Hargrove said. "The grounds are so lovely. If I could make one small addition to them, I should like to see a fountain and some seating there, near the gazebo."

"That's a wonderful idea," Monica agreed.

297

Honor and Grace exchanged a sly look.

"Oh, look, it's Mr. Cleburne to bat," Monica said, suddenly sitting up in her chair and adjusting her bonnet.

The four women turned their attention to the match. Mr. Cleburne struck the first ball with ease and ran quickly to the stumps, then back again. A cheer went up from his team, and all the ladies applauded politely.

"Mr. Cleburne!" Monica called, waving her hand as the gentleman sauntered to another awning and gestured to a servant to pour him ale. He looked up when Monica called, smiled happily and began to walk across the lawn to them.

"Mr. Cleburne, may I present you to my mother, Elizabeth Hargrove," Monica said when Mr. Cleburne reached them.

He took Mrs. Hargrove's hand. "My pleasure." He turned to Honor and Grace and greeted them, as well.

"Good afternoon, Mr. Cleburne. You play very well."

"We might add it to the list of things Mr. Cleburne does well," Monica said eagerly. "I understand you are an excellent pianist, Mr. Cleburne."

"Oh, I am no talent, Miss Hargrove."

"Cleburne!" one of the men shouted at him.

"I beg your pardon, I am wanted," he said cheerfully, and jogged onto the field.

"He seems quite kind, doesn't he?" Monica said admiringly. "I should think he'd make an excellent husband."

"Yes, indeed," Mrs. Hargrove readily agreed.

Monica glanced at Honor. "He is the third son of a viscount, I understand. Well connected in that regard. And he will live in that pleasant cottage on the grounds. You know the one, don't you, Honor?"

Of course she knew it. "Augustine's grandmother lived there. Very cozy, isn't it?"

"Do you think it cozy? I thought it quite large for a couple."

"There is Lady Chatham," Mrs. Hargrove said, and excused herself to go and greet the greatest busybody in all of London.

"He's not married, you know," Monica continued.

"That's a pity, Monica, as you are already spoken for," Grace said breezily.

Monica tittered at that, feigning amusement. "But *you're* not spoken for, Grace, and neither is your sister." She smiled at Honor.

"And I don't intend to be, so you may as well put away this notion of making a match," Honor said.

"Why not?" Monica asked pleasantly. "I should think it a perfect match for the daughter of a bishop."

Oh, but Honor wanted to shriek. "I appreciate your concern for me, Monica," Honor said lightly. "But I think perhaps Mr. Cleburne is better suited for our Mercy."

"Mercy! Mercy is scarcely thirteen years old."

Honor shrugged. "They could grow up together, and then wed."

Monica's smile began to fade. "You think you're quite amusing and will keep us all laughing, don't you?"

"I do try," Honor said sweetly. She turned her attention to the match, aware that Monica was glaring at her. They watched two gentlemen take their turn at bat, neither of them having much luck. But then George Easton stepped up. He braced himself for the swing, the muscles of his broad shoulders evident in the fabric of his lawn shirt. He caught the first ball thrown to him and sent it sailing over the heads of the men in the field. The assembled crown cheered wildly as he ran.

"Oh, my," Monica said. "Mr. Easton is an *excellent* cricket player, is he not?" She suddenly stood and looked at Honor. "He's quite good at games in general, isn't he,

Honor?"

"Pardon?"

"Good afternoon, ladies," Monica said curtly, and walked away.

Honor sat up and watched Monica move away. "Oh, no. Lord help us," she whispered.

"What?" Grace asked.

"I suspected it, but now I'm certain. She *knows,* Grace. Monica knows about Easton!" Honor had a very sick feeling in her belly, particularly now that she wished she'd never started this game.

CHAPTER TWENTY-ONE

Lady Chatham bruised some tender feelings the following afternoon at the horse track with her speculation that Ellen Rivers was besotted with George Easton, and what a pity that was, for now everyone knew of that silly girl's lack of judgment.

When that was repeated back to Ellen Rivers, she was hasty in her attempts to distance herself from a man who, according to a growing chorus, had no business even being at Longmeadow among such august guests.

George was blissfully unaware of the talk, however, as he had forgone the horse racing and escaped into the village, to an inn tucked just off the main road, to imbibe copious amounts of ale.

He was captivated by the serving girl's cleavage, staring at him directly as she leaned quite far over the table to slide him a fresh tankard of ale. It was not the milky mounds of flesh spilling out of her bodice that had him, but the fact that he didn't really care about them at all. His head was filled with the image of a raven-haired temptress, and when he saw this young woman's chest, he thought of another décolletage entirely.

He eased back from the girl. She was pretty. His body was halfheartedly attempting to respond, but there was something else at work in him, something odd and ill fitting that had lodged like a rock inside him. It felt dangerously like a conscience.

He looked down at his tankard, away from her breasts. The girl stood a moment longer at his table before turning and swishing away.

George pushed his tankard aside. He'd lost his thirst. He couldn't seem to rid his mind of the events of these past two days, of that astonishingly intimate interlude on the viewing balcony. He'd lost his mind that night, had allowed himself to sink into the depths of his imagination and feelings that had crept up on him, slipping under his skin.

He couldn't seem to rid himself of the feelings. Big, thick feelings with tentacles had wrapped around his heart and were now holding it prisoner. His instinct was, as always, to ignore those feelings, to tamp them down so far that he might forget where he put them. And here he was, as tangled in thoughts and emotions as he'd ever been in his life, and he didn't know how to get free of them.

But he *had* to get free of them, somehow, some way. Honor Cabot was a dalliance he could not sustain, a woman from a world he would never know. And *she* . . .

She needed to think of her future.

He put some money on the table and gathered up his cloak for the ride to Longmeadow. Why was he still here? Why had he come? Because he couldn't stop thinking about her, couldn't stop dreaming of her. Now he had to return to London, to important things — such as what the devil he'd do if he had indeed lost his fortune to the sea.

The sun was sinking behind the trees when George rode down the long drive to Longmeadow. It was a fine early evening; the front door was standing open, and people were walking back from the track where they had raced horses this afternoon.

He handed the reins of his horse to a young man and instructed him to have his horse ready to depart the following morning. On his way to the entrance, George happened to notice a woman draped in a cloak, the hood pulled over her head. But she was holding her arms tightly across her in a manner that he recognized. He changed course, strolling to Honor's side. He bent his head to peek underneath her hood.

"There you are, Easton," she said, her smile strangely vacant. "Has Longmeadow already lost its charm for you? We missed you and your purse at the races this afternoon."

He wanted to gather her in his arms and kiss her, let her know that he had missed her, too. But he clasped his hands at his back. "Quite the contrary, Cabot. I am completely charmed by Longmeadow. What are you doing out here, alone, cloaked for winter?"

Honor glanced away, toward the lake. "Pru took Mamma for a walkabout, but they've not come back." She squinted in the distance.

George understood the worry in her eyes, and the impact on him was powerful. He did not want Honor Cabot to ever feel the least bit hopeless and thought he'd go to the ends of the earth to keep her from it. "Where did they go?"

"I thought they'd gone down to the gazebo by the lake, but I've just come from there, and no one is about."

"You're sure they've not gone into the

house, perhaps from another direction?" he asked, peering into the gloaming.

She shook her head. "I've searched everywhere." She dropped her arms, her hands in tight fists of anxiety. "I'll have another look," she said, and started to walk away from him.

"Honor, wait," George said, taking her elbow. "It's almost dark. Allow me to help." They walked down to the lake, where a streak of gold and orange from the last rays of the setting sun split the lake in half. "They cannot have gone far," George assured her, sensing her growing unease. He wanted to put his arms around her, infuse her with his confidence. "Your sister will not have let her roam."

"You assume my sister could keep her from it," Honor said, her voice betraying a bit of panic. "Mamma is worse, George, so much worse. It's as if coming here to Long-meadow somehow hastened her along. You can't imagine!"

He couldn't bear it. To hell with propriety and talk. George put his arm around Honor's shoulders and pulled her into his chest. "Take heart, love," he said. "I'll find her. Go back to the house, go and be as happy and carefree as you can be so that no one will suspect, and I shall bring her back to you."

"I can't ask that of you," Honor said wearily. "I've asked far too much as it is."

"Go now," he said, ignoring her protests. "Go before your guests think your entire family is missing. Mercy and Grace need you now."

That seemed to give her pause, long enough that George could turn her around and give her a nudge. He had no idea where he would look for the women, especially now that night was falling. He began to move in the direction of the gazebo.

"George?"

He paused and looked back. Honor was on the path to the house. In the waning light, she looked ethereally beautiful, and a small but powerful tremor of desire raced through him. "Thank you," she said. "From the bottom of my useless heart, thank you." She turned around and moved on, the cloak fluttering out behind her.

He had no idea why she would say such a thing. Honor Cabot had the most useful heart of anyone he'd ever known.

Honor handed her cloak to a footman as she walked into the foyer, soothed her hastily arranged hair and the gown she'd donned so quickly when she'd heard about her mamma.

Why Lady Beckington had become convinced that the earl had been poisoned, Honor could not begin to guess. His lordship had been sitting up in his bed, still very much alive, and yet her mother would not believe Honor or the earl.

"Take her to London at once," the earl had ordered between painful, racking coughs. "I don't care what you must say, Honor, but remove her from Longmeadow before the entire party is aware of her madness."

It was happening so quickly! Like the cuff of her sleeve, Lady Beckington's madness had been a tiny thread, perhaps ignored for too long. But once it began to unravel, it unraveled quickly.

Honor felt as if her entire life was one long unraveling now.

She moved through the crowd gathering for the final night of the soiree. There would be dancing, and supper would be served in two sets to accommodate the large number, the first seating at nine o'clock. Honor put a smile on her face and paused to speak to anyone she knew. She chatted about the fine weather, the horse races next month at Newmarket. She was the consummate actress, and as Lady Chatham prattled on about the latest attractions among the debutantes and the young gentlemen, she thought about how often she'd done this very thing, had made the rounds through crowds, talking and flirting. She'd felt as if she were rebelling, spreading her smiles to gentlemen far and wide. She'd thought herself bold.

Tonight, she felt more like a child, and longed to crawl into George's lap and hide from the world.

She found Augustine reviewing the menu with Hardy. Naturally, Monica was there as well, and for once, she looked almost genuinely pleased to see Honor.

"There you are! We've been waiting for you to come down. Oh, dear, Honor, I expected to see you dressed in something expensive and glittery," she said laughingly as she took in Honor's rather plain gown. "You always shine so."

"Yes, well," Honor said, "we've only one lady's maid between us, and I was rather anxious to come down."

"These past few days have been quite grueling, have they not?" Monica asked cheerfully as Augustine opined about his preference for leek soup over onion soup to Hardy. "I never understood just how difficult it is to host such a large gathering over a weekend."

"It's exhausting," Honor agreed.

"I really must commend Lady Beckington. She's always made it appear so effortless," Monica said. "By the by, where is your lady mother? I've not seen her all day. I worry for her, you know."

Honor tensed, waiting for Monica to say more. *Is your mother mad? Have you noticed that she seems a bit batty?* But Monica merely looked at her, politely waiting a response.

"She is feeling fatigued," Honor said carefully. "I think she will not come down tonight."

"Pardon, what?" Augustine said. "Goodness, it's you, Honor. I really must *insist* that you speak to Mercy about her desire to discuss mummified corpses at breakfast. It's really very off-putting. Lady Marquette was so disturbed she was forced to take to her rooms. What's this about our Lady Beckington?"

"She is resting," Honor said.

Augustine looked confused. "But she's just there, and looking rather well rested, indeed."

Honor whirled about to see what had his attention and managed to choke down a small cry of shocked relief. There was her mother on George's arm, laughing as she explained something to Lord Hartington that apparently involved the muddied hem of her gown, seeing as how she held it out for Hartington to have a look. Her cheeks were flushed, her eyes sparkling with excitement. She looked quite beautiful in spite of her muddied hem.

And entirely lucid. Completely, utterly, *lucid.*

What had George done? How had he managed it?

"Honor, you are a dear and a perfect daughter," Augustine said. "But she seems perfectly well."

"She does, doesn't she?" Monica said, sounding a bit perplexed.

George and Lady Beckington made their way across the room, pausing once to share something with each other that made them both laugh.

"Lady Beckington, good evening!" Augustine said.

Honor's mother inclined her head and smiled brightly at Augustine and Monica as she reached for Honor's hand to squeeze it. "Good evening, all! I do beg your pardon for the state of my hem and no doubt, my hair." She laughed. "It has been a glorious day, has it not? Prudence and I walked down to the old mill, and will you believe it, we were turned this way and that. Had it not been for Mr. Easton, we might never have found our way back," she said cheerfully.

"But where is Pru?" Honor asked.

"Oh, darling, you know your sister. She wouldn't *dream* of coming in the main entrance with a muddied hem. She'll be down shortly."

"You are well, madam?" Augustine asked. "Feeling quite yourself and all that?"

"Yes, of course I am! Who else would I feel?" She laughed roundly at her jest.

"I thought so," Augustine said confidently. "I was just saying to Honor that I thought her concern for your fatigue was perhaps overly cautious, as I found you to be perfectly fine this afternoon."

"Oh, yes, so much to *do*!" her mother exclaimed, apropos of nothing.

"Shall we change gowns, Mamma?" Honor asked, her heart racing madly. She dared not look at George, dared not see the truth in his eyes.

"Oh, we must, mustn't we? It won't do to continue on in such a state."

"Then I shall surrender you to your daughter's care," George said smoothly. He bowed, lifting his head and catching Honor's eye so subtly, she wasn't even certain of it. There it was again, that unholy urge to throw herself into his arms, to bury her face in his collar, feel his breath in her hair and on her skin, the strength of him surrounding her, protecting her from awful truths.

She linked her arm through her mother's. "Shall we go up?" she asked, and led her away before her mother said or did anything that might surprise anyone.

Finnegan had pressed George's formal tails and laid them out, but the man himself was nowhere to be seen. George didn't want to know whose bed that randy bastard might be visiting.

He took his time at his toilette. The thought of another ball, another night of crowded rooms and the scent of a woman teasing him and making him want, did not appeal. But his feelings for Honor could not be put down as he wished. He could not leave Longmeadow without seeing her, without looking into her eyes once more, without remembering those moments on the viewing balcony and feeling the swell of desire in him, the craving to slide inside her and possess her completely.

Where did this unholy yearning end?

He thought of Lady Beckington and the burden of her madness that was now resting on Honor's shoulders. He'd discovered Lady Beckington and Prudence on the edge of the lake — Lady Beckington was laughing wildly at a pair of ducks who were seeking food from her hand . . . food she didn't have. Her madness made his desires even more impossible — Honor would need to marry someone who could protect her mother. How could he? At present, he couldn't say if he would have any funds at all by the end of the year.

George shook his head, angry with himself for having skated onto a very thin patch of ice. Each step brought him closer to falling through, sinking into the murky depths of the dark, cold waters of his desires. *Unwanted, unanswered, impossible desires.*

He was late to the ball; the dancing had begun. He stood in the back, watching the dancers, lost in thought.

"It would seem we find ourselves alone *again,* Mr. Easton."

He was startled by the sound of Miss Hargrove's voice; he hadn't noticed her approach and had no idea how long she'd been there. "How fortuitous," he said, smiling at her.

She cocked her head to one side, studying

him, her brown eyes dancing. "Is everything all right? You seem a bit subdued this evening."

"Do I?"

Her smile deepened. "Perhaps the loss of one's fortune puts a damper on one's ardor."

George blinked with surprise.

"I mean only that you are generally rather eager to seduce me. Perhaps tonight, your mind is on other things."

His gaze drifted to her mouth, sliding slowly and deliberately down to her décolletage. At any other time in his life, he would have been attracted to a woman as handsome and coy as Monica Hargrove. Even in this moment, he was the tiniest bit captivated by his prey, in teaching her a thing or two about disparaging a man's fortune as she'd just done. But a damnably fine pair of blue eyes suddenly shimmered in his mind's eye, and it occurred to him that he could at least do this for Honor. He could at least lure this woman away from Honor's troubles.

He touched Miss Hargrove's hand. "Have you been listening to rumors, love?"

Without shifting her gaze from his face, she laced her fingers with his. "Perhaps one or two. Have you?"

He smiled. "One or two."

She laughed lightly and dropped her hand. "Have you made the acquaintance of Mr. Cleburne, sir?" she said pleasantly, and looked past George. He glanced over his shoulder, saw a thin man with a pleasant countenance standing awkwardly aside.

"Mr. Cleburne is the new vicar here at Longmeadow. Mr. Cleburne, may I present Mr. Easton?"

George nodded. "How do you do?"

"A pleasure, sir," Cleburne said.

"You mustn't allow his charming smile to fool you, Mr. Cleburne," Miss Hargrove said jovially. "Mr. Easton is quite a scoundrel."

Mr. Cleburne laughed. "Mr. Easton, you seem perfectly respectable to me. Please, excuse me," he said, and walked on, his gaze scanning the crowd.

"A scoundrel, am I?" George asked.

Miss Hargrove laughed again. "Mr. Cleburne is such a dear man," she said. "And unmarried. I think he might very well be the *perfect* match for our Honor."

Her gaze was locked on him, watching him closely. How George remained placid, he didn't know, for she might as well have sliced him open. "Perhaps," he said with a shrug.

"He would be an excellent influence, I should think. And of course, he is beyond reproach. That can't be said of every gentleman, can it?" She gave him a coy smile and sashayed away.

George stared after her. Beautiful, exasperating creatures, women were, the lot of them. Monica Hargrove was trifling with him, trying to arouse a reaction from him.

George ignored it, because something much darker had suddenly filled his thoughts — Miss Hargrove was right. As much as George loathed to admit it to himself, Cleburne was a good match for Honor. That slender, smiling man with no more knowledge of the physical pleasures of the flesh than a rock was better suited as a match for the most interesting woman in all of London. He would provide for Honor, and moreover, he was a man of the cloth — his charity at taking his wife's mad mother and caring for her would be exalted. Cleburne's collar would give him access to some of the best facilities for madness, should it come to that.

George, bastard that he was, gambler, womanizer, tradesman, could not have been less suitable for a woman like Honor Cabot. She was so far above his reach that she may as well have been a bloody star.

That truth began to corrode him, eating away at his confidence. No matter how rich, no matter how handsome, or charming, or seductive, there was no happy forevermore for him with a woman like Honor or Monica Hargrove.

And yet George had combed his hair, adjusted his neckcloth and made sure his waistcoat was properly buttoned down with the express purpose of seeing the woman he desired more than life.

If only she would come down.

The wine and whiskey were flowing freely; the musicians began a reel. Lady Vickers appeared, her cheeks flushed, her eyes bright with one too many glasses of "punch," as the ladies liked to call it.

"Where have you been, naughty boy?" she asked, leaning into him, pressing her breasts against his arm. "Dance with me, Easton? I should very much like to dance."

He'd always been powerless to say no to a pretty woman.

He danced with Lady Vickers and then with Mrs. Reston, who spoke endlessly about her recently widowed sister, who lived in Leeds. George supposed that Leeds was far enough removed from proper society that he might be considered a suitable match for her.

He had grown weary of the ball, weary of Longmeadow, of the *ton.* He made his excuses to Mrs. Bristol and had started upstairs to his room when he saw his heart's true desire. How had he missed her? She was a vision of loveliness in the crème silk gown that made her eyes all but leap from her face. She was engrossed in conversation with Mr. Jett, but when she saw him and smiled, a flash of deep warmth filled his chest. She said something to Mr. Jett and started toward him, leaving Mr. Jett behind to stare sourly at George.

"Mr. Easton, you are in the *ballroom,*" she said gaily. "I supposed you would be in the gaming room, winning back your fortune, which everyone seems to be nattering on about tonight."

"And I'd assumed you'd turned in for the night. You've been absent from the dancing."

"I've stood up once or twice," she said with a smile. "You?"

"Oh, well, I've been *quite* occupied with ladies needing dance partners."

"A noble endeavor, sir. None too painful, I hope?"

He grinned. "Perhaps more for my partners than for me."

The music was beginning again, and

George recognized the cadence of the waltz Honor had taught him. How was it possible that the first waltz with her could seem so long ago to him now? It seemed another lifetime. "I think I might bear one more," he said, nodding in the direction of the dancing.

She glanced at the couples. "It's a waltz, which I may attest is not among your best dances," she teased him.

"Then I am doubly fortunate to have you here to lead me once again."

She laughed and placed her hand on his arm, then glanced up at him. When she smiled like that, she looked brilliant, a brilliant star among many dull planets, circling his heart, caught in his orbit.

George led her out onto the dance floor and put his hands where she'd once instructed him. The dancing began; he stepped woodenly into the rhythm.

"Oh!" she said, her eyes lighting with delight. "You're much improved!" He promptly missed a step.

Honor laughed as she righted the ship for him. But then her smile faded somewhat. "Thank you for finding my mother," she said as he moved them along in a straight line.

"It was nothing."

"Don't say that, George," she admonished him. "It was everything. At least to me."

Her gaze was intent and seemed to be searching his. God, how he wanted to touch her, to *be* touched by her. He abruptly twirled her, if only to move those eyes from his. She was peering too deeply, and he feared what she might see in the depths of his eyes. He feared his foolish heart was floating on the surface.

"I've seen our friend," he said, and twirled her once more for good measure.

"Ah. And how did you find her this evening?" Honor said lightly. *Too* lightly. As if she didn't particularly care.

"Animated," he said. "She seemed in good spirits." Honor gasped with surprise when he suddenly twirled her and fell quickly back into step.

"I suppose you charmed her with declarations of your esteem, and she swooned." She smiled lopsidedly; a dimple appeared in one cheek. "Did you look directly in her eyes and say something quite sweet?"

He snorted. "Such as how no one compares, so on and so forth?"

"That would be *too* obvious, wouldn't it? You probably said something quite poignant, didn't you? And yet vague. Something like . . ."

Was it his imagination, or did the light in her eyes soften?

"Something like, 'I have waited a lifetime for someone like you to walk into my life and possess my heart.' With your own particular style, naturally."

The way she was looking at him pulled even harder at George. He understood her, understood what she was saying. He drew a shallow breath, tried to find his footing on that wretched dance floor. "I couldn't possibly say such a thing to her, Honor. Those are words I could say to only one person. And I could only say them if they were true."

Honor's gaze did not waver from his. Perhaps it was the music, or the crowded dance floor, but he could feel a current between them unlike anything he'd ever felt in his life, mysteriously warm, amazingly omnipotent. He could feel what she wanted, how her heart beat, how her blood flowed. He could feel her waiting for him to say those words to her.

But he couldn't say them. How could he say them? How could he say something like that just to soothe her, and at the same time expose them both to untold grief?

When he did not speak, he could see the disappointment cloud her eyes. She shifted her gaze away. "No, you mustn't say such things," she said casually. "You mustn't say anything at all."

God damn him — he'd let this go too far, had allowed his desires to rule him, and he hated himself for it in that moment.

He suddenly twirled her one way and then the other. Honor's smile slowly returned to her. *Good girl.* She understood as well as he that the thing between them could never come to life, must remain buried for all eternity.

"You are a wretched dancer, Easton. And you are holding me too close. No doubt all of Longmeadow has already noticed, for these might very well be the most attentive people in all of England."

George pulled her closer, twirled her around. "I don't care, Cabot."

She smiled up at him. "Neither do I."

They danced in silence a few moments.

"We are to London on the morrow," she said.

"As am I."

George could see the indelible sadness in her eyes, and although she tried to smile, it did not come to her easily. He wanted to kiss her, to kiss the sadness from her eyes, the forced smile from her lips. But he couldn't, and to make the moment even more frustrating for him, the song had come to an end. George did not want to let her go. Ever.

When he did, a strange sensation of emptiness spiraled up in him.

"Well, then," she said. "I suppose I should say good-night."

She stood, waiting for him to respond, to tell her that he would see her in London, which of course he hoped for, madly hoped for. . . .

But George couldn't bring himself to speak. He felt as helpless as a baby, unable to find the words to say. He merely gave her a curt nod and clasped his hands tightly at his back. *So* tightly. To keep from putting them on Honor and drawing her back. "Good night, Miss Cabot."

Her gaze flicked over him, and she lowered her head, stealing one last sidelong look at him before walking on.

George kept his hands clasped until he could no longer see her in the crowd.

And when he turned around, he saw Miss Hargrove standing before him, smiling like a fat cat. "You've become quite the partner in demand, Mr. Easton. Should I expect to see you at more balls in London?"

George suddenly understood that Miss Hargrove suspected his feelings for Honor.

She thought she would have the best of him? Oh, no — George suddenly had a renewed interest in enticing her away from Sommerfield. "I've been told that I am much improved. Would you like to see for yourself?" he asked, holding out his arm.

Miss Hargrove laughed and put her hand on his. "I would be *delighted,*" she said.

CHAPTER TWENTY-TWO

It was half past midnight when the ball's orchestra began to ring bells, signaling something was about to happen. It seemed a good time for George to make his escape.

George was grateful that Finnegan was not about, and shut his door, locking it. He shrugged out of his coat, then yanked at his neckcloth. He had removed his waistcoat and had pulled his shirt from his trousers when he heard a knock at the door. George groaned heavenward. "Not now, Finnegan!" he barked at the door.

A moment passed; the knock came again. "Bloody hell," he muttered, and stalked to the door, unlocking it and throwing it open, prepared to give Finnegan a tongue-lashing.

But it was not Finnegan who darted past him, it was Honor. Stunned, George quickly shut the door and turned to gape at her. "What the devil are you doing here?" he

demanded. "You shouldn't be here, Honor
—"

"It's all right," she said quickly. "Everyone is in the ballroom. Augustine and Monica are announcing their engagement."

He blinked. No wonder Miss Hargrove had been so confident this evening. "Shouldn't you be there, as well?"

"Of course," she said, and smiled sheepishly. "But I had something more important to attend."

He didn't understand her. "What?" he asked, thinking of her mother, of her sisters.

She started toward him. "I couldn't leave it like this."

"Leave it," he echoed uncertainly.

"Oh, George," she said, smiling at him. "There is so much that I . . . that I want. That I *need.* I don't know precisely how to put into words what it is that I need." She moved closer, her steps hesitant, as if she were uncertain where she meant to go in this room.

But there was something about her expression, the hope in her eyes, that caused a bit of panic in George's chest. What was she saying?

"I need you, George. I need you to . . . to *help* me," she said earnestly.

"You need to think of marrying," he said

gruffly, taking a step back. "I can't help you in that."

She paused, blinking up at him. "Perhaps," she said. God, how he wished she wouldn't look at him like that! "Perhaps," she said again, and took another step, reaching up to cup his face. "But I won't think of it now. I can only think of you, George, and the thing that is unfinished between us. Don't you think of it, too?"

"Miss Hargrove?" he asked, confused.

"No!" she cried. "No, no — I hope that you will never speak to her again. I mean that I need *you.*"

It took him a moment to understand her, and the panic surged through him like a storm. He knew himself — he was not strong enough for this, he was as weak as a puppy in this. He frantically pulled her hands from his face. "Don't ask me that," he said. "Anything but that, Honor. *Anything.*"

Her lips parted with surprise. She suddenly surged forward, rising up on her toes to kiss him. Still, George didn't touch her. He tried to pull back, but it was impossible.

Then, just as suddenly, Honor stopped and peered deeply into his eyes. She sensed his reluctance; she dropped her hands from his face and moved back, away from him.

"You don't understand," he said simply.

"Neither do you," she said in a low voice, and reached behind her back with both hands.

George watched her a moment before he realized what she was doing. She was unbuttoning her gown. *"No,"* he said, reaching for her hand. "Don't —"

She jerked away from his hand, her gaze locked on his. She wiggled one arm from its sleeve.

George's heart began to race, his body growing taut. "Goddammit, Honor, don't do this! I mean what I say — you don't understand what I will *do.*"

She pushed the other sleeve down her arm, the gown over her hips, and let it fall. She stood before him in her chemise.

George's heart was racing so hard now that he feared it would explode in his chest. His gaze swept the length of her, her breasts, spilling out of a chemise and corset, her waist, curving into hips. It was as if he'd been starved of all sustenance all his life, and here was a feast before him.

And still, he made no move. If he touched her, put as much as a finger on her skin, he would lose all control.

When he made no move toward her, Honor stubbornly lifted her chin. With one hand, she pulled a pin from her hair, and half of it tumbled down her back. "Do you know how to lace a corset?" she asked as she pulled another pin from her hair. And another.

George didn't speak — he *couldn't* speak. Her dark hair spilled all around her shoulders now, and she very deliberately began to unlace her corset, pulling the strings free, loosening them, until she could shimmy out of it. She let that drop, too. Now all that stood between her and George's raging, frantic desire was a chemise so thin that he could see her body through it. His eyes greedily devoured every curve, every swell, his chest rising with tortured breath and falling with the strength it took to keep from reaching for her.

Honor slipped one finger under the strap of her chemise.

Immobilized by his outrageous desire, George helplessly watched her.

She pushed it down her arm. Then the other, and slowly, almost as if in a dream, the thin cotton chemise floated to the floor. Honor stepped out of it and stood before him with her arms wrapped about her belly, the rest of her completely bare. Her perfect breasts, floating above her arms, the thatch of curls at the apex of her legs.

Such a bold girl. Unapologetic. *Brave.* A woman who sought her pleasure as she sought her place in the world. She was a high-stepping horse, just like him, who looked neither right nor left, who did not care what society thought of her. It was almost as if the heavens had molded her just for him.

She was quivering, he noticed, and moved her arms up, intending to cover her breasts.

That was the moment George fell from his precarious perch. *"No,"* he muttered. He slowly pulled one arm from her body, then the other. "Let me look at you." He gazed down at her body, then moved around her, viewing her back, her heart-shaped hips. He curled his fingers in the heavy tresses of her hair, wrapping one thick strand like a rope around his wrist. "What are you doing to me?" he asked helplessly.

She turned her head slightly to glance at him over her shoulder. "I don't want to leave with all this *want* in me," she said, her hands sliding across her abdomen. "I *want,* George, things I never knew to want. And I don't want my heart to turn to dust."

He didn't know precisely how her heart would turn to dust, but it didn't matter; the dam of emotions that George had held at bay for years broke in him. The flood was so powerful that he felt a little light-headed. At her back, he slid his arm around her belly and drew her into his body, then closed his eyes as he pressed his lips against her hair. "You don't want to throw your virtue away," he whispered hoarsely, even as his body begged him to be silent.

"Throw it away? But I'm giving it to you, George. After that, I don't care what will happen."

His blood was already rushing. He drew a steadying breath and kissed her neck. "Be certain of it," he said. "Be quite certain of it, and God in heaven, tell me you are certain of it *now*, before it is too late for us both."

She twisted in his arms. "I'm certain," she said, and kissed him.

The thousand cautions in George's chest were instantly slain. He flamed where she touched him, burned with the warm, fragrant scent of her skin. He slid his hand up her rib cage to her breast, filling his palm with the weight of it, rolling the hardened point between his fingers. He nibbled her earlobe, pressed his mouth against her temple as her hands fumbled with the buttons of his shirt, then pressing her mouth to his throat, sending a painful shiver through him.

George swept Honor up in his arms and whirled around to the bed, knocking over a small table in the process. She made a sound of alarm, but he silenced it with his mouth and his tongue. With his free hand, he clawed at his shirt until his upper body was bared.

Honor gasped with surprise or alarm. He didn't know, didn't care — his body was aching for her as he stared down at her, expecting her to ask him to stop. But Honor's gaze slowly moved over his chest, her fingers following the path of her eyes, tracing rivers of unbearable sensation across his skin, to the top of his trousers. She looked up as she unbuttoned them.

He caught her hand, pressed it against his wildly beating heart. He wanted her to feel the emotions churning the blood in his veins. This moment felt entirely different to him than any other moment of his life. This was not an afternoon romp that he would remember with hazy fondness in the evening. This had him at sixes and sevens, his heart racing like a filly.

She looked at her hand on his chest, then lifted herself up to him, kissed him tenderly, her fingers fluttering through his hair.

He picked her up again, lowered her onto his bed. Sweet, torturous pleasure built, swirling in his groin, pulsing in his cock as he moved against her. She slid her hand into his opened trousers, her fingers closing around him, squeezing lightly, testing the feel of a man's full passion in her hand. It was excruciatingly pleasurable, and George tensed, fighting his body's desire to take her, to plunge into her wet heat.

When he couldn't bear her tender touch a moment longer, he pushed his fingers into her hot, wet depths, shuddering as he tried to control the need that was beginning to overpower him. He thrust his tongue into her mouth as his fingers danced in the recesses of her body, sliding into her and out again while her hand moved on his cock. "My God, you are beautiful," he murmured against her skin.

She didn't seem to hear him; her eyes were closed, her hands and mouth learning his body.

George suddenly rose up, flipped her over onto her belly and left a line of kisses down her back, to her hips, nibbling at her flesh, his hand sliding between her legs. But Honor was not content to be on her stomach and pushed back, then turned about so that she was sitting up on her knees, facing him. Tiny tufts of dark curls framed her face. Long, silken tresses dropped down her back and over her shoulder.

She was panting, her lips swollen from kissing. "Take them off," she said, and reached for his trousers, pushing them down over his hips.

He did as she asked, rising up to discard them.

Her eyes were fixed on his body — of course they were, she'd never seen a nude man, much less one aroused to the point of bursting, he supposed. George balanced himself with a knee on the bed and took himself in hand, wondering if the sight intimidated her.

But Honor Cabot was not so easily intimidated; she was a bold, risk-taking woman, and she leaned forward, touching her mouth to the tip of him. George sucked in a gasp of air through his teeth; he tried to back away, but Honor caught his leg and held him there as she explored the head of his shaft with her lips and the tip of her tongue, swirling around it, tasting the bit of seed that had pearled at the tip.

He grit his teeth against the exquisite sensation, focused on resisting the urge to push down her throat. When she moved to take more of him in her mouth, George grabbed her, put her on her back and moved in between her thighs.

His lips found hers again as he moved the tip of his cock against the slick folds of her body, the pressure building in him intolerable. He could feel the seed throbbing in him. The only thing standing between him and losing himself in her completely was the sheer strength of his tattered, shredded will. Each touch, each kiss was more tormenting than the last, and each moment weakened him a little more.

He dipped his head to her breasts, sucking one into his mouth, teasing her with his teeth and tongue as he pressed against her, the tip of him sliding slowly in. He moved, forcing her body to open to his, pressing her legs a little farther apart.

She dragged her fingers through his hair and looked him in the eyes. George paused, his heart swimming in those eyes now. She gazed at him so beguilingly, so bewitchingly, he thought he might very well do anything for this woman. *Anything.* Climb mountains, slay dragons, *dance. . . .* Whatever her heart desired. He'd never felt the desire to please a woman so intently, and he'd never yearned for one quite as deeply as he was yearning for her now. He ached for her and wanted nothing more than to pleasure her so thoroughly and fulfill her so completely that no other man would ever compare to him.

Honor's gaze drifted to his mouth, and she tucked a finger in between his lips.

George could endure it no more. He kissed her fingers, her palm, as he began to ease into her, squeezing into the wet recess, his cock expanding to fill it. He moved carefully and steadily, relishing the feel of her body tightening provocatively around his, coaxing him into her depths. Torrents of raw affection flowed through George, and as he slipped his arm beneath her, pulling her into his chest, he pushed against the barrier inside her.

She seemed to sense his hesitation, his fear at taking that from her. *"George,"* she whispered, and reached between them, cupping him.

A purely primal sound escaped him as he pushed past the barrier.

She made a small cry, pressed her forehead to his shoulder.

The sound of her muffled cry alarmed him. *God, what had he done?* He was a libertine, a man who could not control the urges of his flesh. He had just ruined a woman whom he greatly esteemed and even —

Honor shifted against him, her foot running up his back and down again, her body pressing back against his. She wrapped her leg around his waist, turned her mouth to his shoulder and bit it lightly.

Even loved. Loved! God, he loved her, helplessly, completely. She shifted again, pressing harder against him, urging him to continue this extraordinary journey, to press inside her again. George cupped her face, wanting to look into her eyes as he pressed deeper. He could feel her body opening to him, could feel the seductive rhythm of an ancient, primal call. His breath ragged and torn, he began to move in her, sliding out to the tip, then sliding in again, and again, only more urgently.

She began to move with him, clinging to him, her fingers scraping down his back, digging into the flesh of his hip. He reached between their bodies and began to stroke the nub of her pleasure.

She was gasping for breath, pushing against his hand and his cock, her mouth on his chest. But she paused, and her fingers dug deeper into the flesh of his buttock; she gasped as her legs tightened around him.

George's desire took on a new urgency; he pumped into her, wanting her to feel the violent shattering that was building in him. She cried out, her head dropping back, a swirl of dark hair covering her face as her body convulsed around his and she pressed against him.

With a low growl, he threw his head back on one last powerful thrust, burying himself deep inside of her, the moan of sheer ecstasy clawing its way from his throat, spilling hot seed inside of her.

The moment left him spent; he collapsed to the side of her, his arm draped over her middle, his face in her hair, fighting his way back from the fog of euphoria. It wasn't until she traced a light line down his back and up again, that he lifted his head and looked down at her.

Honor's cheeks were flushed, and she was, in that moment, as beautiful as any work of art George had ever seen. She turned her head slightly and opened her eyes with a gorgeously bright smile. She stroked his chin, brushed back his hair then peeled herself up to kiss him, her tongue teasing his, her lips wet on his.

"Are you all right?" he asked.

Her smile deepened, and she nodded. "I'm complete," she said simply.

He wrapped his arms around her and marveled at the depth of his feeling. It was love, he feared. Real and true, raw love.

God, anything but that.

Anything.

Chapter Twenty-Three

Honor felt complete and invincible, as if she'd vaulted over a chasm. Her body was full of vigor. She was a bit sore, but she scarcely cared — it was an exhilarating soreness, and her heart . . . Dear Lord, her heart was heavy with adoration.

She lay on her side, her head propped in her palm, her finger tracing a path down George's chest as he slept. *She loved this man,* loved him thoroughly. She loved the way he looked as he slept, his face free of tension. She loved the way his hand kept reaching for her, finding her, even while he slept. She loved the way he smiled, the way he'd looked at her as he'd entered her body. . . .

A small clock on the mantel chimed, and through the dim light of a single candle, she squinted at it. It was four in the morning. In another hour, Hannah would come to wake Honor to begin preparations to leave

Longmeadow. She had to leave this place of wonder, had to leave the bed where she'd found her heart's true direction.

She leaned down, touched her lips to George's nipple. As he stirred, Honor stood up and went in search of her clothes.

"Where are you?" he asked hoarsely.

"Here," she said softly, and let her chemise slide over her head.

He came up on his elbows, blinking sleepily. He silently watched her dress until Honor donned her corset and presented her back to him to be laced.

George sat up and very deftly began to pull the strings of her corset. Honor couldn't help but wonder how many times he'd done this very thing, had sent a woman along after making love to her. The thought sobered her; she finished dressing and turned to face him as she absently braided her hair.

George sat on the edge of the bed, completely nude, his gaze fixed on her face. "George? I —"

"No," he said brusquely, lifting a hand. "Don't speak, Honor. Don't say aloud words or promises that neither of us can ever reach, or worse, ever forget."

Honor blinked. "But I —"

He stood up, gathered her in his arms and

kissed her. "Don't speak, my love. There is nothing either of us can say that will change anything, is there? Let this night live in your heart, but God help me, please, don't *speak*."

She understood him. . . . At least she thought she did. To say words of love when one could not live in that love was too painful to endure, wasn't it? But there was yet so much to say to him, so much she wanted him to know! She wanted to tell him he was the best man she'd ever known. She wanted to tell him she didn't care about his humble beginnings.

But George turned her around and fastened the last few buttons of her gown before she could say them. He bent his head and kissed her neck. "I will never forget this evening, not as long as I draw breath, and I will cherish it always," he murmured. "Go now, before you are discovered."

Honor stumbled forward. She didn't know how to argue with him, or even if she should. She only knew that her heart was filled with him, utterly and completely.

She had to figure things out. Yes, that was what she would do — she would return to London, settle her mother and consider all her options. *There had to be a way to him.*

Honor didn't look back as she slipped out

of his room, afraid to see the expression on his face, afraid of wanting him again, of saying those things he did not want to hear.

As it turned out, it was just as well she went when she did. There was much to be done, and only a few hours later, Honor and Grace found themselves struggling to put their mother into the coach. Lady Beckington was not of a mind to leave Longmeadow, which she had newly dubbed Halston Hall in her wrecked brain — a place where she'd summered as a girl but had not seen in twenty years. She was combative with her eldest daughters while her youngest two stared in horror.

The ordeal left them all exhausted and dreading the long and bumpy drive to London.

In the course of that drive, Honor's thoughts about George grew confused. Her sunny happiness at being in love and discovering the landscape of pleasures between a man and woman had disappeared under the cloud of her mother. She and Grace were fighting an increasingly hard battle; she could see that.

Her heart's heaviness was becoming painful.

There was so much she'd wanted to say to George last night, so many words of admiration and esteem. But now, away from him, she was glad she hadn't said them. She mulled over what he'd said, the way he'd said it. *Don't speak. Go now.* Is that what he said to the women he'd bedded? Or was there something deeper that he couldn't face?

And what did it matter? George was right — she couldn't be with him, no matter how she loved him. Honor had thought herself above caring what society thought, but she was discovering she wasn't above it at all. The glow of lovemaking had dissipated, and she was growing frightened of what she felt for George, of what it meant. She understood all that she would sacrifice to be with him, and yet what she felt was perhaps the most tangible thing she'd ever felt in her life. It was real, it was powerful. It was entirely irresistible.

Honor adored George Easton. Truly, madly, adored him. But could she give up all for him? Did he even want her in the same way? And didn't she have far greater problems at present than pining for a gentleman?

The first two days in London were unexpectedly and blessedly peaceful. Honor's mother had calmed considerably and seemed mostly lucid once she'd returned to what was, at least for now, a familiar setting. Her only worry was when Augustine would return with the earl to London. There was only one incident, and Honor had not witnessed it. Jericho confided to her that Lady Beckington had mistaken him for a Scotsman and had threatened to see him hanged for stealing the earl's things.

On the third day after their return, Honor was very relieved when Augustine arrived with the earl. Three footmen carried the ailing earl to his rooms, and his painful coughing once again settled into the fabric of the house. Lady Beckington, who had removed the embroidery from yet another sleeve, disappeared into his chambers to see to him.

One cloudy afternoon, Honor found Grace in a pensive mood, staring out a window, her gaze distant.

"Grace? Is something wrong?" Honor asked.

Grace curled a tress of hair around her finger as she once had done when they were girls. "I am cross with you, if you must know. I asked Jericho to give Mamma the laudanum, but you told him he should not."

"Of course he should not," Honor said flatly. "I can't believe you would think otherwise, not after Longmeadow. We

345

agreed."

Grace's jaw clenched. "We didn't agree, Honor. Only you. I suppose you think we should allow Mamma to continue wandering about, muttering to herself and picking at the embroidery in her sleeves."

"If we must," Honor said stiffly.

Grace dropped the strand of hair and whirled about. "You're impossible! We wouldn't be in this predicament had you allowed anyone to court you and accepted an offer of marriage along the way! But no, you preferred to pine away for Rowley."

"I beg your pardon? Our mother's madness is *my* fault?" Honor cried indignantly.

"I didn't say that!" Grace shot back angrily. "But were you capable of thinking of someone other than yourself, we might not be in the predicament we are today!"

Honor gaped at her sister, feeling each word slice painfully into her heart. It was dreadful enough that Honor had thought the same thing herself, but to hear *Grace* say it . . . "What of *you*?" she demanded.

"You know very well Mamma would never allow me to marry before you," Grace said angrily. "And now we have waited too long! We have squandered the time we might have had to make a good match, and we are facing an uncertain future with a mother that neither of us can properly care for and no one — *no* one — will take!"

Honor felt foolish enough for believing that her ridiculous plan would ever work. The only thing that had come from it was that now she longed for a man she could not possibly engage. "And what exactly was I to do, Grace?" she asked, angry with herself, with life. "*You* didn't help."

Grace's shoulders suddenly deflated. "I know," she said flatly. "I've been quite useless. But, Honor, *one* of us must marry, and marry quickly!"

How could she think of marriage when she loved George Easton? Just hearing the word made her stomach clench painfully. "Very well. Who would you suggest I marry?" she asked, resigned.

"Not you. *Me,*" Grace said, and before Honor could roll her eyes, Grace said, "If you have a better idea, say it now, for I am to Bath —"

"Bath!"

"Yes, Bath! Amherst is in Bath."

"*Amherst!*" Honor cried. "There is not a worse rake in all of England. Everyone knows it! Dear God, Grace, don't be as foolish as me! You won't succeed!"

"He's not a bastard, and at least he has a name," Grace shot back.

347

Honor stilled. She took great offense to that and pressed a fist hard against her roiling belly. "This is absurd," she said, turning away, intending to argue, but Mercy suddenly burst into the salon and threw herself facedown onto the settee, sobbing.

"Mercy!" Grace cried, dipping down, her hand on her sister's back as sobs racked her small frame. "Good Lord, what is it, what has happened?"

"It's Augustine!" Mercy said, gasping through her sobs. "He raised his voice! He said I was never to mention grave robbers again and sent me from the room!" She pushed herself up and removed her spectacles to swipe at the tears on her face. "It wasn't a very frightening story. I promise, it wasn't!"

Honor's bleak mood was pushed into full-blown anger by Mercy's tears. "I will speak to him," she said briskly, and reached down to stroke her sister's hair before she swept out of the room, her fist still clenched at her side.

Her slippers were almost silent on the stairs as she hurried down them. In the foyer, she heard voices down the hall and walked purposefully in that direction. As she neared the main salon, she heard Augustine's laugh mix with Monica's. But there were other voices, too.

At the door, she saw Monica and her mother sitting together on the settee, and Augustine and Mr. Cleburne standing. Mr. Cleburne instantly straightened when he saw her and smiled a little nervously.

"Honor!" Augustine said when he saw her. "I was about to send Hardy for you."

"I beg your pardon, I shan't interrupt. Good afternoon," she said to everyone in the room. "My lord, might I have a word?"

She did not miss the look that passed between Augustine and Monica before he said, "Yes, indeed, darling. I should like a word with you, as well. If you will excuse us?" he asked his guests.

"Of course!" Monica sang out. "Take all the time you need."

Augustine came forward, clasped Honor's elbow and wheeled her about, escorting her down the hall and to the butler's office. He ushered Honor inside, then closed the door behind them and opened the curtains to the courtyard for light.

"Why are we in Mr. Hardy's office?" Honor asked, the soft drumbeat of wariness beginning in her chest. "You have your guests, and I want only a moment —"

"But that's just it, dearest," Augustine said, interrupting her. "The guests — well, at least *one* of them, that is — have come for you."

The wariness she'd been feeling began to take wings, trying to fly.

"Mrs. Hargrove and Monica were kind enough to deliver Mr. Cleburne to Beckington House all the way from Longmeadow. He's to be our guest for a fortnight." Augustine's smile was apprehensive, and he nervously drummed his fingers on the edge of Mr. Hardy's desk.

"What has that to do with me?"

Augustine touched his neckcloth and cleared his throat. "Mr. Cleburne is the third son of Lord Sandersgate. You know Sandersgate, don't you? Tall man, crop of ginger hair?" he asked, gesturing to the crown of his head. "He's brought six sons into this world. Can you imagine it? Six sons! What a challenge that must be to see them all properly situated!" He said it as if it were an impossible feat.

"That is quite a lot," Honor agreed. "Still, I —"

"Nevertheless, Mr. Richard Cleburne, his *third* son, is in London to study with the archbishop for a fortnight. Fancy that, Honor, a vicar in our service with personal ties to the *archbishop.*"

She glanced at the door. Her wariness was

now a caged bird, flapping its wings and squawking for release. If she could somehow maneuver herself around Augustine, she might escape before he said whatever dreadful thing he was trying to say.

"My point is that Mr. Cleburne is a good man, an educated man, with an untarnished reputation and a perfectly respectable occupation."

That sounded so rehearsed that Honor's heart was suddenly in her throat.

"Will you say nothing?" Augustine asked.

Honor shook her head, not trusting herself to speak.

Augustine frowned thoughtfully and began to walk in a tight little circle, given the lack of space in the office. "I think we must accept certain truths, mustn't we, dearest? My father is not long for this world. God willing, he will see me happily married, starting a family of my own, but in recent days, I have come to doubt he shall live as long as that."

"Oh, Augustine, you —"

"That means," he rushed ahead, "that it will be up to me to determine how best to settle you and your sisters." He smiled, clearly proud of himself for having delivered his speech properly. "Oh! And naturally, your lady mother," he amended quickly.

"Augustine, what are you saying?" Honor said, choosing a new tack. "Are you turning us *out*?"

"What?" Augustine looked horrified. "*No!* No, no, no, of course not," he said anxiously, and reached for her hand, grasping it tightly. "How could I turn you out? You are my sister, Honor, in my heart as well as in name. But don't you see?" he pleaded. "I shall be making my home with my wife, and it wouldn't do to have six adults under one roof, what with different opinions and . . . and schedules," he said, as if he were uncertain what conflict there was between six adults.

Honor's heart was now sinking away from her throat, passing through her chest, falling, falling, *falling.* "Don't say it, I beg of you," she said. "Don't say that you will put us away from you."

"I would never!" he said, seeking to assure her. "But surely you *must* understand my dilemma."

"And surely you must understand that we've no place we might go, Augustine. We are entirely dependent on the earl, as we have been for many, many years. You know that we are."

"Yes, I know," he said with a sympathetic wince and squeeze of her hand. "Which is why we — that is, *me* — would like to see you and Grace properly matched as soon as possible. That's the best solution for all, I think. You must admit, you've had quite a lot of time to settle things, and now it is time. Really, it rather solves all of our problems, does it not? And frankly, Mr. Cleburne is as fine a match as you might hope to make."

She jerked her hand free. "No!"

Augustine's expression changed. He looked as hard and stern as she had ever seen him. "You will have the husband you need in Cleburne, and he will make you comfortable at Longmeadow. And if you are at Longmeadow, we will see each other quite often."

He couldn't mean it. "A *vicar*, Augustine? Do you think that is the best I might expect? You might at least let the Season take its course!" she said, reaching for anything that might give her time to think her way through this sudden problem.

"But . . . but your father was a bishop," Augustine said, clearly surprised by her objection. "And Mr. Cleburne may be a vicar, but he is a wealthy one."

"I don't care about his wealth," Honor said. "I care that he is a man I scarcely know, a vicar at Longmeadow no less, with no society other than widows and orphans. What do you think, that I shall pass my days embroidering and taking long walks?"

"Do you harbor some *grievance* against Longmeadow? For you have seemed perfectly at ease there all these years!"

"I am very fond of Longmeadow. I should not like to spend all my days in the country any more than you would!"

"*I* would be very grateful if I were to spend my days at Longmeadow and not in a *meaner* house in a *meaner* part of England!" Augustine said sharply, his cheeks mottling with his anger. "And do you not think that perhaps the *country* might not be the best place for Lady Beckington? Away from the society you apparently covet? Have you thought of *that*?"

Honor was shocked.

"Allow me this, Honor. As I am to be the Earl of Beckington sooner rather than later, and you shall be my ward. I want . . . No, I demand, yes, I *demand* that you marry. If you cannot produce someone of your own choosing, then I should very much like you to do your *very* best to find some common ground with Mr. Cleburne with the hope of making a match. Do I make myself clear?"

"I can't believe this!" she protested.

"Well —" he pressed his lips together for

a moment "— believe it."

Honor's head began to spin with the threat of marrying the anxious, hopeful vicar in the salon and, confusingly, George Easton. "You might at least allow the gentleman to make an offer before you command it."

"He has indeed been favorably impressed with you. He has said as much to Miss Hargrove."

"I wouldn't doubt for a moment that the two of them might have said my name, but I assure you, it was Monica who mentioned it," Honor said angrily. "Your father never once imposed his desire for a match on me. You're not yet earl, and here you are, telling me whom I must wed. It's quite unlike you, Augustine! I can only believe Monica has put you up to this. Is that the sort of marriage you will have? One in which your wife directs you?"

Augustine's face darkened. "Monica and I share a common vision. She has not *directed* me. She has merely expressed Cleburne's interest in you, and we have both seen the great opportunities in that match for you, Honor! I would advise against aggravating me," he added brusquely, and yanked the door open. "You know my wishes. I expect you to follow them. I've already arranged for the four of us to ride in Hyde Park on Thursday. So, come now, be a good girl, and take tea."

Honor glared at him, debating what to do. She knew better than to put a man, *any* man, in a corner. She needed to be far more strategic than shouting and complaining to save her future. To save her *life*. And really, she could scarcely think, with so many confusing thoughts swirling about in her head. So she clenched that fist at her side against the rage of helplessness and walked out. She marched ahead of Augustine and into the salon, her face a wreath of smiles.

Until Honor had thought what to do, she had no choice.

CHAPTER TWENTY-FOUR

George's visit with Mr. Sweeney sent him even deeper into the despair he was feeling for the first time in a very long time.

Sweeney had paid another visit to the docks looking for word of the *Maypearl*. "No one has seen her," he said apologetically.

"What does it mean?" George demanded. Not of Sweeney, really, but of life. *His* life. What did it all mean?

Sweeney's chair creaked and moaned beneath him as he squirmed about. "It's hard to know. I think we must prepare to accept that she is lost."

George was not ready to accept it — he couldn't even bring himself to fully accept the *possibility* of it. In that moment, he outright refused to give any credence to it. "If that is what you believe, Mr. Sweeney, perhaps I should find a new agent," he snapped.

Mr. Sweeney paled. "That is . . . that is *not* necessary, Mr. Easton. It is my duty to be as honest with you as I might —"

"Speculation is not honesty, sir, it is merely that — speculation. And I, for one, refuse to accept your speculation as *fact*. Good day," he said crossly, and stormed from Mr. Sweeney's office, ignoring Mr. Sweeney's calls to please wait, to hear him out.

He owed the man an apology, but then again, he thought it hardly fair to surmise that all was lost merely because a ship was now a month late to port. One might argue that Mr. Sweeney's was the more prudent viewpoint, but George had not built his fortune with prudence.

Lost in thought of how he would revive his fortune if indeed it was lost, George thundered back to his home. On Audley Street, his horse trotted down the cobble-stones and came to a halt before his magnificent house without prompt. The house, the symbol of the man he thought he'd become, was the only thing of value that George held now.

He swung down off his mount, tossed the reins through the iron ring where he generally tethered the horse, tying them loosely. As was his habit, he would send a stable boy out to fetch him and take him to the mews. He took one step in the direction of his house and happened to glance up the street as he did so.

He saw the coach with a *B* emblazoned in a swirl of foxes, the sleek black lines of a vehicle familiar to him since stepping into its interior some weeks ago. He paused, squinting at it. She wouldn't have come *here,* would she, in the light of day, for everyone to see? Had she no regard for her reputation at all?

The coach door suddenly swung open. From it emerged a small boot attached to a shapely leg. And then another. Honor alighted without help, dropped her skirts and shook them out. She was wearing a jaunty little bonnet with a trio of feathers artfully arranged, and when she cocked her head to one side to smile warmly at him, they bounced gaily, reminding him of little birds dancing around her head.

He strode forward as she ran daintily across the street. He paused several steps before her, his hands on his hips, wondering if he should kiss her or physically put her back in the coach. "Have you lost your mind? Dispensed with all good judgment? Kicked your common sense off the London Bridge?"

She beamed at him. "Good afternoon, Easton!"

"*What* are you doing here?" he demanded. "I grant you, I'm hardly one to give a whit about what anyone will think, but in this instance, even *I* am concerned that you have crossed an ineradicable line."

"Then perhaps you should invite me in so that I will not be exposed to prying eyes," she suggested without compunction.

Why was it he could not refuse women? Was his creator so cruel as to give him such a terribly vulnerable flaw? He looked her up and down and said, "I shudder to think what my Finnegan will have to say," and gestured impatiently for her to come along.

Honor looked back to her driver and waved. The man instantly set the coach in motion.

"Wait!" George exclaimed. "Where is he going? Tell him to come back at once!"

"He believes I have come to call on a sick friend and that I shall see myself home. It's a lovely walk from here. You might try it! But if you prefer, you may lend me your coach to see me home."

George gaped at her. "You are free with my transport, are you not?"

"I am merely taking your concern for my reputation into account. Anyone might see the Beckington coach sitting before your house. Speaking of that, which one is it? This one?" she asked, pointing up to his white brick townhome.

He sighed.

"It's lovely, Easton!" she said brightly, and moved up the walk to the steps.

"For God's sake, Miss Cabot, at least do me the courtesy of accompanying you into my house," he said gruffly, and caught her elbow, escorting her up the stairs, glancing around them to see who noticed.

"That won't do the least bit of good," Honor said. "Don't you know that women in their dotage do nothing all day but sit about at their windows peering down at houses that belong to men like you?"

George muttered something under his breath, reached for the brass door handle and pushed it open.

Finnegan was there and took an almost unnoticeable step backward when he saw Honor.

Honor seemed to think nothing of it as she glided into the foyer. "Oh, Mr. Easton, your house is so *lovely,*" she said, looking up at the domed ceiling above her head. She took off her hat and handed it to Finnegan without actually looking at him.

Finnegan exchanged a look with George,

a rakish twinkle in his eye. That was precisely what George deserved in taking the ex-lover of his ex-lover as his valet. "Thank you, Finnegan, that will be all," George said.

"Shall I serve tea?"

"Serve whatever you like," George snapped, and startled Honor by taking her by the elbow and marching her into the small salon.

Once inside, she wrested free of his grip and walked to the middle of the room, turning slowly to take in the silk-papered walls, the French gold-leaf furnishings, the portrait of a lady dripping with pearls hanging over the mantel. "Who is she?" she asked, tilting her head back to better see the woman with the piercing blue eyes, the creamy skin. "One of your *acquaintances*?" she asked coyly, looking at him sidelong.

"I haven't the slightest idea who she is," George said, and leaned back against the closed door, his arms folded over his chest. "Honor, look at me."

She glanced at him over her shoulder.

"What are you doing here? I can't believe that even *you,* the most audacious woman I have ever known, would come to the very door of a bastard son with a questionable reputation. Do you *want* to be ruined?"

"My goodness, Easton, when you put it

like that, it sounds so disagreeable. But I will tell you honestly, I hardly care if my reputation is ruined or not."

"Of course you do," he scoffed. "If you wanted to speak to me, you should have summoned me to Beckington House."

She clucked her tongue at him and unbuttoned her spencer. "I wouldn't presume to *summon* you, George," she said, and removed the jacket, tossing it onto a chair. "Well, not like *that,* at least."

George arched a dubious brow at her and tried not to ogle her décolletage. His body was already beginning to stir, and he hadn't even touched her. Damn her for coming. Damn him for being so besotted.

"And besides, I couldn't have summoned you if I'd wanted, as we have a houseguest. It's been difficult enough to keep Mamma from him."

"Houseguest," he repeated, noting that it was a *he.* "Who is this houseguest?"

She waved a hand at him. "It hardly matters." She ran her fingers over a pair of hand-painted porcelain horses that graced a sideboard.

George watched her curiously. There was something a bit different about Honor this afternoon. She was her usual, unapologetic self, yes, but the closer he looked, the more vaguely out of sorts she seemed to him. Anxious. "Honor . . . is something wrong?" he asked her.

"Wrong?" She smiled and put her hand to her nape. "Nothing is wrong other than Lord Sommerfield is still engaged to marry Miss Monica Hargrove." She dropped her hand. "They are practically standing before the altar. They are very pleased to be able to present themselves as a newly engaged couple at the reception for Lord Stapleton."

George knew of that reception; everyone knew of it. Hundreds would attend it, he guessed, as Stapleton was being honored for his bravery in the war. "I hope you've not come here to ask me to engage in parlor games with Miss Hargrove at that reception."

"To what?" She looked surprised, as if the thought had not crossed her mind. "Of course not!" she said, recovering and giving him a withering look. "I told you, I hope you never speak to her again." She sighed, put her hands to her waist. "It was foolish. And in trying to . . . to *dislodge* her, I've only made the situation worse for myself."

He didn't like the look in her eye. "What has happened? I can see that something has."

Honor shook her head. "Oh, George," she

said, sounding almost defeated. "I've no-where else to turn —"

A knock at the door startled them both; Honor turned away and walked to the window, pretending to peer out.

Finnegan entered with a tea service, moving with swift efficiency across the carpet and depositing the heavy silver tray onto a small table. He smiled; his attention was on Honor, and George could see the look of appreciation he gave her figure. "Shall I serve?"

"No, thank you, I will," George said, glaring at him.

Finnegan looked at Honor again, and George was reminded that one day, he would indeed put his fist in his valet's face or dismiss him. But for the moment, he shoved Finnegan toward the door. "That will be all, thank you, Finnegan."

Finnegan grinned and started for the door.

"We won't need you again," George hastily added, lest Finnegan devise some reason to return for another look.

When Finnegan went out, George locked the door for good measure. He turned back to the room and gestured to the tea. "Shall I pour?"

"I don't care for tea, thank you," Honor said distractedly.

"All right. Then will you tell me what has happened?"

"What has happened is that a new vicar has come to Longmeadow, and he is quite unmarried."

A lump of resentment instantly formed in George's chest.

"Augustine has told me, with uncharacteristic determination, that if I cannot produce an offer for my hand, then I must allow the vicar to court me properly, and then . . . then I must marry him."

That news left George speechless. He couldn't imagine Sommerfield insisting on anything, much less *that*. That he had filled George with a sudden and uncontrollable rage.

"In fact, I am to be home by five o'clock," she said, glancing at the mantel clock, "as Mr. Cleburne has invited me and my sisters to attend a church service with him."

George pushed a hand through his hair as a wave of bitter disappointment roiled through him. This was just what he'd expected. So why, then, was it so gut-wrenching to hear? He supposed he'd hoped that nothing like this would happen until after he'd managed to remove himself from the circle of Honor's life. "And if you don't do as he asks?"

She shrugged. "I suppose he'll find another way to remove us from Beckington House. Some way that is far less convenient than marriage, I'd wager."

"I see," he said tightly.

"No," Honor said. "No, George, I don't think you do. *You* may choose who you will marry. Or who you will *not* marry. But that's not a choice I have. I've managed to delay it a year or two, but I suppose I've always known that, eventually, I would be forced to marry."

George couldn't find the words to express his bitter disappointment, even to himself. He was a jumbled mess of raw, unfamiliar feelings, and for a man who had steadfastly avoided *feeling*, he felt decidedly unsteady.

He glanced uncertainly at the tea service, then abruptly turned away, stalked to the sideboard and poured two whiskies. He crossed the room and handed one to Honor, who took it hesitantly, staring down into the amber liquid.

"He seems kind," George grudgingly offered. "You might come to esteem him."

Honor sipped from the glass. She winced, pressed her hand to her chest then sipped again.

An alarming swell of fondness for her bloomed in him, and he felt entirely lost, adrift on a sea of feelings he had struggled to avoid all his life. He suddenly despised Monica Hargrove. It was an irrational surge of anger — this wasn't her fault — but he could see her hands all over this forced engagement. All in retaliation for what he'd done.

He put aside his whiskey glass. "I can fix things, Honor. I can undo this."

"You can't," she said wearily. "No one can. It was bound to happen, and I've no one to blame but me."

"But it doesn't need to happen now. Not like this," George said angrily. "I should have heeded your advice, but I merely toyed with her. Now she will feel the full force of my ardor —"

"George!" Honor said, alarmed. "You mustn't do anything! We've tried and failed, as you yourself warned me we would —"

"I intend to kiss her," he said. How could he even *contemplate* kissing Monica Hargrove? The thought made him shudder. The only one he could think of kissing was Honor. "I will seduce her."

"No!" Honor cried. "No, you mustn't!" She suddenly took his face between her hands. "You can't *kiss* her," she implored him. "You can't kiss her, because I will perish with jealousy."

George lifted his arms, his palms out and away from Honor, fearful of what he would do if he touched her again. "Then tell me, Honor, *instruct* me. Tell me what to do to help you."

"I've missed you," she said softly, knocking him off center once more.

"Pardon? We were speaking of Miss Hargrove —"

She shook her head. "Why did you tell me not to speak?"

He blinked; it took him a moment to recall what he'd said. She was watching him closely, and he could see the doubt in her eyes. "Honor, darling . . . I told you not to speak because I couldn't bear to hear it."

Her eyes suddenly began to water, and she dropped her hands. "Because you cannot return my affection," she said.

He didn't mean to chuckle, but he couldn't help it. Honor blinked; she began to turn away, but he caught her hand. "Because I can only return it tenfold," he said. "I couldn't bear to hear it because I can't have you."

Her eyelids fluttered; she eyed him warily, as if she expected him to declare he was jesting after all. When he did not, she turned to him and said, "Do you want to know how you can help me? You can show me your deepest affection before I am forced to marry the vicar. Before the ache of missing you turns my heart to dust."

Those words were a salve to old, ancient wounds, and he scarcely knew what to do with them, which way to turn. "I can't do that, Honor. You know as well as I that it's impossible for us."

"Impossible?" She laughed. "I don't know which way is up or down anymore. I only know what I feel in this moment, Easton, and I have *missed* you."

"Honor, please," he said, begging her now. "I *cannot* resist you."

She curled her fingers around his, squeezing them tightly. "Then *don't.*"

He reached for her at the same moment she reached for him, slipping into his arms as if she belonged there, had been there all his life. George's heart began to reel. Her lips felt like silk beneath his, tantalizing the beast in him. He crushed her to him, felt her breasts against his chest, the heat of her body mingling with his, flaring in his groin.

He lifted his head, gazing down on the woman who had the power to do this to him. She opened her eyes and smiled so seductively that it was a wonder George didn't fall to his knees. He was on fire, fully engulfed by a woman whose smile could reduce him to ashes. She touched her finger to his lip and whispered, "Did you miss me?"

"More than the air I breathe," he growled, and lust for her flooded into every part of him, hardening his cock to the point of aching. Her hands moved over his body; he grabbed her bottom, kneading it, pushing it against his erection, showing her just how badly he wanted her. She began to move against him, pressing into him, nipping at his lips, sliding her tongue into his mouth. She was a hellion, so brazen in her desire that he was melting with it.

He put her on the settee and moved over her, trapping her beneath his body. Hungry for the taste of her skin, he moved his mouth to her throat, down to her breast, nipping at the hardened nipple through the fabric of her gown. Honor whimpered softly, shoved her fingers into his hair as she instinctually lifted her breast to his mouth. He pulled at her gown, freeing both breasts, uncaring that he was devouring her, uncaring of anything but the dangerously desperate need to touch her, to be in her once more.

He suddenly sat up, clawing at his clothes, his gaze locked on Honor. When he had thrown off the coat and waistcoat, had removed his neckcloth and shirt, he slipped his hand under her back, lifting her up, kissing her deeply with all the emotion that was surging through him, and lowering her down once more as he found the hem of her gown. The need to feel her body surround his was overpowering; when she kissed his nipple, he caught her hands again, pinned them above her head. "Be still."

Honor laughed breathlessly. "Why?"

"Because you drive me to madness."

Her eyes were glittering up at him, her lips, wet and lush, curved enticingly. "Touch me, George," she whispered. "*Touch* me."

George unbuttoned his trousers and freed himself, then lowered her hands to his member. She wrapped her fingers around him, squeezing lightly, feeling him as he slipped his hands between her legs, into her wet depths. The lids of her eyes grew heavy as she lost herself in the sensation. She bit her lower lip as he stroked her — she was so alluring, so seductive. George moved down her body, leaving a trail of kisses over her gown, finding the bare flesh of her thigh and licking his way up, pushing her thighs apart and dipping his tongue into her sex. She bucked at the sensation of his mouth and tongue in her, which in turn sent blood pounding through George, engorging his heart and his cock. Had she been anyone else, he would have hurried his pleasure along. But with Honor, he desired her pleasure almost more than his own. He held on to her, holding her firmly as he carefully explored her every crevice, flicking airily across the core of her desire, then deep into the recesses of her body.

Honor gasped for air as she moved against him, thrilling him, inciting him with small whimpers of pleasure as she neared her release. George stroked her and nibbled as if she were a delicacy, bringing her to the brink of fulfillment, then backing away, finding another way to tantalize her. But Honor couldn't bear it. She grabbed his head between her hands, pulled him up and kissed him wildly before she sought his cock with one hand and pushed against his trousers with the other.

He helped her, pushing his trousers down. Honor drew a shallow breath as she cupped him in one hand, stroking him with the other. Her fire was consuming him, burning him up. George moved between her legs, pushing them apart and pressing the head of his cock against her slick sex. Honor came up on her elbows, her gaze locked on his as he began to slide into her. He held her gaze as he slowly worked his way inside her tight, wet sheath. He felt her body open to him, wrapping firmly around him, claiming him.

God, he was mad for her, utterly mad for her. "I don't know what you've done to me," he said roughly.

Honor smiled as if that pleased her. She closed her eyes, and let her head drop back as he began to move inside her. And then she began to move with him, meeting his thrusts, learning the rhythm of lovemaking. He felt himself filling up with heat, and he moved faster, harder in her, circling his hips, stroking her differently. He was panting, he realized, trying desperately to hold on to the massive climax that was brewing in him. He felt her body coil around him and draw him in, felt her tightening. When he thought he could not endure another moment of it, her body contracted tightly around him, and she shuddered violently as she cried out with an explosive release that convulsed around his body.

It pushed George over the edge. He spilled into her in quick, explosive bursts at the end of almost savage thrusts until he was completely numb. He slowly lowered himself to her, pressed his racing heart against her breast.

He had never in his life been so completely

and wholly satisfied.

He had never loved a woman so.

She reached for his hand, clung to it tightly as she tried to regain her breath. And when she had caught it enough to talk, she opened her eyes, smiled up at him and said, "You *did* miss me."

More than air.

CHAPTER TWENTY-FIVE

Honor cast a deliriously happy smile up at a sky shrouded by the smoke of chimneys as she walked home and thought it never seemed so blue.

She'd refused George's demand that she take the coach, as well as his demand that he see her safely home. She wanted these moments to herself, to relive every moment of it, to marvel at it all again. She wanted to float home with her heart and mind full of George Easton, of the extraordinary command he'd had of her body, of the way he had looked at her and made her feel so very beautiful and desirable.

She had finally agreed that a houseboy might follow her to see that no harm came to her. It was the only way George was willing to let her go. It was difficult enough to take her leave, what with all the kissing and his apparent need to keep her in his embrace, and really, the boy was so small he could not be at all useful if she were set upon by thieves. Nevertheless, Honor had agreed and George had let her go.

She glanced down at her gown. Not only was George capable of lacing a corset, he'd also proved himself capable of pinning hair, at least well enough to tuck it up under her bonnet. Honor had cupped his chin and bestowed a soft kiss on his lips.

George had seemed rather disconcerted by it. He had taken her hand and held it tightly in his, looking at her with concern and affection. Honor had never seen him so uncertain. "Will you be all right?" she'd asked him.

"Me?" He'd said it as if she somehow had it wrong, that she should be the one who was disconcerted. "Yes!" he'd said, flustered. "But I . . ." He'd groaned, closed his eyes a moment then opened them, looking at her intently. "Honor, heed me. This cannot happen again. That is to say, we can't —"

She'd smiled, kissed him before he could tell her it was impossible again. "Calm yourself, Easton," she'd said quietly.

He'd pressed his lips together and nodded. And then he'd gathered her in his arms one last time, held her tightly as he kissed the top of her head, her neck, her cheek, before letting her go. "You astound me," he'd said. "In so many ways, you astound me."

She didn't know why.

"I will fix things, Honor," he'd said to her, her hands clasped tightly in his. "I won't allow them to force you into a marriage you don't want."

She appreciated the sentiment, but it wasn't possible for him to stop a marriage. Unless he —

She swallowed down that impossible, fantastical thought and carried on.

At Beckington House, Honor managed to slip upstairs to her rooms, unnoticed except by Hardy, who scarcely noticed her at all, as he seemed a bit distracted. Later, when Grace came knocking on her door, Honor understood why he'd seemed so.

"Where have you been?" Grace asked, glancing down the hall before shutting Honor's door.

"Walking," Honor said with a shrug she hoped didn't look too suspicious. She removed her bonnet and set it aside.

Grace shook her head and studied the palm of her hand for a moment.

"What is it?" Honor asked.

"I've had a letter from Cousin Beatrice. She is in Bath and writes that she would welcome my visit at any time."

Honor patted Grace's hand. "We hardly have time for a trip to Bath, what with all the weddings on the horizon," she said, gesturing to herself.

"I don't mean you are to go, Honor. I mean to go alone."

Grace sounded the same as she always did, but she looked different somehow, Honor thought. Resolved. When she realized it, a shot of panic jolted Honor. *"No,"* she said instantly. "Grace, you can't desert me!"

"I'm not deserting you," Grace said, and took Honor's hand between both of hers. "Come now, we are agreed that we must *do* something. First, I owe you an apology for laying the blame for our predicament at your door. I was so very frustrated that afternoon, but God knows I am aware how hard you've tried, Honor. I am going to Bath because Lord Amherst is there. He's shown a particular fondness for me. You know he has. I mean to secure an offer —"

"Are you mad?" Honor demanded, yanking her hand free from Grace. "You scarcely know him! You have no *affection* for him."

"Frankly, I am *quite* sane and apparently the only practical one in this room! It is true, I have no deep affection for him, but I do rather enjoy his company. What else is required? He's not a vicar, he's a titled man of means. At the very least, I shan't be forced to live in some cottage in the country."

Honor couldn't abide it. "It's not what you want!"

Grace laughed sourly. "Pray, what do I want, Honor? Please tell me what it is, for God knows I can't name it. I haven't given the slightest thought to what I really *want.*" She shook her head as if she found that mystifying.

Honor groaned with misery and laid her head on Grace's shoulder. "When are you leaving?"

"At week's end."

"So soon!"

"Lady Chatham is to Bath to take the waters, and I . . . I invited myself along. I've waited long enough," Grace said firmly. "Now then, what have you done to your hair?"

Honor sat up with a start. She put her hand to it. "A pin fell from it while I was walking," she said, and stood up, moving away from Grace to her vanity, before her sister could examine her hair more closely. She quickly pulled it down and picked up her brush.

Grace stood and moved to the door. "I'll

send Hannah around to help you repair it. You've not much time, you know. We're to meet the charming Mr. Cleburne in an hour."

When she was alone, Honor folded her arms on the vanity and lowered her forehead to them. She closed her eyes, thinking back to the moments she'd had this afternoon with Easton. It made her a little queasy to imagine Mr. Cleburne in a similar situation. It made her positively ill to imagine it all without Grace.

An hour later, Honor arrived in the foyer in the most demure, lifeless gown she could find in her wardrobe. She wore it as a symbol of her silent protest to this match, to the life that had led her to this moment. It was plain and sedate, just like she imagined marriage to Cleburne would be. This was what Augustine had done to her, she absently mused as she and Mr. Cleburne followed at a bit of a distance behind Augustine and her sisters to the church — he'd taken the desire for fine gowns out of her. She scarcely cared if she ever wore one again.

Honor managed to endure the service and the walk back to Beckington House. She thought she had managed to make it through an interminable evening in the company of the vicar and that she could at last turn her attention to something else, but then Augustine had the audacity to push her once more.

"Mr. Cleburne, you've not forgotten our ride and picnic in the park on the morrow, have you?"

Mr. Cleburne smiled self-consciously at Honor. "I have not. I have heard that you are an excellent horsewoman, Miss Cabot."

Honor said flatly, "I am." Perhaps she would ride away from him. Point her horse north and ride it until it could not carry her another step.

"You must see her," Augustine said cheerfully. "That is, if you dare to be bested by a woman." He laughed as if that were entirely impossible.

"I sit a horse respectably well," Mr. Cleburne said with a modest shrug.

Honor said nothing. Augustine glared at her, and she said, "You must join us."

"Excellent!" Augustine crowed. "We'll have a picnic, the four of us."

"I want to go," Mercy said, and pushed her spectacles up the ridge of her nose. "I'm a good horsewoman, too."

"Oh, but you are needed at Beckington House," Augustine said.

"Why am *I* needed?" Mercy complained.

"Because someone must keep an eye out for the ghosts," Mr. Cleburne said congenially.

That seemed to give Mercy pause, and in that moment, Mr. Cleburne turned his smile to Honor, clearly pleased with himself for showing some attention to her youngest sister.

Honor was entirely certain that her attempt at a smile failed. "Mercy, tell us a ghost story," she said, and looked away, lest Mr. Cleburne see her great disappointment in him.

CHAPTER TWENTY-SIX

Monica's mother believed Mr. Cleburne was a perfect match for Honor in every way, most particularly because it meant Honor would be living at Longmeadow.

Not London, where Monica would be stepping into her role one day as the new Lady Beckington. But at Longmeadow, where Monica would only need see her in summer, when London was unbearably hot and fetid.

Monica didn't ride as well as Honor — none of them did — and she'd assumed Honor would ride far ahead, pausing to speak to acquaintances, then trotting back to the party, where Monica would labor along with her horse. But nothing was further from the truth. Honor rode at a sedate pace beside the vicar and behind Monica and Augustine. She hardly seemed herself.

They were so slow, thanks to Augustine's

clumsy handling of his horse, that Monica could overhear Honor and Cleburne's conversation. The vicar asked what diversions Honor enjoyed. Honor replied she enjoyed gaming. The vicar chuckled indulgently and made a remark about the games of the devil. Honor asked if he ever bet on horses, that everyone at Longmeadow found a coin or two for that purpose.

Mr. Cleburne said he did not.

Monica would have given anything to see the expression on Honor's face at that moment, but alas, her task was to train her eye to her horse, lest she fall.

Monica knew Honor was perturbed when they stopped for their picnic. Augustine busily instructed a footman where to lay the blanket and the basket of food the cook had prepared. Honor stood to one side, tapping her crop lightly against her skirt, staring out across the lake.

Monica asked lightly, "Mr. Cleburne, I've been meaning to inquire, how do you find Longmeadow now that you've been there a time?"

"Oh, very well, indeed," he said, as if he could say anything less before Augustine.

"You've met the fine families there?"

"Naturally. They are my flock."

"I am sure you have discovered many

young, unmarried woman in your flock," Honor said.

Mr. Cleburne blushed. Monica realized then how inexperienced the man was. "Perhaps one or two have allowed an interest," he said modestly. "But none that I found suitable," he quickly amended.

"What do you mean? There were *none* that caught your interest?" Honor asked.

Mr. Cleburne smiled nervously. "No, I . . . I consider myself a man of discernment."

The man was a fool, Monica realized. He hadn't the slightest idea how to entice a woman like Honor Cabot. He was no George Easton, a surprising thought that caused her to chuckle unexpectedly.

Honor and Mr. Cleburne looked at her. Monica gaily remarked, "What a lovely day!"

Honor's gaze darkened.

"We have our picnic!" Augustine said, making a grand gesture to the setting the footman had made for them.

The four of them eased themselves down on the blanket and helped themselves to fruit and cheeses while the footman filled their wineglasses. Augustine had stretched out on his side, and his belly, Monica was chagrined to see, was spilling onto the ground beneath his waistcoat. They spoke of nothing of import, and even when Augustine brought up the reception for Lord Stapleton, Monica resisted a yawn. But then Augustine suggested Honor invite Mr. Cleburne to accompany her.

Honor's head came up. She looked at Monica, then at Augustine, clearly caught off guard.

Mr. Cleburne sensed her fluster, for he said, "I couldn't possibly impose."

"No imposition," Augustine said easily, and stuffed a pair of grapes into his mouth.

"But I should not impose on *you,* Mr. Cleburne," Honor said, recovering slightly. "The reception will be crowded and . . . and noisy."

"Oh, I scarcely mind that," Cleburne said congenially. "I am sure I have suffered worse at the country dances." He laughed.

Honor glanced away, her jaw clenched. "Unfortunately," she said, shaking her head to the wine the footman silently offered, "the building is not well ventilated."

"Then I suppose I shall remove my coat," Mr. Cleburne responded, and smiled at Monica and Augustine, as if they were playing a game.

"Then it's all settled," Augustine said triumphantly. "Mr. Cleburne shall be your guest."

"Yes," Honor said. "Thank you, Augustine, for the idea." She stood up. "Please, excuse me."

Mr. Cleburne hastened to find his feet.

"Oh, no, Mr. Cleburne, do keep your seat. I mean only to stretch my legs." Honor whirled and began to walk. Or march, really, her riding habit billowing out behind her.

Cleburne looked helplessly at Monica and Augustine. "Have I said something wrong?"

"Not at all, Mr. Cleburne," Monica said, and held out her hand so that he might help her to her feet. "Honor can be rather . . ."

"Mercurial?" Augustine offered innocently.

"That was not the word I was searching for," Monica said kindly. *Stubborn* was more in line with her thinking. "She is the restless sort. I'll see to her — enjoy your wine," she said, and straightened her bonnet before marching after Honor to the edge of the lake.

When reached by her nemesis, Honor was ripping apart a rush, one bristle at a time. When they were girls, her mother had brought them to this very lake to feed the ducks. Monica remembered Honor, with her dark hair streaming behind her, chasing the ducks at the edge of the lake, trying to catch them as Monica's mother shouted at her to stop. Monica had been afraid of the ducks, and she was suddenly reminded of how Honor had held her hand while Monica had thrown her breadcrumbs to the honking beasts. When had those young girls parted ways? Honestly, Monica couldn't recall any longer.

She glanced at Honor from the corner of her eye. "You seem rather cross."

Honor bestowed a withering look on Monica. "Cross is the *least* of what I am. You know that very well."

"I suppose I do," Monica said, and shrugged, looking out over the lake. "I don't understand you, in all honesty. Mr. Cleburne happens to be an excellent match for you —"

"An excellent match?" Honor shot back and glanced over her shoulder at the offending gentleman. "Why do you believe that? Because it is *your* idea to broker a marriage? Ah — don't even *think* of denying it," she said when Monica opened her mouth to do precisely that. "I know very well you suggested it to Augustine. He would not have thought of it on his own."

"Even if I did suggest it, or even if you suggested to Mr. Easton that he should court me, it's all beside the point," Monica said pertly, taking pleasure in the flicker of culpability that flashed in Honor's eyes. "Mr. Cleburne is a perfect match for you because he *is*. He is devoted, he is kind and his reputation is irreproachable. Can you really ask for more?"

"Yes!" Honor exclaimed. "Yes, Monica, I can ask for more. Perhaps *you* can't, or won't, but *I* ask for more."

"Why isn't anything ever *good* enough for you?" Monica demanded crossly. "How can you find a man who most women in your position would consider a *very* good match beneath you? Why must you always have *more*?"

"I don't think Mr. Cleburne is beneath me, for heaven's sake. But I think he is as far removed from me in spirit and temperament as a man could possibly be. And furthermore, why don't you ever want more, Monica? Why won't you believe in the *best* possibilities, instead of taking the first offer?"

Monica gasped. "Don't you dare disparage Augustine to me!"

"I wasn't —"

"You were!" Monica insisted. Now she glanced over her shoulder at her fiancé. Augustine, sitting cross-legged, enthusiastically regaled Mr. Cleburne with some tale, judging by the wave of his hands. "I happen to be quite fond of Augustine. And I have done what every woman is exhorted to do, Honor. I have made a good match. There is nothing *wrong* with that. I am happy. Can you not see it? Can you not be happy for me? Happy that I will marry him, happy that the banns have been posted?"

Honor's eyes widened. "They've been posted?"

"Yes!" Monica said crossly. "Must you look so astounded? Augustine told you that we wished to marry before his father . . . Well, you know very well what I mean. I have accepted my life and his offer, and I am *happy.*"

"Do you not hear yourself?" Honor demanded, suddenly turning to face her. "Wouldn't you rather find true, consuming love than merely accept your life and an offer?"

Sometimes Honor was ridiculously childish, and Monica couldn't help but laugh.

Honor's brows sank in a confused frown. "Why are you laughing? Do you *love* Augustine?"

"Will you stop?" Monica exclaimed through her laughter. "I told you, I esteem him!"

"But do you *love* him?"

"For God's sake, Honor! I will come to

love him. Love develops over time, with familiarity, as two people move through life as one. You act as if there is some other alternative! What alternative is there? To wait indefinitely? For what? For a knight to come along and quite literally sweep me off my feet?"

"Yes!" Honor cried with frustration.

"Dear God, you are maddening," Monica snapped, and looked away, angry with herself for allowing Honor to vex her. *Again.*

"We will never have alternatives if we don't demand them," Honor said, and folded her arms tightly over her middle.

Monica rolled her eyes. "And what alternative will you demand, pray? That you do not marry? That you may continue to flit from this soiree to that?" she asked, gesturing around them.

"I mean that unless women demand to follow their heart's true instincts, we will never be allowed to do so. Society will insist we marry *well,* and that is *all* they will ask of us."

"Ah. And your heart's true instincts are not Mr. Cleburne."

"Not in the least."

"Have you ever considered that perhaps your heart doesn't have a true instinct? For surely, if it did, you would have acted on it by now."

Honor's eyes widened. She looked almost insulted for a moment, but that quickly gave way to another expression. She seemed to be considering what Monica had said, mulling it over for a long moment. "Goodness, I think you may be *right,* Monica."

"I am?" Monica said, startled.

"Yes." Honor nodded thoughtfully. "If I don't act, who will?"

Monica suddenly had a sinking feeling she'd unwittingly unleashed a beast from its cage. "Honor Cabot, what are you thinking?" she demanded. "You'd best not cause trouble —"

"Trouble? No," Honor said sweetly. "You've helped me clarify a thing or two. We'd best go back to the gentlemen, do you suppose?" She smiled warmly at Monica, then started back toward the men, suddenly strolling along as if she hadn't a care in the world.

Chapter Twenty-Seven

London scarcely managed to crawl out beneath the leaden skies on the afternoon of Lord Stapleton's reception. A stiff wind and the smell of rain in the air only increased George's uncharacteristically somber mood, and he wouldn't have minded in the least to have remained in bed all day, a pillow over his head, his eyes closed against the world.

But Finnegan had other ideas, it would seem, as he had polished George's boots and laid out his gold waistcoat and navy superfine coat to don for the reception. It looked, George thought, almost naval in appearance.

George was generally annoyed when Finnegan laid out his clothes as if he were addled, but this afternoon he was glad for it, because he doubted he would have been able to dress himself with much care. He'd been walking around in a melancholy fog for two days, obsessed with thoughts of Honor, remembering in exquisite and torturous detail the afternoon in his salon.

There was no help for him. He was a fool, a bloody fool for having agreed to help her in the beginning. He was an even bigger fool because he was mad for her. He'd broken his one cardinal rule: never believe he was one of them. After a life spent trying to be someone, to be recognized, he'd learned to keep proper society at arm's length, to protect himself above all else.

In this case, he'd missed his steps, had fallen out of line, had looked to his left and right and, in doing so, had ruined his life. It had happened so quickly, so easily, too — when a daring, beautiful woman presented a challenge to him, his rule had held up like cotton batting in fire, disappearing completely.

The most enraging part of it was that George did not want Honor to marry a bloody vicar. He did not want her to marry at all. He wanted things to remain as they were, with opportunities to be in her company, to hear her clever mind spinning out wretched ideas to create a bit of mayhem in her society, to keep him properly diverted from the lack of a name, the loss of his fortune. From who he was.

It was an absurdly preposterous wish. And an astoundingly intense one.

To confound his thinking even more, there was part of him that didn't entirely trust Honor. It was a truth he grudgingly admitted to himself. Yes, he loved her. And there was a part of him that believed she loved him, as well. But she was a woman of the *ton,* and she had come to him seeking a way to keep her fortune and standing. In spite of what they'd shared, in spite of his strong feelings — or hers, for that matter — he could not bring himself to believe she would ever truly give that up to settle for someone like him. Or that Beckington would ever consent to someone like him as a possible match for her. And though passion had flared hot and wild between him and Honor, he couldn't help but wonder if this . . . this thing between them, this intangible, intense thing wasn't merely pleasure for her.

How could it be anything but?

Oh, yes, George was a miserable man.

But in that misery, he was irrationally determined to lure Monica Hargrove to him. He told himself it was to keep her from making Honor's burden of her family dilemma any worse by presenting potential offers for her hand. A smaller voice suggested it was even more personal than that

— he'd been rather astounded that his attempts to seduce the debutante had failed. *A kiss.* That's what was required. One small kiss of her lips, and all the reticence would melt right out of Miss Monica Hargrove. She'd be eating from his bag of oats or he'd find another way to tether her.

Dressed like a sailor for the occasion of honoring a war hero, George stalked downstairs so gruffly that the daily maid Finnegan had hired — to clean or to bed, George didn't know — scampered out of his way like a frightened little hare.

Finnegan was waiting in the foyer with George's hat and gloves. "What a splendid surprise," he said, bowing slightly. "You've combed your hair."

George snatched the hat and gloves from Finnegan. "Today, Mr. Finnegan," he said, stuffing his hands into the gloves, "may very well be the day I throttle you."

"Very good, sir," Finnegan said, and opened the front door.

On such a gloomy day, Burlington House was predictably crowded. All of the illustrious guests had crammed inside the gallery, standing shoulder to shoulder, the din of their voices echoing against the cavernous ceiling. George couldn't imagine how he'd find anyone, but he pushed through the crowd all the same, muttering his apologies for stepping on this toe or elbowing that back, receiving some less-than-welcoming looks for it.

He spotted Sommerfield first, his girth affording him a bit more space than most. Standing beside him was Miss Monica Hargrove, her expression full of tedium. George wasn't entirely certain what he would say, but he started for her.

Miss Hargrove turned her head, and when she saw him, she straightened slightly. She seemed perplexed, and then her brows dipped into something of a frown. In a mood, was she? He'd change that. George stepped around a couple in his progress toward Miss Hargrove and was startled by the sudden appearance of Honor in front of him. "Mr. Easton," she said, and put her hand on his arm.

George looked down at her hand on his arm, her touch incinerating his sleeve, marking his skin underneath. "May I have a word?"

"Not now, love. There is another woman I should like to address."

"George . . . please. *Please.*" She smiled as she glanced to her right. George followed her gaze and saw Cleburne standing there.

"Mr. Cleburne, will you excuse us a moment?" she asked.

"Yes, of course. Good day, Mr. Easton," he said, and with a curt bow, he took several steps away. But not far enough that Honor was out of his sight, George noticed.

George didn't speak; Honor tugged him to one side.

"Go back to your suitor, Cabot. You've nothing to fear, I do not intend —"

"I beg of you, don't speak to her!" Honor interjected frantically. "Don't even look her way. It's over, it's done — I should never have begun this madness!"

"It's not your scheme any longer, love. It's mine. I told you I would fix things for you."

"I don't need you to fix anything for me. I don't *want* you to fix it!"

George paused and looked down at her. "*Why?* Is Cleburne suddenly to your liking?"

"*No!*" she exclaimed, and looked nervously in the direction of the young vicar. "That's certainly *not* what compels me. It's that I . . ." She rose up on her toes to look over his shoulder.

"You what?" he asked.

Honor sank down, bit her lip.

George frowned, imagining all manner of nonsense. "What is this sudden shyness?

What is it?"

"I am not *shy,*" she said, as if the very notion offended her. "But I am afraid."

"Of what?"

"Of *you,*" she admitted.

Something toxic began to brew in George. He suspected this was the moment she would say that she had come to realize that theirs was not a relationship she could maintain, not with an urgent need to find an offer for her hand. He stepped back. "Go on, then, say it. Don't let maidenly angst stand in your way."

"I love you," she said.

Stunned, George gaped at her.

"Are you shocked?" she asked, smiling at someone who passed by. "Well, I do, Easton, I love you so, with all my heart," she said, stacking her hands and pressing them against her breast. "What am I to do? I'm not supposed to love you, but I do. I don't want you to seduce anyone but me. I want you all for myself. I want *you.*"

He had never desired to hear those words more, and yet he had never wanted so desperately *not* to hear them. "What you think you *want* is impossible," he said brusquely. "How many times must I tell you so?"

Her eyes widened with surprise. And then

narrowed with anger. "Why must every blessed thing with you be so *impossible*?"

"Because it is," he snapped, feeling inexplicably, inexcusably angry with her. He was feeling the same thing, had been feeling for days that rusty, unfamiliar crank of love in his chest, and it made him furious. As much as he loved her, he wouldn't taint her with the rumors that swirled about him. Worse, he had nothing. He had less than nothing now, thanks to his missing ship. He could offer this bright star in his galaxy *nothing.*

"But I thought . . . You admitted to affection for me. You *missed* me."

He could see unshed tears beginning to glisten in her eyes. It was a rare glimpse of innocence from this young woman, and for some reason it made George even angrier. She was naive in ways he could not begin to fathom, and he'd allowed it, had encouraged it, had *taken* innocence from her. "It is time you accepted life for what it is, Honor. You can't recast it to meet your whims."

She looked truly wounded by that. "A whim? Do you think I *want* to love you?" she asked, heedless of anyone around now. "Do you think that it eases my life in any way?"

George's heart constricted, squeezed by

so many emotions, so many things he didn't want to feel. He gazed into the beautiful face, into the eyes of a daughter of the Quality, who had been trained to high-step into salons and advantageous matches just as surely as he was trained to not desire them. She had been trained to seek fortune and, more important, standing.

She could *not* love a man like him. It was *impossible.*

Her naive ideas of love and noble sacrifices would fade with time.

But then Honor surprised him yet again. It was almost as if she could feel the doubts raging through him. She put her hand on his arm and said, "I *do* love you, George. I know you don't believe me, but I love you in a way I never believed was possible. I beg you, tell me the truth. Tell me you feel the same. *Please.*"

A flash of panic and an age-old ache swept through him. He peeled her fingers from his hand and stepped back. "I beg your pardon, Miss Cabot, but I cannot possibly tell you what is not true." George did the only thing he could do — he turned away and walked. Fled, really. He looked wildly at the crowd in that hall and felt the walls closing in, pushing the air from the room. He stalked from the reception, out into the cold gray day.

He did not look back. He didn't have to. The image of the hurt in her eyes was forever burned into his memory.

And because George left in such a fashion, a prisoner of his birth and his experiences, because he believed that the vicar *was* a good match for her, and that he was the worst match for her, because he took himself to Southwark and gambled and drank the remainder of the day, trying desperately to block her words from his ears, her image from his eyes, he did not hear the Earl of Beckington had died until well into the following afternoon.

Chapter Twenty-Eight

Death had crept in when the Beckington household had least expected it. The earl had been at breakfast that morning, smiling as the girls talked about their plans for the day, and reminding Augustine, when he grew impatient with Mercy, that she was a girl yet.

A congenial Augustine had agreed and had turned the talk to the reception for Lord Stapleton that afternoon, pondering who might attend. Honor had wondered aloud if Grace was still abed after an evening spent at the Chatham residence. The earl had said she must be exhausted, having endured the unending stream of words from Lady Chatham.

Prudence had recalled a silly story about Mrs. Philpot's chickens that had gotten loose in Grosvenor Square, and dissolved into giggles as she'd related how the poor woman had run after them, her skirts lifted to her knees. It had made the earl laugh until he couldn't catch his breath.

After breakfast, Mercy had offered to read to her stepfather — truly the only father she'd ever known — but he'd smiled fondly at her and assured her he'd had quite enough tales of wolves who ate humans.

When Honor thought of that morning, she thought of her mother, not the earl. Her mother had sat beside her husband, quite subdued, staring at her plate. Had she sensed that death was so near them? Or had she slipped into the private world she increasingly inhabited?

There was one more thing Honor remembered about the last time she would see the earl alive. When she'd stood to go, she had leaned down to kiss him goodbye. He'd caught her hand in his and said, "You're a good girl, my love. Never let anyone convince you otherwise." And he'd smiled.

Honor had laughed. He'd been telling her she was a good girl since the day she and Monica had slipped out of the back of the church during Sunday services to meet a pair of boys. Not just any boys, mind you, but stable boys who were charged with looking after the parishioners' horses.

"I think you are the only one who believes

it, my lord. But I shall endeavor to remember."

The earl had patted her hand, then had let it slip from his grip.

Honor wished she was the good girl the earl had always believed her to be. She wished she'd been a better daughter to him, had spent more time with him.

His funeral had been a blur of activity. So many people had come, so many embraces and offers of condolences. So many rituals and so much black.

The day after the funeral, Grace had left for Bath. *"Stay,"* Honor had begged her.

"I can't," Grace had said grimly. "We've no time to lose."

Honor had said goodbye to Grace that morning, holding her sister tightly. She'd told herself that Grace's plan was just as fraught with opportunities for failure as hers had been, and that by all rights, Grace would be home in a matter of weeks. But Grace's departure had felt like the final blow, the last door to shut on the life as they'd known it.

Honor had stood on the street, watching Grace's coach disappear around a corner. And even then, she'd remained standing there, looking down the street. Waiting. Watching.

For what, Honor hadn't known.

She'd felt great despair that morning. She'd lost the most important people in her life in a matter of days. The earl. Her dear sister Grace. *Easton.*

Her disappointment was devastating.

Now it had been a fortnight since the earl's death, a fortnight of grief so deep that Honor had lost her appetite and seemed only to eat when Hardy urged her to do so. It was nonsensical — Honor had known that the earl was not long for this world, had believed herself prepared for his departure. Nothing could have prepared her, however.

His absence was felt throughout the house. Augustine seemed anxious in his new role, and the entire staff seemed to be in the doldrums. Prudence and Mercy whispered to each other, their black clothing making them look tired.

But Honor's grief ran so much deeper than her stepfather's death.

She mourned George just as deeply.

Lord, how she missed him. And hated him, too. At least, she tried to convince herself she hated him. With his rejection of her, he'd reopened old, deep-seated wounds. She felt as if she were reliving the nightmare of Lord Rowley all over again. Honor had been destroyed by Easton's rejection of her, and had it not been for Mr. Cleburne's kindness in seeing her home, she'd feared she might have collapsed at the reception.

Since that horrible afternoon, she'd not seen George and had heard nothing of him. He hadn't come to pay his respects, and even at the funeral service, she'd scanned the dozens upon dozens of mourners gathered, certain she would see his reassuring smile. He did not attend.

At the gathering after the funeral, she happened to overhear two gentlemen speaking of the war. One of them mentioned that Easton's ship was missing and presumed captured or sunk, and with a chuckle added that his fortune had sunk along with it. Honor wondered if he'd truly lost his fortune, if he would be reduced to mean circumstances. She hated him . . . but she wished she could help him, too.

Her heart was whittled away by her hurt, and it had turned to dust. She could feel it — a powdery, insubstantial thing in her chest.

One gloomy, damp afternoon, as Honor and Prudence strolled about the square — they were desperate to be out of doors — Prudence reported that she'd heard Monica saying that she might wed within the next few weeks, but her mother had corrected her to say that likely she would wait another year, given the prescribed period of mourning for the earl.

"Perhaps in theory," Honor said thoughtfully.

"What do you mean?"

"I don't believe Augustine can do without her for a full year," Honor said. "He'll think of some way. Even if it were to take a year, how long will it be before Mamma begins to speak again and the words coming out of her mouth are as mad as her appearance? Her madness will affect us all, Pru. The only thing that has truly changed for us is that the rituals of mourning have added another complication to our lives."

"I don't want to say it, but . . ."

"But what?" Honor urged her sister.

Prudence shook her head. "I am quite worried for Mamma. I overheard Mrs. Hargrove and Augustine talking."

A slight shiver of fear ran through Honor. "Mrs. Hargrove? Or Monica?"

"Mrs. Hargrove," Prudence repeated, and glanced across the square to Beckington House. "She said that she worried for Mamma's health, and, naturally, Augustine agreed. But then Mrs. Hargrove said there was a place in St. Asaph that could provide care for people like Mamma."

"St. Asaph?" Honor said. "I've never heard of it."

"Mercy and I hadn't, either. We looked for it in the pages of the atlas. Oh, Honor — it's in Wales! It is very far from London — it's far from everything!"

Honor's heart skipped a few beats.

"Miss Cabot!"

Prudence and Honor both started and glanced around. Mr. Cleburne was striding across the square toward them.

"God help me," Honor muttered.

"I beg your pardon," Mr. Cleburne said as he reached them. "I hope I'm not imposing. I happened to see the two of you here and thought perhaps you might like some company."

"I was just saying to Honor that perhaps we ought to turn back. Mamma might need us," Prudence said.

"But surely you might use a bit of fresh air," he said hopefully, forgetting, perhaps, that London air was the farthest thing from fresh.

"Go and see after Mamma, Pru," Honor suggested.

Prudence looked at her uncertainly, but Honor winked. "Mr. Cleburne and I will be along shortly."

When Prudence had left them, Cleburne smiled at Honor and gestured to the walk. "Thank you, Miss Cabot." He fell in beside her, his hands at his back. "I am grateful for this opportunity to be alone in your company, in truth," he said. "Your family's tragedy has necessitated my stay in London, but I really must return to Longmeadow and my flock there. I plan to take my leave a week from Saturday."

"I'm certain your parishioners have missed you terribly," Honor agreed.

He smiled sheepishly. "May I compliment you, Miss Cabot? I have admired your strength during this time of great sorrow. You've been a true pillar of comfort for your family."

She hadn't been a pillar of comfort in the least. She'd been stumbling about, completely lost in her grief.

"Miss Cabot, I . . ." He paused midstride. "Miss Cabot, I have come to esteem you," he blurted.

Honor swallowed down a sudden lump of terror. "Thank you for that, Mr. Cleburne, but I beg you not to say more, as I am in mourning —"

"But that is precisely why I must," he said earnestly, and reached for her hand. Honor looked at his hand. "I beg your pardon, am

411

I too forward?" he asked.

She blinked. Were he any other gentleman, she would have laughed, for that question would have been a jest. But Cleburne mistook her hesitation for fear, and smiled reassuringly. "You have nothing to fear from me, Miss Cabot. I would protect your virtue as my own. Think of this as a touch of comfort."

What Honor thought of was her night with George. In comparison to him, Cleburne was an unswaddled babe left in the woods.

Her silence made him nervous, she could see that. "Do you think that perhaps we might — after a suitable period of mourning, naturally — come to an understanding with one another? I'll be frank — Sommerfield is perfectly satisfied with the idea. I know I am not a London dandy, or . . . or any of the men you might have consorted with prior to our acquaintance, but I am a good man, an honest man and I would cherish you all our days."

Honor didn't know what to say to him. She didn't dare speak her heart for fear of angering Augustine or hurting Mr. Cleburne. But neither could she encourage him. She thought frantically as she pulled her hand free. "I can't say that this . . . conversation comes as a surprise," she said, and the poor man actually blushed. "There is much to consider, Mr. Cleburne. My sisters and my mother not the least of them."

"Of course. They are welcome at Longmeadow."

"You may have noted that my mother is unwell," she said bluntly.

He smiled. "I would consider it my Christian duty to help in any way that I might."

Of course he would. She nodded, her mind spinning, her thoughts on George, who had told her flatly that her love for him was "impossible." She should accept Cleburne's offer, should accept the truth of her life as George had so boldly told her to do, and yet . . . yet she couldn't seem to shake the thoughts of George from her mind. "May I have a day or two before . . . we talk?"

Cleburne seemed a bit disappointed by her request but rallied gamely and said, "Yes, of course. One must thoroughly consider all aspects."

Cleburne accompanied her to the house, but he did not come in, claiming he had some calls he must make.

She made her way upstairs, feeling heavy in her limbs and her heart, and walked down the long hall to her mother's suite of rooms. She knocked lightly on the door; Hannah opened it instantly. Just behind Hannah, Honor could see Mercy, her arms outstretched, practicing dance steps as she hummed a tune.

"How is Mamma?" Honor whispered.

"The same, miss. Says little and hasn't an appetite."

Honor nodded and stepped inside. Her mother was dressed in her widow's weeds, standing at the window, looking out over the square. "Mamma?" Honor said.

"She's not listening today," Mercy said, sinking into a deep curtsy.

Honor walked across the room and touched her mother's arm. She started, then looked at Honor and smiled. "Darling," she said.

"Are you all right? May I get you something?"

Her mother didn't answer, just turned her gaze to the window again.

"Mercy, you'll stay with Mamma?" Honor asked as Mercy twirled again, the black ribbons of her mourning dress flying out behind her.

"When might I have my dance lessons again?" Mercy asked, dipping and swaying to one side.

"When we have properly mourned our

stepfather," Honor said. "Where is Pru?"

"Playing another dirge on the pianoforte." Mercy sighed.

Just as Mercy had said, Prudence was playing a lugubrious song when Honor found her.

"Have you come, too?" Prudence asked. "Mercy has already tried to persuade me to leave off."

"I wouldn't think of it," Honor lied. "But I need your help. Will you keep an eye on Mamma this evening?"

Prudence stopped playing. "Why? Where will you be?"

"I have something I must do."

"What is it?" Prudence pressed.

Honor really didn't know the answer to that. She only knew she'd not accept Easton's rejection of her. Unlike her experience with Rowley, this time Honor was certain of the feelings Easton had shown her, and she wasn't going to walk away as if she had no say in it. "Darling, bear with me. I shall return by nightfall."

"All right," Prudence said lightly, and began to play again. "Do remember what the earl always said of you, Honor — you're a good girl."

Honor looked at her sister with surprise.

Prudence smiled a little. "You think me a

child, but I'm not," she said, and played a heavy chord.

Honor smiled fondly. "No, Pru, you're not. You've grown up far too quickly."

"Grace warned me. She said someone must remind you that you're a good girl, or you will forget it entirely."

Honor laughed. She missed Grace so! "I shall remember. But this afternoon, you really must bear with me."

"I will," Prudence said lightly. "I always do." She smiled playfully at her sister and resumed her playing. "Have a care, Honor."

As she went out, it was not lost on Honor that even the children were telling her to be careful now.

CHAPTER TWENTY-NINE

In a cloak, with the hood pulled over her head, Honor used the alleyways and mews to wend her way to Audley Street. A fine mist hung over the street. She hurried up the steps and rapped on George's door. It seemed several long, torturous minutes passed before the door swung open. Mr. Finnegan stood there, looking at her curiously. He stooped down and peered under her hood to see her face. "Miss Cabot?" he said, his voice full of surprise.

"Yes, I . . ."

He abruptly grabbed her arm, pulled her inside then glanced up and down the street before shutting the door.

"I beg your pardon," Honor said breathlessly, her anxiety having the best of her now. "I know this must seem highly unusual, but it is important that I speak to Mr. Easton. Is he at home?"

"He is," Finnegan said warily.

"Then . . . then could you please tell him I have called?"

Finnegan sighed. He shook his head.

Honor's heart sank. She'd come only to be rejected again.

"I shan't tell him you've called — I think it best that it come from you, madam," Finnegan said, and put his hand to the small of her back, ushering her deeper into the foyer. He pointed to a long hallway. "Walk until you see a green door on your right. That is his study, and you will find him within."

She looked uncertainly at Finnegan, then peered down the dimly lit hallway. "Should you not warn him?"

"If I tell him you've come, he might very well draw a pistol." He smiled as if amused by that. "When you see him, you will understand. Green door," he reminded her, turning away. "Don't knock. It will do no good. Just enter."

Honor clenched a fist against the swell of nerves and started down the hall. She found the green door easily enough, and when she glanced back to the foyer, Finnegan had disappeared.

Honor looked at the door. She pushed the hood off her head, smoothed her hair and considered the door handle. When she thought of all the things she'd done, of all the risks she'd taken and then laughed about, she could never recall being afraid. Not even the night she'd gone to Southwark. But tonight, her fear was almost choking her. She didn't know how she would ever bear it if he turned her away. But she wasn't going to marry Cleburne without hearing the truth from his lips. Either he loved her, or he had used her. The man had to tell her the truth.

She reached for the handle and slowly turned it, opening the door only partially. She put her head into the opening and looked in.

The only light in the room came from the hearth. She could see the back of George's head over the top of a chair, his feet crossed and propped on an ottoman. One arm was draped over the side of the armchair, a snifter of brandy dangling from two fingers, the amber liquid glowing in the soft light.

She stepped in and quietly shut the door behind her.

"Damn you to bloody hell, Finnegan!" he snarled. "I've told you to leave me be. Do you *want* me to shoot you? Come round here, man, and I will happily oblige!"

Honor undid the clasp of her cloak and let it fall to the ground.

"Don't creep about behind me," George

snapped. "Do you know that you are perhaps the *worst* valet in all of England? God help me to understand why I ever accepted you into this house."

The beast in him had certainly come out to play, hadn't it? Honor smoothed her gown and started forward.

"If I'd had half a wit, I would have turned you out as Lord Dearing did. I could have brought a goat into my house and been assured of less trouble than you give me."

Honor cocked a brow at that. Finnegan seemed a perfectly nice man to her. She moved to stand directly behind George, debating what she would say. All of her carefully rehearsed words had flitted out of her mind.

"Get *out*," George growled. "I don't want to hear you. I don't want to *smell* you. I don't want your food or wine or whatever it is you've brought me now. I do well enough with my whiskey and brandy. Take a good look around this room and see what I mean. They are my friends."

"They are not your only friends," Honor said.

George came up so quickly at the sound of her voice that he knocked over the ottoman. He whirled around, and his eyes went wide with shock at the sight of her. His gaze scraped over her face. And then he carelessly dropped the snifter onto the carpet as he surged forward, catching Honor in his arms, burying his face in her neck, her hair. "Dear God, where have you *been*?" he moaned into her hair.

A tear coursed Honor's cheek. If he hadn't held her so tightly, she would have slapped him. "I would ask the same of you!"

He kissed her, his hands on her body, in her hair. He crushed her to him, kissing her hard and holding her tightly, as if he feared he would lose her if he let go. "My God, I have missed you."

Honor's fear gave way to desire. The way he was holding her, looking at her, kissing her — she'd never felt so desirable, and she would not shy away from it. She would take what she could for as long as she could.

There seemed so much to say, but it was lost in the onslaught of his passion. George sank back into the chair, carrying Honor with him. His mouth was warm and wet on hers, as tormenting as it was pleasurable. Every touch of his mouth, every caress of his hand jolted her to her marrow. She clung to him, to the strength in his arms and his torso, to the heat that radiated from him.

He groped for the hem of her gown and slid his hands up, finding her waist, lifting her and settling her on the hard ridge of his erection. A shiver of yearning shimmered down her spine, and she moved against him, gasping at the sensation of his hardness against the softest part of her. As his tongue swirled around hers, his hands caressed her sides, her torso, her breasts.

Honor forgot about everything else — she saw, she felt, she thought, of only George. Sparks of desire flared through her as she pressed against his body, riding on a crashing wave of affection and love for him, a need to make him happy, to please him. It seemed as if the sensuality washed over them both, forming a curtain between the world and her and this man.

George eagerly explored her body with his hands and his mouth, sliding over warm skin, pressing and kneading her to a peak of pleasure. He sank his fingers into her hair, pulled a tress free and brushed it against his face. He put his mouth on the hollow of her throat and sighed against the wild beat of her pulse. Honor's heart galloped, heedless of its direction or speed.

George clawed at his trousers, lifting up, sliding them down his powerful hips and thighs, his cock standing erect and eager. He lifted her again, then guided her to slide down onto it.

White-hot sensation slammed at her ribs and her groin. Honor closed her eyes and bowed over his head as George began to move in her, pressing up and sliding down, making her pant with anticipation of her release.

He cupped her face, pressed his forehead to hers. "You cannot imagine the power you hold over me, woman."

She pushed a lock of hair from his brow, kissed his temple. "I love you," she said.

"No," he said, sliding deeper into her, filling her up, shifting her about to slide even deeper.

"I *love* you," she said stubbornly. He growled against her skin, dipped a hand between them, stroking her to madness. Honor matched the rhythm of his body in hers, eagerly meeting each thrust of his flesh into her. She encircled his neck with her arms, teased his lips and tongue with hers. Her craving for him was building, filling her up, reaching for more and pushing her over the edge of reason and decorum. She rode him, wanting to feel it all, to experience the fall from as high a point as she could reach.

His fingers swirled around the core of her pleasure, sliding deep inside her, moving faster. He grabbed her chin with his hand. "Open your eyes." She did as he asked, looking into his eyes the very moment he pushed hard into her, and she fell from the mountain, tumbling down, head over heels.

She went limp, but he surrounded her with both arms, pushing harder into her, making her feel all of it, every last moment of it, riding her to an explosive climax that shattered with a guttural cry against her breast. A moment later, he sagged into the chair, still holding her, seeking his breath, his cheek against hers. His heart was beating so hard that she could feel it in her heart.

"You have destroyed me for any other," he said. "There is only you, Honor."

Those words meant more to her than the physical pleasure he'd just shown her. Honor sat up, cupped his face in her hands and tenderly kissed his lips, lingering there.

He kissed her cheek, her forehead, and shifted, his body falling out of her. Honor rearranged herself so that she was sitting on his lap, her head on his shoulder. Neither of them spoke; they gazed into the fire, watching the flames dance with every gust of wind down the flue.

But the blood continued to pump through Honor's veins, flowing hot. George must have felt it, too; he put his palm to her cheek, kissed her temple.

"How did I come to love you so?" she

asked with wonder.

"You mustn't love me," he said.

She sat up and twisted about to look at him in disbelief. "Do you think to tell me it is impossible *again*? If so, you must tell me that you don't love me as I love you."

He shifted his head, as if to look away, but she caught his face in her hand. "*Say* it," she demanded. "Say you don't love me, and I will leave and I will never bother you again. But if you do love me, then for God's sake, stop telling me it's impossible!"

George's eyes rounded. And then the corners of his eyes crinkled with his smile. "Bloody hell," he said, and gathered her to him again. "You're far too brazen for your own good. You will have your way, for God knows I love you. I love you more than I think is possible for my heart to bear."

Honor gasped with delight. She feathered his face with kisses. She could see his love in the way he looked at her, could feel it in the way he stroked her arm.

"But you *mustn't* come here. If anyone saw you —"

"I don't care if they do," she said.

"*I* care."

"Why? If it bothers you so, you should be offering for my hand —"

"Bite your tongue!" he said gruffly. He

moved her off his lap and stood, stooping down to pick up the snifter he'd dropped. "The new Earl of Beckington would never allow a marriage, and besides, you have a perfectly good match in the vicar." He walked onto the sideboard.

Gaping at his back, Honor gained her feet. "The vicar!" she exclaimed crossly. "Why is it that everyone believes Cleburne is best for *me*? How can anyone possibly know what is best for me? It is an infuriating assumption, especially coming from *you.*"

He seemed properly chastised for that and held up a hand. "You're quite right. But, Honor . . . *darling* . . . Beckington will never allow it. Your affection, my affection does not change who or what I am. It does not change the fact that my fortune is sitting at the bottom of the sea."

She did not like what he was saying. She wanted him to rebel with her, to believe as she did that they were meant to be together, somehow, some way. "Doesn't love count for anything?"

"Of course it does," he said softly, and walked across the room to clasp her face between his hands. "But it's not enough, Honor. Not in the world you and I live."

"Why isn't it enough?" she demanded, and pulled his hands from her face. "What matters *more* than that, really?"

"You know very well. Influence matters. Money matters. You have lived a life of privilege. You are welcome in any parlor in London. Your clothing is of the best quality, you have the finest shoes —"

"They are all just *things,*" she exclaimed angrily. "Do you really think so little of me? That I would put gowns and shoes above love?"

"Honor . . . how could you possibly understand? Those are things you've possessed all your life, and at present, they are things that I can't give you."

"I'm not asking —"

"You're not asking for any of it, I know," he said, and stroked her cheek with his knuckle. "But I have nothing. I invested all but this house in a ship that has gone missing. You deserve better than the likes of me. The love between us was never meant to be, darling. You must accept it."

He wasn't listening to her, and she was sinking into a pit of anguish. "How many times must I say it? I want to be with you always, to lay with you, eat with you, tell you that your dancing is wretched —"

George shook his head.

Honor felt her heart all but explode. She reached for his lapels, grabbing them. "I've

427

never felt so sure of anything in my *life* —"

"Dear God," he said, wrapping her in his embrace, forcing her to be still. He tenderly kissed the top of her head. "Neither have I. But there is far more at stake than you are willing to admit. Deep down, you know what I am saying is true. Deep down, you know very well that Honor Cabot cannot marry a bastard son who dallies in trade. One day you will thank me for making you see it."

She shoved against him. "I will *thank* you?" she said angrily. "I don't care if I ever step foot in a ballroom again! I know only that I love you, George. Perhaps you don't love me as you say. Perhaps you have made me believe it so that you could use me —"

"Don't be foolish," he snapped.

"Then what has you so afraid?" she exclaimed.

"Afraid!" His smile faded. His gaze roamed her face, searching, seeking . . . what? What was it this man needed to love her as she loved him? George suddenly grabbed her arms and yanked her to him. He kissed her, a hard, possessive kiss. And then he held her, cupping her head against his shoulder.

Honor closed her eyes and held her breath.

"I don't deserve you," he muttered.

"That's not true — you deserve the best of everything. You are the son of a prince and the nephew of a king, and you deserve all the things that have been denied you."

"No one believes that," he scoffed.

"I do." She looked up at him. "I believe it."

He gazed tenderly at her. "Do you?"

"With all my heart."

"God, but I do love you," he said with a sigh.

Honor could feel a smile forming on her lips, could feel it light the darkness around them.

"Don't smile at me, Cabot," he warned her. "It's hopeless to deny that bloody bright smile of yours."

Her smile only deepened. *He loved her.* She leaned into him. "I know," she said happily.

CHAPTER THIRTY

It was true. George was incapable of telling the woman no. At last, he convinced her to go home before search parties were sent after her, and he ate a meal that a smug Finnegan presented him. His belly full, his heart fuller, he wondered if there wasn't a way to cast off the shackles of his upbringing, his deepest fears about his place in the world, and perhaps find a way to be with the woman he loved?

He could picture the shock on even the affable face of Sommerfield — now Beckington — if he was to properly offer for Honor.

Perhaps, George thought, if he had something grand to impress with — a large country estate, or expensive jewels, something deemed acceptable to the *ton*. . . .

There had to be a way, but damned if he could think of what that was.

The answer came to him quite by accident. He'd found Mayfair tedious, and had ventured out to Southwark and his favorite gaming hell one evening. He reasoned that perhaps he might postpone selling his furnishings to feed his small household and pay his debts if he could win a hand or two at cards. He'd meant it only as a lark, as he really wasn't as desperate as that. *Yet.* By the end of the year, without income, he would begin sliding into poverty.

Indeed, that night, he won fifty pounds in the first game he entered, which, he thought in the first jovial moment he'd had in a fortnight, would at least pay the wages of that god-awful Finnegan for a year more. George had a pair of whiskies and won two hands more. His outlook on life began to improve. He felt his swagger return, his confidence in himself to persevere no matter what the obstacle.

One of the gentlemen at his table retired after losing another ten pounds, and it was as if the heavens opened up and shone their bright light on George's head, for none other than the elusive Duke of Westport took the empty seat.

Westport was a man who was reputed to have little use for society.

The duke was not particularly talkative as they began to play, but he didn't seem to mind the endless chatter from Sir Randall Basingstoke, the third player. George hadn't heard much of anything he'd said this evening, but in the middle of a round in which George was winning the duke's money, Basingstoke happened to mention the duke's abbey in Bedfordshire. "Had occasion to ride by there," Basingstoke said. "It looked empty."

Westport glanced up over the tops of his cards at Basingstoke. "It is indeed empty, as it is in desperate need of repair."

"Aha," Basingstoke said, as if some riddle had just been solved. "Quite a lot of work, then, is it?"

"Quite," the duke said, relaxing a bit. "And frankly, I haven't the inclination for it at present."

George guessed he didn't have the money for it at present. The old estates were notoriously so entailed that they often were cash poor. An idea wormed its way through George's thoughts. A grand old abbey was precisely what he needed. A respectable country estate, worthy of Honor Cabot. He was playing well, his luck running high tonight, the duke's luck all but run out. *What if . . .*

What if he were to raise the stakes?

What if he were to gamble for an abbey

432

and win?

George played his card, trumping the duke's. "The abbey sounds more burden than treasure," he said idly and watched Basingstoke fold his hand.

The duke turned his shrewd gaze to George. "Perhaps," he said with a shrug, and laid out several banknotes, raising the bet.

George matched it and laid out his cards. He had three kings.

"Would you care to make a more interesting wager, my lord?" he asked as he shuffled the cards.

"Interesting!" Basingstoke said, and laughed. "Can't say I find losing more money interesting."

George ignored him. So did the duke. "What have you in mind?" the duke asked.

"I find myself in need of an abbey," George said congenially.

The duke chuckled "And what would you have that would make the game more interesting for me?"

"Money, my lord. Enough to refurbish the abbey." It was a calculated risk. To lose it would be to lose the last of his fortune.

The duke gestured for George to deal.

Basingstoke looked between the two men. He lifted his hands. "I beg your pardon —

I'll leave it to you," he said, and quickly stood from the table, leaving the duke and George alone.

George dealt the cards. "Good luck to you, my lord," he said congenially.

Word that two gentlemen were playing for an abbey spread rapidly through the hell, helped along by Basingstoke's flapping jaws. And for the first two rounds, George was jovial, confident. He'd amassed a small fortune tonight and felt as if the abbey were already his. Easton Hall, he would name it. A monument to men who were born to dukes and kings and left to fend for themselves. Look how he had fended. Look what he'd become.

But as men began to gather around to watch the game, something awful happened: George began to lose. Spectacularly.

It began on the round where the stakes were higher than what George felt comfortable losing. A small tic of panic erupted in his gut, and as much as he tried to quell it, he could not. That tic of panic was not new to George — he'd felt it many times before and had pushed ahead, ignoring it, knowing that one had to push past discomfort for the greatest victories. It had worked for him time and again, but tonight, perhaps, the stakes were too high.

The more George lost, the more desperate he was to win. The duke was smiling, smelling the blood of his enemy. He made jesting comments about where he would begin the renovations to his abbey.

The tic of panic grew, filling George's throat, forcing him to swallow time and again, if only so that he might catch his breath. While Westport smiled and made small talk with his acquaintances around the table, George wagered more.

Another round, and more men had gathered to watch, exclaiming loudly and drunkenly at every card that was laid. George suddenly couldn't keep track of the cards that had been played. He made mistakes in doing quick calculations of odds in his head. The happy future he'd allowed himself to envision began to crumble away like a pile of ashes. The sound of laughter — at him, at his misfortune — clanged in his ears. He lost sight of himself, of what he'd become.

In the end, he lost, quite literally, everything.

CHAPTER THIRTY-ONE

Honor had grand plans one brilliantly sunny morning to visit some shops. If she were to be destitute, she was determined to at least be the most stylish of the destitute.

She was fitting her gloves when Hardy opened the front doors, and Mrs. Hargrove and Monica walked in. "Oh, good morning, Honor!" Mrs. Hargrove said as she removed her bonnet and handed it to Hardy as if she were the lady of the house. "And where are you off to?"

Honor stuffed her black bonnet onto her head. "To Bond Street, actually."

She saw disapproval glance Mrs. Hargrove's features before she walked on. Monica startled Honor by slipping her arm through hers and pulling her away from the door. "I've something to tell you," she said quietly, glancing back at Hardy.

"What is it?" Honor asked indifferently.

"I mean to help you," Monica whispered.

Honor stilled. "*Help* me?"

"Listen to me, Honor. I am aware that you are not particularly pleased with Mr. Cleburne's interest, but you must agree he is a perfect match for you. And you will lose all hope for it if you do not put an end to the rumors."

Honor's heart leaped. *Mamma.* She decided instantly she would appeal to Monica's sense of decency, to their mothers' mutual affection all those years ago. "Please, Monica," she said softly, mindful that the walls in this house had the hearing of an elephant. "You must see how difficult this is for me. Put yourself in my shoes."

Monica blinked. "You yourself have tried to put me in your shoes, and without success. I *will* marry Augustine, Honor, and you must marry, too!" She glanced nervously at Hardy again and dragged Honor deeper into the foyer. "You *know* you must, so why you resist it I cannot fathom. I am warning you as a friend to be mindful of the company you keep before all hope is lost."

Honor was set to argue, but something about Monica's reasoning didn't make sense. "Pardon?"

Monica rolled her eyes. "I would that you not pretend to be so innocently unaware, at

least now with me. You've never been innocent *or* unaware."

"And I would never pretend to be so, with
you especially. But I have been rather occupied with my sister's departure and my
stepfather's death, and I honestly haven't
the slightest idea what you mean or whose
company I have kept."

"For heaven's sake! *Easton,* of course."

Now Honor's heart leaped even harder.
She could feel it racing as she imagined
Monica standing on the street, watching her
go into Easton's house. "What of him?" she
asked as evenly as she could.

Monica blinked. She looked at Honor,
wide-eyed. "You've really not heard?"

"Heard *what,* for God's sake?"

"That he tried and failed to win an abbey."

"A what?"

"An *abbey.* Montclair Abbey, to be precise. He tried to win it in a gambling game
of some sort from the Duke of Westport.
But he didn't win, and moreover, rumor has
it that he lost *everything* in the attempt."

The news sent Honor reeling. What had
happened? Why had he done something so
precarious? She shook her head. "I don't
believe it."

"Believe it, darling. It was witnessed by
many. I would not like to see your reputa-

tion tarnished by association. And Mr. Cleburne . . . Well, he is above reproach. You must be mindful of that. He's heard the rumors, and now you'd best assure him." She smiled sympathetically and let go of Honor. "I truly am trying to help," she said, and walked on.

Honor blinked after her.

Her plans to shop abandoned, Honor sent a note round to Easton's house on Audley Street with Foster. When the footman returned, she was waiting anxiously for him in the foyer. "Is there a reply?"

Foster shook his head and held out the note she penned. "Mr. Easton sent it back unopened."

Honor flushed; she snatched the note from his hand. "He did, did he?" she asked smartly, and whirled around, bounding up the steps in high dudgeon.

The following afternoon, Honor walked out the front door of her home and marched across the square, bound for Audley Street. This time she would not take the alleys and mews. She would walk straight up to his door and demand entrance. He would not refuse her.

George didn't refuse her, but Finnegan did. At least he had the decency to look pained when he said she was not to enter.

"Mr. Finnegan," Honor said, trying to appear innocent and sad. "You surely don't intend to leave me standing on the steps and reject me for all to see, do you?"

"I would never, madam," he said with a wince. "But Mr. Easton is just as determined not to see you as you are determined to see him."

"Why?" she demanded, all pretense of innocent flower gone out of her. "What have I done?"

"He's not confided in me, Miss Cabot. But I would speculate that you smiled at him and insanity ensued."

"I smiled —"

"Good day, Miss Cabot. Please, do hurry home before even more talk flies about London."

She glared at him. "London has not even begun to *talk,* Mr. Finnegan," she said, and whirled around, bounded down the steps, and brushed past two gentlemen who were staring at her with surprise.

How dare he. How *dare* he!

Honor was so angry she could not take tea. She paced her rooms while Prudence sat on the chaise, watching her, and Mercy went through her jewelry, trying on this necklace and that bracelet.

"Why are you so anxious?" Prudence

asked curiously. "Has something happened?"

"It's difficult to explain," Honor said, and wished, for once, her sisters would find some other diversion and leave her be. How she longed for Grace!

"You might *try* to explain," Prudence groused.

Honor whirled around to the both of them. "Would you like to know what vexes me, Pru? Then I shall tell you. I am hopelessly, completely, *irreversibly* in love with a man whom society frowns upon and Augustine would never agree to allow me to marry. Does that answer you?"

Prudence was taken aback. But not silenced. "Must you have Augustine's permission?"

Honor groaned. "Of *course* I must. He is the one who has charge of our dowries now."

Prudence and Mercy exchanged a look. "And if you marry him, is that the worst you might expect? To lose your dowry?" Prudence pressed.

Grace was so much better than she at explaining these things to their sisters. She tried again. "If I do not marry someone of standing, I will lose my dowry. Furthermore, without a husband of some means, there will be no money to properly present you

441

and Mercy into society, and therefore, who would *you* marry? And there is the question of Mamma," she said. "You surely understand that with Mamma's . . . problems, it will be difficult enough to find matches for any of us."

"I don't care," Mercy said with a shrug. "I will never marry. I mean to sail on ships and search for ghosts."

Honor rolled her eyes.

But Prudence stood from the chaise and folded her arms, and looked uncannily like Grace when she did. "If you would like to know what *I* think —"

"Not now —"

"I think you should marry who you love, and the devil take the rest of it."

Honor gave her sister a dubious look. "Even if it means that you will not be presented? Even it means that no gentleman of standing and fortune will offer for you?"

"If what you say is true, I won't have to make the *right* match, will I? I shall be free to marry who pleases me."

Prudence had a point, Honor thought. But still, she shook her head. "I can't do that to Mamma."

"Don't be silly, Honor. Mr. Easton would care for her, would he not?"

"I quite like him," Mercy agreed. "He likes ghoulish tales. He thinks them diverting."

"How . . . how have you guessed?" Honor exclaimed.

"Oh, really, Honor." Prudence sighed. She held out her hand to her younger sister. "Come along, Mercy. Honor wants to be alone without bothersome children underfoot."

"Pru!" Honor said as Mercy willingly followed Prudence out.

But it was too late — her sisters had gone, leaving Honor alone in her misery.

For a half hour.

The more Honor thought of it, the angrier she became. How dare Easton cast her aside? She grabbed her cloak. He wouldn't allow her in his house, which meant that she would have to stand on the sidewalk until he came out. If she had to stand all night, she would. Grace was right — Honor could be very stubborn when she was of a mind, and, by God, she was of a mind.

CHAPTER THIRTY-TWO

It had begun to drizzle when George rode up to his house and tossed himself off his horse. The weather, he mused, was as bleak as his future. He'd just come from Sweeney's offices, and had finally conceded — his ship was lost. The men he'd sent with his fortune and his hopes were no doubt in their watery graves.

Everything was lost, including his bloody heart.

He swung down off the horse and threaded the reins through the iron loop. He went up the steps, opened the door to his house and stepped inside, removing his cloak to hand to Finnegan.

But Finnegan wouldn't take it.

George looked at him. "What?" he demanded.

"Will you allow her to stand in the rain?" Finnegan asked, his voice full of censure.

"Who?" George demanded.

"You know very well who," Finnegan said, and turned about, marching from the foyer.

George jerked around, pulled the door open and looked down to the street. He saw Honor then, standing across the street from his house, an umbrella high over her head.

She was as persistent as a curse, and George had had quite enough. He stormed out through the open door, striding down to the walk. "Go *home,* Honor," he said sharply.

"Not until you explain to me your sudden change of heart!"

"What do you want?" he roared, startling her enough that Honor took a step back. "Is it not enough that I lost everything trying to win an abbey for you? That's right, Cabot, an *abbey.* It was to be a consolation for you when I told you that I could not return your esteem."

Honor's mouth dropped open in shock.

"Are you surprised? Does your debutante's heart believe every man she meets will fall at her feet? You thought I would offer for *you?* No, madam, I never intended to do so. I have no more use of you, so you may move to the next bachelor. But choose wisely. Someone who will keep you in privileged circumstances and who you might conduct about on a whim seems appropriate."

She was speechless, her blue eyes filled with shock and pain. He'd never believed he could say such wretched things to anyone, much less Honor. He'd loved her from the moment she'd sat down at the gaming hell and won one hundred pounds from him. But he could not have her, *especially* now.

He would not be responsible for ruining her life.

But Honor was so bloody stubborn, he could see no other way than to say these things. "Perhaps it is time I said what *I* want," he said angrily. "I want you to leave me be, do you understand? You were right — I've had my use of you, and now I want you gone. Did you really think I would somehow become respectable because you deigned to befriend me? The truth is that I am a bastard and I enjoy playing games, and I enjoyed winning what I wanted from you. But there is no more than that, so go and marry your vicar and leave me *be,*" he said, and whirled around, striding for the door.

He jogged up the steps, walked inside and slammed the door at his back. Finnegan appeared from the corridor, and George pointed a menacing finger at him. "I will kill you. I will quite literally tear you apart with my bare hands if you so much as *think* of speaking." He took the stairs up to his rooms, two at a time. He burst into his darkened room, stalked to the window and parted the drapes to see.

She was still there, still standing in the rain, still staring at the door. Even from this distance, he could see the rise and fall of her chest with the breaths she struggled to take. As he watched, she slowly turned around and began to walk.

He could feel his heart shattering in his chest, could feel the pieces of it littering his limbs. He'd never felt so numb, so useless, so *cruel.* He whirled about and drove his fist into the wall, hearing a small bone crack when he did.

George Easton was not only a wretched dancer, he was also a wretched actor. And he was a bloody fool if he thought Honor would believe any of what he'd said.

Well . . . besides the part of losing everything.

And she believed that he'd tried to win an abbey for her. An abbey! Her heart swelled with tenderness just thinking of it.

In spite of her initial shock, the walk home had given her the time to think things through, and she was actually smiling a little when she entered Beckington House as she imagined George now, pacing his study — drinking brandy, no doubt — working to convince himself that he'd somehow done a noble thing in setting her free.

She was so lost in thought that she didn't notice Mr. Cleburne in the foyer.

"Miss Cabot!" he said loudly.

"Oh! Mr. Cleburne!" She dropped her umbrella in the stand. "I didn't see you there."

"I am so glad to have happened on you. I am to Longmeadow in the morning."

"Oh, is it — so soon?" Honor asked, trying to recall their conversation.

"So soon," he said, smiling. "If I may impose . . . If you would be so kind, I should like a private word with you."

Honor froze; she wasn't ready to hear his offer, wasn't ready with her response to him.

"If I may," he reiterated.

"Ah . . . well, I am rather soaked through," she said, gesturing to herself.

"Perhaps if you remove your cloak."

He had her there. She slowly removed the cloak, revealing a dry gown underneath. She smiled a little as he put out his hand for her cloak and hung it on a rack. And then he gestured to the hallway that would take

448

them to the small receiving room, where Honor had first attempted to instruct George in the art of seducing Monica.

In the receiving room, Mr. Cleburne indicated she should take a seat, but he remained standing, his hands at his back, his head lowered. He looked almost as if he were offering up a prayer until he lifted his head and said, "Miss Cabot, I should very much like to express my good opinion of you —"

"Oh, Mr. Cleburne," Honor said, and quickly stood, turning at first toward the bookshelves and then toward the hearth, half walking, half stumbling there, her hands clutched at her abdomen.

"Please, hear me," Mr. Cleburne said. "It is no secret to you that your family desires a match —"

She steadied herself with a hand to the mantel, her thoughts racing around what exactly she would say.

"But I cannot, in good conscience, extend an offer for your hand in marriage."

"Oh, Mr. Cleburne, I do so appreciate . . ." Honor paused as his words sunk in. She raised her head and looked at him. "I beg your pardon?"

"Please, don't be cross," he said quickly.

"Cross!"

"I've had time to reflect," he rushed, "and I have come to the conclusion that we are not suited to one another."

Honor had not once imagined that Mr. Cleburne would not *want* to offer for her.

"I do not mean to . . . to *hurt* you," he said, clearly looking for the right word, "but I cannot help but think that it would be a grave mistake."

Honor was so surprised, so relieved, that a burst of mad laughter escaped her. She instantly clamped a hand over her mouth.

Mr. Cleburne smiled. "I had rather hoped you might feel the same."

"I beg your pardon, Mr. Cleburne. I am certain you will make a fine husband —"

"And you a fine wife —"

"But you are right, we are not suited."

He laughed again, with great relief. "I felt certain you were not in favor of the match, but then again, Sommerfield has been rather insistent."

"Augustine? Or Miss Hargrove?" Honor asked with a bit of a smile.

"Lord Sommerfield. I understand that Miss Hargrove's family is rather keen to see you all properly matched and wed, but your stepbrother is fond of you. He has in mind that you suffered heartbreak in the hands of Lord Rowley and had lost your confidence along the way."

Honor blinked. That was rather astute of Augustine. "It's true," she admitted. "I did suffer, but it was my doing. And . . . I seem to have found my confidence again." She put a hand to her heart and laughed with relief. "You can't imagine how I've dreaded this moment —"

"So have I," he said. He looked at his hands. "I have particular esteem for a young woman in my church."

"Oh," Honor said, smiling.

He grinned and shrugged. "However, when one's benefactor suggests a match, one does not ignore it."

"Yes," Honor said, smiling. "I understand *completely.*"

He smiled. "What of you, Miss Cabot? Is there anyone in particular?"

She thought of Easton today, his expression haggard, the dark circles under his eyes. "There is," she admitted sheepishly. "But I am waiting for him to realize it." How different her feelings for George were compared to what she'd had for Rowley. Her feelings now were so much deeper, so much more complex. She believed Easton's feelings for her ran just as deep, if only he could find the courage to admit it!

Mr. Cleburne laughed. "I am certain he

will come around."

"What do you think, Mr. Cleburne? Would you give up this," she said, gesturing to the opulent room they stood in, "for love?"

"This?" he asked, looking around them. "What do you mean, the brick and mortar?"

What, indeed. Honor smiled. "Something like that."

"You are a handsome woman with a fine heart, Miss Cabot. My best wishes for a happy future. Shall we go and explain our decision to your brother?"

"I think we ought," she said, and took the hand he offered her.

The person who took Honor's news the hardest was not Augustine, as Monica might have guessed, given how hard he'd worked to convince the vicar that Honor was the perfect match for him. It was her mother. She cried out at the news, then paced about the small parlor where Monica sat and her brothers watched, muttering all the things she found objectionable about Honor Cabot.

The list was longer than Monica had realized.

As for Monica, the fight had gone out of her. She was happy with Augustine, secure in their affection for one another. She'd come to realize that she didn't really mind if the Cabot sisters were about. "It's really not such a bad thing," Monica said in an effort to soothe her mother. "Someone will offer for her."

"Not before she's spent her stepbrother's inheritance! And honestly, Monica, I think you don't realize how difficult it will be to find four husbands with a mad mother."

"Mamma!" Monica exclaimed and looked nervously at her brothers, who were not generally praised for their ability to keep secrets.

"Well?" her mother angrily demanded. "There's something quite wrong with her. It's very obvious. No one will want to introduce the possibility of madness into their family, will they? You'll be shackled with the lot of them all of your days."

Monica quit the parlor that afternoon feeling slightly ill.

That feeling did not go away in the next two days when when she heard her brother and mother plotting to save the Beckington fortune. How had she been so blind to them? How had she not understood that their enthusiastic support of her match with Augustine had nothing to do with *her* happiness, but the Beckington fortune?

Honor had been right to suspect her.

Monica had believed her mother wanted what was best for her, but what she wanted was connection and money, just like everyone else in London. At least Honor wanted something pure. Honor wanted love. What else might explain her esteem for Easton?

That was why, then, when Monica heard from Augustine the very next day that Easton was desperately gambling every night, trying to piece together the fortune he'd lost, she told Honor. Only this time, she didn't tell Honor about it to warn her away from Easton. She really hoped Honor would find some way to help him.

As it happened, Monica rather admired the charming George Easton.

CHAPTER THIRTY-THREE

Honor instantly suspected trickery when Monica came to her at Lady Barclay's tea with the news of George's desperate gambling. "Why are you telling me this?" she asked, eyeing her shrewdly.

Monica shrugged. "I thought you'd want to know."

There was nothing in Monica's expression or demeanor to suggest otherwise. But then again, Honor didn't understand Monica any longer. It was as if her old friend had changed overnight. She'd become gentler, more accepting of Honor and her sisters. And especially of her mother.

"What am *I* to do?" Honor asked, frustrated by the news.

"I don't know," Monica said. "But if anyone would know, I believe it would be you." She smiled and walked away to join her friends.

Honor could only wonder at Monica's

motives, but later, at the same tea, she overheard Lady Vickers speaking about Easton. Laughing at him, actually. It seemed that Lord Vickers had frequented the gaming hell in Southwark and had witnessed George being turned away from tables as no one believed he could honor his bets any longer.

"That's not true," said Lady Stillings. "He certainly divested *my* hapless husband of a large sum." The ladies tittered.

For days afterward, Honor could think of little else. After one long sleepless night, she awoke to the answer of how to make Easton admit the truth and stop losing all that he had. He was a gambler; he would never freely offer something so personal as she had offered herself and her love. She also knew him well enough to know that he had to prove to himself that he deserved happiness.

Once Honor realized it, she knew precisely what she had to do. It was an enormous risk, one that could truly ruin her forevermore. But Honor had never shied from risk, and if she was right, she would win her happiness. If she was wrong, well . . . She'd just as soon be put away in St. Asaph with her mother. She'd be no use to society or anything else. She wouldn't care what happened to her after that.

That night, she dressed in the peacock-blue gown she'd worn with the bonnet Monica had commissioned. She summoned Prudence to her room to fasten the buttons.

"Where are you going?" Prudence said. "You're not allowed to wear something so colorful, are you? Only black."

"I think the earl would approve," Honor said.

Prudence stepped back. "But . . . *where* are you going?" she asked again, her voice low and serious.

Honor smiled at her sister. "You were right, Pru."

"*Pardon?* When?"

"When you said I should marry for love."

Prudence gasped. "Are you *eloping*?"

"No. But I am going to offer for Mr. Easton's hand."

Prudence's mouth dropped open. She looked so shocked that Honor couldn't help but laugh. "Wish me luck, darling. If he refuses, I doubt I will ever have another offer. I certainly won't want one."

Prudence folded her arms and studied Honor a long moment. "He couldn't possibly refuse," she said solemnly. "And if he does, you'd not like to be married to him because he is a wretched fool."

Honor smiled gratefully at her sister and embraced her. "Thank you. I am in need of all encouragement, for my knees are shaking, and my stomach is quite in knots."

"Shall I come with you?" Prudence asked.

Honor shook her head. "I would not want you anywhere near what I will do this evening."

On her way out, Honor stopped in to see her mother. Lady Beckington smiled with pleasure at the sight of Honor. "Oh, my," she said, nodding approvingly. "How lovely you look, my love."

"Thank you, Mamma!" Honor said, pleased that this was a lucid moment. She walked to her mother's side and crouched down beside her. "Mamma, I would like you to know that I intend to marry for love."

"Do you?" her mother asked, and stroked Honor's hair. "Very good, for anything less than that is a waste of some very good years."

Surprised, Honor blinked at her mother.

Her mother smiled. "Don't look so astonished. I married for love once." She glanced back at Hannah and said, "Didn't I, Mother?"

Hannah smiled. "Indeed, you did."

"Thank you, Mamma." As far as Honor was concerned, she had her mother's blessing, as much as she was able to give it.

Jonas looked at her askance when Honor told him she was to Southwark, but Honor ignored him and settled back against the squabs and clutched her reticule tightly, her belly churning with nerves. She kept drawing deep breaths in a futile effort to soothe her racing heart. Her entire life had been building to this night. She hoped that she would remember everything she'd been taught, that she could find the courage to reach with both hands for the one thing she wanted — to love a man with all her heart and be loved by him, no matter what.

No matter what.

In Southwark, she asked Jonas to wait. "I may be a while," she said.

He looked at the building and at her. "You're certain, miss? You'd not like me to come in with you?"

"Thank you, but, no. I'd best go in alone." She wasn't certain of that at all, really, but it seemed something she had to do alone. She stepped into the dimly lit club, saw the many male heads turn toward her. Expressions of shock and disgust, bafflement and lust began to dance before her eyes. She felt as conspicuous as she must appear to them all — a fish out of water, a woman who had crossed some invisible line.

Please, God, let him be here. Honor lifted her chin and began to walk through, looking at every table.

"Miss Cabot!"

It was Mr. Jett, and Honor almost swooned with relief at the sight of a friendly face.

"What are you doing here?" he demanded, glancing back at the door. "Are you alone?"

She nodded.

"Oh, no, Miss Cabot. This is *far* too brazen," he said, as if she didn't know it. As if she'd somehow stumbled into the gaming hell by accident.

"Is Mr. Easton here?" she asked.

Something flickered over Mr. Jett's eyes. "I fear this time you've gone too far, Miss Cabot," he said low.

"Mr. Jett . . . is he?" she asked again.

He sighed and glanced over his shoulder. "The last table," he said. "He's there every night."

"Thank you."

Mr. Jett shook his head and stepped back, as if he did not wish to be associated with her.

She could scarcely blame him. She did not look into the faces of the men who eyed her as if she were prized game, but kept her gaze ahead of her, stepping around one or

460

two men who deliberately stood in her way as she progressed to the back of the room.

George didn't notice her at first — he was intent on his hand, intent on the coins in the middle of the table. He looked thinner than when she'd last felt his arms around her. His hair had not been cut, and his right hand was wrapped with a bandage.

As Honor moved near the table, his opponent threw in his cards. "Bloody hell," he groused, and said something else that was unfamiliar to Honor but sounded quite vile. The gentleman lifted his ale to his lips, at which point he saw Honor and spilled a bit of it in his haste to stand. "Madam."

George's head came up at that. He quickly came to his feet, and Honor saw a glint of emotion flash in his eyes. It was quickly overshadowed by his surprise and anger, but she *saw* it, and she knew that he loved her yet.

The knowledge emboldened her. When he demanded to know what she was doing there, she said, "I have come to play, Mr. Easton. As you might have guessed, with the passing of my stepfather, my dowry has shrunk."

"No," he said instantly, and pointed to the door. "Leave at once. This is no place for a lady."

Honor held out her reticule, aware that several gentlemen had made their way to this table to see what was happening. "I have ninety-two pounds. I should like to use it to play."

"You won't shy from a lass, will you, Easton?" someone called, and the gentlemen laughed.

George's eyes narrowed on her, his gaze almost murderous, and Honor was suddenly grateful that others were nearby.

"These are not games for debutantes," he said tightly. "It is ten pounds to enter."

Honor swallowed down a lump of nerves. "I have ten pounds."

The gentlemen around her howled. Honor could feel the crowd growing at her back, and it frightened her. She had not counted on the uneasiness of being the only woman in a room of men with money and liquor in their gullets. George was aware of it, too, apparently, because he suddenly yanked out a chair and gestured with exaggeration for her to sit.

Honor took the seat, her reticule tight on her lap.

"Have you lost your mind?" he said low as he resumed his seat.

"No," she said. "Have you?"

He glared at her as he gestured for a footman. "Wine, madam?"

"No, thank you, Mr. Easton. I should like to keep my wits about me."

His gaze flicked over her, and if Honor wasn't mistaken, she saw the tiniest hint of a smile at the corner of his mouth.

"May I assume Commerce meets with your approval?" he said, picking up the cards.

"Certainly." She withdrew ten pounds from her reticule and placed it on the table.

"May I introduce you to Mr. MacPherson," he said, and as Honor greeted the other player, George began to deal the cards.

The din around them was increasing, and it felt to Honor as if twice as many people were gathered around their table than when she'd first entered. She felt a bit queasy as she picked up her hand and saw the pair of aces.

They played the first round without talk. Honor had been taught how to gamble by her father. He'd thought it quite diverting to introduce his young daughters to games of chance and even more entertaining to watch them giggle and trick his friends. She still remembered a trick or two.

It was quickly apparent that Mr. MacPherson was no match for her or George and bumbled his way through the first round, betting on cards blindly, even when Honor withdrew.

As George raked in his winnings, he looked at Honor, silently assessing her.

They played the second round, and while Honor had the winning hand, she allowed George to believe it was his. But as he took the winnings, he frowned at her. "You are careless tonight, Miss Cabot."

"Am I?" she asked innocently.

"How much is left of your infamous ninety-two pounds?" he asked.

"Enough," Honor said pertly. "How much money do *you* have?"

The men around them hooted with delight, and even George smiled a little. "Enough," he said.

When George won the third hand, in spite of her obviously superior draw of cards, he looked at her with exasperation. "I can't guess what you are attempting to do, but if you want to give me your money, by all means, give it to me and go. Let the gentlemen here play a gentleman's game."

This was her moment, her turn to deal, and Honor's hand shook as she accepted the deck of cards. "Shall we increase the stakes, Mr. Easton?" she asked lightly. "That might speed things along."

He laughed. "With what? I've taken most

of your purse."

"I had in mind something other than money."

There were a few audible gasps, and with it, Honor understood that what tatters remained of her reputation had just fluttered out the window. She had to win now. Her heart raced, her palms were turning damp. She'd just anted everything she had — *everything.* Her heart, her future, her prospects.

George was looking at her as if he were trying to work a puzzle. "Go on."

"If you win," she said, speaking as if she were playing a parlor game with children, "I will leave this gaming hell and I will never see you again."

Men around her bellowed with delight, calling out to George that he was a fool. He leaned forward and said, "And if *you* win?"

Honor swallowed and somehow managed to shuffle the deck without shaking. "If I win —" she glanced up, looked him directly in the eye "— you will extend an offer of marriage to me."

That remark was met with utter silence. For a moment. And then pandemonium erupted in that room. Suddenly everyone was shouting as men called friends to come and witness, others shouted at Honor to leave the gaming hell, that she had brought dishonor on the Beckington name.

But George . . . *George* . . . He regarded her stoically, his eyes boring through hers. "That's impossible. I've told you, Cabot — *impossible*!"

"Only because you refuse to believe in the possibilities."

"I withdraw," MacPherson said, standing. "I will not be party to this . . . Whatever *this* is."

Neither Honor nor George noticed his departure.

"You are making an abominable and *foolish* bet," he said angrily.

"I don't agree."

"Then allow me to instruct you on just how foolish it is," he said angrily. "If you win, I will indeed make that offer. And you will be forced to live in a style to which you are *quite* unaccustomed. By that I mean there will be no servants. No gowns. No pretty things. There may not be a roof over your head."

She hoped she wasn't shaking.

"Ah, Easton, at least a pretty thing," someone said, and others around him laughed.

She was back on her heels, but nonetheless determined. There was no other man

466

for her, no one who was of a like mind, who understood the sort of woman she was. She did not relish a life of hardship, but neither did she fear it. Her heart raced even harder. Honor had walked her private plank, and she wasn't turning back now. She began to deal.

"You will not be invited to fancy Mayfair salons," he continued. "You may not even have meat on your table."

Honor finished dealing and picked up her hand. "Do you intend to play or prattle, Mr. Easton?"

He swiped up his cards and said, "Gentlemen of standing will have second thoughts about your sisters."

Honor's heart stopped beating altogether for a moment. But she carefully laid her first card, a deuce.

George looked at it and sighed. "God help you, Honor Cabot. You have no idea the mistake you've made."

They played on. More than one spectator pointed out Honor's hands were shaking, just as she'd feared. George watched her closely, making her quite anxious. Just when it seemed all was lost for her, Honor hesitated before playing the last of her hand. She looked up at George and smiled. "If I may, Mr. Easton, I don't care who your father is or is not, or the size of your fortune, big or small."

The crowd suddenly grew quiet, leaning in to hear what she said.

"I don't care if there are gowns or balls, and while my sisters may have a difficult road ahead, I am confident they will follow their hearts and persevere. That's what we Cabots do. We set our sights. I have set mine, and the only thing I care about is you. Only you." She laid her hand, a trio of queens.

The crowd erupted with cheers and jeers. George looked at her hand and sighed as if he'd expected it. "I don't know who taught you the art of gambling, madam," he said, and began to lay down his card. One king. Then two. "But your teacher may have neglected to explain that one should never attempt to cheat." He laid down a third king, and then a fourth. "Unless one knows precisely how to do it."

The crowd suddenly stilled, all of them leaning in to see his hand. Honor was stunned. She could feel the emotions and tensions begin to leech out of her body, spilling out of her, taking the last of her strength with them. She watched as George stood up, raked in his winnings, and put them in his pocket. He stared down at her, his eyes dark and unreadable, and pushed a man aside to leave the table.

Honor couldn't draw a breath, much less move. It felt as if she'd just been snapped clean in two. There was nothing left of her. *Nothing.* How could he have done it? How could he refuse her, so publicly, so dreadfully?

She didn't even realize Mr. Jett was shaking her until he said her name loudly, and she glanced up into his face. He was frowning, holding her reticule. "Come along," he said, and grabbed her by the arm, pulling her up from her chair.

Honor stumbled along beside him, almost blindly. The only thing she could see was George's winning hand, the way he'd stood and left the table without looking at her, without looking back. He had *left* her. He had rejected her public appeal, had rejected her completely. He'd broken her heart, and the pain was intolerable.

Mr. Jett put Honor in her coach. She cried all the way to Mayfair, and then cried on Augustine's shoulder when Jonas handed her over to him. She cried into her pillow as Prudence and Mercy petted her leg, trying to help.

There was no help for her. No hope. Now Honor had truly lost everything.

CHAPTER THIRTY-FOUR

George walked into his house and went directly to the salon, poured himself a whiskey, downed that and then hit the wall with his fist again. The pain was excruciating, driving him to his knees.

It did not compare to the pain of humiliating Honor before half the *ton.* But what could he do? Dammit all to hell, *why* had she come? She thought she could publicly challenge him, force him to her will? She thought she could *cheat* her way into his heart? She thought she could make such an unreasonable, impossible demand and *win*?

On all fours, gasping at the pain, George smiled a little. That brazenness, that absurd sense of righteousness, was why he loved her. No other woman could compete with that audacity, and he found it alarmingly arousing.

But that did *not* change the fact that he was in no position to offer for her. He was working the gaming hells to keep food on his table — it was hardly anything to settle on a wife. There would be no servants, no gowns, no hats. . . . "She'll never agree," he whispered through his teeth.

"Agree to what?"

Finnegan had entered without George hearing him. George groaned with exasperation, fell onto his side and rolled onto his back. "She'll not agree to marry a man with nothing, that's what."

Finnegan stepped over him, picked up the glass George had dropped before hitting the wall, and as George tested his fingers, Finnegan filled it. "Are you certain?" he asked as he crouched beside George. "Rather seems to me that the only thing the lass wants is you."

George sat up, took the whiskey and downed it. "Because she is young and in love, Finnegan. After a time, she'll want her gowns and shoes, and at present, I can't even pay *your* bloody wage, much less provide for her and all the Cabots as they ought to live."

"She has a dowry, does she not?" Finnegan asked practically.

George snorted and waved a hand at him.

"I suggest, sir, that if you want this lass as you apparently do, judging by the number of times you've slammed your fist into a wall, that you find employment so that you can provide for her and all the Cabots, as you say."

"Pardon?" George asked.

"Employment," Finnegan said, as if the word was foreign. "Work. It is an activity that other, less fortunate persons such as myself find necessary to do."

George snorted. "What, do you suggest that I become a valet?"

"Absolutely not. You'd be utterly useless in that capacity. It would appear that your talents lie in the buying and selling of commodities. Cotton, for example. Were I you, I'd begin there." Finnegan stood up, stepped over George again. "Shall I send for the physician to set your hand again?" he asked as he walked to the door.

"Yes." George sighed and settled on his back, his injured hand on his chest, looking up at the painted ceiling.

Employment. A wage. It had been quite a long time since he'd worked for wages. But if he had even a modest income, he might sell this house — the symbol of the man he'd become, which, in hindsight, had been a bit of a cruel joke — and put himself, a wife and even a bloody cock of a valet in a respectable manor.

Honor would find the notion reprehensible, and if she didn't, she was a bigger fool than he'd believed. But that was all he could do. Without a ship, without sufficient funds in the bank, his hands were broken. Quite literally.

George sat up, picked himself up, shoved his good hand through his hair. He'd lived through worse than this, that was certain. And he'd never been afraid of honest work. If there was one thing he might say for himself, it was that he believed in his ability to pull himself up.

Employment. He would call on Sweeney on the morrow. Perhaps he might partner with his agent. George certainly had the connections to buy and sell cotton, which Sweeney could use.

George went to find a comb to make himself presentable before the physician arrived a second time.

Three days passed before Honor finally stopped crying or lying listlessly about, staring into space. But it was Mercy who finally convinced Honor that the time for grieving had passed. "I think you should ring for a bath," she said, wrinkling her nose.

"Fine," Honor snapped. She wound her hair up, pulled on her dressing gown and stumbled down to the breakfast room while a bath was drawn.

Augustine and her sisters were in the dining room. Augustine came instantly to his feet, his fork clattering to the floor in his surprise. "Honor, darling," he said, his eyes wide as he took her in. "You're all right, aren't you? You're on the mend? You'll return to yourself, will you?"

"She's not going mad, if that's what you think," Prudence said.

Of course they all knew what had happened to Honor that night in Southwark. All of London knew it. Mr. Jett, her savior, had been unable to keep from telling the tale — casting himself in the role of hero, naturally.

"I'm all right," Honor said, and sat heavily in a chair beside him. Augustine slid his plate to her, offering her bacon. Honor shook her head and turned away from it. The sight of food made her ill.

"I think you must pick yourself up," Augustine said. "Rally and all, that sort of thing. Monica and I thought perhaps it might be best if you had a rest at Longmeadow."

Honor gave him a wary glance.

"It would seem best until the Season is done, do you not agree?" he asked, wincing a little at the suggestion, as if he expected her to lash out at him.

"Actually, Augustine, I do," she said, surprising her stepbrother. "I would like nothing more than to leave London and hopefully never see George Easton again." She shook her head at the breakfast Hardy offered her, but allowed him to pour tea.

Augustine munched on his bacon, studying her. "Shall I send for anyone? Grace, perhaps?"

"No!" Honor said quickly, sitting up. "Please, no, Augustine. She will be quite cross with me, and besides, she should have a few weeks of happiness before word reaches her of what will surely be the Season's most infamous scandal."

"I suppose," he said uncertainly. "Oh, Honor, I cannot help but ask — *why* did you do it? To Southwark, of all places! *Alone!* Mrs. Hargrove was quite beside herself, but I told her if you went, there was a *very* good reason for it. There *was* a very good reason for it, wasn't there?"

"I had a very good reason for me," she said flatly. "My feelings are entirely too complicated to explain properly, but perhaps you will understand if I ask if you've ever admired someone so completely that you believed you couldn't possibly draw your next breath without them?"

Prudence and Mercy looked curiously at each other, but Augustine nodded enthusiastically.

"Or loved someone with every bit of yourself, and convinced yourself there is no point in carrying on without them?"

Again, Augustine nodded adamantly.

"Truly, Honor?" Mercy asked. "You wanted to *die*?"

"Not die, precisely," Honor said. "But I can't explain how I feel for Mr. Easton, darling. It seemed so . . . important," she said with a weary shake of her head. "I went to tell him how I felt. To *prove* it. But the only thing I accomplished was my complete humiliation and ruin."

Augustine leaned forward. "But . . . but might you have told him somewhere besides Southwark?" he asked carefully. "Perhaps without a lot of gaming and such? Perhaps a more private venue."

Honor smiled for the first time in days. "No," she said with a slight shake of her head. "That's the peculiar thing. Southwark was a perfectly natural place for George and me. That's the sort of people we are — swashbucklers."

"Oh, dear," Augustine said, looking truly distressed.

"But —" Mercy leaned forward, pushed her spectacles up the bridge of her nose "— doesn't he want to marry you?"

Honor ran her hand over her sister's head. "No," she said, her voice so low she scarcely heard it herself. Tears filled her eyes at the admission.

"Oh, *dear,*" Augustine said again. "It's the Rowley business all over again."

"This is nothing like the Rowley business," Honor corrected him. "Lord Rowley didn't love me. The worst thing about this tragedy is that George Easton truly loves me."

"That makes no sense," Mercy said, squinting up at her through her spectacles. "If he loves you, why will he not marry you?"

"Mercy, leave her be," Prudence said gently.

They didn't ask her more, all of them falling into contemplative silence.

Honor took the bath Mercy had recommended. She donned her mourning garb, left her hair loose, having no energy or desire to put it up. She padded aimlessly and barefoot about the house, staring solemnly at portraits, wondering after their wretched romances. She picked up books and put them down again.

She had no idea what to do, where to go after such colossal ignominy. There seemed no place for her life to go.

Honor wandered up to her mother's suite to read to her. Lady Beckington stood at the window, staring out as Honor read listlessly from a book.

"He's come," her mother said as Honor read.

Honor looked up. "Who, Mamma?"

"That man. The earl!" she said, and smiled brightly. "He's come. Oh, dear, have you any shoes?"

"I'll put them on later," Honor said, and returned to her reading.

Her mother was not listening, however. She leaned forward, her hands on the window, her nose pressed against it. "He's coming, Juliette!" she said excitedly, calling Honor by her deceased sister's name. "The earl is coming *here.*"

Honor sighed and put aside the book. "Come and rest, Mamma."

Her mother hurried to her vanity. She opened a drawer and rummaged through it, and turned around, her smile bright, and held out an emerald drop necklace to Honor. "Here, then. It will go very well with your gown."

Honor looked down at her black gown.

Her mother was quickly at her side, turning her about, pushing her hair away to fasten the heart-shaped emerald at her throat. She turned Honor around again and stood back, nodding her head with approval. "You want to look your best for the earl!" her mother exclaimed. "Who stole your shoes?"

"No one stole my shoes —"

"Honor!"

It was Prudence, calling to Honor from down the hallway. "Honor, where are you?" She burst into her mother's room, her eyes wide. "It's *him*!" she exclaimed in a loud whisper, and for a moment, Honor almost believed the earl had come back from the dead.

"Who?"

"Easton!"

Honor gasped. She unthinkingly stepped back, bumping into her mother. "No! No, Prudence, you must send him away! I don't want to see him!"

"You must!" her mother said, pushing her forward. "You can't deny the earl!"

Prudence looked confused by that, but said, "Augustine told him you'd not see him, and Easton said, very well, he would stand in the foyer until he was forcibly removed."

"What?" Honor's heart began to pound painfully in her chest. She frantically looked down. "I can't see him!" she said. "I can't endure it!"

"Honor," Prudence said, and grabbed her hand. "I must tell you, he was *very* stern with Augustine. He insisted that he see you, that he owed you this, that you deserved this call."

Something snapped in Honor. She would never be entirely certain what it was Prudence had said that put the steel in her spine, but she was struck by a rare moment of clarity when all of the knowledge she possessed about the world and people came into sharp focus. The pieces of her life, of her heart, rearranged themselves into a crystal understanding.

Honor looked at her mother. Lady Beckington was smiling serenely. "You mustn't keep the earl waiting, darling. That will only make him more determined."

Truer words had never been spoken, and with newfound strength, Honor surged forward, wrapped her arms around her mother and held her tight. When she let go, she looked at Prudence. "How do I look?"

"A fright," Prudence said.

"Good."

She swept out of the room, marching

down the corridor, then pausing at the top of the stairs. He was standing there, his legs braced apart, his arms folded over his chest. He had the growth of a beard on a clenched jaw. Her heart leaped, somersaulting in her chest. "Easton!" she shouted down at him.

His head came up. Augustine was standing to one side, looking as if he might faint. "Honor!" Augustine cried, "I tried to turn him away, but he'd not go!"

"He'll go," she said confidently, and ran down the stairs, her feet landing silently on the marble floor as she marched up to him, Prudence right behind her.

"What do you want?" she demanded. "Haven't you done enough? As Augustine has said, I do not wish to see you. I've said all that I have to say to you, so, go!"

"Good God, someone should have taken you in hand many years ago," he said flatly, his gaze traveling the length of her. "What did you think, Cabot, that you would dance into Southwark and force me to your will? That you would cheat to get your way?"

"You *cheated*?" Prudence exclaimed.

Honor ignored her. "What would you have had me do? You are so convinced of your own inferiority, it makes you blind and deaf to all reason!"

He took a menacing step forward. "Allow

me to instruct *you* for a change, *madam.* Generally, it is the gentleman who makes the offer for the hand in marriage."

She folded her arms. "Unless the gentleman is as stubborn as an old pig."

A light sparked deep in his eyes. "And the *gentleman* generally makes the offer with an idea of how he might support the woman when she becomes his wife. Am I right, Sommerfield?" he demanded without looking at Augustine.

"Me?" Augustine squeaked.

"Yes, you!" Easton bellowed, his gaze locked on Honor's.

"It is, yes, most certainly it is," Augustine quickly agreed.

Honor's eyes narrowed with her ire. "Is there a *point* to your call, sir? You have rejected my declarations not once, but *twice.* Am I to be rebuffed a third time? If that is your intent, it is not necessary, for I heard you *quite* plainly the first two times!"

"The first two times you assumed the role of the gentleman in this affair between us. I was not in a position to make that offer, Honor, but did that give you the slightest pause? No — you insisted on shaming me in front of all of London."

Honor gasped with outrage. "*Shame?* You will talk to me of *shame*?" she cried, her hands curling into fists as she rose up on her toes.

"No one invited you to Southwark. In fact, my recollection is that several told you to leave!"

"Sometimes one must take matters into her own hands!"

"Oh," he said, almost jovially. "And we've *all* seen how well taking matters into *your* hands has done for you, have we not?"

She gaped at him. "At least I'm not *afraid.*"

"I never feared you!" he cried to the ceiling. "But I was not prepared for you. I don't know that I shall ever be prepared for the likes of you, Honor Cabot, but nevertheless, I have done my best by seeking employment —"

"You see? You insist on making things impossible!" Honor cried, poking him hard in the chest.

"Employment!" Augustine said, confused.

"And I have obtained it."

Honor had no idea what he was talking about. "Obtained *what?*"

"Employment, I think," Prudence said, sounding as confused as Augustine looked.

"That's right," Easton said, nodding. "I have sought employment. I am the new agent at Mr. Sweeney's offices. I lost my fortune, and I could not provide for you, Honor. Now, at the very least, I can provide you a modest home. I can feed you. I might even feed one or two more of the virtues," he said, gesturing at Prudence. "I can clothe you . . . somewhat. But I cannot allow you to buy bonnets for eight bloody pounds."

"Pardon . . . what?" Honor said, as her heart began to flutter in her chest.

"And I must warn you, this loss of fortune may happen again and again. I live my life by taking risks. Sometimes my pockets are full. Sometimes they are not."

Honor's fluttering heart changed tempo. It began to race, feeling as if it might lift her off the ground.

"Do you understand?" he demanded, taking her by the elbow.

"*Yes,*" she said, her voice full of wonder. "I understand that this is a very bad offer for my hand."

Easton smiled. "Do you still feel the same?" he asked softly. "Can you accept what I am telling you?"

She nodded. Tears began to fill her eyes again, only these were tears of utter happiness. "Yes," she said. "I can accept it all as long as you are there."

George stepped back and went down on one knee. "Honor Cabot," he said, "will you do me the honor of becoming my wife?"

Honor wasn't certain what happened after that. She believed she shouted *yes*. She remembered George sweeping her up, and there was much more shouting, which she believed came mostly from Augustine, something about how he could not possibly allow it. She remembered George kissing her so completely that she was light-headed with relief, with love, with lust.

And with much happiness. Euphoric, ethereal happiness. And a wild belief that with George, *anything* was possible.

George kissed her neck. "You're a bloody fool," he whispered. "I'm near to penniless."

"I don't care," she said dreamily.

"You might have very well done the most heart-warming thing anyone has ever done for me, do you know that?"

"I did?"

"You cheated to try to win me, Honor. I've never been so flattered. But good God, lass, learn how to cheat," he said, and smothered her with his kisses again.

CHAPTER THIRTY-FIVE

Augustine was completely flummoxed by what had happened in the foyer of Beckington House. "It was a theatrical event!" he exclaimed to his fiancée.

"He may not be the man you had in mind for her," Monica said soothingly, "but Honor seems very happy."

Augustine squinted a little as he pondered that. "She does seem happy, doesn't she?"

"And I rather think, after all that's gone on, no one else would have her."

"Oh, no," Augustine said, nodding in furious agreement. "*No* one would have Honor now."

"Then I think perhaps you should ask that they marry sooner rather than later, given all the speculation that is flying about Mayfair just now."

"Yes, of course, you are absolutely right," Augustine said. "I shall demand they marry straightaway!" He suddenly brightened. "I know just the thing! We'll all go to Long-meadow. It's out of London, isn't it? And Mr. Cleburne might do the honor."

"Oh, dear, that might be a bit much," Monica said with a slight wince.

"Well. We'll devise some sort of cer-emony."

Augustine used his new title of earl to obtain a special license. Honor and George were wed at the end of that week in a private ceremony. There was no time to prepare properly, much to Prudence and Mercy's horror, as they both would have liked to have commissioned the latest fashions for the ceremony.

Honor, however, scarcely cared what she wore, and arrived in a plain gray gown with no adornment. Clothing had slipped her mind — all she could think was that she was to marry a man she loved above every worldly thing, and that was all that mat-tered.

Augustine insisted, given the events lead-ing up to their so-called engagement, that they perhaps not go out into society for a time, which Honor and George were happy to oblige. After the ceremony, they retreated to the house on Audley Street; they spent most of the first few days in his bed, occasionally allowing Finnegan to bring them food.

George taught Honor things about her body and his that both astonished and pleased her. She loved the way his mouth moved on her skin, the way his tongue slipped into her body. She loved the way he caressed her when he was making love to her, as if reassuring himself that she was there, all of her, still in his bed, still beneath him or on top of him, still part of him. She adored the things he taught her — how to take him in her mouth and please him, how to ride his cock when she was on top of him while he helped her find fulfillment with his hands.

But mostly what she loved after they'd both found their fulfillment in one another — or, in Honor's case, more than once — was the tenderness between them. His body spent, he would still cover her with kisses by the light of the fire, slowly making his way down one leg to her toes, and up the other to her breasts, and to her mouth again, whispering his love for her, the realization that his life had been so empty before she'd intercepted him on Rotten Row that fateful afternoon.

Honor felt the same way — her life had consisted of gowns and gatherings, but until

George, there had been nothing substantial to anchor her to this earth, to this life. Now she had him, and, God willing, they would have a large family. Nothing could make her happier than living in a cottage or mansion with him, presiding over a table that was filled with laughing children, and seeing this man across from her.

One evening, as they lounged naked in his bed with a tray of roasted chicken, cheese and fruit, they talked about their future. "I should think five children in all," she said casually.

"Good Lord, darling, that number is a small village."

"Don't you want them, too?" she asked, kissing his nose.

"I want six."

She laughed.

He wrapped her hair around his bandaged hand. "How shall I feed an entire village?" he mused. "Well, I shan't fret over it. I've always managed to land on my feet. Mr. Sweeney is searching for a new ship —"

"Another one?" she asked, surprised.

He shrugged and allowed her to stuff a bite of chicken into his mouth. "Someday. I'm afraid it will take a grand attempt to dig out of our present hole."

Honor giggled. "I love our hole," she said,

and leaned down to kiss his mouth. "I have enormous faith in you, husband," she said, because she liked calling him that. "I know you will do it. And when you do, we'll find a place that will fit all of my family and all of our children."

"Even Grace?" he asked casually as he traced a grape around her nipple. "You've written her, haven't you?"

Honor winced. "Not yet," she said.

"Honor —"

"I know." She sighed. "I've been avoiding it. She will be so cross with me, George, and I dread her reply. But it's only been a fortnight since we were wed."

"Only?" he said dubiously. "She should know, love," he insisted, and sat up to kiss her breast.

"You're right." Honor sighed and closed her eyes, enjoying the feel of his lips and tongue on the peak of her breast. "You're always right."

"Mmm, say it again," George said. "It arouses me to hear you admit it."

"You're right, darling. You're right, you're right," she whispered as he began to suckle her.

George pushed the tray of food aside and rolled them over so that Honor was beneath him. "Once we have the Cabot girls under one roof, we'll work on our house full of children, the great-grandchildren of a king." He smiled as he leaned down to kiss the hollow of her belly. "With a name that no one can deny."

Honor stroked his head and smiled up at the canopy as he began to drag his mouth down the hollow of her belly and to the apex of her legs. "I like the sound of that."

"There is really no time to waste," he said, moving lower, pulling her legs apart and dipping his head between them. "No time at all," he muttered, and ran his tongue up her cleft.

Honor threw her arms above her head and smiled with delight as he began to lave her. They had a lifetime of making children, a journey unfolding that she'd never understood she'd wanted until faced with the prospect of not having it.

Oh, but Honor wanted that. She fiercely, deeply, passionately wanted it.

She would write to Grace and tell her . . . tomorrow.

At the moment, she was pleasantly and thoroughly occupied.

CHAPTER THIRTY-SIX

Grace wore a plain blue gown with a collar, as instructed by Cousin Beatrice. She'd been sitting on a wooden bench for more than an hour, waiting. Her limbs ached, her head ached more. It was a small, dark office, and she wished someone would open the blinds. The only light was that of a single candle, making the room as bleak and as dark as her mood, even though it was only midday.

She stared at the crumpled vellum in her hand. She'd received it this morning, Cousin Beatrice pressing it into her hand when the carriage had come for her. Grace had read it three times, maybe four, and each time tears had streamed down her face.

Oh, Honor.

The door opened; a dark-haired man with fierce green eyes strode inside. He stood just at the door, one fist clenched at his side, lightly tapping against the jamb. *One two three four five six seven eight.* He dropped his hand. "It is time, Miss Cabot," he said simply.

"Shouldn't you call me Grace?"

He did not respond, but tapped the jamb again. *One two three four five six seven eight.*

Grace shoved the letter into her reticule and stood slowly. She looked at the man with the fierce green eyes and swallowed down a small lump of trepidation.

His jaw was clenched, his expression distant, cold and angry. When she did not move, he glanced at a small mantel clock. "Please, do come. It is time," he said again.

She cast down her gaze as she moved past him, and winced when she heard the door shut resoundingly behind her.

How in heaven had she managed to create such a prodigiously complicated shambles of her life in such a short amount of time? She didn't really know, but it looked as if she would have quite a lot of time to contemplate it and sort it all out before she wrote to Honor to tell her what had happened.

If she was allowed letters, that was. Grace wasn't entirely certain what to expect any longer.

Fierce green eyes paused at the next door and knocked. As they waited for it to open, he tapped the jamb with his fist.

One two three four five six seven eight.

Grace glanced heavenward and sent up a silent prayer for courage.